"Who, exactly, is this fellow?" asked someone to Kyrtian's left.

"My cousin, Kyrtian," Aelmarkin said lightly. "Son of the late Lord Darthenian, my uncle."

"Lord Darthenian . . ." a voice murmurmed behind him. "That name sounds familiar. Don't I know it from some old story?"

"Try coupling the name with *daft,*" drawled another smugly. It was all Kyrtian could do to keep from going for the fellow's throat. "Daft Darthenian, excavator of things better left buried, and pursuer of useless old manuscripts. Missing in pursuit of same, decades ago."

Kyrtian gritted his teeth. He knew he was meant to overhear all of this. Aelmarkin had accused him of being mad; if he attacked his cousin or any of the others, it would only prove that he *was* mad. An Elvenlord issued a proper challenge, and settled it with trial-by-combat by their slaves. If *his* fighters were better-trained—

It might be worth dealing with these dolts in a way they'll understand.

THE HALFBLOOD CHRONICLES

BY ANDRE NORTON AND MERCEDES LACKEY

The Elvenbane *Elvenblood* *Elvenborn* *Elvenbred* (forthcoming)

Tor Books by Andre Norton

The Crystal Gryphon
Dare to Go A-Hunting
Flight in Yiktor
Forerunner
Forerunner: The Second Venture
Here Abide Monsters
Moon Called
Moon Mirror
The Prince Commands
Ralestone Luck
Stand and Deliver
Wheel of Stars
Wizards' Worlds
Wraiths of Time

Grandmasters' Choice (EDITOR)
The Jekyll Legacy (WITH ROBERT BLOCH)
Gryphon's Eyrie (WITH A. C. CRISPIN)
Songsmith (WITH A. C. CRISPIN)
Caroline (WITH ENID CUSHING)
Firehand (WITH P. M. GRIFFIN)
Redline the Stars (WITH P. M GRIFFIN)
Sneeze on Sunday (WITH GRACE ALLEN HOGARTH)
House of Shadows (WITH PHYLLIS MILLER)
Empire of the Eagle (WITH SUSAN SHWARTZ)
Imperial Lady (WITH SUSAN SHWARTZ)

BEAST MASTER (WITH LYNN MCCONCHIE)
Beast Master's Ark
Beast Master's Circus (2003)

THE GATES TO WITCH WORLD (OMNIBUS) including:
Witch World
Web of the Witch World
Year of the Unicorn

THE WITCH WORLD (EDITOR)
Four from the Witch World
Tales from the Witch World 1
Tales from the Witch World 2
Tales from the Witch World 3

WITCH WORLD: THE TURNING
I Storms of Victory (WITH P. M. GRIFFIN)
II Flight of Vengeance (WITH P. M. GRIFFIN & MARY SCHAUB)
III On Wings of Magic (WITH PATRICIA MATHEWS & SASHA MILLER)

MAGIC IN ITHKAR (EDITOR, WITH ROBERT ADAMS)
Magic in Ithkar 1
Magic in Ithkar 2
Magic in Ithkar 3
Magic in Ithkar 4

THE SOLAR QUEEN (WITH SHERWOOD SMITH)
Derelict for Trade
A Mind for Trade

THE TIME TRADERS (WITH SHERWOOD SMITH)
Echoes in Time
Atlantis Endgame

THE OAK, YEW ASH, AND ROWAN CYCLE (WITH SASHA MILLER)
To the King a Daughter
Knight or Knave
A Crown Disowned

CAROLUS REX (WITH ROSEMARY EDGHILL)
The Shadow of Albion
Leopard in Exile

Tor Books by Mercedes Lackey

Firebird *Burning Water* *Children of the Night* *Jinx High* *Sacred Ground*

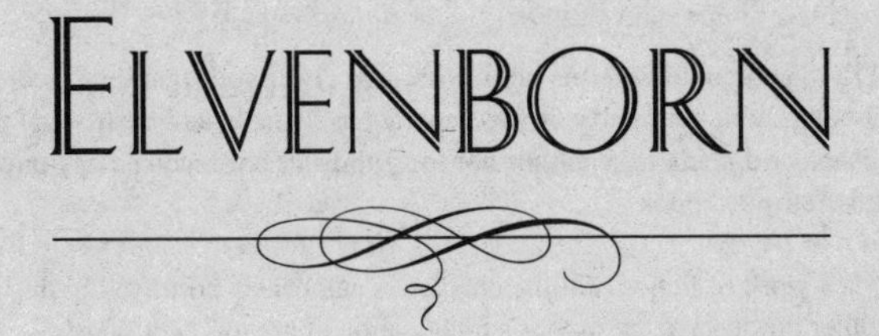

Book Three
of the Halfblood Chronicles

Andre Norton and Mercedes Lackey

A TOM DOHERTY ASSOCIATES BOOK
NEW YORK

ELVENBORN: BOOK THREE OF THE HALFBLOOD CHRONICALS

Edited by James Frenkel

A Tor Book
Published by Tom Doherty Associates, LLC
175 Fifth Avenue
New York, NY 10010

www.tor.com

ISBN: 0-812-57123-1

First edition: August 2002
First mass market edition: October 2003

Printed in the United States of America

0 9 8 7 6 5 4 3 2 1

Dedicated to the memory of the following men of the FDNY
September 11, 2001

Whose motto could have been: "I will, because I must."

RETIRED:
William X. Wren
Philip T. Hayse
James J. Corrigan

PARAMEDICS:
Carlos Lillo
Ricardo Quinn

CHAPLAIN:
Mychal Judge

HAZ-MAT:
John Crisi
John Fanning
Dennis Carey
Martin Demeo
Thomas Gardner
Jonathon Hohman
Dennis Scauso
Kevin Smith

RESCUE 1:
Dennis Mojica
Terrence Hatton
Gary Geidel
William Henry
Kenneth Marino
Michael Montesi
Gerard Nevins
Patrick O'Keefe
Brian Sweeney
David Weiss

RESCUE 2:
Peter Martin
William Lake
Daniel Libretti
John Napolitano
Keven O'Rourke
Lincoln Quappe
Edward Rall

RESCUE 3:
Thomas Foley
Thomas Gambino, Jr.
Raymond Meisenheimer
Donald Regan
Gerard Schrang

RESCUE 4:
Kevin Dowdell
Brian Hickey
Peter Brennan
Terrence Farrell
William Mahoney
Peter Nelson
Durrell Pearsall

RESCUE 5:
Harvey Harrell
Louis Modafferi
Carl Bini
John Bergin
Michael Fiore
Andre Fletcher
Douglas Miller
Jeffrey Palazzo
Nicholas Rossomando
Allen Tarasiewicz

PROLOGUE

V'kel Lyon Lord Kyndreth stood up, and loomed over the Council table and the Councilors seated there. Most of his fellow Elvenlords would not meet his eyes; those that did so shared a congratulatory glance with him. The Council Chamber was not a comfortable place today, and he had ensured—with a few orders to the slaves who had prepared it—that it would remain so. Cold. Dim. The cushions on the seats pounded flat. And even the refreshments were ill-served—at a uniform temperature that could only be described as "tepid." All to keep everyone here wishing he was elsewhere, and less than pleased with the one—*not* Lord Kyndreth—who was nominally in charge.

Lord Kyndreth's star was in the ascendant once again, and this time he would see to it that it did not fall a second time.

"How is it," he asked, to empty air, "that a rebellious pack of children and former slaves have managed to hold off our allegedly well-trained, well-led and well-supplied *armies?* And have done so for long enough that people are beginning to call this—temper tantrum—the Young Lords' Rebellion?"

"Lord Kyndreth—" ventured V'kel Anster Lord Rechan, scrambling mightily for the upper hand he had—if he had only known it—just lost, "this *is,* exactly as you say, no more than a temper tantrum. Inconsequential. No more than a handful of estates have been lost, our supplies continue to move without more than the occasional ambush, there is no more than a trickle of slaves escaping, and *our* lives continue as they always have. In balance, the threat—"

"A trickle here, a loss there, the *complete* inability of our so-called 'invincible' army to bring our *own offspring* to heel, and you say it's *inconsequential?"* Lord Kyndreth roared, and had the satisfaction of seeing his chief opponent wince. "By the Ancestors, you fool, can't you see that a so-called 'trickle' is all that is needed to bleed us to death?" Kyndreth saw with some satisfaction a subtle and unspoken shifting among the other Council members, and watched as power came over to his side. "And what, may I ask, do you propose to do if these so-called 'errant children' of ours decide to ally with the Elvenbane and her wizards and dragons?"

There. It was out in the open, the thing that no one had dared to say, and he watched as a chill passed over all the rest of them. Yes, even Lord Rechan.

"They wouldn't—" someone whispered.

"Don't ever believe that," one of Kyndreth's supporters said, sharply. He took note of the speaker and reminded himself to single *that* one out for some special favor. "Why shouldn't they?"

"Because—because—because they're Elvenlords!" the first lord spluttered, looking so horrified by the very notion that one would think he'd been accused of fathering halfblooded children himself.

"And when whatever magic they've discovered ceases to prevent *our* magic from reaching and punishing them?" Lord Kyndreth asked. "What then? Do you think, do you *really* think that they will hesitate for one moment before going over to the halfblood side?"

Silence.

"Now," Kyndreth said, into that silence, changing his voice from challenging to calm, "I have some suggestions. The first of which is one I think none of you will anticipate. I suggest that we continue to allow our *loyal* offspring to continue their lives as usual. I do *not* propose interfering with their pleasures. In fact, if anything, I suggest a slightly looser leash for now. And you may well be asking yourself why—"

"Well—yes," replied Lord Rechan, looking gratifyingly puzzled. "If, as you say, the inroads are slowly bleeding us to death—"

"Firstly, we don't want the brats to *know* it's bleeding us to death, and rest assured, they must have ears and eyes among us, and it's probably *some* of our apparently-loyal children. Secondly, we want to remind our apparently-loyal children just how pleasant life is, when one's sire is pleased with one." He smiled, slightly. "It is easier to catch a fly with a sweetmeat than with vinegar. And meanwhile—" his eyes narrowed. "—I will be a-hunting for a better commander."

And to his immense satisfaction, there was not one single objection.

1

V'kel Aelmarkin er-Lord Tornal smiled down at the slave who rested her pale-tressed head on his knee. She was his current personal favorite, a delicate young human female nestled trustingly against his leg. Her thin, fine-boned face and porcelain complexion pleased him with their flawless symmetry and perfection. She returned his smile shyly, yet with a touch of the coquette, her round, blue eyes reflecting her callow, unsophisticated nature. No rebellious thoughts dwelling in *that* narrow skull—in fact, he would be surprised if she managed to conjure up more than one or two thoughts of any kind in an average day! Her pedigree was immaculate, out of a long line of carefully chosen slaves famed for their beauty and delicacy to be nothing more complicated than any other ornamental object.

He sighed with contentment, and smoothed the pale gold, silken hair away from her brow with a gentle caress. She was exquisite; lovely, eager to please, pliant, graceful, innocent and incredibly easy to manipulate. Exactly the sort of slave that gave him the most pleasure. He carefully cultivated that innocence, and none of his other slaves would dare his wrath by spoiling that naivete. No tales of floggings or more extreme punishments, no harem-stories of his other "favorites" and what had become of them—nothing to hint that he had aspects she had never experienced. So far as she was concerned, he was the gentle, loving, ever-kind master that she believed him to be.

He turned his attention back to his most important guest. "There, you see?" he said, gesturing expansively to the hall before them and its raucous occupants. "Did I not promise you would be far more amused here than in dancing attendance on all the dull, hopeful maidens at your father's fete?"

Elvenlord Aelmarkin did not possess enough magic to create a fanciful illusion in his Great Hall, so the luxurious surroundings here were all quite real; guests at his entertainments would always find themselves in the same opulent room that they had graced at the last entertainment, rather than a new and exotic setting vastly different from their last. He made up for the lack of novel surroundings by the lavishness of his entertaining, which had begun to earn him something of a reputation.

Take this room, for example: fortunately it had been beautifully constructed in the first place, and he had only needed to embellish it when it came into his possession. The north and south walls were mostly of glass—northwards lay a natural lake, artfully landscaped, and southwards were the pleasure-gardens. The east and west walls, paneled in wood bleached to silver, held silver-rimmed doors that led to the rest of the manor. The ceiling with its bleached-wood beams from which hung great silver fantasies of lights, crystals, tiny glass sculptures and silver filigree, also boasted vast transparent skylights; just now the reflection of the myriad lights made it impossible to see anything of the outside world, but later, when the lights were dimmed, the stars would shine impassively down on the celebrants. The black carpet of the floor was kind to the bare feet of the slaves, but Aelmarkin had selected black carpeting largely because it was easy to clean after one of his entertainments and was far more forgiving a surface for a drunken reveler to fall on than marble or wood. The east and west walls were hung with silver draperies, and the silver dining-couches were upholstered in black to match the carpet. Between each couch and the next stood an enormous silver censer, from which came sensuous and intoxicating incense-smokes. Silver tables stood before each couch, and the guests provided the only touch of color in the room. The couches themselves each held two occupants, an invited guest and a companion of his (or her) choosing—either a fellow guest or one of Aelmarkin's harem-slaves dressed in silver gossamer and matching silver collar. Picturesque wine-slaves, dressed in abbreviated silver tunics, stood at each couch with their silver pitchers, and more slaves dressed in silver tunics and gossamer skirts or trews served the guests with plates of dainties. Enough wine had been drunk by this time that the guests were starting to raise their voices in less-than-delicate jests, and lose what few inhibitions they had when they arrived here.

V'sher Tennith er-Lord Kalumel raised one long, silver eyebrow sardonically as he surveyed the occupants of the dining couches before and below him. "I must admit," he drawled, "that seeing Varcaleme making a fool of himself is far more entertaining than fending off would-be brides and their anxious fathers."

Aelmarkin laughed and continued to caress the platinum tresses of his slave, chosen out of all the possible candidates presented to him, because she most resembled a delicate Elven maiden. He dressed her like an elven girl, too, in flowing gowns of delicate pastel silks with huge, butterfly sleeves and long embroidered trains, ordering her attendants to weave strings of pearls in her silver-blond hair—and to arrange her hair so that it covered the round tips of her ears. So long as one didn't look too deeply into her eyes, the illusion was complete; and he *could* use his magic to change her blue eyes to Elven-green if he chose. Her name had been "Kindre" until he ordered it changed to the Elven "Synterrathe."

The aforementioned Varcaleme was chasing one of the wine-girls around his couch; the flower-wreath she had bound around his brows had slipped sideways and was obscuring one eye, and the fact that he had drunk most of the wine in her now-empty flask was not aiding his ability to catch her. She had cast one look at her master when she began eluding those clutching hands, to see if he objected to her evasions; he had nodded slightly, and she needed no further encouragement to keep dodging his advances. Varcaleme's couch-companion, one of his personal concubines, a tall, dark-haired wench gowned in brilliant emerald that matched the beryl of her controlling collar, seemed relieved that she no longer had to entertain him, and was nibbling on spiced fruit, wearing a bored, but wary, expression.

Now the rest of the guests had taken an interest in the proceedings, calling out encouragement to Varcaleme or the slave, taking bets on whether or not he would catch her, as she dodged his outstretched hands and outpaced his stumbling feet. Most of Aelmarkin's guests were male, with a scant pair of Elven ladies. One of the ladies, clad in pearly silks that revealed scarcely less than the slaves' costumes, had brought her own couch-companion, a muscle-bound human gladiator; the other Elven lady, swathed from nape to ankle in skin-tight black satin, had come with another of the Elvenlords—who was *not* her affianced. Of the remaining twenty guests, half had brought their own concubines, and half had made a selection from the slaves offered to them by Aelmarkin.

All of the Elvenlords present, with the exception of Aelmarkin and the lady who had brought her own male concubine, were the sons of ruling Elvenlords—but had *not* joined the Young Lords' Rebellion. Most of them saw themselves as losing far more than they would gain by rebelling, and the rest were cynically hoping for the rebellion to eliminate their fathers for them.

Aelmarkin and V'dann Triana Lord Falcion—who, despite being female, was Lord of the Falcion holdings in her own right, and thus (it recently had been ruled) was entitled to the title of Lord rather than Lady or er-Lord—were the only Elvenlords in the room with their own estates and property. Aelmarkin, however, was hardly a Great Lord—his property was a fraction of the size of any of those with real power; most of his wealth came from the sale of the exquisitely bred and trained concubines who were literally worth their weight in gems. That gave him a certain status, but no real power. As for Triana, her standing had plummeted after her involvement in the debacle of the Second Wizard War, and she was no longer a desirable ally to anyone on the Great Council. She generally kept to herself on her own estate. He suspected that she was biding her time, waiting to see which way the wind blew in the Young Lords' Uprising, before she tried to worm her way back into the good graces of the powerful.

As a party guest, however, she was still of value; an acid wit and a reputation for depravity gave her all the fascination of a captivating serpent, and people enjoyed seeing what she would say or do next. Any time Aelmarkin invited her to one of his entertainments, he knew he would have full participation, and her own parties continued to be extremely popular among the younger sons, those who did not possess great power, and those who did not have a Council seat.

Aelmarkin was by no means as certain as the Great Lords that Triana would remain out of power for the foreseeable future. She was clever, resourceful, and learned from her mistakes. The Wizard Wars and the Rebellion were changing everything; it was always possible that Triana would prove to be a potent ally at some point. It was even possible that she would somehow claw her way to power entirely on her own. The extent of her boldness was demonstrated in her dress tonight; gowned in transparent silks like a concubine, she knew very well that however tempting she might be, there was no one here with sufficient power to dare touch her without her consent—and so she taunted them with her very appearance.

Besides, she had no scruples to speak of; he liked that in a woman—provided he didn't have to marry her.

"Have you heard anything more from the Council about your petition?" Triana called to him from across the room with a half smile. Her gladiator offered her a choice tidbit with a servile gesture; she allowed him to feed it to her, nibbling at it with white, sharp teeth. He was new to Aelmarkin, but that was hardly surprising; Triana went through male slaves at an astonishing rate.

He concealed a wince; Triana had a vested interest in the outcome of that petition, and it was one quite opposite to his. She *would* bring up the subject; he'd cherished the notion, when he'd scheduled this entertainment, that it might be a victory celebration. Since it wasn't, he had hoped no one would bring up the subject.

"They denied it," he said, trying to sound as if he didn't care about the outcome, even though his defeat ate at him.

Triana made a little pout of sympathy, and Tennith turned his head to gaze at Aelmarkin with astonishment. "No, really? I should have thought that your cousin had proved himself mentally unbalanced a hundred times over by now!"

About half of the guests looked puzzled; they didn't know who Aelmarkin's cousin was and he really didn't wish to enlighten them.

"Really!" chimed in another, sending away a server with a flick of an impatient hand, "Your cousin is quite a piece of work, Aelmarkin. Playing soldier with human slaves as if he was still an infant playing with toys! It's ridiculous! If he was going to have an obsession, it at least ought to be a dignified obsession!"

"Oh, I don't know," purred Triana, running her finger along the arm of her gladiator. "Some of us *like* to play with soldiers." The slave blushed from the top of his head to well past his waist.

"On what grounds did they deny you?" Tennith asked, and Aelmarkin wondered if he detected a certain malicious enjoyment in Tennith's tone. Tennith might not be a lord in his own right, but he outranked Aelmarkin, and he wasn't above flaunting that fact and embarrassing Aelmarkin at the same time.

But Tennith would find out for himself what the Council had said if he simply bothered to ask his father. Aelmarkin's best protection lay in pretending the decision meant very little to him. "They did a very tiresome thing; they had the production records from the estate for the last fifty years brought out, and nothing there shows that cousin Kyrtian is neglecting his estate or his duties. They decided that he isn't unbalanced, merely eccentric, and that eccentricity is hardly grounds for taking his inheritance and giving it to the next male heir."

"Next *male* heir?" Triana asked significantly, with a little frown. "Isn't his mother still alive? Wouldn't she be the appropriate heir even if he was disinherited on the grounds of insanity?" That was Triana's interest; anything that barred another female from inheriting could eventually be used against her.

"His mother is not *my* sister," Aelmarkin replied. "She's not the next heir of blood-descent, as you so clearly were for clan Falcion. If Kyrtian were removed, the estate would come to me, naturally and legally."

"She's probably the one running things, then," Tennith pointed out. "If she doesn't want to be sent back to live in her father's household, she has to make it look as if your cousin is competent."

"That may be, but I've no hope of proving it," Aelmarkin growled, wishing that Lady Lydiell had resembled the child at his feet rather than the clever creature she was. He recalled his intended pose, and forced a laugh. "Well, I suppose the Council had to rule the way that they did. Lord Jaspireth told me rather tartly that if fitness to hold title and property was to be judged on the basis of unusual hobbies, half the Council would lose their seats."

"Half?" Tennith laughed. "More like three-quarters! Looked at in that light, it's obvious you are a victim of necessity."

Aelmarkin signaled to his wench to refill his goblet, and sipped at the vintage with deliberation. "Much as I would like to see the lands of my clan administered properly, I suspect they will come to me in time, anyway. Kyrtian shows no sign of marrying, which in itself ought to prove his unfitness, and it's entirely possible he'll manage to break his neck, or do something equally foolish to himself, as he careens around the countryside."

"Break his neck?" queried the second lady, looking puzzled, as did her escort. "I'm afraid I'm rather lost, Aelmarkin. I don't know anything about your cousin. Who is he? Is he doing something dangerous?"

That triggered laughter among some of the others, who were more familiar with Aelmarkin's cousin than she was. Triana took pity on her—probably because the lady's escort was neither clever nor outstandingly handsome—and explained.

"We've been discussing Kyrtian V'dyll Lord Prastaran," Triana said, giving Aelmarkin's cousin his full name and title. "Surely you've heard something about him?"

The lady shook her head. "Not really," she confessed, then realized that Triana was patronizing her, and put on a cool air as she tried to save the situation. "But I don't pay much attention to the provincials."

Aelmarkin snorted. "He's certainly *provincial,* I'll grant you that, Lady Brynnire. He never leaves the estate unless he absolutely has to. He *could* get a seat on the Great Council if he only worked at it, but he won't even try! Instead, he spends all of his time collecting books and studying—of all the nonsensical subjects—military tactics!"

"Military tactics!" Triana erupted in peals of laughter. "Oh, Aelmarkin, even if he is serious and not seriously unbalanced, just who does he think he's going to *use* military tactics on? Everyone knows the humans and the halfbloods don't have *real* armies! They don't fight proper battles! And as for the Young Lords—"

She stopped, because it was entirely possible that this was a touchy subject for some of Aelmarkin's other guests. But Tennith, whose father was highly placed in the Great Council and thus was the highest-ranked Elvenlord present, finished her sentence for her.

"The Young Lords are a disorganized pack of rabble," he said loftily. "Once a solution is found that negates their ability to nullify magic, they'll dissolve and come crawling back to their fathers, begging forgiveness. In the meantime, it is impossible to use *tactics* against someone who doesn't know what the word means."

"Oh, that isn't the best of it," gloated Lord Pratherin. "He not only studies this nonsense, he *practices* it! Personally, I think he's never gotten over playing in the nursery with toy soldiers; he just does it now on a grander scale." When Brynnire still looked confused, he leaned over the couch in her direction and explained. "He makes up two opposing armies out of slaves, my dear, and personally leads one army into battle against the other, if you can believe it! Not to settle a grievance or for any other reasonable purpose, not even for the entertainment of watching them slaughter each other! No, he does this just to see how strategies work out with living subjects!"

As the others chortled, howled, or simply looked smug, according to their natures, Lady Brynnire looked startled, then shocked, then amused. "Aelmarkin! If I didn't know you, I'd be tempted to think you were making this up!"

"Sadly, my dear, I am not," Aelmarkin replied, and looked to Tennith, who nodded in confirmation.

"Really!" Brynnire giggled, a little nervously. "Well, *eccentric* is not what I would call him!"

"He takes after his father, dear lady," said Tennith smoothly. "Which might be said to demonstrate that, sadly, madness is inherited in his family. Surely you recall that poor demented fellow who vanished several years ago, out hunting some obscure relics of Evelon?"

"Yes!" Brynnire replied, brightening. "Ancestors! You don't mean to tell me *that* was Kyrtian's father?"

"The same," Aelmarkin told her, with a heavy sigh. "A sad case indeed. And it should have been obvious to the Great Council from that fiasco that the estate should not have been put in the hands of his son."

"I should say not." Lady Brynnire nodded her head, after exchanging a look with her escort. "At least, I would not have."

"Nor anyone else with any sense." Aelmarkin thought it more than time to change the subject, and signaled for the dancers.

The musicians, who had been playing soothing, quiet background music until this moment, abruptly changed mood and tempo, startling the guests with a thunder of percussion.

The lights dimmed, and a mist arose from the censers, a scented, cool mist that relaxed and yet stimulated the senses, even as it obscured the couches and their occupants. Only the space in the middle of the couches remained clear, lit from some invisible source.

The dancers ran in from all directions, dressed in the merest scraps of animal-hide, paint, beads, and feathers, and meant to represent wild humans. Not that any of Aelmarkin's guests had ever seen wild humans—nor had Aelmarkin himself, for that matter—but that would hardly matter. Most entertainments featured dancers mimicking the graceful and ethereal dances of their masters, or dancers changed to resemble animated flowers, birds, or flames. Aelmarkin wanted to startle his guests with something different.

The dance began with astonishing leaps as the performers hurled themselves across the floor with total abandon, their unbound hair streaming out behind them. Then, as drums pounded, the females hurled themselves at the males, who caught them in various positions, whirled them around, and flung them on to the next partner. There was frank and unflinching eroticism in their choreography. Even Aelmarkin, who had seen them practicing, felt his pulse quicken at their raw sensuality.

"Ancestors!" Tennith muttered under his breath, his eyes wide. "What *is* this?"

"An ancient fertility rite, so I'm told," Aelmarkin said casually. "I thought it might be interesting to watch."

Tennith didn't reply; his eyes were glued to the dancers.

Half combat, and half mating-frenzy, it was sometimes difficult to tell if the dancers intended to couple or kill each other, and the performance built to a pulse-pounding crescendo that ended in a tangle of bodies suggestive of both.

By Aelmarkin's orders, the lights dimmed gradually as the dance ended, leaving the room bathed only in star- and moonlight. As he had hoped, the performance had achieved the arousing effect he had intended. His guests had turned their attentions to their couch-companions, and as the dancers and servants slipped away, Aelmarkin turned his attention to the censers, increasing the mist rising from them. The slaves already knew to dust more of the intoxicating drugs over the coals therein.

Magic did not come easily to him, and he had to close his eyes in concentration even to perform so minor a conjuration. As he opened his eyes, he realized that he and his little slave were no longer alone. A slim form sat on the end of his couch.

"Well, Triana," he said blandly, concealing his surprise. "Whatever brings you to my side? Forgive me if I doubt that you have erotic intentions."

She made a pouting motion with her lips. "Aelmarkin, I do believe you haven't a romantic particle in you!"

"Neither do you," he countered. "So?"

"I just wondered what it would be worth to you to see your cousin unseated," she said casually, casting her eyes down and tracing a little path on the fabric of the couch with her finger.

"I suppose that would depend on the circumstances," he replied just as casually. "It would do me no good at all if, for instance, his estates were ruined in the process. Why do you ask?"

"No real reason. Just that women often have sources of information that are closed to the men." She gave him an arch smile, but he refused to rise to the bait. The last thing he wanted was to give Triana something she could use to manipulate him!

"Just as men have sources that are closed to women," he countered, with an arch smile of his own. "Especially someone like me. *Do* recall what my stock-in-trade is, my dear. Concubines don't speak to *ladies.*"

She smiled with malicious delight. "If I hadn't made a vow never to marry, I swear, I would propose to you on the spot, Aelmarkin! You and I are two of a kind."

"You and I would kill one another before a year was out," he replied, and touched his finger to the bottom of her chin, drawing her to him for a brief, dangerous kiss. "Now, you've left that handsome stud all alone. Better get back to him before he pines away."

"Or falls asleep." She rose with a sinuous grace worthy of any of his dancers. "I'll tell you what; I'll lay a bet with you. I bet that *I* can find something to discredit him before you do."

"And the stakes?" he asked.

Her smile was so sweetly poisonous that it took his breath away. "Something we both swore never to do. If you lose, you train a male slave for *me.* And if I lose, I train a female for you. But you can't limit me as to means. Is it a wager?"

The idea of owning a slave trained by Triana made his head swim and his breath come short. Now here were stakes worthy of the play!

"Done," he said immediately. She laughed, and glided away into the mist.

He felt a tentative touch on his wrist, and belatedly returned his attention to his current favorite. He looked down at her, and saw by the furtive color in her cheek, her moist lips, and her shining eyes that the dance—and the sighs and vague shapes moving in the mist around them—had produced the effect he had anticipated on her, as well.

"Lord," the slave breathed, looking up at him coyly from beneath her long, fluttering lashes, "Do you wish my—further service this evening?"

Though untouched, she was by no means unaware of the duties of a concubine, and it was clear from the moist eagerness in her eyes that she was ready to fulfill those duties.

He closed his eyes for a moment, savoring what he was about to do. He had ways of controlling the slaves he trained that went beyond, far beyond, the slave-collar and magic coercion. He had subtle tortures that were far more sophisticated than anything Tennith dreamed of.

"I don't believe so," he said, just as casually as if he were rejecting a not-quite-ripe fruit. Then he looked down at her and frowned. "My dear child—is something troubling you? You seem to be a little—puffy tonight. Or perhaps you have just gained a little weight? Perhaps you should return to your quarters."

The girl put her hand to her mouth, stifling a sob; her eyes brightened further with tears. Quickly as a fluttering bird, she fled into the mist.

He chuckled to himself. He had carefully manipulated her mind for weeks now, and this carefully chosen moment was the beginning of a delightful interlude.

He had made a point of praising her slender figure, of leaving no doubt that he treasured her slimness. Doubting her own mirror, certain that she had lost her real beauty, and desperate to gain his regard, she would begin starving herself from this moment. At first he would taunt her by references to plump arms and chubby cheeks, by inquiries if she thought she ought to change her diet. Once she truly began to starve herself, he would switch to the next phase. She would begin refusing food. He, of course, would urge all manner of dainties on her, which she would eat unwillingly, only to purge herself of them at the earliest opportunity.

His lips curved in a slight smile. Watching her torture herself, all the while certain that *he* was still as gentle and considerate as ever, would be highly amusing. Eventually, she would probably die, of course, but not before he gained a great deal of pleasure from watching her ridiculous sufferings. If he was feeling generous, he might even save her, wiping out her memories of everything up to this moment so that he could sell her to someone else. In any case, there would be weeks, possibly months, of pleasure ahead.

And further pleasure. Between the two of them, he and Triana would almost certainly find a way to bring his cousin Kyrtian down.

He laughed softly; how his fortune had suddenly turned! This might well turn out to be the victory celebration he had hoped for.

His appetite suddenly aroused, he reached for the nearest wine-wench to satisfy his needs of the moment.

Poor Kyrtian. He had no notion even that he *had* an enemy, much less how formidable that enemy was.

One did not normally see an Elvenlord smudged with dirt, twig-scratched, and rather the worse for several hours of tramping through untamed forest. *I wonder how much scandal I would cause if even one of the Great Lords saw me in this state?* Kyrtian mused, as he held aside an errant limb of a bush, taking care that it did not rattle, and making certain the human behind him had a firm grip on it before he released it. It was impossible to see the man's expression behind his helm, but the fellow sketched a respectful salute with his free hand. *Ah well; knowing my reputation, they would probably not be at all surprised.*

Kyrtian V'dyll Lord Prastaran led his skirmishing band of lightly armed humans in person; very few Elvenlords would ever have put themselves in that inferior and vulnerable a position. Especially now, with humans, halfblooded Wizards and younger Elvenlords all in revolt against the Great Lords, the mere notion of leading a group alone, without the presence of a fully collar-controlled and loyalty-spelled bodyguard, was something that would never occur to most of them.

Kyrtian cared nothing for their opinions, since little secret was made of the fact that they cared nothing for his. His reputation was as eccentric as his hobby, and that was the way he preferred things. His Grandfather had eschewed politics when the Great Lords disdained his advice; by now, staying out of politics was something of a family tradition, and Kyrtian was quite prepared to continue that tradition.

At this moment, as always when on maneuvers, all of his attention was focused on his battle-strategies and his surroundings, to the exclusion of everything else. His initial battle-plan was so vague that at this point he was rather recklessly making decisions moment by moment. He suspected that his opponent was counting on that, assuming that Kyrtian's well-known caution would also make him inflexible. It was a reasonable assumption; Kyrtian just hoped that he could prove that it was an incorrect one. That was the point of this exercise, after all. This was the first time he had ever met an opponent in anything other than a set battle. Where was the right balance of caution and initiative? Nothing in all of his books and studies had dealt with that magic formula.

Sweat trickled down the back of his neck, but a headband under his helm kept it from dripping into his eyes. He felt a brief flash of superiority as he climbed the steep and rock-strewn slope before him with no sense of strain, not even an increase in his breathing. How many of the pampered Great Lords would be able to do as much? Certainly he was sweating, but he wasn't in the least tired, and if at last he managed to bring his skirmishers to a fight, he would be as ready for action as any of them.

Senses alert for the least sign of warning, he picked his way one careful step at a time through the sparse underbrush of the forest. His men spread out in his wake, carefully following his example. His sword was out and ready in his left hand; that would give him a little advantage against an opponent, should one suddenly appear before him, but not much. The enemy fighters lurking somewhere ahead knew him and some had fought hand-to-hand against him before.

The enemy—all that he knew for certain was that they were here in his patch of pristine, old-growth forest, and that their numbers were equal to his. The most logical place to find them, the weathered remains of an ancient fortification, had been empty. He assumed now that they probably planned to set up an ambush for his skirmishers somewhere; they knew he was coming, and he doubted that they intended to make a pitched battle of it. In their place, *he* wouldn't.

His advantage was that he knew these woods as well as his opponents did; he should, since everything for leagues around here belonged to him. He had made a mental tally of all the obvious places for an ambush, and he hoped he could approach such places from unexpected angles, and with luck, catch the foemen by surprise.

An ambushed ambush—hardly sporting, I suppose. He smiled, knowing the expression was hidden by his helm. Well, first he would have to pull this off. *Then* he would worry about whether it was "sporting"—assuming he'd won the encounter, of course.

After all, it is the victor who writes the histories, and he is the one who gets to determine what is fair, after the fact.

A movement to one side caught his eye; only one of his men, trying to shoo away an irritating fly with a minimum of obvious movement. They knew better than to slap at insects, lest the sound betray them to the enemy, and he felt sorry for his human fighting-men. For all that he sweated as heavily as any one of them, insects seldom plagued elves, perhaps because elves, not native to this world, did not smell "right" to the pesky bugs.

Kyrtian froze and raised his hand to signal to his men to do likewise, as he thought he caught a murmur of voices up ahead. Holding his breath, he closed his eyes and concentrated on *listening.*

Perhaps—perhaps. He opened his eyes again, and considered their present location, frowning as he did so. He and his fighters were approaching a ridge overlooking one of the lesser-used pathways through the forest. The ridge was an obvious location for an ambush placement on the part of his foes, *if* they assumed he and his men would take that path below. It would be very difficult for his party to creep up upon the enemy unseen if that was where they were.

He raised his right hand above his head to describe three circles with his index finger. The fighter immediately behind him made the same motion, and in due time, a slightly built, lithe young fellow by the peculiar human name of Horen Gosak moved cautiously and noiselessly into place beside Kyrtian.

They locked eyes, Kyrtian's green ones meeting the human's brown; Kyrtian nodded towards the ridge in the direction of the voices and made the hand signal for *ambush.* Horen nodded, and leaving his sword and sword-belt behind in Kyrtian's keeping lest they catch in the brush, dropped to his hands and knees to snake his way up towards the ridge, moving so low to the ground that he looked like a crawling lizard.

It was always a wonder to Kyrtian how young Horen managed to disappear into landscape that was so barren of obvious cover. Sometimes he wondered if the ability was some unique application of the so-called human magics. That was entirely possible, and would have caused far more scandal among the Great Lords than Kyrtian's little eccentricity of leading his fighters in person. Although it was the law that all human slaves be fitted with collars that inhibited their own peculiar magic, no slave on the Prastaran estates had ever worn anything but a decorative collar since the Elvenlords came to this world. And no "slave" on the Prastaran estates had ever *been* a slave in anything but name.

Humans make very poor slaves; Grandfather tried to tell his arrogant compatriots that, and they wouldn't listen, and now they're paying the price for ignoring such sage advice. The first Lord Prastaran had retired to the estate he'd been allotted, proceeding there to put his own theories to work in regard to the aboriginal inhabitants of the place. Before he drowned in a flash flood—while nearly twenty of his devoted "slaves" also drowned in frantic attempts to save him—he had formed the loose confederation of primitives that had been living on the property into a thriving and prosperous community that not only accepted him as their overlord, but were absolutely devoted to his welfare.

Kyrtian's father had inherited that community, and had cherished and fostered it, recognizing it for the valuable resource that it was. Now it was Kyrtian's to guide and guard, for in guarding the humans under his protection, he was all too aware that he was guarding his own prosperity.

His wandering thoughts were abruptly recalled by Horen's return, as the young man wriggled into cover beside him. With the aid of twigs, pebbles, and a few hand-signals, Horen swiftly laid out the disposition of the enemy forces ahead.

Kyrtian studied the arrangement for several moments, grinding his teeth a little in frustration. As usual, the enemy commander showed brilliant skill. It was an appallingly superior disposition. Obviously one couldn't approach them from the front *or* the rear, so what did that leave *him?*

We could retreat, but that would leave them in possession of the woods, and they would win this without a fight. That was unacceptable. *Is there enough room on the top of this ridge to flank them?*

He didn't want to divide his force if he could help it, and he'd have to if he wanted to use a classic pincer maneuver. That wouldn't be a good idea anyway; one that the ground didn't encourage. He'd have to send his men to fight against both ends of the enemy ambush-line in a way that would only allow one or two fighters to close in at a time; that would put them at an immediate disadvantage.

Finally Kyrtian decided on something truly unorthodox; waiting until the enemy commander was frustrated enough to come looking for *him.* Short exploration by Horen produced the place where any opposing force was most likely to descend from the ridge. After careful deliberation, he set up an ambush of his own.

Of course, the weakness of this plan was that the opposition might not decide to come down on this side of the ridge. That would leave him, in his turn, waiting to spring an empty trap. Still, the occasional murmur of voices through the hush of the forest told him that his opponents were getting tired of waiting.

Probably they had been in place ever since his own force had entered the woods. Horen went out again to spy, so that Kyrtian's troops would at least know if the foe moved off in some other direction. Kyrtian settled into his own position and held off boredom by making an informal bird-count based on the calls he heard.

Time crawled past, but his patience was finally rewarded. Horen slithered back to take up his weapons. Kyrtian pumped his fist in the air once, and heard a faint rustle of leaves as his men caught the signal, relaying it down the line, and readying themselves for action.

He *had* chosen his own place perfectly. Another faint rustle of leaves and the occasional snapping of a twig warned that the enemy was on the move, and shortly after, the men appeared filing cautiously down the slope below them, flitting from bits of cover to their next position. Kyrtian waited until he was certain that all of the enemy skirmishers were immediately below their own position, his nerves so taut that his skin tingled, muscles were afire, his pulse pounding in his temples and his ears.

Wait for it—

If he sprang the ambush too soon, his own men would be surrounded. He didn't know exactly how many men the enemy had, so he couldn't count heads. . . .

Wait for it—

He didn't dare permit his force to be outflanked.

Now!

His throat cracked with a yell as he broke out of cover and charged, his men streaming down the slope behind him. The startled skirmishers whirled to face them.

Kyrtian skidded to a halt on the slope as he nearly ran into a fighter who was considerably taller than he. In that moment, as was always true for him once the fighting started, everything narrowed to this single opponent. Their swords clashed together, his opponent countered with a clever parry that sent him leaping away lest the fighter try to grapple with him. Next the man tried to circle him, but that was the last thing that Kyrtian was going to allow—at the moment he had the slight advantage of being uphill, and that was the only advantage he really had over this bulkier opponent.

Kyrtian retreated as fast as the other advanced; nothing was going to force him to turn if he could help it. Somewhere in the back of his mind he was dimly aware of shouts, the clashing of metal, and all the din of battle, but he was too seasoned to ever be distracted from his own line of combat. Giving up on the ploy of forcing Kyrtian off higher ground, the fellow swung low, hard and wide, scything at Kyrtian's legs; Kyrtian used the opportunity to slash at the man's sword-hand as he himself skipped backwards.

He really hadn't expected the luck of a full strike, but his opponent had evidently anticipated a blow to the head rather than the hand. The fighter ducked to one side and didn't get his hilt up in time to deflect Kyrtian's blow.

The blade passed through the other's wrist, leaving behind a glowing line. The fighter cursed, transferring the sword to his left hand, tucking the "disabled" hand into his belt at the small of his back, as per the rules of combat. If he hadn't, he'd get a warning after the battle was over—and the second time he refused to accept a blow, the marked area or limb would truly go completely numb and useless until Kyrtian removed the magic that rendered it so.

He was by no means as good a fighter with his weak hand as Kyrtian was. A clumsy attempt at an overhand blow left his armpit unprotected, and the Elvenlord executed a fatal thrust. The blade vanished up to the hilt with no resistance, and the man jerked in reaction to the all-over tingle that the "death-wound" gave him as the sign that he was "dead."

Now the fighter glowed the color of new leaves all over; with a good-natured curse, he saluted Kyrtian, sheathed his blade, and removed his helm, joining five of his fellow "dead men" on the sidelines. All of them were glowing the same yellow-green, which meant they were all out of the enemy forces. Kyrtian made the mistake of allowing himself a brief pause to gloat without looking behind him.

A moment after that, a sudden electric jolt told Kyrtian that he had been taken from behind. Ruefully looking down at himself, he saw that he, too, was glowing.

"Galkasht!" he cursed, in the Old Tongue, and heard Sargeant Gel's familiar laugh in answer. He sheathed his own sword in disgust, pulled off his helm, and went to join the other dead.

Gel did not get a chance to enjoy his victory for long; Horen rose out of a bush behind him and caught him across the neck as he turned. Gel swore even more colorfully than Kyrtian had, while his own men jeered and catcalled from the sidelines.

"Who is it has never been hit from behind?" called one, in feigned innocence.

"You owe me beer for the next moon, Sargeant," one of the others heartlessly reminded him. "And you owe Horen three night-watches."

"Don't remind me." The human pulled off his helm and threw it to the ground, glaring at them—but they knew they were safe. The "dead" could say anything they liked as long as the battle was on. That was another one of the rules, meant to be sure that no one turned mock-combat into a real fight.

"Temper, temper," scolded a third, as Horen vanished to seek a new opponent. "A true warrior never fights with anger."

"I'm not fighting," Gel pointed out sourly, his jaw clenched tight.

Gel picked up his helm after another scorching glare and stamped his way down the hill to the sidelines. Kyrtian hid his own grin, and gave Gel a commiserating slap on the shoulder.

"Too bad, old man," he said, with what he hoped was a good counterfeit of sympathy. "That's combat-luck for you."

"That's carelessness, you mean," Gel growled, as he ruffled his sweaty, grizzled brown hair to dry it. "Don't coddle me, Kyrtian; I got you when you stopped to gloat, then I was served the same dish. What's more, you ambushed me when I lost patience. You're going to win this one. I underestimated you."

Since at this point, those who glowed yellow-green outnumbered those who glowed red-orange by three to one, that was fairly obvious, so Kyrtian held his tongue and tried assume a modest expression.

"I think we can count this experiment a success," he said instead. "I wasn't sure we'd be able to make the transition from arena-fighting and set-battles, but it's obvious this mode is going to work."

"I'd keep it at the skirmish-level for a while," Gel cautioned.

"I intend to," Kyrtian assured him, as more of the "dead" on the sidelines cheered the surviving fighters on or showered them with abuse. "At least until everyone's gotten a fair amount of practice at this. I don't want people stumbling around breaking ankles in rabbit-holes or running into an alicorn and getting skewered. We're out here to fight, not get hurt." He loosened his throat-guard and yanked it off.

Gel barked a laugh at that, and Kyrtian had to grin. "That's as true as it sounds absurd," Gel chuckled. "And it's true you'd have less luck getting people to volunteer to fight for us if too many of the boys started coming back with broken bones, or worse." He stuck his thumb in his sword-belt and watched the fighters with pardonable pride. "I'll tell you what, though—I'd pit these lads against any of the professional fighters I've seen when it comes to combat rather than gladiatorial games. They'd win."

"That's rather the point, though I hope it doesn't come to that. There'll be far less blood shed if they go up against conscripts." Kyrtian watched as the last of his men surrounded the last of Gel's and demanded their surrender. "The Elvenlords can compel men to fight, but they can't compel them to fight *well.* Speaking of volunteers—the field-folk are going to need another holiday before too long."

"We'd better think about organizing a melee, then," Gel sighed. He hated setting up melees, as they were a great deal of work, and as in real battles, most of the people who took part in them had no idea how to actually fight. A good percentage got muddled and did the opposite of what they'd been ordered, and when they got muddled, they generally confused those who were trying to obey the orders correctly. Still, everyone on the estate enjoyed the mock wars and were happy to volunteer for them; there was great excitement in battle when there was no chance of dying and little chance of getting hurt. A war-day meant a general holiday with feasting and music, and dancing for those who were "killed" before they were completely exhausted.

Not that anyone got killed deliberately just so he could go dancing, since those who *were* too exhausted to dance were pampered and treated like heroes regardless of which side won.

Ever since the first time that Kyrtian and his right-hand man had expanded their war-games to include the general population of the estate, the exercise had proven so popular that humans and elves alike had come to expect and anticipate a war-day every two or three moons or so. Kyrtian just couldn't bring himself to disappoint them—and the one time he'd tried to hold a feast without a war, there had been such protest that he'd never dared do it again.

"I don't suppose it could be a woods-battle, could it?" he asked wistfully. "Or—oh, what about a siege?"

"With the manor as the target? No, better yet, the Dowager-House; no one's used it in decades, and it's been years since it was cleaned and aired out. It'll give your Lady-Mother an excuse to get it set to rights in case we need it for something. Ancestors know *what,* but we might." Gel mulled that over as his men declined to surrender, electing to fight to the last one standing. "That could be done—if you could manage mock-arrows and mock-stones; perhaps mock-boiling-oil."

Kyrtian stared at him, aghast at the picture *that* conjured up. "Ancestors! *You're* certainly bloody-minded!"

"If you want a siege, you might as well do it right," Gel argued. "That means that the besiegers will use bows, and the besieged will pelt them with whatever they can from the walls. Now, can you produce the proper material, or can't you?"

"I probably can," Kyrtian admitted. "But you do realize what this will mean, don't you?"

"Huge casualties early on, which means the battle won't run long, which means we'll get to the feasting sooner." Gel grinned. "Which means less work for me and more for your obliging Lady-Mother in arranging the entertainment."

"And probably a population increase in nine months unless I make sure to dose every particle of food on the estate against conceptions," Kyrtian sighed. "Which means more work for *me,* both in concocting the new magic-weapons, and in seeing to it that we *don't* get that flood of new births. You *know* what happens when the women get to be in on the combat! Why it is that mock-fighting gets them so stimulated—" He shook his head. "Sometimes I think that you humans are so different from us that I'll never understand you. Still—"

"A siege would be fun," Gel said, persuasively, as his men dropped, one by one, beneath the swords of Kyrtian's fighters. "We've never done a siege before with live fighters. Things that work on the sand-table with models don't always work with living people."

The temptation was too great to resist. "All right," he decided. "Start planning and working toward it. I'll research the magic needed. If it doesn't look as if we can pull it off in a months' time, we'll have the usual field-melee instead."

"Done!" Gel crowed, and slapped him on the shoulder, just as the last of his men fell. At that point, Kyrtian's remaining fighters rushed up, cheering, and there was no point in trying to talk until the victory celebration was over.

3

As was usual, the two groups of combatants trudged out of the forest together as a single fraternal mass with no sense of marching order. The forest could well have been devoid of life at this point; birds and beasts were probably frightened into immobility by the laughter and talking. At any rate, Kyrtian couldn't spot so much as a rabbit or a sparrow as they followed the faint track of an old road beneath the trees. The sun was just setting, and a thick, golden light poured through the branches, gilding the edges of the leaves and touching the clouds. Tired, but cheerful, friends and comrades traded congratulations, boasts, and outright lies as Kyrtian and Gel brought up the rear. Kyrtian never permitted anyone to carry his armor for him; like his men, he bore his own equipment, at least as far as their transportation. There were wagons and a carriage waiting just outside the woods to carry them all back to the manor, since it would have taken them hours to return on foot; Kyrtian was very glad to be able to toss his helm to his driver and allow his body-servant to take the heavy armor off before he climbed into the cushioned comfort of the carriage. As a token of his privileged rank, Gel shared both the attentions of the servant and the carriage; the men helped each other and made do with the cushioning effect of a thick layer of hay in their wagons. "Ah, the benefits of rank," Gel sighed as he sat back in the carriage opposite Kyrtian. Kyrtian grinned.

As soon as Gel got himself seated, the driver turned the horses and sent the carriage on its way while the wagons were still being loaded with men and armor. "Ancestors!" Kyrtian exclaimed, as the servant handed him a flask of cool, sweet water. "I've been looking forward to this all afternoon!" He took a long draught, timing his drink with the jolting of the carriage so he didn't break his teeth on the neck of the flask, before handing it to Gel.

"You'd think we'd get tired of this nonsense," Gel responded, leaning back into the soft, dark brown velvet cushions after he'd corked the flask and handed it back to young Lynder, Kyrtian's body-servant. "Your dear mother keeps saying we're too old to play at being soldiers, and sometimes I wonder if she's right, at least about me. Every time we come back from one of these games, I ask myself if it isn't time to stop."

"You only think that as long as it takes for you to get your wind back." The young Elvenlord grinned at his companions, and Lynder chuckled. "And mother has a different set of priorities from you and me. What do you expect her to say? She's not just a female, she's a *lady,* and if she had her way we'd all be drifting around the estate in clouds of tranquil music, perfume, and refinement. If it were up to her, *you'd* be cultivating roses, and *I'd* be cultivating illusions and courting some fragile little lily of a maiden." He accepted the flask back and took another drink. "Not that you need to apologize for having a knack with roses—but I don't think you'd want to spend your life among the flowers."

Gel rolled his eyes. "Gods forbid!" he exclaimed. "I'd die of boredom in half a day! Roses are all right for a hobby, but not as a life's work!"

"I'd prefer tending roses to being forced to spend my time cultivating a highborn maiden." Kyrtian laughed, the sound interrupted oddly by the jouncing of the carriage. "At least you don't have to make conversation with a flower, even if you do have to be careful of the thorns. It's easier to avoid thorns than try to keep a strange woman from seeing things she shouldn't."

He tried to keep his tone light, but his laughter sounded a bit strained in his own ears. The subject of wives and heirs had been much on his mother's mind and tongue lately; hardly a day passed without her alluding to it at least once. It was a subject he was not easy with. He enjoyed his life the way it was, and had no real wish to bring a stranger into his home. "Ancestors! I'd have to set up an entirely separate part of the estate to keep her properly secluded, and that would be as much of a bore as courting her would be! I swear, if it weren't forbidden I'd wed a stout-hearted human wench from right here."

Gel made a sour face. "At the least, we'd need the Dowager-House set to rights just to confine the girl in, and somehow keep her mewed up there indefinitely. If Tenebrinth, Selazian and Pelenal had daughters—things would be a great deal easier on all of us. You'd think *one* of your clients would have the good sense to take care of that little problem for us!"

Kyrtian replied with complete seriousness. "I wish they had. Nothing would have pleased me better to take one of them into my family line; they're all fine gentlemen. As it is—well, someday soon I suppose I'll have to please Mother and go looking amongst someone else's underlings for a wife. Eventually I'll find a maiden who's of sufficiently low rank to be too overawed to notice my eccentricities."

"She'll have to overlook more than that," Gel warned him,

"Or you'll have her running back to her Papa with stories of how you can't keep your slaves properly under your thumb."

Kyrtian felt compelled to give his mother's counters to those arguments, which were the same that he himself had raised. "Elven maidens in most households are kept close-confined, Mother says. And a maiden of low rank should be dazzled by her new surroundings and too much in awe of Mother ever to question things. We think that as long as her servants obeyed her, she'd never know we do things differently here." He compressed his brows in a little frown. "I'd have to make sure that she was never allowed to abuse them, though . . . and that could take some management."

Gel looked dubious, but only said, "If you'd just leave the wife-hunting up to your Mother, you can be sure she won't choose someone we'll have to worry about. *She* has entry to all the bowers, and if she can't find someone sympathetic to our ways, she can at least find someone who is too timid to speak up about anything, too stupid to care, or has been too closely sheltered to know what is and is not usual."

"I suppose that's the only real solution," Kyrtian sighed, and winced at the thought of a mouse, a dolt, or a frail flower as a wife. *What a disgusting situation,* he thought, frowning. *And I'm going to have to do something about it fairly soon. Mother isn't going to allow me to put it off much longer.*

Gel snorted at his rueful expression, as a particularly hard bounce sent them all in the air for a brief moment. "Don't mope," he replied sternly, then added, with a crude chuckle, "At least you aren't going to be saddled with a wife who has the hips of a cow, the manners of a pig, and the face of a horse. You Elves are never less than handsome, so you won't have to wish for a bag to put over her head when you do your duty to present the estate with an heir."

Kyrtian flushed, feeling the tips of his ears burn. Gel had been his teacher, companion, and friend for as long as he could remember, but the human could be amazingly coarse, sometimes. How on earth could he explain that what made him dread matrimony was the fear that he'd find himself bound for centuries to a dull, insipid idiot? How could he possibly get up enough interest in a maiden like that *to* do his duty by the estate and the clan? Gel would only laugh, and tell him that it wasn't what was between a girl's ears that mattered—

If I could find someone like Mother, he thought wistfully, *I'd wed her no matter what her rank was. Did Father ever really know how lucky he was to find a maiden with wit, courage, sense, and intelligence? What are rank and magic worth, compared with qualities like that?*

"We'll have to tell Milady about the new scheme for a siege," Gel said cheerfully, interrupting his thoughts. "She'll probably want to have a hand in it herself this time—and I think you ought to give her a bit of a command. Maybe then she'll stop teasing us about our pastime."

"You know, you could be right." Kyrtian braced himself as the carriage hit a series of ruts that threatened to bounce them all against the ceiling, rattling his very teeth. This was the worst part of the road; in a moment, everything would suddenly smooth out as they reached the paved section. "Maybe if she gets a taste of this, she'll realize just how challenging it is."

My only other choice would be to tell her the truth—that it isn't a game, that Gel and I are training the humans to defend the estate if—or when—combat comes here. I don't want to do that; I don't know *that danger is coming, I just feel it in my bones.* Their estate was relatively isolated, and he and his mother certainly were *not* in the first social circles, but still . . . first had come the Elvenbane, that weird wizard-girl who had, by all repute, single-handedly engineered an uprising of totally unsuspected halfbloods. Not that *he* expected any trouble from the halfbloods—his people were perfectly free to join the Wizards any time they wanted to, and none of them did. Still, to have a dreaded legend come to life and take down the *most* powerful Elvenlord on the Council, and do it with the aid of Lord Dyran's own son, who she somehow subverted—well, it had all of the Elvenlords looking for more halfbloods-in-disguise in their midst.

And when the Great Lords were looking for one thing, they might find something else they didn't care for.

Then had come a second rebellion, this time of the Elven

lords' own disregarded second and third offspring, the "spares," which apparently involved a new sort of magic that disrupted even the most powerful Elven magic. That war was not going well for the Great Lords. It wasn't so much that they'd lost a great deal of territory, for the relatively small number of Young Lords who had revolted had only taken a few estates; the problem was that they'd taken and held them, and continued to hold, and although Kyrtian didn't know this for certain, he suspected they were making themselves felt. They were a thorn, not in the side, but in the foot, and one which was felt with every step the Great Lords took. That made them edgy; always a dangerous thing. Kyrtian didn't like the idea of having an edgy, inquisitive Great Lord nosing around anywhere near *his* estate. Or his people.

And if anything happened because there was an inquisitive Great Lord sniffing around—well, he wanted to be ready for it.

"Maybe she'll want to take up the sword for herself," Gel suggested, with a sly twinkle. "You know she'd be good at it. I think if she ever got a feel for fighting, she'd be as addicted to it as we are."

"Oh, there's a thought!" Kyrtian laughed wickedly. "I could make *her* my second-in-command. Then what would you do?"

"Go on my knees and submit," Gel admitted. "And bow to the inevitable. I've seen her move and I've seen her at the hunt—she's got better reactions than you do. Ancestors! Put a bow in her hands, and I'll surrender on the spot rather than face her!"

The carriage jolted one last time, as the wheels bounced up onto the pavement, then Kyrtian and Gel settled back with identical sighs of relief as rough ride gave way to smooth rolling that was as comfortable as sailing on a smooth lake.

"I trust you've taken care of things for the men as usual?" Kyrtian asked Lynder. The young human had only been Kyrtian's body-servant for two months, but he'd been meticulously trained by Kyrtian's previous man, and the Elvenlord was confident he could handle his new responsibilities as invisibly as his predecessor.

The man looked a little anxious. "The bathhouse is cleared and ready, dinner's been held, there's to be music and late-leave for the other servants to join the entertainment—" He hesitated, and glanced pleadingly at Gel, clearly wondering if he'd missed something.

"Exactly right, Lynder," Kyrtian said soothingly, to take the look of anxiety out of his eyes. Lynder had probably missed one or two details, but the other servants would see to it that everything went smoothly anyway. After years of these mock-battles, everyone knew what was expected afterwards. The house-and field-servants were expected to reschedule their own baths so that the returning fighters could have the place to themselves. Dinner had been held back so that it would reach the tables hot and fresh as they came out of the bathhouse—and it wouldn't be the usual bread and stew, but something a little fancier. Roast meat or chicken, usually, a choice of side-dishes, and something in the way of a sweet. There would be a little extra beer—not enough to cause problems, but a glass or two more than usual for everyone. Some of the household musicians would come down after dinner, and there would be some lively music and dancing, and if beds had two occupants or none in them tonight instead of one, no one would be taken to task. Tomorrow would be a quarter-holiday, work and drill to start a bit later in the morning than usual so that the men could sleep in a bit. All in all, the men would feel themselves well rewarded for their hard work today.

And we need to begin planning the next holiday by tomorrow at the latest, Kyrtian reminded himself. He didn't like to make the intervals between holidays too long; he didn't want the house-and field-servants to start feeling aggrieved at the special treatment the fighters received.

The carriage slowed and came to a stop; in the dusty gold light that was swiftly fading, a servant in emerald-green tunic and trews opened the door, and Kyrtian got out, followed by Gel and Lynder. Round, blue-white lights hanging in clusters of four from bronze posts already blazed on either side of the white stone staircase that led to the front portals of the manor. More green-liveried servants took possession of the armor and arms as Kyrtian looked about. Gel saluted and stalked off towards the barracks in that tireless, ageless stride that Kyrtian could never imitate, with the final rays of the setting sun illuminating him like some god-touched hero of human history.

Kyrtian ran up the alabaster steps of the manor with Lynder close behind, deep shadows now giving way to blue dusk. At the top of the stairs, double doors of cast bronze would have swung open at the merest touch of his magic, but he ignored them entirely, intending to take the inconspicuous doorkeeper's entry at the side. The green-clad doorkeeper had expected just that, and was holding open the smaller portal for him, bowing slightly as he passed through.

"Beker!" Kyrtian greeted him. "Is your wife better?"

The human's long face brightened at the question. "Oh, much better, Lord Kyrtian! We cannot thank you enough—"

"You'll thank me by not letting things get to such a pass before you say something," Kyrtian replied, with just enough of a stern tone to his voice that the doorkeeper would know he was serious. "Don't keep going back to the 'pothecary; when the simple cure doesn't work, go to Lord Selazian. That's why I keep him as a retainer, Beker; make the lazy lout work for his living!"

"Yes. Lord Kyrtian," the doorkeeper whispered, bowing further. "I will, my lord."

"Carry on, Beker," Kyrtian replied, and moved on, leaving the doorkeeper to shut things up behind him.

"Lynder, remind Lord Tenebrinth to have a talk with the apothecary, will you?" Kyrtian said in a quiet aside as they strode down the middle of the entrance hall. A thick, pale-grey carpet beneath their feet muffled all sound of footfalls, and although the alabaster ceiling and grey-veined marble walls were not *imposing,* Kyrtian thought they had a great deal of dignity about them. "I can't have my people getting sick and relying on that—that herb-shaman for everything! I wouldn't have had him at all, if you humans hadn't insisted on him."

"Lord Kyrtian—it is frightening for some of us to ask a Lord for anything, much less ask him to treat us for our ailments," Lynder replied with hesitation. "You forget sometimes that although many of us have been born and raised in your service, many more come from outside the boundary of your estate, and things are very different in the greater world."

"Well, that's why I want you to remind Lord Tenebrinth to talk to the apothecary. I suspect the man might be encouraging those fears, and if that's true, I want it stopped." Kyrtian frowned. "Ancestors! The last thing we need is to get a plague started because a man who thinks rattling bones and brewing teas can cure everything won't give up trying till his patients are dead!"

"With your permission, Lord Kyrtian, I'll ask Sergeant Gel to have a word with him first." Kyrtian saw out of the corner of his eye that Lynder was smiling a little. "The Sergeant can be very persuasive."

Kyrtian nodded, as they turned down a side corridor to the family-quarters. "I trust your judgment, Lynder. But do feel free to bring Tenebrinth in on it; he is my Seneschal, after all."

Lynder moved ahead to smoothly open a door on the right-hand side of the corridor before Kyrtian could touch it himself. "Yes, Lord Kyrtian," he replied, and as Kyrtian stepped through the door into his private quarters, he was engulfed by servants.

In other households, they would have been called "slaves," and it was true that Kyrtian was their titular owner—but if any one of them wanted to leave, he would have only to petition the Elvenlord and permission would be instantly granted. Somehow, some way, Kyrtian would find a way to smuggle the human out to the territories held by the Wizards or the free humans. Not that anyone would ever ask for that permission—the world open to free humans was hostile and uncomfortable, and entirely too dangerous to be much of a temptation.

As had been the case with Kyrtian's father and grandfather, Kyrtian and his mother were respected, admired, even beloved, not only by the humans of the estate, but by the few Elven retainers who called them their liege-lords. There were three who were of the most importance; the aforementioned Tenebrinth whose position as Seneschal predated Kyrtian's birth, Selazian the Physician who had been studying the diseases of humans as well as Elves for literally centuries—and Lord Pelenal, Kyrtian's Agent, who handled all the affairs of the estate that needed to be conducted outside the walls of the estate.

Kyrtian and his mother were as dependent on Pelenal's good will as he was on theirs, but he had never given them even a moment of unease. Pelenal bought new slaves, negotiated contracts, and haggled to get the best prices for the foodstuffs produced by this most fertile of estates. Pelenal was one of those most despised of creatures, an Elvenlord with so little magic he might just as well have had none at all. Despite the fact that there could not possibly have been a better Agent in all of the estates, Pelenal would never have attained that position of power in the service of anyone other than Kyrtian's family. He knew that; saw Elves with more magic than he groveling for crumbs at the tables of greater Elvenlords, and demonstrated his gratitude in the most tangible of terms on a regular basis.

That was just as well, because where real power, the political power of the Council of the Great Lords was concerned, Kyrtian had none. His only power was economic, and that was in no small part due to Pelenal's clever management.

Still, that power could be formidable.

As servants swarmed over him, stripping him to the skin as they propelled him towards the bathing room, he allowed himself the luxury of feeling just a little smug. Political power came and went—even magic power could fade with time, or be lost to further generations—but economic power was a much more dependable, if underrated force. His grandfather had understood that, even if his father hadn't—but his father had the services of Tenebrinth to ensure that the estate's prosperity continued. Pelenal had simply built on that foundation.

The bathing-room, of green-veined marble with shining silver fixtures, featured a sunken tub longer than Kyrtian was tall, and deep enough for him to sink in up to his chin. Just now it was so full of steam it was difficult to see across it. Kyrtian stepped into the tub carefully. *When father vanished, things could have been very bad, if mother hadn't had the good sense to ask Tenebrinth if he knew someone he could trust to become our outside Agent.* Kyrtian eased himself down into the hot, juniper-scented water of his bath, thinking as he did so that his Mother was almost as remarkable in her way as his Grandfather had been. The more he learned about running this estate, the more amazing it was to him that nothing had gone wrong. Thanks to Tenebrinth and Pelenal, who studied the demands of the other estates and the resources of their own with the fierce dedication of a warrior for his craft, Kyrtian's estate was so prosperous that even his worst enemies would never dream of forcing a confrontation with him.

He closed his eyes and fragrant steam rose up and filled the room further with scented fog. *No one Lord would ever dare challenge me,* he thought contentedly. *And probably not two or three together. Not that they're likely to, since I don't meddle in politics, but they still wouldn't dare. Not when these lands feed and clothe a third of them. Not when the fruits of* our *labors are served up on* their *tables, when* our *wines are the choicest, our silks the fairest.*

Granted, an Elvenlord with powerful magic could transform water and ashes into the finest wine and choicest meals—but it was still water and ashes, and wouldn't nourish any better. It took a great deal of magic to create such illusions, magic which could be put to better use. Illusory gold had no commercial worth—but the gold in Kyrtian's treasury was real enough.

No, no one is ever going to try any political games with us, he told himself, as the heat of the bath warmed and soothed all of his tired, strained muscles. *They wouldn't dare. Pelenal wouldn't sell to them, and then where would they be? Half the stuff that goes to feed their slaves comes from here; most of them don't bother growing grain anymore, or raising sheep for wool and flax for linen.*

As often as he asked Tenebrinth if there was anything the Seneschal wanted as a reward for all his good service, Tenebrinth had never asked for anything but the most trivial of favors. Lord Tenebrinth often seemed to Kyrtian the most contented of beings; he had a wife who adored him, and the freedom to manage the estate as he saw fit. Tenebrinth's chief pleasure outside of his family came from trying out little theories of management. Over the decades, he had weeded out all the ones that didn't work at all, or didn't work well, and now he was in the process of fine-tuning and balancing everything. The one thing that Tenebrinth would have wanted that Kyrtian couldn't give him was a child.

And if I could, I would. I think we pay for our long lives in our lack of children. It was sad, really, for if there was ever an Elven lady born to be a mother, it was Tenebrinth's wife, Lady Seryana.

And of course, it would be so much easier on all of us if they just had a daughter. It wouldn't have mattered how young the girl was; Kyrtian would be more than willing to wait for her to grow up. After all, he had all the time in the world before him; Elves *did* age and die eventually, but "eventually" was several centuries away.

Maybe what he ought to do would be to investigate those rumors that some Elvenlords had discovered ways to enhance their fertility with magic. If that were true, and he could find a way to purchase the services of such a magician—

That would solve everyone's problem, wouldn't it?

It was an easy solution on the surface, but like deep water, such a "solution" could cover more than was immediately apparent.

The favor might cost more than I'm willing to give. What if the mage wanted slaves? How could I send off any of my *people into real slavery? What if he wanted some of my fighters? What if he wanted Gel?*

Even if that difficulty never came up, there was the imaginary girl to consider. *She might not like me. She might like me, but not enough. She might fall in love with someone else—even Pelenal.* He winced away from the idea of forcing a maiden to wed because she'd been betrothed to him in her cradle. How could any good come out of such a bad bargain?

Gel is right. I should leave it up to mother, he decided, with a slight sinking of his heart and a contradictory feeling of relief. *I'll tell her so at dinner. That should make her so happy she'll let us besiege her very bower if we want!*

4

As Lynder replenished the goblet of cool water at Kyrtian's right hand, the young lord soaked until the aches in his tired, sore muscles eased. He'd have remained in the bath until he was in danger of falling asleep, if not for two factors. His stomach complained that it hadn't gotten anything but water for some time, and he knew his mother was waiting for him to have dinner with her and out of politeness would not touch a morsel until he appeared. Servants sent off for a platter of finger-foods would have taken care of the hunger, but he was not going to be rude to his mother!

It isn't wise to be rude to one's mother. She knows everything about your childhood that is potentially embarrassing.

Reluctantly, he stepped up out of the water, dripping onto the marble floor, and waved off another attentive servant, taking the soft, snowy towel the lad held out to him. Wrapping the towel around himself, he returned to his bedroom to find clothing laid out over a stand and waiting for him to don. This clothing had been selected by Lynder to complement whatever his mother was wearing for dinner. It was a small gesture, but one that his mother appreciated, and it only cost a little extra attention on the part of the servants; such attention was no burden to them, for she was as beloved to her staff as she was to her son.

To his relief, the waiting clothing was casual, a comfortable tunic and trews of heavy amber silk with a simple geometric design in bronze beadwork trimming the collar and belt. That meant his mother was in a casual mood; in fact, with any luck, she had arranged to dine on the balcony outside the lesser dining-room, where they could watch their human dependents dancing and listen to their music.

He knew, because she had told him, that other Elvenlords

generally chose to dine amid self-created, fantastic settings built of illusion, a simpler version of the illusions he'd seen at the few Elven gatherings and fetes he had attended. He had never been able to fathom why they would wish to do such a thing. How boring must it be, surrounded by something so utterly controlled, in which one knew to the moment exactly what would happen? He preferred real weather, real sunsets, and the spontaneity of live performers. But then, he'd never cared much for even the most elaborate of illusions, far preferring the beauties of the real world to gossamer fantasies. Even his suite held a but single illusion, to bring the outdoors that he loved inside regardless of weather or season. He had created an ethereal forest glade and waterfall, illuminated in a perpetual twilight, in the corner of his sitting room. This illusion opened his suite and made the room seem to extend far beyond the actual walls. He could easily have had a real waterfall put in, but that would have made the sitting room rather more humid than he liked. The three rooms of his suite—sitting room, study, and bedroom—were otherwise all as they had been built: grey carpet, white walls and ceiling, simple, unornamented furnishings with frames of pale birch-wood and fat cushions in grey-blue, grey-green, and slate-grey. Sourceless, gentle light bathed the rooms, but could be extinguished with a single command—magic, yes, but hardly illusion.

He donned the soft, comfortable silk garments, slipped on a pair of buttery leather indoor boots and belted the tunic with a matching sash. After a quick glance at himself in a mirror to ensure that he had not forgotten anything, he set out for the dining-chambers, leaving the servants to clean up behind him. The same sourceless light as brightened his rooms illuminated the hallways whose only ornaments were small tables placed at intervals against the wall. He noted with approval that now that it was summer, someone had replaced the statues that had stood on each table with arrangements of flowers which gently scented the air without being cloying. *So* much better than all the incense and heavy perfumes he'd encountered in the few other manors he'd occasionally visited! His mother made life here into an art form, something that appeared effortless and was anything but. It required a small army of their faithful servants, working in careful harmony, to achieve the "simple" effects that others created with illusions.

As he approached the dining chambers, the light subtly changed, growing warmer in tone, and the flower arrangements here were no longer made up of blooms of white and pale pastels, but of richer colors. This was clearly the work of his mother's hand and mind. The impression now created was that of cheer and welcome, and he noted proudly that once again, it was accomplished without the use of a single illusion.

Lynder waited patiently outside the door of the lesser dining-chamber, confirming Kyrtian's guess that he and his mother would be dining without the company of any of the other Elves of the estate. Lynder opened the bronze-edged door for him, and he passed through with a nod of thanks. Subdued lighting and an empty table greeted him, and the open casement door to the balcony beyond beckoned him onward.

Out on the alabaster balcony, a pair of bronze lamps gave just enough light to be useful without being obtrusive. A servant with a cart laden with covered dishes waited beside a small table flanked by two chairs. His mother rose from the furthest of these as he stepped onto the balcony, and held out her hand to him with a welcoming smile.

V'dyll Lydiell Lady Prastaran was not the most beautiful of Elven women; her green eyes were a touch too shrewd, her cheekbones too sharply defined, her mouth at once too generous and too sardonic, her winglike eyebrows too inclined to arc upwards in wry amusement. Her figure was too slight to be called "generous," and too muscular to be called "delicate"; in fact, she was a notable dancer and athlete. And she was too tall for the current fashion, with fully as much height as her son. Tonight her moon-pale hair was caught at the back of her head in a single, practical knot, only relieved by three strands of bronze, moonstone and amber beads threaded onto slender locks of hair behind her left ear. Her clothing was virtually identical to her son's, except that she wore a divided skirt instead of trews. She followed no fashions, and set none; she was a law unto herself, and as such, fit the Prastaran estate and clan perfectly.

Kyrtian took her hand, dropped a filial kiss on it, and assisted her back into her seat before taking his own. He sniffed appreciatively at the savory scents arising from the first dish as the servant uncovered a thick soup and offered it for their approval.

Lydiell took the ladle herself, and measured out two porcelain bowls full. "I've already quizzed Lynder, so I know that you beat Gel," she said with amusement. "And I also know that he managed to kill you in the process of beating him. A rather dubious victory, don't you think?"

"I suppose it would depend on whether you were the captain who was killed or the general who sent him," Kyrtian pointed out. "My imaginary superior would have no reason to be unhappy about the outcome of our battle."

Lydiell made a little grimace of distaste. "Your not-so-imaginary relations would either be very grieved or very pleased if your demise had been genuine," she countered. "Your obnoxious cousin Aelmarkin in particular—"

Kyrtian knew what was coming, and this time decided to preempt the little speech about his duty to the legacy left to him by his father. "My obnoxious cousin in particular is going to be very *un*happy as soon as you finish the project I'd like *you* to undertake, Lady-Mother," he interrupted, tapping her hand playfully with his index finger. "I want you to go hunt me out a couple of suitable females so I can make a selection for a bride. I'd likely only bungle the job; you, however, will manage it brilliantly."

Lydiell stared at him with her mouth slightly open, her eyes wide and her eyebrows arched as high as they would go. "Are you serious?" she demanded. "Are you really ready to wed?"

She didn't say "at last" but she didn't have to.

He shrugged. "As ready as I am ever likely to be, and with all the unrest about, it would probably be better to get it over with before it becomes impossible for you to travel around to find me someone."

Lydiell's expression assumed a faint cast of guilt. "I swore to your father I would never pressure you into marrying someone for whom you had no affection," she began. "And—"

"And you aren't going to now," he replied firmly. "I've just gotten over the expectation that the perfect woman will somehow drop out of the sky on gossamer wings, emerge nixielike from the river, or materialize spirit-wise out of the forest, and make me fall into passionate love with her. A girl who won't become a risk for us is far more important, and you're the best judge of that. So far as my own needs are concerned, someone I can tolerate over breakfast will do nicely. If we have some things in common so that we don't baffle or bore each other, better still." He put his hand over his mother's as it rested on the table, and he felt it tremble. "To my mind, it is far more important that she feel love and affection for *you,* my lady."

"If you found a wife whom *you* loved but who didn't care for me, I could always retire to the Dowager-House," she began bravely, but he shook his head.

"I know Grandmother loved the Dowager-House and retired there because she found too many memories in these halls, but that won't be the case for you. I couldn't care for anyone who drove you out of your own home, so I rely on you to find me someone sensible. I will be happy with safety, sense, and intelligence, in that order. Now," he continued, seeing the light in her eyes and deciding to take advantage of the situation, "Gel and I want to stage another holiday-battle, and we thought we'd have a siege of the Dowager-House instead of the usual woods-battle or field-melee. Do you think we could arrange that?"

As surely as if he had the human magic for reading thoughts, he knew she was engrossed in running over the various matrimonial possibilities in her mind, and that the moment he had said Gel's name, she dismissed the rest of the sentence as irrelevant to the all-important task of matchmaking. "Oh, certainly," she said absently, allowing the servant to take away her soup and serve her a portion of baked eel, a dish she normally never touched. She ate it, too, taking dainty but rapid bites, all of her thoughts occupied with more important things than food.

He grinned to himself, and devoured his own portion without further comment, congratulating himself on his clever maneuver. He'd gotten her approval of the siege—which she would belatedly remember, some time late tonight as she went over the dinner conversation in her mind. By that time it would be too late to retract the approval. And it hadn't cost him anything other than something he'd already made up his mind to do. Satisfaction gave him a hearty appetite, and he enjoyed every bite of his dinner.

Down below the balcony, the lawn stretched out in a plush, velvety slope for some distance before it flattened out and became the village green shared by all of the human servants who had earned cottages in the manor-village. Surrounded by lanterns suspended from stands plunged into the turf, it was brilliantly and festively illuminated. The green served as fairgrounds, dance-floor, and feast-table in fine weather, and it served the latter two purposes tonight. The warriors, victorious and defeated both, celebrated at long wooden tables that had been carried out from their barracks. Other servants and fieldworkers, their dinners long over, slowly came by groups of two and three to join the fun. Festive torches burned brightly at either end of each table, and a little band of musicians had set up at the far end and played raucous dancing-tunes that were unlike anything ever heard at an Elven celebration. Kyrtian rather liked human music, himself, and he knew his mother was amused by it—but to compare human to Elven music would be like comparing a noisy forest stream to an illuminated water-sculpture. They were both made of moving water, but with that all resemblance ended.

Gel and a dozen others had already finished their dinner and found themselves partners, and were dancing with great enthusiasm and abandon, if not skill. From the rosy cheeks and sparkling eyes of the girls, none of the partners were inclined to complain if their toes got trodden on, occasionally. Kyrtian finished his meal in silence, and settled back in his chair with a glass of wine, watching the swirl and chaos of the ever-increasing crowd of dancers.

"About your obnoxious cousin—" Lydiell murmured unexpectedly, startling him.

"What about him?" Kyrtian replied, glancing at her. "He

doesn't want to visit again, does he? I thought we'd managed to cure him of that after the last time."

Lydiell winced. "It almost cured *me* of wanting to stay here," she said, shuddering. "If I'd had to sit through one more evening of you droning in that flat voice—! You'd have made erotic poetry unbearably dull with that voice!"

Kyrtian grinned. "I thought the monotone went with the subject matter. You can thank Gel for that, by the way. I had no idea he knew so much about the tactical importance of camp supply and sanitation; by the time he was done filling my head with the information, I could have written a monograph on the subject."

"Remind me to have him served a nice dish of live scorpions," she said, with a touch of exasperation. "He *might* have taken care to recall that I was going to have to endure that evening too! But, to go back to the subject—no, your cousin Aelmarkin has no intention of visiting. Evidently, however, he does want to make up for trying to disinherit you."

"Oh, really?" Kyrtian felt his eyebrows rising in an imitation of his mother's most sardonic expression. "How fraternal of him. What, exactly, does he want?"

Lydiell's face gave no hint of her feelings. "He wants *you* to visit. He's invited you to a—a gathering, of sorts. Lord Marthien and Lord Wyvarna are settling their dispute at his estate."

Kyrtian was unpleasantly surprised. "Two Great Lords are settling a feud and Aelmarkin wants *me* there? Whatever for?"

Lydiell shook her head. "I don't know," she replied, sounding honestly perplexed. "Perhaps he has decided he should change his behavior, in the hope you'll forget his petition. Or forgive it, at least."

Kyrtian made a sour face. "Perhaps he just wants to show the Great Lords that I'm as crazed as my father. After all, I have the same obsession with the past that father did. He's probably hoping I'll start droning about Evelon history, or asking if any of them have ancient books in their libraries that I could have copied."

"Darthenian wasn't crazed," Lydiell said softly. "And neither are you. It isn't madness to be concerned about the past—it's madness to try and pretend it never happened. Look at the situation the Great Lords have created—at war with their own sons! If they had remembered the past, and the feuds that sent us fleeing Evelon in the first place, they might have avoided this tragedy."

"I sometimes wonder if it isn't a little mad to pursue the past so relentlessly," Kyrtian replied, his mood suddenly shadowed. "Why else would father have disappeared?"

Lydiell's cheeks flushed delicately with anger, but she did not give rein to it. "Why else?" she asked, and answered the question herself, forcefully. "A combination of dedication and bad luck—or, perhaps, the acquisition of a ruthless enemy. I don't know what Darthenian was hunting when he vanished, my love, for he kept it a secret even from me, but I *do* know that it was important and potentially very powerful. That made the secret a dangerous one, and that was *why* he kept it from me. It is possible that he met with an accident. It is also possible that someone besides me took him seriously—and wished to learn what he knew, or prevent him from discovering anything that might have given him an edge in the endless jostling for power."

"Are you suggesting that he was—murdered?" Kyrtian asked slowly. It was something that had never occurred to him.

Lydiell sighed. "I don't know. It is possible—but I cannot even guess at how *likely* it is. I have never seen or heard anything to allow me to dismiss the idea, or that confirmed it." Her expression was haunted by that very uncertainty. "Nevertheless, let others remember him as an unstable dabbler for delving into the oldest of our records—I know better, and so should you."

Kyrtian immediately felt ashamed, and bent his head in mute apology. "And I should not allow the views of V'kel Aelmarkin er-Lord Tornal to shade my opinion of even so trivial a question as wine selection, much less anything important." He frowned. "I've half a mind to turn his invitation down. It's come too quickly on the Council's decision, and Aelmarkin is nothing if not persistent. He surely has something planned as an attempt to embarrass me."

But Lydiell shook her head. "That, you mustn't do. He has more political power than you, and he could make things difficult if you offend him. Do you really want to waste your time countering his petty nastiness with the Council, when you could avoid having to do so by attending his gathering?"

Kyrtian sighed, knowing with resignation that he was going to have to go and play the fool to keep Aelmarkin happy. "Not really. When is this farce scheduled?"

"In three days," Lydiell told him, and patted his hand comfortingly. "Cheer up," she offered. "It's only for an afternoon. How hard can it be to maintain your composure for an afternoon?"

How hard can it be to maintain my composure for an afternoon? Kyrtian asked himself savagely, as he glared down at the sands of the arena to avoid meeting any more contemptuous or amused glances. *Harder than getting the better of Gel in a sword-bout, that's how!*

From the moment he'd stepped out of the Portal into Aelmarkin's manor, he'd realized two things. The first: Lydiell had been absolutely right; if he hadn't shown his face—and his sanity—at this function, Aelmarkin would have been able to say whatever he liked and be believed. The second: it was going to stress his patience and his acting ability to the limit to put up with the attitude of every other guest that Aelmarkin had invited. He had never felt so utterly out-of-place in his life. Why, he had more in common with the humans of his estate than he did these strange creatures of his own race!

A great many of them were approximately his age—much younger than Aelmarkin—the idle offspring of Great Lords who didn't care to attend this particular challenge-fight themselves, but wanted to send representatives. Of course this meant that he was surrounded by those with little to do except chatter about others of their set, current fads, useless pastimes, and new fashions. The people of their social set were people he didn't know anything about, and the pursuits they found so important—well, he couldn't imagine why anyone would waste time on such things. But in their eyes, he was clearly impossibly backward, out-of-step, and provincial.

None of them knew anything about any of the subjects he cared about, which made him sound both a bore and a boor.

And after he'd shown a flicker of startlement at statements he considered outrageous, they probably put him down as callow and a prig.

Well, by their standards, I am a prig. I don't consider an afternoon spent in having my jaded appetites aroused by poor human girls who only exist to serve as my concubines to be particularly amusing.

After the first hour, they snubbed him openly, and with unveiled contempt.

This, strangely enough, made him very uncomfortable. He hadn't expected them to make him feel that way. He could try to tell himself that these people didn't matter, that all he had to do was remain polite and comport himself like a gentleman and nothing they reported back to their fathers would do any harm—but that didn't make the sneers and the sniggering any easier to bear. He didn't like them, but they were many and he was one; it was all too easy to feel the hurt of the scorned outsider. He truly hadn't anticipated that sort of reaction from himself, and he wished there was a way he could gracefully extricate himself and go home.

As he stared fixedly down at the wooden-walled arena below him, he heard whispers behind him, and snickering, and felt the back of his neck grow hot. He was just glad that Gel was here with him, in the role of bodyguard; somehow it was easier to stay composed with Gel's stone-faced example to copy.

I'm on their choice of ground; the best I can hope to do is get out of this without making any major blunders. Mother couldn't possibly have known how slippery this situation could become. He was acutely aware that *they* had far more experience than he at the maneuvering of intrigue and politics. He felt horribly young, shallow, and naive; these people had drunk machination with their first milk, and he had no idea how to deal with situations they wouldn't even hesitate over.

Kyrtian had taken a seat in the first row to avoid meeting their eyes any longer, but they continued to speak to each other in voices pitched for him to overhear, taunting him to respond.

"Who, exactly, is this fellow?" asked an arrogant young male a little to Kyrtian's left.

"My cousin Kyrtian," Aelmarkin said lightly. "Son of the late Lord Darthenian, my uncle."

"Lord Darthenian . . ." someone murmured behind him. "That name sounds familiar. Don't I know it from some old story or other?"

"Try coupling the name with *daft,"* drawled another, sounding so smug that it was all Kyrtian could do to keep from standing up and going for the fellow's throat. "Daft Darthenian, pot-hunter, excavator of things better left buried, and pursuer of useless old manuscripts. Missing in pursuit of same, and presumed dead, oh, decades ago."

"Now, Ferahine, there's nothing wrong with having a hobby," replied Aelmarkin, in a tone so *tolerant* that Kyrtian clenched his hands on the armrests of his chair to keep himself in his seat. "Isn't insect-collecting as silly? I've *seen* you send slaves out bobbing about in fields and forests with a net and a bottle—and all those boxes of dead beetles are just as useless as unreadable manuscripts!"

"Point taken. Still, hobbies are all very well, Aelmarkin," said the drawler, "But no gentleman and no *sane* fellow goes off *himself* to dig up nasty old discards in parts unknown, now, does he? *I* certainly don't go rambling through briars with nets and bottles! That's what slaves are for! And he went out alone, too! Why, that was simply insane, if you ask me."

Kyrtian gritted his teeth. He knew he was meant to overhear all of this. He knew they were trying to provoke him. And they were only saying in his hearing what they told each other—and what their elders said. If he just kept his temper, he would learn a great deal. If they thought he was too dull to understand—or too cowardly to respond—what possible harm could it do?

Still, it was the hardest thing he had ever done, to sit there and let strangers abuse the memory of his own father, without challenging them.

"Alone!" exclaimed the first speaker. "Why didn't he *take* slaves, if he wouldn't send them to do his hunting for him? Aelmarkin, admit it, he must have been deranged!"

There was an audible rustle of fabric, marking Aelmarkin's careless shrug. "He was always secretive about these hunts of his, and never more so than on the last one. He was hunting the site of the Great Gate that brought us from Evelon, and the things that were discarded as useless because they no longer functioned after passing the Gate. Why? I haven't a notion."

"Yes, well, it's obvious he was an obsessive, at the very least," said the drawler, dismissively. "And judging from the disaster of a conversation I had with Kyrtian, yonder, obsession runs in the family blood. All the poor fool can talk about is military matters! History, tactics, battles no one cares about." A sneer crept into the drawl. "As if anyone would ever give the likes of *him* command over so much as a squad of latrine-diggers."

By now Kyrtian's neck burned, his cheeks were nearly the same temperature, and his jaw and shoulders ached with the strain of tightly-clenched muscles. He gladly would have given half his possessions for the opportunity to come at any of those foppish fools in barehanded combat!

And that's just what they expect from you, he reminded himself, trying mentally to throw a little cold water on his overheated temper. *They think you're an atavistic barbarian, and they may very well be waiting for you to stand up and attack them physically! They* would *have the right to challenge you or bring you up in front of the Great Council.*

And that, beyond a shadow of a doubt, was what Aelmarkin wanted him to do, for such an attack would prove to everyone's satisfaction that he, Kyrtian, was just as mad as Aelmarkin claimed in his petition. An Elvenlord and a gentleman did not settle differences hand-to-hand. An Elvenlord and a gentleman issued a proper challenge, and settled it as this feud was being settled.

I have to keep my mouth closed and my eyes open and find out just how these things work! he told himself vehemently. *So that if I get a chance, I can arrange for these fools to eat their words without salt!*

Beside him, Gel stood at wary attention, as impassive as any statue, and as invisible to these fools as any other bodyguard. Gel had heard every word, too—but you would never know it by looking at him.

Copy Gel, he told himself. *Stay quiet, if not calm. Wait, and watch.* He knew only that these feuds were settled in trial-by-combat, using slaves as proxies. If *his* fighters were better-trained than these—

Then it might be worth dealing with these dolts in a way they'll understand.

Abruptly, conversation behind him ceased, as some signal he didn't recognize warned the idlers that the combat was about to begin. Abruptly caught up in spite of himself, Kyrtian leaned forward with the rest, as the light in the arena brightened, and the lights above their seats dimmed.

5

Two bronze doors, one at each end of the arena and decorated with hammered images of armored fighters, opened onto the sands of the arena. Two lines of heavily-equipped fighters paced through them, moving ponderously into the light. There were fourteen of these humans in all, seven to each side. One set was armored in pale green, with a winged serpent badge in brilliant blue on their breastplates and shields, the other in emerald green with the badge of a rearing alicorn in white.

The armor was impressive; the men inside it were less so. Kyrtian studied each of the fighters minutely, weighing and measuring their general strength, noting the kinds of weapons each man carried. He assumed that Gel was doing the same.

"Ancestors!" came another whisper from behind. "What can be so fascinating about a handful of fighters? Is he *so* provincial that he's never seen gladiators before?"

Kyrtian's neck burned again for a moment, but he calmed himself quickly. With something before him to study and analyze, he finally managed to think of his own situation in terms of tactics rather than emotions.

Most of them are taking me for a provincial boor, but those are the ones who are ignoring me. The comments might be coming from those who are suspicious of me—thinking that the "provincial fool" might just be a pose. They would be trying to prod me into either doing something typical of a fool—such as lose my temper and insult them back—or to do or say something that will give them more information about what I'm really here for. If I do neither, I'll confuse them further. It's even possible that Aelmarkin is behind the prodding. The possible number of plots and counterplots going on behind his back made him feel dizzy.

And these strangers seemed even more alien to him. How did they do it? How could anyone live like that, spending most of every day in guarding against treachery, and the rest in planning treachery? It would drive him mad in no time. He could not imagine how they coped with the constant paranoia.

Perhaps that is why they spend so much time in debauching themselves. Only by immersing themselves in pleasure can they relax for a few moments. If that was so—he felt suddenly sorry for them. But not *too* sorry.

The best weapon he had to use against them was the uncertainty he represented, the very fact that he was unknown. No matter what Aelmarkin had told them, they probably wouldn't really believe it until they had proved for themselves what he was. They would tend to judge him against the standard of their own behavior. What would one of them do in a situation similar to his? Play the fool? Try and find an ally?

Probably look for an ally or a protector; hopefully by doing neither, he had confused them further. He wished he could talk openly to Gel; of all the times he needed advice—

Then again, Gel might not have any better notion of how to handle these effete creatures than he did.

Well, others have mistaken my caution for a lack of imagination in the past—so perhaps that is what is going on now. I can only hope so; it will make them underestimate me further.

All he really knew was how such situations would have been handled in the far past, as recounted in the history books he spent so much time perusing. In the days of long ago, there had been less time and leisure for long plots and political machination. The Elvenlords of old had dealt with problems with their own kind in ways that "human barbarians" would find perfectly familiar.

If one of the First Lords chose to deal with the insults instead of tamely accepting them, he would have called his enemy out for a duel-by-magic.

That makes a satisfying fantasy these days as well—providing you picture yourself as the winner rather than the loser.

In law, that was still an option, but it was one that very few ever took anymore. More than ninety-nine times out of a hundred, insults were answered and arguments settled by proxy, in the arena, at the hands of human gladiators like the ones below. Hardly fair, since clearly someone whose means were limited couldn't afford to keep and train as many fighters as someone of greater rank and power, but someone of greater rank and power would also be much stronger in magic than a lesser lord—so it wouldn't make a great deal of difference to the outcome, whether it was settled by combat or magic duel.

It's even possible for someone with weak magic to become wealthy enough to afford first-quality fighters, or to gain an ally with access to such fighters, but nothing increases the power of the magic that someone is born with. I suppose combat-by-proxy is marginally more fair than combat-by-magic.

It wouldn't be quite as viscerally satisfying, though.

I wonder how I'd fare if I decided to challenge one of the charmers behind me to a magic duel? Have any of them even bothered to practice and train their power? There was no way of judging how strong they were by the way they were acting, and he really didn't know how strong *his* magic was in comparison with theirs. Going into such a challenge blind would be the stupidest thing he could do.

He didn't use magic except when there was no way to accomplish something without it. He really didn't have much use for illusions, so he'd never really practiced them, but there was no reason why even an illusion couldn't be used as a weapon. Other Elvenlords seemed to waste a great deal of power on outward appearances—for instance, as Aelmarkin had, turning his manor into an impossible confection that hardly resembled a dwelling at all. But was that the waste that it seemed to be?

Is it a kind of bluff—or even a way of demonstrating power without the risk entailed by combat?

For a moment, he felt a flicker of concern that *he* hadn't done likewise; should he have created an opulent illusory costume like theirs? What would these people think if they saw his unadorned home? Did they think him weak, and of little account, because he didn't create and maintain fantastic illusions?

It doesn't matter, he told himself quickly. *No one ever comes to visit who needs to be impressed, and I'm not the only one here wearing ordinary clothing.*

He reminded himself that his status, and that of his family, remained secure—because they produced what others needed, and they had no power that anyone else coveted. It was a reassuring thought, and one that calmed his new-born concerns. He *wanted* to look harmless and inconsequential; he'd nearly forgotten that. He wanted people like these friends of Aelmarkin to underestimate him and his family.

He gave himself a mental shake. These people were contaminating him—he hadn't been among them for even half a day, and already he was thinking about challenges and status, worrying because they thought he was a provincial, insular bumpkin! So what if they did? That was what kept him and his safe! *Let them jockey with each other* he reminded himself. *Let them ignore us. As long as they consider us politically insignificant, but too useful to disturb, we'll remain secure and safe.*

Unless, of course, the family holdings looked *so* prosperous that they became a choice plum, ripe for picking. Certainly Aelmarkin thought so; was it possible that some other, more dangerous opponent would come to share that belief?

Perhaps—perhaps he ought to consult with Lydiell when he returned home. Maybe it was time to create a few carefully-crafted bluffs. Lydiell was clever; surely she would be able to concoct an excuse for Kyrtian to demonstrate his powers in such a way that would make it appear that Kyrtian had incredible ability. Or, at least, that he had enough magical power to make challenging him more costly than the prize was worth.

Something to make it appear that it isn't worth upsetting the way things are now, that's what we need. Something to show that there is nothing to be gained and a great deal to be lost in a direct confrontation.

It might be all to his advantage that most conflicts were settled in the arena. He knew for certain that in strength and agility, his own worst fighters were the equal of even the best of the fighters down there on the sand—and were superior to most of the men waiting to fight. If it came to a challenge-match like this one, Kyrtian was confident that his side would not lose.

That realization made him relax a little. Really, he was worrying for no reason. As long as issues were settled by human gladiators like those below him, he had nothing to fear.

In fact, the more he studied those fighters, the more confident of that fact he became. It was odd; those gladiators all seemed a good bit younger than he would have expected. This was an important match, or so he had been led to believe. So why weren't the two antagonists fielding their older, more experienced gladiators? *What is it that Gel says? "Experience and duplicity will overcome youth and energy every time."*

He had managed to lose track of what the gossips behind him were chattering about while he mulled over his own situation and studied the combatants. When he turned a fraction of his attention back to them, he discovered they were placing bets on the outcome, not only of the whole combat, but on the fortunes of individual fighters. Mildly intrigued, he eavesdropped without shame.

"You must know something, if you're betting *that* high," the drawler said suspiciously. "Don't take the bet, Galiath! He's too confident! I think he bribed the trainers to tell him something!"

"Nonsense, he doesn't know anything—he's just bluffing, and I've wanted a chance to get that horse for ages!" replied a new voice, one that Kyrtian thought was slurred just a little with drink. "I'll take that bet; your racehorse against my red-haired concubine and two jeweled armlets that the one with the two swords draws first blood before he's marked!"

It took a moment for the sense of what they were saying to

sink in, and when it did, he felt a little sick. The idea of equating the value of a human with that of a horse—no, as *less* than that of the horse . . . it hit him with the force of a blow to the stomach just how foreign their way of thinking was to his. He'd known it intellectually, of course, but this was the first concrete example he'd witnessed. Up until now, Aelmarkin's slaves hadn't behaved any differently than his own servants at their most discreet.

I truly am the alien here. If they knew how we treat our humans, they wouldn't hesitate for a moment to bring us all down. He would be considered a traitor to his race, and worse than the Wizards and the wild humans. He had to remember to keep his guard up!

The two feuding parties finally arrived, with great fanfare, at exactly the same moment. With each of the Elvenlords came an entourage of glittering, fancifully-costumed hangers-on. There were box seats at either end of the arena, directly above the two doors that had disgorged the combatants; those boxes were now occupied by the newly-arrived lords and their entourages. Kyrtian found that he could not for the life of him remember their names and Houses—not that it really mattered to him. He would, if he was introduced later, congratulate the winner and be properly sympathetic to the loser. It wasn't likely, though, that Aelmarkin would make such an introduction, unless he thought he had a way of making Kyrtian lose face.

How they took their seats and in what order was clearly as choreographed as an elaborate ritual. Neither of the Lords wished to be seated first, and there was much arranging of the chairs and jockeying of seating before the two Great Lords sat at precisely the same moment. They glared at each other across the span of the arena, before turning away with studied indifference to speak with a companion.

Now Aelmarkin, as host, stood up; Kyrtian caught the movement out of the corner of his eye, and turned just enough so that he could watch his cousin without being obvious about it.

"Most noble Lords," Aelmarkin said, his smooth and impersonal words carrying effortlessly above the whispers of those seated all around him, "You have determined to settle your differences in trial-by-combat, and have accepted my offer to host this venture. Are you still of the same mind to accept the outcome of this combat as the settling of your feud?"

He of the azure serpent replied with a gruff, "Aye" while he of the white alicorn simply nodded.

"Very well," Aelmarkin said calmly. "Let the record show that both agree to be bound by the outcome here below us. Let all who are assembled here so bear witness."

"We so bear witness," came a chorus of voices, some indifferent, some full of tense excitement. A hush came over them; all whispers and movement stopped. So profound was the silence that the slightest rustle of fabric came as a shock.

As if this had been a signal, the fighters below tensed.

Aelmarkin surveyed the two opposed lines of fighters for a moment, an odd smile on his lips. "Very well," he said at last, into the stillness. *"Begin."*

Kyrtian's full attention immediately turned to the arena. The two lines of fighters leapt at each other, hurling themselves across the sand to meet in a clangor of metal and harsh male shouts. The noise echoed inside the arena, making Kyrtian wince involuntarily. Added to the noise of fighting was the clamor of shouts and cheers behind him and to either side of him, as the onlookers cheered the combatants on.

Kyrtian was still trying to figure out how Aelmarkin intended to score this combat, when the swordsman nearest him managed to beat down his opponent's guard and laid open the other's sword-arm from shoulder to wrist with a single blow.

The man screamed, and dropped to his knees, a torrent of shockingly scarlet blood pouring from the wound into the sand as his blade fell from his slack fingers.

For one moment, Kyrtian was startled by how realistic the wound was—then he realized that it wasn't "realistic," it was *real.*

He felt as if someone had rammed him in the midsection and knocked all the breath out of him. He started to shake, as a wave of sick horror twisted his throat and stomach.

It's real—it's real. They're trying to really kill each other.

They're dying, and all so a couple of idiots can settle an argument! Senseless—useless—insane!

Then, strangely, it all dissolved under a flood of blinding rage. He lost caution, lost focus, lost everything except the will to make it all *stop.* He rose abruptly to his feet.

"No!" he shouted, spreading his arms wide, his voice somehow carrying above the noise of combat. His powers, leaping to answer his will, poured out; an angry and violent burst of magic tore out of him.

It flung the combatants to their own sides of the arena, and dropped every man in the arena to his knees—except the injured one, who was frantically trying to close his gaping wound with his good hand.

The sudden silence, heavy with anger, seemed louder than his shout.

For a moment, no one moved—no one seemed able to believe what he had done.

Then in an instant, both of the Great Lords turned to stare at him with an anger as overwhelming as his. Kyrtian felt the weight of that anger, all of it directed solely at him, and came to his senses with a start.

This might have been a tactical error. . . .

The lord of the white alicorn was the first to rise from his seat; there was lightning in his gaze and thunder in his voice as he addressed, not Kyrtian, but his cousin.

"Aelmarkin," the Elvenlord said, enunciating each syllable with care, "I trust you did not anticipate this?"

Aelmarkin also rose, and his voice fairly dripped apology and concern. "Good my lord, I assure you, I had no idea that my cousin would indulge in such *bizarre* behavior! I do apologize, I would never have invited him if—"

Kyrtian, who had been staring down at the wounded fighter, now being aided by one of his companions, felt fury overcome his good sense again; he swung around to face his cousin, twisting his lips into a snarl, a red haze settling across his vision.

"Bizarre behavior? *Bizarre?* I call it sanity—stopping utterly senseless and wanton waste! What—"

"Waste?" shouted the other feuding lord, furiously, the ice in his voice freezing Kyrtian's words in his throat. "Waste? What do you know of waste, you impudent puppy? You provincial idiot, who let you in among civilized beings? I—"

"I apologize again, my lords," Aelmarkin protested, waving his hands about frantically. "Please, take your seats and the combat can resume—"

"Resume? *Resume?*" At that, Kyrtian's rage sprang to full and insensate life again, and grew until it was beyond anything, he had ever felt before. He went cold, then hot, then cold again, and a strange haze came over his vision. "Haven't you heard a word I've said? This idiocy will *not* resume, not while I'm standing here!"

"That can be remedied," muttered someone, as Gel finally put a calming hand on Kyrtian's arm. Kyrtian had the sense not to throw it off, but he was quite ready at that moment to snatch up a sword himself and take them all on single-handed.

"Don't back down," Gel muttered, "but get hold of yourself. Think fast—if you can't salvage this situation, we're going to have *three* feuds on our hands, two with them and one with Aelmarkin."

Aelmarkin was so angry he could scarcely think. When he'd invited that fool Kyrtian here, he'd hoped the puppy would make some sort of blunder that would prove he was as foolish as Aelmarkin claimed. Well, he'd blundered all right—but he'd managed to do it in such a way that now *Aelmarkin* was potentially in as much trouble as he was! How had he managed to stop the combat? *Where* did he get all that magic power?

To the desert with that! How am I going to save myself?

This was nothing short of a disaster. The amount of status he stood to lose over this debacle was incalculable. This might even cost him his Council seat.

"Please, my lords," he said, entreatingly, to his two furious guests, "my young cousin has never seen one of these exhibitions before and—"

"Exhibitions?" Aelmarkin blinked at the tone of Kyrtian's voice—a moment ago it had nearly cracked with strain, and Kyrtian was clearly a short step from losing control entirely.

Suddenly now—the anger was still there, but it was controlled anger, and overlaid with calculated scorn worthy of an experienced Councilor. He turned to see that Kyrtian's face was now a carefully haughty mask.

Could Kyrtian actually salvage this situation?

"Exhibitions?" Kyrtian repeated. "Is that what you call these senseless slaughters?" His lip curled in what was unmistakably a sneer. "I suppose if your idea of 'sport' is to take tame pets and line them up for targets, then you could call something like this an *exhibition,* but I certainly wouldn't dignify this idiocy with such a term."

Aelmarkin saw with hope that the two feuding lords had forgotten all about him. Kyrtian's declaration and attitude had caused them to focus all of their insulted rage on him.

"I suppose it's too much to expect you to answer that statement of utter nonsense with anything like a challenge?" asked Lord Marthien, his voice dripping with sarcasm.

"Yes it is," Kyrtian replied, answering sarcasm with arrogance, "Because your fighters are no match for mine. You would lose before the combat began. *That* is why I say this is senseless. The least of my fighters has four years of combat experience—the best of yours can't possibly have more than one. No, less than one, since I doubt your men ever survive even that long."

That arrogance took them rather aback; Lord Wyvarna glanced at Aelmarkin as if asking for confirmation of the astonishing statement. Aelmarkin made a slight shrug.

"And are we supposed to accept this bluff at face value, impudent puppy?" Lord Wyvarna demanded.

To their astonishment, Kyrtian laughed, albeit mirthlessly.

"You would be wise to, since it is hardly a bluff," he replied. "Consider what you already know about me and my—hobby. Consider that I have very little to do except train and drill my fighters in every possible style and manner of combat, and that I do not and never have sold any of them for any price. Consider that I have been doing this every day for the past ten years at least, *personally* overseeing the training and practice in every aspect. Meanwhile, what have you been doing? Entrusting the training and practice of your gladiators to others, quite without supervision, and slaughtering the best of your men in useless *exhibitions*. And what stake do those you entrust with this training have in your success or failure? What personal incentive have they to make certain that nothing is left to chance? And how many of your gladiators die or are crippled in training? For that matter, what incentive do your gladiators have to succeed? The best and cleverest of them are surely contriving to get themselves mildly crippled in the first week of your so-called 'training!' It would seem to me that the very smartest ones, the ones who would make the very best fighters, would see to it that they were *always* crippled in training, in order to avoid being slaughtered in one of your so-called *exhibitions!*"

Kyrtian cleverly left the questions hanging in the air, and now Aelmarkin saw a certain wariness creep over the expressions of the two feuding lords.

"And I suppose you have a better idea?" boomed a new voice.

Both Aelmarkin and Kyrtian turned to face the new speaker, who stood up from among his son's entourage. Aelmarkin was startled; he hadn't realized that Lord Lyon had come with his son Gildor—

Damn! Has he been there all along, or did he just arrive for the combat? Did I somehow insult him by not noticing him? Can anything else go wrong here today?

Aelmarkin's thoughts scurried after one another, like frantic slaves trying to clean up a terrible spill. V'kel Lyon Lord Kyndreth—Lord Lyon of the Great House of Kyndreth—stood wrapped in a scarlet cloak embroidered with leaping stags, his arms crossed over his chest. Aelmarkin shivered; the man was one of the most powerful lords of the Great Council. A vote from Lord Lyon was worth three from anyone with a lesser Council Seat. The number of allies he had—the number of people he could make or break with a single word—

Aelmarkin held his breath. All his own prayers might be answered in the next few moments. If Kyrtian insulted Lord Lyon badly enough—if he convinced Lord Lyon that he was as insane and unstable as Aelmarkin had been claiming . . .

Then before this day was over, Aelmarkin might be organizing his slaves for the move to his new properties.

Kyrtian looked at Lord Lyon, a veritable icon of power, as if he were no more important than any of the lesser sons and hangers-on.

"Yes," he said, simply, "I have. And I'm quite prepared to demonstrate it, here and now in front of you all."

6

"That's V'kel Lyon Lord Kyndreth," Gel hissed in Kyrtian's ear. Kyrtian made the finger-sign for *I understand,* but did not look away from the tall, powerfully-built noble who had addressed him. That was one name he definitely recognized, and the half-formed plan he had thrown together in an instant of panic-ridden thinking took on a new importance and urgency. If he could persuade Lord Lyon to use *his* methods, not only in training, but in challenge-matches, how many thousands of lives would be spared? For if Lord Lyon decreed it, all training and matches would be performed Kyrtian's way.

So he turned his half-formed plan into a bluff. "In fact," he continued, as calmly as if he spoke the truth, "I came here hoping to stop this nonsense for all time with such a demonstration."

"Really?" Lord Lyon looked amused, which boded well for Kyrtian. "And how is that? I take it you intend a live demonstration, and not some illusory shadow show."

"Pit one fighter of your choosing against my bodyguard," Kyrtian said, boldly. "They will use my methods of fighting. They will fight to a death-wound, but neither will be harmed by the experience. You can use the best of your men—the one you would least care to lose—without any fear that harm will come to him and you will be without his services."

"Indeed." Lord Lyon looked from one side of the arena to the other. "Wyvarna, Marthien—if I proposed using *my* bodyguard in this combat, would you accept the results of such a duel instead of using your gladiators as settling your dispute?"

The lord of the white alicorn looked sullen; the lord of the blue serpent responded first. "How would we decide which fighter represented which of us?"

"Draw lots," Lyon said carelessly. "I know my man takes second-place to very few, and I hardly think Lord Kyrtian's man is less expert." He turned back to Kyrtian. "I agree in principle that this is a waste of fighting-strength. The training is expensive, and it's all gone to waste when a fighter is killed—or runs off to join those damned renegade Wizards. Before the current unpleasantness, there were no Wizards to run off to, of course, and there was no need to field battle-troops, but our present situation does call for some changes in our own customs. In fact, some of the members of the Council have even asked openly if it might be wise to outlaw challenges altogether to save the waste of trained fighters." He smiled thinly. "Some have even suggested that if challengers are unwilling or unable to conduct duels-by-magic, that they should take sword in hand themselves to settle their quarrels."

Astonished mutters and a few gasps followed that announcement, and Lords Wyvarna and Marthien looked openly dismayed.

Lord Lyon looked down his long, aristocratic nose at Kyrtian with a hint of sardonic interest. Kyrtian raised his chin and reminded himself that his lineage was as long and proud as that of the House of Kyndreth. "How much better, then, if you can have your challenges without the loss of a single fighting man or spillage of a single drop of blood?" he demanded. "Maybe your gladiators will stop running off if they know they aren't going to be killed in a senseless grudge-match. And I know I need not point out to a Lord of your experience and wisdom that such training will make better field-forces than anything our foes can create. Think of the kind of fighters you will field, when you can breed the best to the best, then give them real combat experience where they can learn from their mistakes!"

"Bloodless matches? Where's the sport in that?" someone behind Kyrtian muttered.

Kyrtian ignored the comment—and ignored the fact that the spectators were leaving, one by one, grumbling. He had Lord Lyon's attention, and he was not going to give it up. "I am well aware that many consider my interest in the past to be eccentric," he continued, "but because of that interest, I have learned at least one of the secrets lost when we passed the Gate from Evelon. I *know* how the Ancestors conducted their duels-of-honor and their training sessions—how they taught and practiced combat without pulling blows, without using blunted weapons, yet without spilling blood. Didn't it ever occur to you that they *must* have had some way to learn sword-work themselves without risking hurt? After all, unlike *us*—" here he looked down his nose at the young Lords around him with a bland expression "—*they* engaged in sword-duels themselves, and not by proxy. Their method is what I use to train my own fighters. Furthermore, I give every able-bodied human on my properties a basic training in fighting-skills, against the day that they may need to defend the manor until my real fighters can come to their rescue!"

He did not say *what* foe he trained his humans to fight—he figured that Lord Lyon would assume that he meant the army of the Wizards or of the Wild Humans, not an army commanded by his fellows. Not a flicker of mistrust appeared on Lord Lyon's face, only a growing interest—and if anyone here had been thinking about the idea of taking his holdings by force, that last statement would give them a reason to think better of the plan.

"If all this is true—" Lord Lyon turned to a silent, black-clad, flame-haired human who stayed at his side like his shadow. "Kaeth—get down to the arena and get some armor and weapons. I want to see how this works."

The human saluted, and left Lord Lyon's side, jumping down into the arena and walking past the gladiators as casually as if they were statues. Kyrtian caught Gel's eye and nodded; Gel followed him.

"I believe that you will find this well worth your time, Lord Lyon," Kyrtian said evenly, then turned to the feuding parties. "My lords, will you make your choice of combatant?"

There was more grumbling, but finally it was settled that Lord Marthien would be represented by Gel, and Wyvarna by Lord Lyon's man Kaeth. Since it was obvious that there was no longer going to be the bloody spectacle that everyone had planned on, no one really wanted to remain any longer, and both lords lost most of their entourages, leaving only their human bodyguards and one or two other slaves in attendance.

As for Aelmarkin's guests, they had all departed as well, probably returning to the Great Hall and the food and drink and other pleasures they had abandoned to watch the combat. That left only Aelmarkin, Lord Lyon and a young er-Lord who was probably his son, a couple of young lords who looked to be friends of his son, and Kyrtian. Those who remained seated themselves, and waited with varying degrees of impatience for something to happen.

Gel was no stranger to getting into armor quickly, and neither, apparently, was Lord Lyon's red-haired bodyguard. Both appeared at the same door of the arena a remarkably short time later; Gel must have told Kaeth not to bother about weapons, for neither man carried any. Kaeth looked up at his master, who nodded to Lord Wyvarna; Kaeth immediately picked up one of the discarded shields stacked at the side of the arena bearing the azure serpent, and Gel took one of the discarded white alicorn shields.

"We've agreed to longsword and shield, master," Gel called up, in a servile voice that Kyrtian hardly recognized. He suppressed a nervous chuckle, and nodded.

Then Kyrtian fixed his gaze on a point on the sand at Gel's feet, and concentrated, drawing motes of power out of himself, and spinning them into the fabric of a pair of his very special blades.

He'd conjured up longswords so many times, that it was hardly any effort at all to spin out a mere pair of them. The air above the sand misted briefly, then shimmered, and a pair of fine blades condensed out of the mist as Kyrtian felt a slight inward drain of power. He looked up to see that Aelmarkin was watching closely, with a look of intense concentration on his face.

I wonder if he can follow what I'm doing? Has he the talent to read all the special modifications I've made?

Gel gestured to the identical swords and let Kaeth pick first.

The bodyguard picked up the nearest, and gave it an experimental swing, then rapped his shield with it. The shield gave off a perfectly normal metallic clang, and Kaeth nodded with satisfaction. "Feels like a regulation longsword, Lord Lyon," he called up into the viewing stands, squinting against the light. "Maybe a bit better balanced than most."

"These blades will act in all respect like a normal battle weapon," Kyrtian assured the few who were left in the stands, but concentrating on Lord Lyon. "With a single exception, that is. They will not cause any physical damage. Gel, please offer your opponent a target."

Gel held out his sword-arm with a grin, knowing that Kyrtian would eliminate the shock of being struck for this part of the demonstration.

"Kaeth, if you would swing at Gel please, and cut off his arm?"

Lord Lyon's slave did not hesitate; he took a full, overhand swing at the arm Gel extended for him as Lord Lyon leaned forward a little with interest. The blade passed through Gel's arm, leaving a glowing line, and making about half his body glow.

"Wounds cause a slight shock to the wounded man to tell him that he has been wounded, and the blade leaves a mark that he and any referees can see," Kyrtian explained. "There is no other effect on the fighter so struck, but for the purposes of scoring, there is full attention paid to the realities of battle. The longer Gel stands there, the more of him will glow, representing how close he is to death by blood-loss from such a massive wound. If he had only gotten a slight wound, there would only have been a mark and a shock. Eventually, according to the rules we follow, he will glow all over and be forced to retire."

"And if the wound was immediately mortal, he'd glow all over as well?" Lord Lyon supplied.

"Yes, and he would get a larger, quite unmistakable shock."

Kyrtian replied. He permitted himself a smile. "We allow for the heat of combat causing people to forget themselves, and the shocks they receive *will* get their attention." He negated the glow with a moment's thought, and Gel shifted his feet in the sand.

Lord Lyon nodded thoughtfully, and even Wyvarna and Marthien looked more interested than they had been. "I'm sure there are more details that I will want to ask you about later," Lord Lyon said after a moment of silence. "But meanwhile—let's settle this quarrel and have our practical demonstration, shall we?"

At this point, Kyrtian caught a decidedly unfriendly expression on Aelmarkin's face. It was there for only a moment, but it reminded him that his cousin *was* the host of this combat, and that Kyrtian had done him a fair amount of damage.

But maybe there was a way to begin repairing that damage—or at least, doing something to make up for it. *Never make an enemy that you don't have to,* he reminded himself, *and never give an enemy you already have another excuse to act against you.*

"Cousin?" he said, gesturing to the arena. "As host, yours should be the honor."

Aelmarkin looked briefly startled, then suspicious, but stood up. He bowed to the two for whom this entire combat had been arranged. "Lord Marthien, Lord Wyvarna, will your feud be settled by the outcome of this challenge?"

"Aye," came the reply—grudgingly, but without much hesitation.

"Be it witnessed," Aelmarkin intoned.

"We so witness," came the chorus of Kyrtian, Lord Lyon, Lyon's son, and a pair of hangers-on, thinner than before, but enough to satisfy custom.

"Very well," Aelmarkin continued, as Gel and Kaeth eyed each other and settled into nearly identical stances. "*Begin.*"

Aelmarkin seated himself, and crossed his arms over his chest. Kyrtian leaned forward to watch what he suspected would be a very fine show.

There was no rush to combat and clash of weapons this time, not with two such seasoned fighters. They circled each other warily, taking careful measure of each other, making tiny feints and gauging the speed of response. Gel and Kaeth were a good match for one another, and although Aelmarkin leaned back in his seat and looked dreadfully bored, Lord Lyon and the two feuding Elvenlords were quickly on the edge of their chairs, recognizing the level of skill each man represented. Kyrtian felt a thrill of pride as he watched Gel's catlike, powerful moves; it was obvious that Kaeth was an extremely well-trained and probably very expensive slave, and regarded Gel as his equal in ability.

When the first exchange came, it was sudden; Kaeth thought he detected a weakness and drove in, making Gel's shield and blade ring with a flurry of blows. Gel countered successfully, and when Kaeth sprang back, both of them had tiny glowing marks, Kaeth along the back of his sword-hand and Gel across his forehead.

Well used to the rules of the game, Gel did something that surprised Kaeth; he sprinted backwards out of reach for a moment, just long enough to pull a scarf from around his neck and whip it around his forehead. Kyrtian risked a glance at Lord Lyon, and saw him frown suddenly in puzzlement, then just as quickly nod and smile slightly.

Good. He understands that if Gel hadn't done that, the glow would drop over his eye, obscuring his vision as blood would without a scarf to stop it. He's beginning to understand how complex the rules-magic is.

Kyrtian abandoned himself to watching the fight, able to enjoy it as a demonstration of grace and expertise. He noticed that Kaeth was grinning, just as Gel was; evidently, Kaeth seldom found himself with an opponent of comparable ability, and without needing to worry about crippling injuries or death, had given himself over to the exhilaration and visceral pleasure of such a duel. With each exchange of blows, one or both of the combatants came away marked, but only superficially—and by the time they'd acquired half a dozen "cuts" each, Lord Marthien and Lord Wyvarna were on their feet, cheering their representatives on with as much vigor as they would have used if their contest had gone as planned. Kyrtian's own heart was pounding at this point, and his fists clenched with excitement. It was a terrific combat, and he honestly wasn't certain who he wished to see win it.

Kyrtian noticed a pattern in Kaeth's shieldwork, a weakness, a tendency to push an oncoming blow to the outside rather than hold up under it. That spared the shock to the shield-arm, yes, but it left him open for a sliding parry under the shield or a feint and a drive straight to the chest. If *he* saw it, certainly Gel did—

Gel made a little dance to the side, another blow towards the shield—but it wasn't a blow, it was a feint, and he followed it with a lunge straight for Kaeth's unguarded throat!

But *Kaeth* was ready for him! The pattern had been a ruse, a lure to see if Gel would take it! He dodged aside, moving just enough so that Gel's blade slid over his shoulder without harming him, and slashed *up* in a vicious gut-thrust.

Gel stiffened, and burst into glowing light. Obedient to the rules (and his own sense of high drama), he toppled over and dropped to the ground, "dead."

Lord Lyon rose to his feet, applauding enthusiastically, as Kaeth saluted him, then saluted Lord Wyvarna, who was also on his feet and cheering. So, for that matter, was Kyrtian—

—and oddly enough, Lord Marthien.

"By the blood of our Ancestors, Lyon, I haven't seen a better fight in decades!" Lord Marthien shouted, as Kyrtian banished the weapons, and Kaeth offered his now free hand to Gel to help him up. "It's worth losing the challenge to have seen it!" He turned his attention briefly to the arena, and waved graciously at Gel. "Well fought, boy! I couldn't have had a better champion!"

He gathered up the remains of his entourage, and in amazingly good humor, led them out.

Kaeth and Gel left the arena in a similar state of accord, and Lord Wyvarna made his way to the area of seating where Lord Lyon still stood, clearly in a high flood of euphoria. After a moment of hesitation, Kyrtian followed to join them.

When he reached them, he found them involved in a rehash of the combat, but Lord Lyon broke off when he noticed Kyrtian's approach.

"Well, you impudent young puppy, you were right and I was wrong!" Wyvarna exclaimed, laughing. He showed Kyrtian a friendly face for the first time since he'd entered the arena. "Ancestors! That old fool Marthien was right for the first time in his life—even if I'd been the one who lost, I'd have thought it was worth it to have seen a fight like that!"

He shook his head, and now that he was closer, Kyrtian realized that Wyvarna was much older than he had thought. It was often difficult to tell the age of an Elvenlord, but a hint of lines at the corners of his eyes, and a certain sharpening of the tips of his ears indicated that he was older than Lord Lyon. If Lord Marthien was just as old—

Then I've gotten myself two very well-entrenched allies; maybe not as powerful as Lord Lyon, but certainly respected by the Council. This is coming out better than I dared hope!

"And I think it was just as well that it never came to a challenge with young Kyrtian, here, hmm?" Lord Lyon asked, slyly. "Given how well his bodyguard fought—what must his trained fighters be like?"

Kyrtian's respect for Lord Lyon rose a notch. *He's reminding Wyvarna that this could have been very expensive—and he's making sure that Wyvarna will spread the word. So although I might be considered a dolt, I'm a dolt no one will want to challenge.*

Lord Wyvarna gave an exaggerated shudder, and laughed again. "Damn me if you aren't right about that! His men would have cut mine to pieces without even breathing hard!" He clapped Kyrtian on the back, hard, trying to make him stagger. Kyrtian, who had been expecting something of the sort, braced himself and stood firm, smiling.

"It was a pleasure to show you the secret I discovered, my lords," he replied blandly. "Of all the things I dislike the most, waste is highest on the list, and there is no reason other than losses in a real battle to have to replace a gladiator or a fighting-slave before his time. Humans are hardly difficult to breed, but it takes time and resources to train them, resources that could more sensibly be put to other uses! Besides, if we keep killing the strongest and cleverest of our breeding-slaves, what do you think we'll end up with? These techniques are quite easy to learn, and even easier to apply; if you can set a collar-spell, you can create these training conditions."

Wyvarna gave a half smile, and glanced over at Lord Lyon. "Then I expect we'll be getting a mandate from the Council about using them shortly, eh, Lyon?"

"I believe that you can count on that, Wyvarna," Lord Lyon replied, just as blandly as Kyrtian.

Wyvarna coughed, and then shrugged. "Well, times change, and the ones who won't change with them are fools," he said to no one in particular. "I'll be off; Marthien will be sending his conciliation-party, and I should be there to receive them properly, or there'll be another feud on my hands."

With that, Lord Wyvarna turned and led his own entourage out of the arena, leaving Kyrtian standing beside Lord Lyon.

"Well, either you are the cleverest young lordling I have ever seen, or the luckiest," Lyon observed softly. "I wouldn't have given you any odds of getting out of that situation intact."

"The luckiest, my lord," Kyrtian replied quickly—hoping that he sounded modest. "I fear that although I had come to this event intending to demonstrate my discovery, I made a profound mistake in permitting my feelings to get the better of me, initially. I am, I fear, a very provincial fellow, and this was the first combat-trial I have ever attended. And if I offended you with my untutored manner, I do apologize, for I had no intention of offending anyone."

And once again, he turned to his cousin. Aelmarkin's expression was so bland it could not have been anything other than a mask. He was probably still infuriated.

"Cousin, I must ask your forgiveness for using *your* premises as the intended venue for my display, but—well, not to put too fine a point upon it, this is the only combat-challenge I have ever been invited to, so opportunities have not exactly been thick upon the ground." He had no real hope that this would pacify Aelmarkin, but at least it would make it look as if he'd tried.

"I wouldn't worry about it if I were you, Aelmarkin," Lord Kyndreth told the stone-faced Elvenlord, with a raised eyebrow. "I can promise you, this little demonstration is only going to reflect to your glory. If you like, I can even spread it about that you colluded with young Kyrtian here—"

"To what end, my lord?" Aelmarkin asked dryly.

"Ah, well, to a most proper end. *You* are aware of the dreadful wastage of fighters we've had in this campaign against the so-called Young Lords. And I assume, given the age and rank of your two main guests, you were aware that *I* would appear at this combat. Of course you are aware of my keen interest in new methods of training our fighting-slaves faster." Lord Kyndreth smiled; the smile reminded Kyrtian of a large cat with its prey beneath its paw. "So you decided to help your cousin and yourself at the same time, by giving him a venue to demonstrate the fruits of his hobby for me. Hmm?"

Aelmarkin's expression remained as bland as cream, but he bowed. "As you say, my lord, and I am deeply grateful to you."

"No more than I am to you." This was clearly a dismissal, and Aelmarkin took it as such.

"I must return to my guests, my lord, if I may excuse myself?" Aelmarkin bowed.

Lord Kyndreth waved him off, and Aelmarkin departed; the line of his backbone suggested further trouble to Kyrtian. But that was for the future; there was a larger and more dangerous predator in front of him still. Aelmarkin was a jackal at best. Lord Kyndreth was a lion in truth and not just in name.

"Thank you again, my lord," Kyrtian said, meaning it.

"Hmph." Lord Lyon eyed him as if suspecting further cleverness. "Well, I shall be wanting to come visit you within the next few days. I want to discuss your training methods—and other things."

"I am at your service, Lord Lyon," Kyrtian replied, stunned. "I will send a Portal-token to the Council Hall in your name." Before he could think of anything else to say, the Old Lord had sketched a brief salute and turned away, leading what was left of his entourage off through the exit.

7

Every trace of the bloody conflict that had preceded Gel's fight had been cleared away from the preparation room by the time that he and the other lord's bodyguard retired to it. Even the armor was gone; all that remained was the presence of the liveried gladiators themselves, divided into two tight groups with a careful space between them. Divested of arms and armor, to Gel's eyes they looked absurdly young, barely out of boyhood. The two sets of gladiators hovered at a respectful distance from Gel and Lord Kyndreth's man as they took over the preparation room for themselves. Gel suppressed a smile of amusement; there was more than a touch of hero-worship in those young faces. He and his opponent had not only saved these children from injury and death, they had probably put on the most skillful combat the callow lads had ever seen. He was just glad that he was going to be able to return to his own estate and get away from all those admiring eyes.

As Gel followed Kaeth Jared's example and divested himself of armor, clothing, and walked naked into the white-tiled water-cascade cubicle as if he belonged there, he was thoroughly conscious of gratitude for being able to clean up after their strenuous bout. With all of the youngsters still watching, awe-filled eyes glued to him, Gel was more than a little uncomfortable as he plunged under the warm cascade of water and let it soothe muscles that had been asked to work without a proper warm-up. He wondered why the other fighters didn't say anything to him—or at least, to Kaeth Jared. They might not know him, but surely they knew Kaeth at least by sight. *Well, they've got tongues,* he told himself, as he ducked his head under the steaming water and let it pour down his neck and back. *If they don't want to use them, that's not my problem.*

Kaeth Jared must have been more used to this odd, semi-frightened treatment from his fellow humans, as he *acted* on the surface as if the other fighters simply weren't there.

On the surface, anyway.

To Gel's experienced eyes, he moved as if he noted and analyzed every move any of them made, however inconsequential. That spelled "assassin" as well as "bodyguard" to Gel, which actually made a great deal of sense, considering Lord Kyndreth's prominence and the uncertain times. There was no telling if the Young Lords or his own peers might decide to revert to the ancient ways of dealing with an obstacle in the form of another Elvenlord. Who better to guard against assassins than another assassin?

Still. It aroused his suspicions. In all his lifetime, Gel had encountered no more than four assassins, and he himself was one of them.

And I wonder if Kaeth Jared has made the same conclusions about me that I have about him. . . .

The first had been his own teacher, the third had been his teacher's teacher—a succession of trained men to guard the estate's lord, just in case. The fourth had been on the auction block, and that particular set of skills hadn't been mentioned in the auction catalog. Although it momentarily tempted him—to have someone else he could trust with his lord's safety—he had said nothing to the Seneschal who had been looking for a few choice youngsters to introduce to the freedom of the estate. It was a bad idea; like his own teacher he would train his own successor. There was no telling where that man had been, or why he was on the block.

For a moment, Gel recalled his teacher with great fondness—Hakkon Shor had not been Gel's father, but he might just as well have been. He'd helped raise Gel from the moment that Gel showed the sort of athletic potential that made him the skilled fighter he was today. Hakkon hadn't had sons, only daughters—not that one of them wouldn't have served perfectly well as Kyrtian's bodyguard, but none of them took after Hakkon; in point of fact, they were sweet-natured and absolutely oblivious to half of what went on around them. Now

Tirith Shor, who'd been Hakkon's father, felt that was just as well, but Gel knew it had been a great disappointment to the Old Man that his son wouldn't be the one to stand at the next Lord's side. . . .

Kaeth Jared was an unlikely sort for an assassin, if you only saw him clothed. Tall and slim, pale, with hair of a dark auburn and long, clever hands, he didn't look particularly strong. If you saw him nude, however—or in combat—you realized that he was a great deal stronger and more agile than he seemed. There wasn't an ounce of superfluous flesh on him anywhere, and the muscles he had were wire and whipcord; tough, and powerful.

Gel wondered if the others had noticed Kaeth Jared's unusual alertness and caution, and decided that they probably hadn't. They were just ordinary fighters, and wouldn't be trained or practiced in such careful observation and deduction. They were probably just impressed by the bout that he and Gel had completed—and perhaps a little stunned at its bloodless outcome.

Part of their awe might very well have been due to the *lack* of scars on Kaeth's body and his own. In the old methods of training, at some point, when two fighters met, they would covertly read true expertise in martial arts not by the number of wounds collected over the years, but by the absence of scarring. An unmarked body in their world meant either that one's lord valued one so highly that he granted the use of magic in healing, or that a fighter's reflexes were so swift and movement so agile that no opponent ever got a chance to land a blow. Neither he nor Kaeth were marred by more than a few trivial lines, long healed.

As Gel emerged from the cascade of water and shook his head like a dog, he caught Kaeth watching out of the corner of his eye; Kaeth knew he'd been caught, and unexpectedly grinned. "You gave me the best bout I've had in a long time, friend," he said, pitching his voice just loud enough to be heard over the sound of the water-cascade. "I'm impressed."

"So am I," Gel admitted freely, as the circle of silent gladiators strained their ears to hear every syllable either of them spoke. "And I don't mind saying that if you'd had the benefit of

Lord Kyrtian's system to train under, you'd be so much better than me that it wouldn't have been a contest."

"I wouldn't know about that," Kaeth replied, quickly enough to salve Gel's bruised ego. "But if I'm any judge of Lord Kyndreth, he'll be using this system of yours before the month is out. And if *he* does, every other lord will do the same, or be thought hopelessly provincial and out-of-step. With enough approval behind him, he might well mandate this system through the Council."

The encircling men let out a suppressed sigh; so *that* was what they had been waiting to hear, and perhaps Kaeth had known that. Gel sympathized; such news would be like a reprieve from a death-sentence.

Like? By the Stars, it is a reprieve from a death-sentence! I wonder how many of their comrades were killed in training, and how many more killed in feud-combat or their masters' entertainments? Now the only thing they'll have to fear is being drafted into the Old Lords' Army and sent up against the rebels or the Wizards.

"I dare say you're right," Gel agreed, waving his hand in front of the cascade to stop it, then reaching for a towel from the rack behind him. At that point, a servant appeared to summon the gladiators to their respective lords for the return to their home estates, and with palpable disappointment, the two groups of men filed out of the preparation room.

Kaeth waved his own hand at the cascade beneath which he'd been standing, and the sound of rushing water was replaced by silence. He seized a towel and dried himself, then wrapped it around his waist as Gel already had and exchanged a wry smile with his companion. "Alone at last!" he said.

Gel chuckled, warily. For an assassin, this man had a remarkable sense of humor and no reticence about showing it. "I would hardly have thought my conversation was *that* entrancing."

Surely he's here by accident. Assassins are normally sent against key humans in an Elvenlord's entourage, and there was no way of knowing who would be playing bodyguard to Kyrtian. Was there?

"It's better than theirs." Kaeth jerked his head in the direction of the exit door. "Those poor blockheads don't have much to talk about except fighting, food, and sex. If they'd gotten up the courage to speak to us, you'd have found that out."

Gel raised an eyebrow. "Well, they're young," he pointed out, as he followed Kaeth carefully into the main room.

"And under the old system, not likely to get older," Kaeth retorted, getting his clothing off the shoulder-high shelf beside him, and laying it out on a polished wooden bench. "How old's your oldest fighter?"

Gel considered his reply carefully before answering, using the opportunity to lay out his own gear as a chance to stall a little. "If you count *retired* fighters who could still pick up a weapon in defense of the estate—the oldest just turned seventy-eight."

Kaeth was actually taken aback, and let out a low whistle as he reached for his trews. "I don't know that I've ever *seen* a human that old, much less a fighter! You mean your lord actually puts his old men out to pasture instead of putting them down? Great Ancestors, man, how many of these *retired* fighters have you got?"

"I'm not sure," Gel replied, his suspicions aroused. *He's asking too many questions. He's a trained assassin, I* know *he is—what if he's targeting Kyrtian?*

It was possible—Lord Kyndreth could be a patron and ally of the obnoxious Aelmarkin. It might be that he would wait just long enough to learn Kyrtian's training-technique, then eliminate Aelmarkin's inconvenient cousin.

In fact he might have been brought to get rid of Kyrtian right here and now, which was why Kyrtian got the invitation in the first place! Maybe that's why Lord Kyndreth wants to come to our estate now, to get the secret, then get rid of Kyrtian where there aren't any witnesses—and maybe get rid of the Lady at the same time!

By now, Gel had gotten his second wind, and such alarming thoughts only increased his energy. And Kaeth, all unsuspecting, had actually turned his back to him. If there was ever a time when a trained assassin would be vulnerable, this was it.

Gel didn't even pause for a breath; he acted. He had been

bent over, tying his boots; now without warning, he turned his pose into a charge, staying crouched over and rushing Kaeth, shouldering him into the wall face-first. He heard Kaeth grunt as he hit the wall, but before he could secure the assassin, Kaeth writhed loose a trifle. His reactions were as swift as a serpent's, and he managed to get himself turned around, but not before Gel grabbed a wrist in either hand and smashed them into the wall, then got his knee up to reinforce his hold. Now Gel had Kaeth pinned against the wall with both wrists imprisoned over his head and Gel's knee in his gut.

His legs are still free. If he can kick my leg out from under me—

Flushed, but impassive, he stared into Gel's grey-violet eyes for a long moment as Gel waited for him to speak or act. His wrists under Gel's hands showed no sign of tension, nor was there any indication that he intended resistance or struggle.

But that could be a ruse to get me to drop my guard.

"I suppose it's too much to ask what prompted this—ah—rather unexpected action of yours?" he finally asked mildly, a bit out of breath, but completely polite, in spite of the situation.

Gel glared at him, but he didn't drop his eyes. "I suppose you're going to deny you're an assassin," he replied flatly.

"Ah!" The expressionless eyes now reflected understanding, and the mouth relaxed a trifle in a faint smile. "*Now* I understand! You think Lord Kyndreth has targeted me at you—or perhaps, your master! Be at ease, friend; Lord Kyrtian is in no danger that *I* know of, other than from his own conniving cousin. And you're in no danger at all, least of all from me."

It felt honest. Gel wanted to believe him.

"But you don't deny you're an assassin—" Gel's instincts warred with his intellect. His instincts and his senses swore that Kaeth was telling the truth—his more cynical mind warned him that this was just a trick. Still, he was very tempted to release the fellow; this just didn't seem like a lie.

"Hardly, since you seem to have caught me as one," Kaeth replied, with a surprising amount of humor. "Although my own Lord isn't nearly as observant as you, since he is totally unaware of my training; I went to him, bought at auction after the unlamented death of my old lord. Still, once an assassin, as they say, the cloak never drops from your shoulders—so I'll qualify it by admitting for Lyon Lord Kyndreth, I'm an active *agent,* but an inactive assassin, nor am I ever likely to let him know of my more esoteric abilities."

"Huh." Slowly, carefully, Gel rocked his weight back onto his own feet, and released Kaeth's wrists. Just as slowly, Kaeth dropped his hands from the wall and rubbed, then flexed, his wrists, testing them. "And just how did you become an *inactive* assassin?"

"Look for yourself." Kaeth reached up and pulled the neck of his tunic open, then tilted his chin up so that Gel could see his slave-collar clearly. It wasn't the seal of Lyon Lord Kyndreth there, but that of the deceased—and, as Kaeth had said, unlamented—Lord Dyran.

Things were beginning to add up.

The noble Lord Dyran, who trained all manner of slaves in skills best left unexamined . . . and whose estate was broken up and divided among his relatives, with what was left going to auction. And that *was where I saw another assassin!*

That seal couldn't possibly be counterfeited, either. The fact that he was still wearing Dyran's collar meant that he'd been claimed after Dyran's death—otherwise the new master would insist on having the old collar removed and his own put on. Gel backed up, giving him a little more space. "Interesting."

"My beloved former master," Kaeth said, with a touch of ironic inflection on the word "beloved" that did not escape Gel's notice, "Was not the sort of Elvenlord to forget the traditions of his Ancestors."

"Including assassination?" Gel replied evenly.

Kaeth nodded with a dignity that impressed Gel in spite of himself. "Even so. I was trained from childhood, having shown unusual ability for getting into and out of supposedly guarded spaces and places without being caught. Whether or not you choose to believe me, I will say that my training was never employed against Elvenlords. . . ."

"Not that Dyran would have hesitated if he'd thought he

could get away with it," Gel interjected. Again, Kaeth nodded, this time with a shrug.

"Be that as it may, my *usual* tasks were to act as his intelligence agent, which is how I was employed at the time of his demise. And, not knowing any better, that is how my talents were advertised when the estate was broken up and the slaves went to auction, as an agent and bodyguard." Kaeth turned his palms up, and shrugged his shoulders again.

"And you, of course, were under no compulsion to enlighten the auctioneers." Gel felt a reluctant smile creeping over his lips; if this story was true, Kaeth was a very clever fellow indeed. *Hardly likely he'd tell them, when it was a lot more likely that the other Elvenlords would order him destroyed rather than take the chance of one of their number getting his hands on a trained assassin.* "I don't suppose it ever occurred to you to bolt?"

"Of course it did," Kaeth replied, and sat down on the bench, indicating to Gel that he should do the same. "Oh, don't worry about anyone overhearing us. If there had been anyone listening or watching, they'd have been in here the moment you went for my throat. I cost Kyndreth a *very* pretty penny, and he'd take it personally if someone deprived him of my services."

And this could be a set-up, but it's getting rather too unlikely and complicated—no, I think I'll go with my instincts and take him at his word.

"Naturally, it occurred to me to flee to the Wizards and the Wild Humans," he repeated, "But—well, I learned a few things about these collars that I wasn't supposed to. Only Dyran could *compel* me magically, and once he was dead, no other Elvenlord can harm me through this collar, unless he is Dyran's equal or better in power. That was a reason to run. But Dyran was as clever a bastard as his reputation claimed—I can still be traced and pursued through the collar, and any attempt to take it off will deprive me of my head. That was Dyran's little fail-safe in case anyone ever decided to subvert me."

Gel winced; that took *powerful* magic, and it took a particularly cruel mind to think of it.

"So, on the whole, it seemed better for everyone that I turn myself in as one of Dyran's slaves and go up for auction with the rest," Kaeth concluded with a lazy smile. "After all, I still had the option to bolt if my new master proved unbearable, and I'd be able to plan my escape so that I'd have a decent chance to get so far away before they discovered I was missing that it wouldn't be worth pursuit. At the time of Dyran's death I was in a position where that wasn't a possibility."

"What if Kyndreth ever finds out from another of Dyran's slaves—" Gel began, but Kaeth interrupted him with a gentle shake of his head.

"It's not likely, since everyone who ever knew what I was trained for is dead—mostly at Dyran's hands, I might add." For just a moment, there was a shade of bitterness in his voice, but he quickly covered it. "And of all the Old Lords, frankly, Kyndreth is the *least* likely to use an assassin. He's powerful enough to do his own dirty work, and ruthless enough to enjoy doing so. No, I'm out of the business, unless for some reason it becomes necessary to re-enter it long enough to protect myself. On the whole, I'm rather enjoying myself. Kyndreth treats expensive property well, and my duties are light, compared to those I had under Dyran."

Gel didn't miss the veiled threat in those words, but he shrugged them off. "I don't give a flying damn what you do with your skills, as long as you're not targeting Kyrtian." He couldn't help it; a note of fierce protectiveness crept into his voice.

Kaeth blinked slowly, and looked deeply and penetratingly into Gel's eyes for a moment. "Interesting," he murmured. "I'd heard rumors about Lord Kyrtian's people . . ."

Then he shook his head, as if it was no consequence. "I overhear a great deal, as all bodyguards do, and Kyndreth has the usual failing of our masters that he forgets how much his slaves see and hear. I hope you will believe me when I tell you that Kyndreth's plans are such, and so complex, that it is unlikely he could *ever* fit a trained assassin into them with any degree of confidence."

"Maybe against the Old Lords, and the lords that haven't revolted," Gel objected, "but what about the Young Lords who are still in revolt?"

"A bare possibility if they actually developed a leader with enough charisma to make them all work together," Kaeth admitted. "But it's more likely that cattle will fly before *that* happens. And besides, even if he did, sons aren't so thick on the ground that the victim's relatives would be very happy that the errant lad had been eliminated rather than returned to the parental fold." He smiled, but this time there was no humor in it. "After all, a youngster who has had all thoughts of rebellion neatly wiped from his mind can still function to sire the next generation, even if the rest of the time all he does is sit in a corner and drool."

That shocked Gel; he'd heard rumors that some of the Old Lords had the ability to tamper with another Elvenlord's mind and memory, but this was the first time anyone had said anything that confirmed what he had privately thought was a rather wild tale.

He did his best to seem as nonchalant about it as Kaeth was, however. "Putting it that way—I suppose you're right. Kyndreth would get no joy from the surviving relatives if he wiped out an heir, no matter how they felt about that heir when he was alive." He shook his head, and allowed his disgust and bafflement to show. "Damn, but this is as twisted as ball of snakes! How do you make it all out?"

"Early training, mostly." Now Kaeth actually *relaxed,* and for the first time, Gel saw him drop all of his defensive mannerisms. He knew that he was meant to see that—and he instinctively knew that Kaeth now trusted him as far as he had ever trusted anyone but himself. "Politics among the Elvenlords—it's considered a high art. Sometimes I think it's a pity that no one will ever know how accomplished an artist I am but myself."

Gel had to chuckle at that, and Kaeth smiled—a real, unmasked smile—in answer. "Well, I'm a plain man, and I tell you now that I'd rather map battlefield strategy than political strategy any day."

"It's cleaner." The regret in that voice was so deep that Gel could have drowned in it. For a moment, they both fell silent, then Kaeth coughed. "Well—before Lord Kyndreth wonders what is taking me so long, and summons me—what can *you* tell me about this training method of Lord Kyrtian's?"

Gel studied his expression, and came to an interesting conclusion. *He approves. Granted, if his master asks what we were talking about, this will give him something to feed to him, but he also approves of this and wants to know for himself. Fascinating. I wouldn't have thought that an assassin would be interested in preserving lives.*

"He's doing something with his magic that's initially complicated to set up, but doesn't take a great deal of power," Gel admitted. "That's what he's told me, anyway. Not being a lord, I don't know the mechanics of it." He brooded a moment, thinking back to the first time that Kyndreth set the spells. "There are two different pieces of magic involved: one to create a weapon that looks and feels real, but has no more substance than an illusion; and the other that he sets on the fighter that works with the weapon and reacts to what the weapon does."

"Senses it, you mean?" Kaeth asked, his eyes intent.

"I guess that's close, as close as anything a human can understand." Gel licked his lips. "Anyway, that second spell is what makes the glow and the shock when you're hit. The first time he did it, it took him most of the day; he says it gets easier as you get used to it. And according to him, it's almost as simple to work the spells on a lot of people as it is to cast them for one—he said something once about giving the magic extra energy and it copies itself for as long as you feed it." He laughed with embarrassment. "That probably sounds stupid, but that's the best I can tell you."

"No, no, it makes sense," Kaeth told him. "I've heard them talking about that, when they want to create a lot of something, like trees or flowers—doing the first one, then setting it to copy itself. That's how they can tell the difference between the illusion that a really powerful lord creates, and one created by an underling. You never see a powerful lord making copies; in his illusions, every tree, every flower is different."

"Whatever. That's the best description I can tell you." He pondered a moment, then decided to give Kaeth some information that, should he feed it back to Lord Kyndreth, would be a protection for Kyrtian rather than a danger. "Kyrtian has as many regular fighters as any other Great Lord, but I have to tell you, *all* we do is practice—either in daily drill using his method, or in actual battle-simulations. That's the *regular* fighters. Once a fighter is over forty, he goes on light-duty; he has some other job, but keeps in practice—archery practice, mostly, though some of them keep their sword and spear work right up to their old standards."

"Which means you don't just have gladiators, you have an *army,* trained to fight together." Kaeth pulled on his lower lip. "And you have a back-up corps of those older men. Interesting. Only a fool would challenge your Lord."

That was said as a statement, not a question.

Good. Let Kyndreth chew on that! "Exactly," Gel nodded. "That's because Lord Kyrtian likes to see how battle-strategy really works, rather than just reading about it. We work out new combat simulations fairly often, because unless someone steps into a hole and breaks a leg or something equally stupid, we come out of combat with the same number of fighters we went into it with."

"It's a damned good system," Kaeth agreed, finally. "So good, it makes me wonder what the advantage is to Lord Kyrtian. Trained fighters could revolt, if they put their minds to it."

Gel laughed easily. "Well, for one thing, there aren't any *real* weapons around where we can get hold of them. They're all locked up in the armory under Kyrtian's seal."

"So he doesn't have to worry about a slave-revolt." Kaeth's face cleared, and he nodded.

"And, of course, knowing you aren't going to get injured or killed makes the men willing to practice."

"He wouldn't have the expense of buying or raising replacements, either." Kaeth sighed in open admiration. "Brilliant strategy, especially for someone with no political allies. After today, no one will *dare* challenge him to a feud; his position is secure against all normal avenues of challenge. I would never have thought it, given his reputation."

"Not exactly *bad* strategy to make the others underrate him until he was ready, was it?" Gel said slyly, and Kaeth actually laughed.

Gel had the impression now that despite his sinister training, Kaeth Jared was a pretty decent sort, and that surprised him, more than a little. He'd always considered assassins to be—

To be scum, actually. I suspect most of them are. This one, though—well, he's got my respect.

His thoughts were interrupted by a discreet cough from the door, where a pair of young lads in Aelmarkin's livery stood uneasily. "Your Lords—" the nearest said, a tremor in his voice.

"Our Lords require us," Kaeth supplied with a nod. Suddenly the mask dropped over his face and he was all cool surface again, remote and unreadable. "Of course, immediately."

Gel stood only a fraction behind Kaeth, who turned and offered his hand. "It was a pleasure in every sense," Kaeth said, the warmth of his tone belying his lack of expression. "I would like to meet you again under similar circumstances."

Gel clasped the offered hand solemnly. "I hope that we can," he replied as warmly, "and I look forward to it."

And with that, they parted. As Gel followed his guide, he wondered what Kaeth's emotions were. He didn't think he was mistaken; something had resonated between them.

Maybe not friendship, at least not yet, he decided, as he saw Kyrtian waiting up ahead with a sense of relief that the ordeal was finally over. *But definitely admiration. And neither of us wants to ever have to kill the other. That has to count for something!*

8

Kyrtian passed through the Portal, which on Aelmarkin's side was a great gilded bas-relief gate wide and tall enough for a cargo-wagon to pass through, and on the manor side was an ornately-carved wooden door with a high lintel featuring the family crest. He had been in a profoundly thoughtful state of mind from the moment that he had parted with Lord Kyndreth, and Gel didn't interrupt his musings by trying to talk to him. Then again, it was entirely likely that Gel was too tired to talk, which didn't hurt Kyrtian's feelings in the least.

Longstanding family tradition of caution situated the Portal inside a small chamber with walls of stone and a locked door of fire-toughened bronze as insurance against an enemy using it to penetrate the heart of the manor. Invited guests were met here by an escort and let out, and the chamber itself would hold no more than ten at the most. The "key" to unlock the door was the presence of a family member or someone else (like Gel) to whom the lock had been sensitized. Of course, it was possible to overpower the escort and open the chamber door that way, but the door was guarded every moment of every day, and at least one guard would be able to raise an alarm. There would be no invasions of the estate through *this* Portal—or so it was hoped. After all of his studies in military tactics, Kyrtian was only too aware that a clever commander could think of ways to get past their precautions. His only comfort was that most of the Elvenlords were not very clever commanders.

Kyrtian parted with Gel just outside the Portal Chamber, as the guards tried to pretend they weren't eavesdropping. "Well, we're in for it now," he said, in mingled pride and chagrin. "I think this is the highest-ranked member of the Great Council to come here since Grandfather's day, and we're going to have to make certain everyone is totally prepared and understands what they need to do. The sooner we start preparing the staff and servants for Lord Kyndreth's visit, the sooner we can get it over with, and then everything can go back to normal."

"And the longer we delay, the more we risk an insult. Don't worry, I'm on it," the Sergeant said with a wave. "You go break the news to the Lady."

Gel made for the training-quarters at a trot, and Kyrtian reflected that the Sergeant was probably already five steps ahead of *him* in planning things. And one thing was absolutely certain; the visit could *not* take place until every servant on the estate was so well-rehearsed in the appropriate conduct of a slave that nothing would force him to depart from it, not insult, not punishment, and certainly not carelessness. Those servants closest to Kyrtian and his mother would have to be the best actors of the lot, which meant that certain of the younger and less experienced house-servants (such as Lynder) would be replaced for the duration with others who had been promoted to other positions or had even retired. Kyrtian would certainly be doing without most of his personal servants, who would be attending Lord Kyndreth, but that was a small price to pay for keeping up the deception that this was a normal Elven household.

All that would be in the hands of Gel, Lady Lydiell, and Lord Tenebrinth the Seneschal, and the sooner he let the last two know what was about to descend on them, the better. Gel was right; Lord Kyndreth's visit could not be postponed for long without offending him.

He paused for a moment to locate both his mother and the Seneschal; this was no time to waste precious moments hunting for them by ordinary means. The merest whisper of magic told him that, as was often the case at this time of day, Tenebrinth was with his mother in the latter's office, probably going over the household and estate accounts, making plans for the next couple of months, or dealing with issues of the servants. That could not possibly have been better for Kyrtian's purposes. By catching them together, Kyrtian would only have to go over the prospective visit and the reasons for it once.

Lydiell's office was literally at the center of the manor, overlooking everything. The manor boasted five towers, one at each corner and one at the center, with the center-most being a good two stories taller than the others—a full twelve stories tall. The towers gave the manor a look of delicacy and attenuation that Kyrtian found both attractive and amusingly deceptive, for the building itself had been constructed to survive a long siege, and had been built to withstand siege weapons that for the most part no longer existed. Lydiell's office was a glass-walled room at the very tip of the center-most tower, a place that would, in wartime, be occupied by at least four lookouts. Even in the worst weather, it was a snug and welcoming place, as the tower was one of the few places in the manor that depended on magic for more than lighting and a decorative illusion or two. Magic, and not mechanical contrivances, heated and cooled the tower and protected it from the worst weather. Magic also ensured the safety of any occupants of the transparent tube he entered at the bottom of the tower, powering the little platform under his feet that slowly rose through the tower to the top. No human could use this contrivance by himself, not even if that human was blessed with the humans' own form of magic. In this way, when she worked, Lydiell could be assured that no one could interrupt her without having to go first to one of elven blood. There were drawbacks to being as approachable as the lords of this manor had always been; the short-lived humans tended to come to them with any problem that had them stymied for more than a few moments, assuming that long experience granted unfathomable wisdom.

If it did that, there wouldn't be a Young Lords' War now. The Old Lords would have known better than to let them get as far as they did. And there wouldn't have been a second Wizard War either.

The intervening floors of the tower were, for the most part, unfurnished, although this was the oldest section of the manor and everything else had been constructed around it. The round rooms were too small to use for anything but offices, and only Lydiell and Tenebrinth had need of an office. So Kyrtian passed room after round, empty, alabaster-walled room with nothing more to entertain him than brief glimpses of the outside through the weapon-slits that served in place of windows. Even the look of alabaster was deceptive; the tower was built of something far stronger, though too much magic went into the construction of the material for anyone to use it these days. This tower was an artifact of the first fifty years after the Elves crossed out of Evelon, when no one knew if this world would prove to be as dangerous as the one they had left, a time when the elven-born existed as closely crowded together as any of the primitive humans in their huts, and waited for something infinitely more dangerous to descend without warning than a mob of weak, short-lived humans.

Tenebrinth's office, just below Lydiell's, was empty and untenanted as Kyrtian had anticipated. That office, and Lydiell's, were nearly double the size of the rooms below them. The walls swelled out here, giving the tower the look of a deep plate or shallow bowl balanced on a candlestick and covered with a round, pointed silver dish cover that was the overhanging (and projectile-proof) roof. The windows in Tenebrinth's office were only half the size of the ones in Lydiell's, but were glazed with the same impervious substance used instead of ordinary glass in every opening of this tower. Light that came through this substance lost some of its color and strength, making it appear as if the office lay underwater.

Now Kyrtian heard voices, and as he rose through the ceiling of Tenebrinth's office into that of Lady Lydiell, Lord Tenebrinth himself got up from his chair to greet him. Lady Lydiell remained seated, but welcomed her son with a smile and an extended hand.

Tenebrinth was a little older than Kyrtian's father would have been had he still been alive, having apprenticed in the position of Seneschal under Kyrtian's grandfather. He had served in his official capacity for as long as Kyrtian had known him, and as one of Kyrtian's tutors as well. As with all Elvenlords above a certain age but below the point of being considered ancient, it was impossible to tell exactly how old he was. Tall, thinner and less muscular than Lady Lydiell, with a long jaw and nose and prominent cheekbones, hair confined with a silver clasp at the nape of his neck, he looked exactly like what he was, a studious creature, serious and careful in thought and speech, a true scholar and thinker who preferred to joust with his mind and not his body.

"Well, I see you survived your encounter with the young tygers," the Seneschal said genially. "Permit me to congratulate you."

Kyrtian stepped out of the tube, kissed the back of his mother's hand, and took the chair that the Seneschal offered him. "Believe me, it *felt* like being in a tyger-pit," he replied with feeling. "I can't imagine how anyone enjoys these so-called social occasions."

"They aren't all as bad as combat challenges seem to be," Lady Lydiell said with a touch of sympathy and a shrug. "Some of the fetes can be positively pleasant, especially the fetes for unwed daughters. The presence of women seems to make the young tygers sheath their claws and hide their teeth, at least long enough to look civilized while in the company of the ladies."

Kyrtian had debated whether or not to tell his mother everything, and decided now that on the whole she was better off not knowing about how he had interrupted the challenge-combat, since only good had come out of his near-blunder in the end. "Well, I know you don't care who won the dispute—but Gel and I managed to pull off a little triumph that I think you two *will* approve of."

Tenebrinth blinked, and his mother raised an eyebrow. "Oh?" she said. "Now what have you two gotten into?"

"Well, there's good news and there's inconvenient news," he replied, "The inconvenient news is that Lyon Lord Kyndreth wants to visit for long enough to learn my training and combat methods. The good news is that the reason he does is that we persuaded the two feuding lords to have their differences settled in a combat *my* way, between Gel and Lord Lyon's man. Lyon was impressed, and not only wants to know how the spells are set, but said in the presence of the other lords that he intends to make this *the* way in which fighters are trained and disputes settled from now on. After seeing bloodless combat, he says that he agrees with me; the old ways are too wasteful to continue."

With every word, Lydiell and Tenebrinth grew more and more astonished, eyes widening and mouths dropping slightly open. It was Tenebrinth who could not restrain himself as Kyrtian leaned back in his chair, a satisfied smile on his face.

"By the Ancestors, boy, that isn't good news, it's *wonderful* news! Do you realize what this means to the humans out there?" Tenebrinth waved his arm at the world outside the windows.

"Well—mostly," Lady Lydiell interjected gently. "There are going to be those of our race whose thirst for blood and cruelty will not be satisfied with bloodless combat and who will continue to waste the lives of gladiators. Not even Lyon could get a law through the Council forbidding them to kill their own slaves. That strikes at the heart and soul of what nearly every Elvenlord sees as his basic rights over creatures he considers to be no better than beasts and property." At Kyrtian's nod of agreement, she smiled. "Nonetheless, Tenebrinth is right. Most of the Elvenlords will be only too pleased with the notion that they can settle differences through bloodless combat. It's a great drain, breeding and buying expensive fighting stock. The further expense of training gladiators and keeping them in training is bad enough; it's worse to have their expensive property massacred *during* training, and nearly as bad when the massacre happens in settling a petty argument, leaving them to train gladiators all over again if they wish to maintain their position and status."

Tenebrinth nodded. "That's been a complaint of the Lesser Lords against the Greater for the past two generations—very few have the resources to toss away slaves without considering the expense! Lord Lyon will gain a great deal of support among the Lesser Lords for this, if he makes it policy—and almost as importantly, he *won't* aggravate the Greater. He stands to win all around."

Lydiell patted her son's hand. "I'm so pleased that I won't even ask what trouble you tumbled into in order to achieve this remarkable goal!"

"Mother!" Kyrtian objected, hoping he didn't sound guilty.

"But the price of this is that we are to expect Lord Kyndreth some time in the immediate future?" the Seneschal interjected. "Did you actually set a date for the visit?"

"No date has been set, and I told him that I would send him a Portal-key when I had things ready for him. I tried to give the impression that, as we were a small household, reclusive and unused to visitors, we needed time to prepare for the visit of so prominent a guest. He was satisfied with that so far as I could tell, and I have no intention of letting him set foot here until *everyone* is prepared. That won't be until you two and Gel have gotten the servants and field-hands ready to hold up the illusion that this is an ordinary estate," Kyrtian assured him. "He didn't seem all that impatient and he wasn't offended that I couldn't offer him our hospitality immediately."

"No doubt he has business of his own to take care of before he can afford a formal visit," the Seneschal murmured, as if to himself.

"More likely he is taking the time to see who is and is not our ally, going back to the time we all left Evelon," Lydiell replied tartly. "Someone of his rank and status can't afford an ally with an inconvenient number of deadly enemies."

"Well, the only enemy we have that I know of is Aelmarkin. . . ." Kyrtian said, letting his voice trail off and looking at his mother questioningly.

"Correct; Aelmarkin is our only open enemy, with the remote possibility that *his* allies might choose to throw in on his side," his mother confirmed. "Though once they see that Lyon has thrown in with us, however briefly, they are unlikely to back Aelmarkin against us in anything important. Thank the Ancestors we never meddled in politics on either side of the family! We'll have a clean slate, so far as Lord Lyon is concerned. All we have to worry about is keeping up appearances for a few days at most."

"I—don't intend to ask anything of Lord Lyon for this, Mother," Kyrtian said, hesitantly. "And I don't intend to make it seem as if *I* consider it a great favor on my part to teach him my methods. I want it to seem as if I consider this to be—how shall I put this?—something that I truly believe *should* be offered, part of my duty to the Elvenlords as a whole. I want to give him the impression of a solemn young man who is devoted to the welfare of his people. Which I *am;* just not the people that he thinks." He smiled. "There's no point in disillusioning him on that."

"Exactly right; any of the ordinary status-grubbers would do the opposite," she confirmed. "By acting differently than he expects, you'll catch him off guard and he won't know quite what to think of us. At best, he may decide that we're worth having as a permanent ally. The worst he'll assume is that we are so quietly provincial, so wrapped up in our own ways and life, with such quaint ideas of loyalty and duty, that we are no threat or challenge to anyone. We'll be safe to patronize, and he'll be motivated to protect us from any more of Aelmarkin's maneuverings."

"For my part, I would say that this would be the *best* thing he could assume," Kyrtian replied, relieved. "Can I take it that you approve?"

"Completely," Lady Lydiell said, as Tenebrinth nodded. Kyrtian smiled, a little thrill of pleasure tickling his spirit at the notion that his first foray into the dangerous world of Great Lords and politics had come off so successfully.

Even though I almost turned it into a disaster, he reminded himself. *This is not the time for hubris!*

He took his leave of both of them and stepped into the tube, which held him in place until the platform rose to receive him. Once he had been deposited on the ground floor, he headed straight for the West Tower, which held all five floors of the great library.

He planned to do a little genealogical investigation himself before his own plans went any further.

In the home of every Elvenlord, Great or Lesser, there was always a Great Book of Ancestors, kept up to date by either the Lady of the clan or a clerk she personally supervised. Every birth, death, and wedding was promptly reported to the Council, which sent out immediate notification to every household, however small and insignificant. No marriage or alliance could be made without consulting the Great Book, which dated back to the exile from Evelon.

Kyrtian sat at the table holding the Great Book on its slanting stand, and drew it closer to him. As he always did, because those First Days fascinated him, Kyrtian opened the Book to the first page where the names of all of those who had dared the Gate out of Evelon were written. Fully half of them were inscribed with death-dates that came within days or weeks of the Crossing. Some had died of the strain of the Crossing itself, or of injuries sustained in Evelon before the Crossing.

Few in these days realized that those who had made the Crossing had been the *losers* in a war that had split Elvenkind and set one half warring against the other. The Crossing had been the desperate attempt of the defeated to escape rather than surrender, not the valiant and bold move of those who were in search of a new world to conquer. That was one fact that those who ruled here now preferred to forget and bury in the past.

Of the survivors that remained after the Crossing, none were still alive at the present day. Elvenlords lived long, provided no accident, illness, inherited weakness, or murder disposed of them before the normal span of four or five centuries, but they were hardly immortal. Kyrtian's paternal great-grandfather had been one of the longest-lived survivors, as (he now learned) had Lyon Lord Kyndreth's great-grandsire; most other Elvenlords in these days were yet a further generation down the line from the original inhabitants of the new land.

He turned the page to trace his mother's line, rather than his father's. *Odd,* he thought, as he noted something that had never seemed important before. *I'm literally the first male any woman of her line has produced since Evelon—*

"That is why there was no great objection when I wedded your father," said Lydiell, behind him, as if she had the human gift of reading thoughts. He was too used to her uncanny ability to do this with him to be startled; he simply turned and smiled at her as she stepped forward another pace and placed her hand affectionately on his shoulder.

"No one—least of all Aelmarkin—ever thought I would produce a male heir," she said quietly. "That was why there was no objection raised to the marriage, and why Aelmarkin is so intent on dispossessing you of your inheritance now. He assumed that the ripe plum of our estate would drop into his lap without any effort on his part—or that he could somehow connive or force me to wed my presumed daughter to him." Lydiell smiled down at her son, whose birth had spoiled Aelmarkin's plans.

"But he's really a cousin in name only," Kyrtian objected, tracing back Aelmarkin's line. "His people haven't been directly related to ours since Evelon itself! It was our great-grandfathers who were cousins, and there's been no closer marriage since then."

"But if you trace carefully, he's the only other male heir to the Clan," Lydiell pointed out. "That's as much your great-grandfather's and grandfather's fault as anything else. Once they had a single, living child, the need to protect what we had built here took precedence over trying to sire any more children. They each had *one* male heir by *one* marriage and no further children; no daughters to wed outside the Clan, no second sons to secure alliances. Granted, they were exceptionally long-lived, and that's what saved us, but I was the first bride to come from a family not bound in any way to your Clan, and if your father was still with us, by now you would have at least a younger sister or brother, because *I* would have personally seen to it, rather than accepted the edict that there was no need for further children."

Now Kyrtian noted something else that had somehow escaped his attention. His ageless mother was nearer in age to his grandfather than his father! She saw his eyes resting on the birth-date under her name, and chuckled richly.

"I wondered when you would uncover that!" she said. "Yes, I'll admit it; I robbed the cradle! When your grandmother—wiser or more pragmatic than her husband—knew that she would not survive your father's birth, she had enough time to handpick a successor. She turned to our family, who had been her friends; she wanted my sister, but the family had already wed her off, so she chose me! But she had reckoned without your grandfather's love and devotion; he refused to take another wife, especially one as barely-nubile as I was. Still, for the sake of my friendship with her, I visited often and long, trying to amuse your grandfather and possibly even persuade him in time that I was fascinating and desirable! I wish you had seen me, still barely past my presentation fete, slinking around here as if I was a hardened seductress!"

Since Kyrtian couldn't imagine his mother slinking around like a seductress at *any* age, he spluttered a little and reddened.

"Well, when seduction failed, I thought I would win him by showing him what a devoted mother I could be to his son," she continued. "There was one little wrinkle in that plan; by the time I thought of it, your father was hardly of an age to need mothering! But I persisted in cultivating him, only to find that his son and I were mutually falling head over heels in love as soon as he was old enough to think of such things! Your grandsire was much amused, and so was my sister, Moth."

"Moth," of course, was V'tern Morthena Lady Arada, nearly a full century Lydiell's senior, and the only surviving relict of Lord Arada's tiny Clan. She held a small estate granted her by her late husband in her own right, with no inconvenient cousins to pester her.

Kyrtian sighed. When he looked at the Great Book, in the complicated web of intermarriages and second and third marriages, his family stood all alone, like a single strand of silk off to one side of the greater pattern.

"I have not told you this before, but Aelmarkin tried to force a marriage on me when your father first disappeared," she continued, as calmly as if it had happened to someone else. "That was when Moth came to my rescue; she dug up an obscure law preventing a man from marrying the widow of his cousin if she already had a male heir. She visited each of the Great Lords herself and pointed out to each one of them—with examples—how that law would protect their own sons from certain of their opponents if anything happened to the lord himself. Needless to say, they upheld the law to a man, and Aelmarkin had to slink away with his tail between his legs."

"No wonder he hates you," Kyrtian replied, enlightened.

She sniffed delicately. "Personally, I prefer not to waste an emotion as empowering as hatred on that worm. It was obvious from the start what his plans were when he came slinking around here, oozing false sympathy and groomed and jewel-bedecked to within an inch of his life. Even if I had been the foolish woman he thought I was, I would quickly have seen that such an alliance would mean *your* death. No matter what my personal feelings were on the subject, I would never have placed you or our people in the hands of the odious Aelmarkin!"

"Thank you for that!" Kyrtian laughed.

"And sometime you might thank your aunt for devising the

means to protect us both," she replied cheerfully, with a light squeeze of her hand on his shoulder.

"Well, however much you play at modesty, I think that you would have found the solution just as quickly as Lady Moth if you hadn't had her help," he told her. "You are two out of the same mold, as clever as you are beautiful, and far more intelligent than any mere males."

"I only needed to be clever enough to take advantage of our isolation," she said, with a laugh at his attempt to compliment her. "After all, we *are* out back of beyond of nowhere, and I doubt that anyone other than Aelmarkin would even consider wanting our estate for that reason." Her tone turned scornful. "And frankly, I think if Aelmarkin knew how much work it is to keep this estate so profitable, he'd quickly change his mind about wanting it."

"I only wish that were true," Kyrtian sighed. "It's only a lot of work because of the way we treat our human friends; if this estate were run on the same lines as any other, the profits would probably be much higher. At least," he amended, "That's what Tenebrinth told me once."

"That's beside the point," Lydiell said resolutely. "The point now is to make sure we get the most out of Lord Lyon's visit, without making any blunders and without sacrificing any of our independence. You go off and consult with Gel over dinner; I'll do the same with Tenebrinth. We're going to want to please Lyon without dazzling him, charm him without making it look as if we have anything he really wants other than your knowledge and expertise. And you and Gel ought to put your heads together to see if you can think of anything else he *might* want out of you in particular."

Kyrtian closed the Great Book with a determined *snap.* "You're perfectly right, as usual," he said. "I'll go change into something less ostentatious and find Gel, and we'll get down to business."

But in spite of the excitement of the moment, there was one thing he had realized as he walked off in search of Gel. With all of the conversation about marriages and alliances, for the first time since he'd come of age, Lydiell had *not* even mentioned the prospect of his own marriage!

And that was enough of a relief that his steps became noticeably lighter.

9

Over the next several days, he and Gel were so busy with preparations for Lord Kyndreth's visit that he hardly had time to do anything other than eat and sleep. He certainly didn't have any time for staging even combat-practice, so the fighters were left to fend for themselves until Gel could take over their practice-sessions using the old, blunted wooden weapons instead of the magic ones.

He already knew that he did not have to worry about the fighters taking advantage of his inattention. Thanks to a very real sense of what Gel would have to say—and do—about it, if they spent their time idle, they took it upon themselves to follow the usual course of exercise and simple drill, varied with hand-to-hand, unarmed contests, in which the worst accident that could befall would be a broken bone or two.

Kyrtian also knew that the fighters would not give the game away by acting out-of-character. *They* were military, heart and soul, and would no more speak out-of-turn or hesitate to obey an order than fly. No, the fighters could be counted upon to play their parts like the professionals that they were.

It was the regular servants and field-hands who had to be drilled in subservience until it became second nature, and many times Kyrtian was strongly tempted to meddle with their minds by means of magic to keep them from forgetting. It was finally Gel who came up with the excellent solution of actually working through the elf-stones on their seldom-worn collars, setting up a warning tingle whenever the wearer altered his or her posture from that of complete servility.

That worked, and far better than Kyrtian had expected. The servile pose, with shoulders slightly hunched and eyes on the ground, forcibly reminded people of how they were expected to act. "It won't matter if they look cowed and afraid all the time," Gel pointed out. "Lord Kyndreth won't know it's all acting a part, no matter how exaggerated it seems to us. A real slave just can't *be* too servile; if they grovel a lot, he'll only think you're keeping their leashes short and using the whip a great deal. Now—much as I hate to bring this up, but what if Kyndreth doesn't bring along some of his own women? He'll expect to be offered entertainment, even if he turns it down."

"I don't have any concubines to offer him," Kyrtian pointed out. "I suspect that's one of the things Aelmarkin tries to use against me with the other Lords, that I'm—ah—"

"Virginal and chaste—and probably sexless, hence no fit heir," Gel growled bluntly. "Well, you may not have a harem to offer him at the moment, but what are you going to do? Have you made any plans?"

"Mother had an idea," Kyrtian replied, but made a face of distaste. "I don't like it, mind you, but . . . she thinks it's just that I'm too fastidious. She's going to send Tenebrinth to the slave markets and buy a pretty concubine or two just before the visit; she'll meddle with their memories to make them think they've been here for the last couple of years, keep them isolated in a tiny harem of their own and have me offer *them* to Lord Kyndreth."

"You're too fastidious," Gel told him bluntly. "It's perfect. They won't know anything about us, and they won't be related to anyone here. If there's an . . . accident . . . we won't be losing any of *our* people."

Kyrtian's distaste grew, but he couldn't deny that Gel's pragmatic view was at least practical. "And what do we do with them afterwards?" he asked sourly.

Gel shrugged. "Hardly matters. Concubines aren't the brightest as a whole, and I suspect any that your mother picks will be very pretty and *very* dim—much safer that way. We could probably marry them off to someone, if you've got no taste for having them around. Or sell them again." He raised an eyebrow at Kyrtian's expression, and snorted. "Do yourself a favor; let your mother and Tenebrinth deal with it. Keep your hands clean if you dislike it that much."

As if my not knowing makes it any better, he thought grimly. *No, that's no answer.* "I'll tell Mother you agree with her idea, and even though I don't *like* the idea, I agree it's necessary, there really doesn't seem to be a better solution."

"There isn't," Gel said, with emphasis. "What else do you want to do, ask for volunteers?"

That was definitely no answer. He shook his head. "I'll do the memory manipulation—mother isn't going to be able to impart many convincing illusions about—um—I mean, it's not as if she's a male—" He flushed, and didn't complete the sentence, but got the distinct feeling that Gel found his embarrassment highly amusing. "We'll do what we have to, all of us, and try to make things up afterwards if there's anyone hurt by this." He just hoped that Lord Kyndreth wasn't one of those who left women damaged. "I can always make the girls forget everything when he's gone," he added, as much for his own benefit as for Gel's.

Gel looked relieved. "You'll never be a real commander if you can't make the difficult decisions *and* carry them out," he reminded his erstwhile superior—perhaps just a touch smugly.

"I just did, didn't I?" he replied, irritated. "Enough; we're spending more time on this than the issue warrants, and it has *nothing* to do with your part in this, which is getting the fighters ready. Well?"

Gel grinned. "Oh, they're ready. Very eager to show their paces, and just as eager to see you vindicated. Have no fear, they know their parts. We'll give Lord Kyndreth a show he isn't likely to forget for the next three centuries."

Triana considered the slave dispassionately—a rare state of mind for her. There were several considerations here, not the least of which was this; how far could one trust a human?

As she had told Aelmarkin, she seldom trained female

slaves. *Never* was not the operative word; *never* was not a word to be used at all among the Elvenlords, whose long lives had no room in them for *never*. Sooner or later, whatever it was that had been vowed against would happen. Mind, there were Elvenlords so rigid in their thinking that they actually believed that they could say they would "never" do something—but Triana knew better.

This woman was *not* of her breeding; the female slaves that Triana bred on her own estate were strictly utilitarian, and while not plain (she couldn't bear to have anything plain or ugly about her) were about as animated as statues in the presence of their mistress. This girl, bought, not at auction, but handpicked from among the offerings of a private sale, was the opposite of stoic and unanimated. She was trained as a dancer as well as in harem skills; she was very intelligent. Triana needed a woman who was intelligent, but with intelligence came the liability of thinking for one's self.

How far to trust her? That was the question.

"Would it surprise you very much to learn that I need a spy?" she asked aloud.

The slave shook her head slightly, enough to indicate that she was *not* surprised, but not so much that the mute reply could be considered impertinent.

"The mother of a certain young lord is purchasing harem slaves, and I intend that you should number among them," Triana continued. "I need to know what goes on in his household, and harem slaves are in a unique position to find that out."

"But harem slaves are kept in isolation—" the girl responded tentatively.

Triana smiled. "But men do not heed their tongues when among them," she corrected. "I *could* have merely planted a teleson-ring on you and sent you on as a passive listener—but I would not learn a tenth as much as I will when you work for me in full knowledge of what I want." She considered the girl further. "It is your duty to give me that, but your previous master indicated that you are bothersomely intelligent—"

Here the girl flushed and looked down at her feet.

"—and as a consequence, I am aware that mere duty is not

going to extract what I want from the place to which I am going to send you." Triana chuckled, and the girl looked up again in surprise. "Oh, come now—I am not one of those lords who prefers slaves to have no thoughts of their own! You little mayfly humans may not have the capacity to appreciate what your masters can, but you are still as motivated by the prospect of *gain* as we are. I know full well that once planted in this household, your leash will be slipped and you can and will do as you please in this matter." She leaned forward, catching and holding the girl's gaze with her own. "I have an incentive to offer you, so that you will work that dear little mind of yours to the fullest on my behalf."

A flicker of emotion passed across the girl's face, and she flushed again. "Incentive, Mistress?" she ventured breathily.

Satisfied that she had found the correct key to the lock of the girl's ambition, Triana leaned back. "A reward, if that word pleases you better; a reward for exemplary service. Exert yourself to the utmost on my behalf, find a way to convince Kyrtian to leave the harem door unbarred to your comings and goings, and above all, report *everything* you see and hear, however small and seemingly inconsequential, to me. Do that, satisfy me, and at the end of a year in his service I will have you retrieved. You can retire here, and name what you will for your conditions of living, never again being required to do anything you do not care for. From a cottage and mate of your choice to the suite and service of a young Lady. *Or*—if this is more to your liking—you may go to your wild brethren among the Wizards. I can arrange for that as well."

From the slight quickening of the girl's breath, Triana knew she had caught her. *Mine,* she thought, with satisfaction, and nodded to set the hook, now that the bait had been taken. "This will not be easy," she warned. "You will have to bend your whole mind to the task, and you will have to keep Lord Kyrtian and his mother from ever guessing that you are not what you seem. If you do not satisfy me—" she shrugged "—I will not be able to punish you, obviously, but I can and will leave you in place, and you will live and die the concubine of a minor lord in a tiny harem with unvarying routine. Kyrtian does not often have guests, so you would not even have that prospect to brighten your days. I believe that someone like you would find that sort of life maddeningly restrictive."

The slave did not hesitate even for the smallest part of a moment. "I will serve you, Lady," the girl replied decisively. "You will find nothing lacking in my zeal."

Triana laughed aloud, with a glance at the girl to invite her to join in her good humor. *Ah, Aelmarkin,* she thought, as she settled down to instruct the girl in the use of the teleson-ring and her initial duties. *This wager is already won!*

Gel knew his business, none better. Kyrtian left the matter of the household to his mother, and took charge of the rest. Now that the warnings were in place and the attitude of the field-hands and farmers had been established, he judged that it was time to prepare the general outward appearance of his people. They must look self-sufficient and prosperous, but not *too* prosperous. The servants must not look too healthy, too happy. In fact, the ones in the fields must not look happy at all.

He spent a day considering how to accomplish that, researching spells of illusion, wondering what he would do if Lord Kyndreth detected them or broke them. Kyndreth had not gotten where he was by being a fool, and if he detected illusions, he would want to know what they hid—he would first suspect treachery, but he would definitely want to know why there were illusions on human slaves.

Finally, in the twilight, he decided to take a walk to see if the fresh air would clear his head out and let some fresh thoughts in.

The stars were just coming out, and a fine breeze carried the scents of the gardens on its wings. He took a moment to extinguish the glowing globes illuminating the pathways, for he knew the garden paths by heart and had no need of the lights. At the moment, he would rather enjoy the darkness, not because he was brooding, but because he wanted his mind to rest.

How did Aelmarkin's servants look? That would be the sort of thing to get his own people to emulate. Despite their servile stances, there was still something wrong about them that he could not put a finger on. He took slow, deliberate steps and cast his mind back a few days, trying not to frown in concentration. It wasn't an exact memory he wanted, after all, but an impression. How did the ordinary servants, the ones who cleaned the rooms and brought the food from the kitchen, seem to an observer?

It was easy enough to remember the pretty ones, the upper-level slaves, whose duties included being decorative. Those weren't the ones he wanted, at least in part because he wasn't certain any of his people could manage a convincing imitation of a pleasure-slave, and in part because it wouldn't do any harm for Lord Kyndreth to believe that his household was on the austere and sober side. Let Kyndreth think of him as hard-working, somewhat obsessed with his hobby, and not really interested in the opulent life. That would do no harm at all.

It will also reinforce the impression that we aren't worth the attempt to take us over. Profit can only be stretched so far; we might be austere because we can't afford too many luxuries.

Try as he might, all he could come up with was a vague impression of *sameness,* as if the lesser servants were all as alike as ants, and as interchangeable. They could have been furniture, floor-tiles, the plinths upon which statues stood, they blended so well into the background.

With a flash of insight, he realized at that moment that *this* was what he wanted!

They must have all been in some drably uniform tunics, or the like, he decided. *They aren't supposed to stand out—they should be invisible. Drab tunics would do that.* No matter that he didn't know what such a tunic or what-not should look like—any of the seamstresses could deal with that detail. He'd take the need to them first thing in the morning, and let *them* decide how to make everyone on the manor lands uniformly drab.

As for making people look unhappy . . . he grinned as another idea came to him. *I'll have the field-workers stick a burr or a pin somewhere in their clothing where it'll irritate them without really hurting them—or put stones in their shoes, or wear shoes too tight or too big. That'll give them all sour expressions, should any of Kyndreth's people come snooping about.*

He yawned, and realized that he'd been up far too long—but they were all going short on sleep, trying to get themselves ready. *Bed,* he decided. *And first thing in the morning, the manor seamstresses.*

Even though he woke very, very early—just at the break of dawn, in fact—when he showed up unannounced at the seamstress's workrooms, they were already well into the day's labors. That surprised him; he'd always known, in a vague way, that his people began their work early, long before he awoke, but he hadn't ever given much thought to what that meant.

Here was a large, well-lit room, furnished with comfortable chairs in which several women were seated, sewing diligently. There was a large table covered with a piece of fabric at the far side of the room, and a woman with a wickedly-bladed pair of scissors made deft cuts in it, folding and laying aside the pieces she had made as she went along. Bolts of fabric were arrayed in a rack along one wall, ribbons and other trim were wound around wooden cones on pegs, and spools of thread were arranged in little racks beside them. He put his need to the chief of the ladies, a formidable dame with silver-streaked hair, explaining the effect he wanted, and why. She pursed her lips and frowned.

"My lord—do you realize what you are asking when you request common uniform tunics for the entire estate? Aye, we've enough seed-sack material about, but no *time*—even a simple tabard with no hems would need side and shoulder seams, and it'd be so crude it would *look* makeshift—"

"Dye," interrupted one of the women engaged in some mysterious task that seemed to involve the edges of a great deal of fabric that pooled on either side of her. "Don't bother with making anything *new,* just fire up dye-pots and have everyone come in and dunk an old tunic and trews, so you get the look of wear as well as having it look uniform."

"Oh, well-thought!" the older woman exclaimed, her brow clearing. "That might be a problem, mightn't it—if it looked as if everyone in the place had new clothes!"

"For color—black'd be best, walnut-black the cheapest, and

we've got plenty of that; soon or late, everybody needs some bit of black, and that way I doubt there'll be much complaining about spoiling something good." The woman was very pleased with her ingenuity, and so were Kyrtian and her supervisor.

"Aye, that's the way! Thenkee, Margyt!" The head seamstress beamed and patted Kyrtian on the shoulder as if he was a small boy. "Don't worry your head about it, my young Lord, we'll handle this for you; when the day comes, everybody'll be making a nice depressing background." She actually *pushed* him—gently, but pushed him, nevertheless—out the door. He didn't resist; in fact, he was rather amused at the situation. He'd had no idea how things were run on the domestic side, but clearly this woman was as much a "commander" in her own ranks as Gel was in his!

And he had no doubt that she would get the job done, either. She had the air about her that said she would ride right over the top of anyone and anything to complete whatever she'd promised.

He went back to his own preparations, calling in each of the supervisors of work-parties and explaining to them what he wanted done—the burrs and all—and why. He'd discovered a very long time ago that if people knew *why* they were being asked to do something that seemed senseless, they were much more likely to comply.

"Now, I don't want anyone to start getting *too* creative," he warned. "Don't let anyone go maim himself, or try to counterfeit plague or something, but if people get other ideas about how to look less than happy and healthy, let them go to it. Particularly I'm a bit worried about the little children giving things away—the older ones will be all right if you put it to them as being important, but the littlest are used to running right up to any stranger and saying what they think."

"There're several of the parents figuring on that now, my lord," one of the supervisors assured him. "If nothing else, everybody's agreed that we can hide the littlest off somewhere nobody'll see them, all in a group. Perhaps we could take them out into the woods, and let them have a camping-excursion. Leave it to us, we'll take care of it. Tell them it's a holiday treat, and they'll be good as lambs."

So many details—as soon as Kyrtian thought he'd dealt successfully with the last, another occurred to him. It wasn't until days later that his mother approached him as he was arranging with one of the building crews to make "alterations" to the workers' quarters. It had occurred to him by then that it was unusual enough for his people to have their own little homes and villages instead of being herded into vast warehouses when they weren't working—and he'd better have their quarters look shabby and ill-made!

Lady Lydiell waited patiently as he and the builders quickly worked out what was needed; it was pretty clear that she wanted to speak with him alone, so he dismissed them as soon as he could, and closed the door of his own new office behind them.

She sat with a rustle of silk and a swirl of scarlet skirts. "You told me to come to you when I had your harem, and I have," she said simply, and the words hit him like a splash of cold water in his face. "They're ready for you to prepare them."

He didn't allow the shock to freeze his thoughts, though. "I don't have anything on my plate at the moment, so I had best see to them, then," he told her, and was pleased to see a bit of surprise in her eyes that he was willing to deal with the unpleasant duty so quickly. She *knew* that he hated meddling with humans' minds through their collars, especially for a purpose like this—

But on the whole, he'd rather just get it over with so that he wouldn't have to dwell on it.

"That's fine," she replied quickly, getting to her feet with that grace he admired so much and was so much a part of her. "Come along; I've converted your old nursery to a harem; it was the most secure suite in the manor and the only one not in use."

"It had to be the most secure, didn't it?" he chuckled, opening the door for her. "Not only did you have to worry about something getting in at me, you had to worry about me getting out!"

"And a mischievous escape-artist you were, too," she retorted. "Well, I can tell you that I am *very* proud of Tenebrinth, and you will be, too, when you see these women. With all of the upheavals, the slave-trade has been very much disrupted—"

"Which *I* will not shed tears over," he responded, with a hint of a frown.

"Nevertheless, it has made *his* task harder." The look she gave back to him was one of reproach. "Many of the slave-markets have been closed down, and others have only the most meager of selection. On the other hand, if it hadn't been so disrupted, I doubt we would have found three women so perfectly suited to our purposes. I doubt that even the great Lord Kyndreth will wonder why your harem is so small, once he sees these girls."

"Oh?" Now his curiosity was piqued.

She nodded, her hair falling in a graceful curve across her brow as she did so. She pushed it back with an impatient hand. "Firstly, I very much doubt that *anyone* other than their trainer and former owner have ever seen them, which makes it much easier to carry off the fiction that you would have owned them yourself for several years. Secondly, if the trade were not so disrupted, I doubt if we would have been able to get them at all; they'd have been snapped up before they reached the greater markets."

Now he was surprised. "Are they that attractive, then?" he asked, his curiosity more than piqued.

"They are not precisely great beauties, although they are quite handsome—well, make that judgment for yourself." By this time they had reached the door—and now guarded—of his former nursery. The guards stepped aside, faces as expressionless as statues, and Lady Lydiell opened the door, gesturing to him to go in ahead.

He did so, feeling the faint tingle of a second "door" as he crossed the threshold that would prevent the women from crossing it until it was taken down. That was usual enough in harems to keep them out of the Lady's Bower; it was necessary here, to keep them from wandering and seeing things they shouldn't.

The three women had clearly been told to await him, for they were standing in poses that were a little too contrived to be natural. That was when he understood what his mother had meant.

There could not possibly have been three women more strikingly different. The first, tall, with pale gold hair and vivid blue eyes, had an angular face and a figure as slender and willowy as any Elven lady, and a far-away expression as if she lived entirely in a cloud of dreams. She had posed herself beside a giant vase of flowers, musing on a single enormous lily-blossom, her frilled and lacy gown echoing the pastel colors of the blooms. The second, a brunette with brown eyes full of passion, full lips, and a sensuous body, fairly radiated promises; she lounged against a pillar in a way that thrust her bosom forward—straining the silk of her scarlet, form-fitting wrap—and allowed her to watch him with a provocative, flirtatious, sideways glance. The third had a tumble of flaming curls and merry green eyes, a dancer's body of strength and agility clothed in a simple blue tunic that left her legs bare, and the expression of a completely innocent child; she looked up from the kitten she was playing with to smile at him with a face full of laughter. It seemed that in these three, all the variety of an entire harem was encompassed. And only a statue could have failed to respond to the silent invitations each of them sent to him in her own way.

"You see?" Lady Lydiell said quietly, as the three sank to the ground in deep curtsies. He glanced at her, and saw that she had a glint of mischief in her own eyes. "Well, dearest, is it safe to leave you alone with them?"

He couldn't help it; he flushed—but he covered it with a half-mocking bow. "You're going to have to if I'm to give them convincing memories," he told her, causing *her* to blush. It was with a bit of satisfaction that he bowed her out, and turned to face his new "acquisitions."

He was trying to think of something to say when they descended on him as a body and made speech irrelevant, at least for that moment, and the many that followed.

Sergeant Gel followed Lord Tenebrinth into the Old Tower, his mood not precisely apprehensive, but tinged with that emotion. Lady Lydiell rarely spoke to him face-to-face, and this was the first time that she had ever required him to attend her in her private office.

He had never been inside the Old Tower; few humans had, only the one or two required to clean Lydiell's, and Tenebrinth's, offices. One of the lords, or the lady herself, would have to have brought him personally; there was no other way for him to use the only means of access, which was a bizarre transparent tube. He couldn't imagine how he was supposed to climb it and entered it with Tenebrinth rather dubiously—only to suppress a start as the floor beneath him began to rise. It gave him a queasy sensation, despite his familiarity with magic, to ride this contraption. It just didn't seem . . . natural. Round, empty room after room passed him—or rather, he passed them—as he rose with no real sensation of movement.

He began to wonder if he would ever reach the top, when finally one of the rooms showed signs of occupation—as did the next after that—and then the platform slowed and came to a stop at the topmost level.

Lydiell's office, at the top of the tower, had a dizzying and unrestricted view that he, as a military commander, could see was of incalculable value for the chatelaine of the manor—or the commander of its defenses. The office walls were all window, and he wondered as he stepped gingerly off the platform what a storm would be like up here.

Lydiell greeted him with a smile, which made his apprehension vanish. She even rose; that was an unexpected honor, and he bowed as deeply as he could without looking ridiculous. The Lady did not like groveling; none of her clan did.

"Sergeant Gel, please, make yourself easy," she said, as she gestured with that grace only the Elvenlords possessed towards an unoccupied chair. "This is not an official summons—rather, it is a personal one. I have a desire to consult you."

Tenebrinth evidently took this as the signal to depart; he stepped back on the little platform and discreetly dropped back to the next level, leaving them alone.

Gel took his seat and examined the Lady's face, and swiftly understood why she wanted to see him. "Kyrtian?" he asked, wasting no words.

She nodded, and took her place behind her desk, clasping her hands on the surface before her. "I had hoped," she said, hesitantly, as if she was voicing thoughts long held in secret, "that I could keep Kyrtian isolated from the politics of the Great Lords and the Council. Unfortunately, it seems that the times conspire against my hopes."

"It does look like he's going to get tangled up whether he likes it or not," Gel said cautiously, his eyes never leaving her face, unnerving as it was to look her straight in the eyes. "My Lady, I don't mind telling you that I don't like the idea any better than you do."

"I'm not certain you realize just *how* tangled he's likely to get," Lydiell replied, a faint frown-line creasing her ageless brow. Gel couldn't for the life of him read those odd emerald eyes the Elvenlords all had, but at least she wasn't trying to hide her facial expressions. "Lord Kyndreth is not going to be content merely to learn a few tricks with magic to help train humans—when he realizes just how extensive Kyrtian's knowledge and practical experience of military matters is, he is going to want my son to exercise his talents in the service of the Old Lords. He will certainly want Kyrtian to command a force against the Young Lords, and possibly keep him on after the Young Lords are crushed, to move against the Wizards and the wild humans."

Gel swore under his breath, angry at himself for not thinking of that himself. And it was far too late to try to talk Kyrtian out of abandoning the full-scale maneuvers he had planned. The boy was determined to prove to Lord Kyndreth that this was the *only* way to train fighters, and nothing would do but to show him how easy it was to hold the spells needed on entire armies.

Lady Lydiell sighed. "Your face tells me that my fears are likely to be realized. Oh, *why* couldn't he have been an artist or a musician, or obsessed with—with—oh, *horticulture* or something equally frivolous?"

"At least he isn't bent on being the dead opposite of his father, my Lady," Gel replied grimly. "You'd not like him as a fop, or a lazy layabout. Or worse, falling in with—"

He hesitated; after all, he was a human, and Lydiell was Elven. Blood was blood—

But Lydiell surprised him with a bitter smile and a light answer. "Falling in with the pampered perverts that most of my kind are. You don't need to spare my feelings, Gel; we cannot afford to be less than honest with each other if we are going to be able to keep Kyrtian out of the pitfalls lying before him."

Ah, cowflops. Why do I have to feel like it's me *that's his father? I'd rest easier at night.* He might be only a few actual years older than Kyrtian, but in real terms, he might just as well have been the Elvenlord's father. By the standards of his race, Kyrtian was the equivalent of a stripling, although by human reckoning he was in his late thirties. In knowledge and general responsibility, he was certainly that—but in the unconscious things that characterized an adolescent, he was very much Gel's junior. His boundless energy, his enthusiasm, his tendency to act rather than sitting back and waiting for events to come to him—those were the characteristics of the young, and made Gel feel very old.

The strength, speed, and endurance of youth were also his, and might be for the next century or two, which made Gel feel even older. He'd noticed of late, much to his chagrin, that he was slowing down, losing some of his edge; in fact, he and that man of Lord Kyndreth's had talked about that. Kaeth wasn't getting any younger either, and if he ever had to actually foil a fellow-assassin, that could be fatal if he didn't take steps to compensate.

We'll both just have to be sneakier to make up for what we're losing, he reminded himself. *Youth and enthusiasm are no match for experience and treachery.*

"I hate to admit this, my lady," he said, feeling ashamed that he had not anticipated this situation, "but I've kept him as ignorant as you have of the way things are—" he waved his hand vaguely at the windows "—out there. And I did it for pretty much the same reasons as you, I figure. Why throw something at him that he couldn't change and would only worry about?"

Ah, all those old lessons came back to him now, of being taken *off* the estate as Tenebrinth's page, so he could see just how the other Elvenlords really acted and thought. Tenebrinth had collared him, of course, and if he'd done something even slightly stupid—which, even as a child he hadn't been likely to—the Elvenlord could have quickly controlled him. And in a peculiar way, that, too, had been part of the lessons in just how fragile and precious the life humans led *here* was.

Lydiell nodded. "And at this point, if we try to tell him that Lord Kyndreth is no more to be trusted than Aelmarkin, he would only make the wrong decisions. He'd try to put Kyndreth off, or—or something. And now that he's aroused Kyndreth's interest, he can't do that without arousing suspicion as well."

"Damn all politics anyway," Gel said sourly. "Kyndreth is going to use him, make a tool out of him, and give him nothing but fine words and empty praise for his troubles—"

"Yes—but—" Lydiell began.

Gel waited, but she didn't complete the thought. He spoke into the heavy silence. "But it might not be bad for him; so long as he's valuable to Kyndreth, he's not going to be wasted. And as long as he's valuable, Kyndreth will see that we're left alone, no matter how peculiar some things around here may look to him."

Lydiell nodded, and Gel felt a certain relief that she agreed with him. There was selfishness in his motivation, and he knew that; as long as Kyrtian was not only alive and well but under the open protection of someone like Lord Kyndreth, Gel and the other humans on the estate would be perfectly safe. Aelmarkin wouldn't *dare* try to interfere or continue in his attempts to gain control of the manor and lands.

As for the humans living elsewhere—humans that Kyrtian would be very concerned about if he knew how bad things could be on other estates—Gel found it difficult to worry about the well-being of people he didn't know. The sufferings of human slaves on other estates were just stories to him, and although he believed them in the abstract, he just couldn't make himself care when people he *knew* needed his whole concentration and concern.

He couldn't really believe in anything he hadn't seen with his own eyes, not deep down where it counted.

Those are all old stories, anyway, and it makes no sense these days that the Elvenlords would wantonly waste or mar their own possessions. With wild humans on the border, drag-

ons in the sky, the Wizards threatening to start the war up again and their own children in armed revolt, they can't *afford the sort of goings-on they did in the past.* Slavery—yes, there was no doubt that the Elvenlords were harsh masters, and kept their humans under complete control. It was a terrible thing that humans elsewhere had every action controlled by someone else, that they could make not even the smallest decision about their own lives. But starvation, torture, abuse—why? *There's no reason to do any of those things; a starved, abused, or injured slave works less, and is worth less, than a healthy one who is punished only when he deserves it.*

"Lady, I pledge you, I will not let the boy out of my sight or care, no matter what Lord Kyndreth wants of him," he promised, coming back to concerns he could understand and see for himself. "I'm a treacherous old bastard, and if I think he's in trouble, I'll dose the boy's wine, make Kyndreth think he's had a fit, and drag him home myself." He surprised himself with his own sudden fierce protectiveness, and tried feebly to smile. "Once we've got him safe, we can talk him into playing witless. If he's lost his senses, he might not be of value to Kyndreth, but he won't be a threat, either."

And that was the best promise he could think of to give her, poor as it was.

Lydiell sent Gel back to his work without feeling much comfort from his words. She was very troubled, and could see no immediate way out of the dilemma that had come at them out of nowhere. *I had hoped to keep him isolated from all of this, but events have conspired against us,* she thought somberly, staring out the window at the placid fields spread so invitingly below. *Thanks to the two latest Wizard Wars, Kyrtian's obscure skills are no longer without value; he will be drawn into Elvenlord politics whether he likes it or not. But Gel is right; telling him some of the realities of the situation won't help him. He might be better if he remains in ignorance. If he knows what the Elvenlords are really like, his own sense of honor just might drive him to make some very dangerous choices. If, however, Kyndreth feeds him what the Old Lords want him to know, and con-*

vinces him to help them—then keeps him ignorant of the truth—he will serve them well and stay out of trouble.

There was one positive effect of all the warfare and quarreling; there were nowhere near as many of the Old Lords as there once had been, and those that remained were mostly very shrewd. *They have little power to spare, and won't waste any tool that comes to their hands when it costs little to keep that tool content. There are very few Dyrans about in the higher councils these days.*

She sighed, tasting the bitterness of her own expedience, the sour knowledge that by keeping him ignorant she was playing the same manipulative games as those she despised.

Kyrtian would be used, indeed, but wasn't it better to be an unwitting tool than a dead hero?

I cannot see any other options.

Keeping him purposefully blinded about the true nature of his fellow Elvenlords might have been a mistake, but she could not see how she could have done anything else.

Gel did have a good idea, she reminded herself, *if it looks as if Kyrtian is in danger. Everyone thinks his father was mad, and no one would be particularly surprised if he went mad under the strains they will probably put him under. Oh, Ancestors, why did I try to keep him sheltered? Why couldn't I have given him some armor against the thorn-maze he is about to walk into?*

She only prayed that her decision would not cause more harm than she had ever dreamt possible.

10

"I hope I don't look as nervous as I feel," Kyrtian muttered to himself, as he re-checked his appearance in the gilt-edged mirror to his right. He'd lost count of the number of times he'd glanced into mirrors today, making certain—of what? He wasn't quite sure; he only knew that he didn't want to look like Lord Kyndreth's son Gildor and his cronies, nor did he want to ape the appearance of Lord Kyndreth himself. He wanted to look mature, sober, perhaps a touch on the scholarly side, but able to hold his own in physical combat as well. Looking prosperous, but not necessarily opulent, was as important; on reflection, perhaps what he wanted was to look as if he could be Lord Kyndreth's intellectual equal, but not as if he already assumed that he was. After going through at least four changes of clothing and nearly driving his poor servants mad, he finally settled on a conservative tunic and tight-fitting trews of soft doeskin dyed a rich blue and slashed to display the silver satin of his shirt. Matching boots suitable for some hard walking completed the outfit, with a heavy silver chain and fillet confining his hair as his only jewelry. Jewels would not impress Lord Kyndreth, who was a powerful mage and knew how easily such things could be produced by illusion.

The mirror he kept glancing into was just outside the Portal Chamber; at any moment now Lord Kyndreth and his entourage should be coming through. The door to the chamber was open; it was really too small to allow for a graceful exit of so large a group. Servants in the household colors lined the chamber and the hall outside, but Kyrtian was the sole representative of the family; he was the head of the Clan now, and it would betray an unhealthy influence from his mother if she were here to receive the guests as well as he.

The servants, well-schooled in their roles, kept their eyes cast down as Kyrtian fidgeted with the chain around his neck. At long last, the Portal shimmered with energy, and Kyrtian snapped to attention, presenting a mask of calm, the perfect picture of a welcoming host.

The first figures through the Portal were, naturally, Lord Kyrtian's bodyguards, one of whom was the fighter called Kaeth that Kyrtian remembered from the combat. They deployed themselves on either side of the Portal with smooth, efficient, and practiced movements, making a barrier of themselves between the Portal and Kyrtian's servants. They must go through such maneuvers constantly; what surprised him was that they looked alert and suspicious, not bored. The servants took no notice; Gel had lectured them on what they could expect and what they should—or more appropriately, should not—do. They kept their places, as if this sort of quasi-military invasion happened every day.

Lord Kyndreth was next through the door, followed by his son Gildor. Kaeth moved in closer to his lord, standing unobtrusively nearby, close enough to intercept any aggressive action. Kyrtian moved immediately to welcome the Elvenlord, making sure that his own movements were non-aggressive.

"Welcome, my lord," he said, pitching his voice low, but putting warmth into it. "And thank you for being patient enough to wait until we could welcome you with all the honor and comfort that is your due. I hope that you will be pleased with what we have to show you."

Lord Kyndreth took Kyrtian's extended hand in his, in a firm clasp that was clearly a test. Kyrtian returned an equal pressure, and Lord Kyndreth smiled, ever so slightly, as he released Kyrtian's hand. "It is I who should be thanking you for your hospitality, Lord Kyrtian," he replied, as they moved forward to permit the rest of the entourage to come through. "Your household is a quiet one, and I understand that you have few visitors; we are creating quite a disruption for you."

Kyrtian made the expected disclaimers, as he kept one eye on Lord Kyndreth and the other on Lord Gildor and the part of the entourage that was composed of Gildor's friends. "I hesitate to mention this, my lord, but we were not expecting so large a group—perhaps some of the guests would accept accommodation in a pavilion?"

Lord Kyndreth cast an eye back at his son and his son's followers, who were clearly intoxicated and likely to remain that way for some time. "Lord Gildor and his associates are not remaining," he replied smoothly. "They came only to view the pitched battle, and will depart as soon as the demonstration is complete."

Kyrtian did not let out a sigh of relief, but some of his concern left him. Housing Gildor and his cronies was the last of his potential problems, and the only one he hadn't anticipated.

Lord Kyndreth and his servants should behave in predictable ways, but Gildor and his drunken friends were neither predictable nor safe for the servants to be around. They were used to getting their way in all things, used to taking what they wanted, and it was entirely possible that what they wanted would invoke automatic, unthinking rebellion in the human servants, who were not used to being treated as objects to be used and discarded at will. But if Gildor and his cronies were already planning to leave right after the demonstration—well, Kyrtian was confident his people could hold things together for that long.

"The demonstration is ready, my Lord," he said, and gestured, bringing several pre-selected servants forward. "My people will guide your servants to your quarters, so that all will be in readiness for your comfort when the battle is over."

"Excellent." Kyndreth did nothing, but Kaeth made a gesture, sending two of the bodyguards and several of Kyndreth's slaves laden with baggage to join Kyrtian's servants. Kyrtian's people quickly took over most of the burdens of the luggage and led the others down the corridor towards the guest-quarters. Lord Kyndreth gave an expectant glance at Kyrtian, who took the hint and led the rest of the group through the maze of corridors to the balcony outside the lesser dining-room. This same balcony overlooked the field usually used for celebrations; today it would be the site of a battle.

For this occasion, the balcony was sheltered from the glare of the sun with an awning made of tapestry, giving it the look of a viewing-stand for a formal tournament. Banks of comfortable seats awaited the visitors, and refreshments had been prepared and set out to greet them, all under the watchful eye of Lady Lydiell. Out of the corner of his eye, Kyrtian saw the smugly superior expressions of Gildor and his friends changed to looks of gratification and pleasure. Obviously they had not thought to find a sophisticated level of hospitality in this provincial household.

Now Kyrtian presented his mother to the guests; Lydiell had gone to great effort to appear as a typical Elven lady. Gowned and coiffed as her son had seldom seen her before, her expression that of a flawless statue, she resembled her everyday self very little indeed. Kyrtian had not seen her until this moment, and winced inwardly as he thought how long she must have spent in the hands of her servants to achieve her appearance. Her silver hair had been divided into hundreds of tiny braids, which had then been arranged in a series of draped loops and knots held in place with jeweled pins. Her pastel-hued gown, of multiple layers of misty, cobweb-like blue fabric, with sleeves and train that trailed behind her, could not possibly be more impractical for her normal duties. Each and every hem had been edged in lace so fine it was close to transparent, and likely to snag on everything unless great pains were taken to prevent such a disaster. Tiny, sparkling motes of gems winked amid the misty folds of the gown, and more gems strung on gossamer strands of silver wreathed her neck. From her toes to the last hair, Lydiell's costume was so fragile it invited ruin in the mere acts of moving and walking.

That, however, was not an Elven Lady's business to worry about; it was the duty of her slaves to manage sleeves and hems, and see to it that her gown remained perfect and pristine at all times. So it was today; any time Lydiell moved, she was trailed by four women whose only purpose was to see that she could move about as easily as a graceful image in a perfect daydream.

This, of course, was exactly what Lord Kyndreth expected to see, so he simply bowed over Lydiell's hand and escorted her back to her chair while Gildor and the rest chose seats. Lord Kyndreth took the place of honor at Lydiell's right hand, and Kyrtian assumed the seat at her left. As soon as each guest was in his chosen seat, a servant presented him with a chilled glass of sparkling wine and a platter of dainties from which to make a choice. Gel and Kyrtian had left nothing to chance, not even the number of guests; a young page had sprinted to the balcony while Kyrtian and Lord Kyndreth spoke to report the exact number of Elvenlords that had arrived. There was neither one chair too many, nor too few, and precisely the correct number of servants, one to each guest. The human slaves, Lord Kyndreth's bodyguards included, all stood, of course. No slave sat in the presence of his masters.

Only when everyone was settled, did the two "armies" move out onto the field. Lord Kyndreth leaned forward in his seat immediately, his attention riveted on the combatants. For his part, Kyrtian tried not to fidget nervously, though not because the success of the combat was in doubt. No, it was only that he was not on the field himself; this would be the first time he was only an observer rather than a participant. He found, somewhat to his own chagrin, that he did not make a very good observer.

As the two forces charged towards each other, shouting taunts and battle-cries, Gildor and his friends were momentarily diverted. But as the combat continued—and it was clear that it would be a bloodless combat, as man after man glowed scarlet or blue and had to retire to the sidelines—they quickly lost interest.

"How many men can you hold this magic on at a time?" Lord Kyndreth asked quietly, as Kyrtian ignored the muttered jeers and scornful laughter of Gildor and his friends.

"I don't know for certain, my lord," Kyrtian said honestly. "I've never had occasion to try it on more than a thousand, so I have not yet found an upper limit."

"A thousand!" Kyndreth was clearly impressed, even if his son was underwhelmed. "By the Ancestors, that is remarkable! There should be no difficulty then in training battalions of fighters in field maneuvers so long as several mages are used to hold the magic in place!"

"I should think not, my lord," Kyrtian responded deferentially. "Especially if the mages concerned are powerful ones such as yourself. I am certain that you would find it a trivial task to hold the magic on twice that number."

Behind them, Gildor and his friends were making deep inroads on the wine, showing quite clearly just how bored they were with the combat. Nevertheless, given Lord Kyndreth's interest and approval, they didn't dare be too vocal in their contempt.

Finally their restlessness got to the point where it annoyed Lord Kyndreth himself. The battle had devolved into a mass of single combats between the most skilled of the fighters, and it was obvious it would be some time before sheer weariness became the undoing of many of the fighters. Lord Kyndreth abruptly stood up, and Kyrtian took that as he was meant to, blowing the shrill whistle that signaled the end of the demonstration.

Obedient to the signal, fighting ceased immediately, and in the sudden silence, Lord Kyndreth turned to his host with a broad smile.

"This has been a most impressive demonstration, Lord Kyrtian," he said, with as much warmth as Kyrtian had ever seen him display until now. "Even more so than the single-combat you originally showed us. I am looking forward to learning this new application of magic in the next few days—but I fear than my son and his friends have previous commitments and must be on their way—" Now he leveled a gaze on his bemused son that shook the young Elvenlord into momentary sobriety. "Mustn't you, Gildor?"

The younger lord, startled by his sire's abrupt change of mood, stammered out his reply. "Of—of course, certainly," he babbled. "Previous commitments, pressing engagements, and all that. So sorry. Excellent show. Be on our way now—"

"My people will show you the way back to the Portal Chamber, Lord Gildor," Kyrtian replied, with as fine a display of the height of good manners as anyone could have asked. He gave no hint that he had heard the disparaging remarks, nor that he was well aware that Gildor was so drunk he probably could not have found the door without help. "I cannot tell you how gratified I was by your presence, or by your appreciation. I hope that we will be able to give you a better demonstration of our hospitality at some time in the future."

Gildor and his friends filed back into the dining hall, subdued by Lord Kyndreth's enthusiastic reception of the demonstration. There were no more jeering asides, no more snickers. Kyrtian was under no illusions about this; he fully expected that the moment the younger Elvenlords passed the Portal, they would begin their scornful gossip again. But for now, it was obvious who the master was, and what the master approved—and all the young lords fell obediently into line.

Odd, Kyrtian thought, as Lord Kyndreth exchanged some

polite compliments with Lady Lydiell and the last of the unwanted visitors passed through the doors of the lesser dining hall. *I would have thought, given the way he likes to puff himself up and bluster, that Gildor would have sided with the Young Lords against his father. Lord Kyndreth isn't going to pass over power any time in the foreseeable future, and I would have thought that by now Gildor would be hungry for that power.*

Perhaps, though, Gildor liked comfort better than power. Perhaps he already knew he didn't dare to challenge his father. Or, perhaps Gildor was less ambitious than Kyrtian would have been in his place. As it was, Gildor had prestige, status, and a carefree, pampered existence. If he sat where his father now held sway, he might actually have to work.

Kyndreth turned to Kyrtian, who collected his scattered thoughts. "I believe that I would like to retire to my quarters to prepare for dinner and think about all you have shown me," he said. "Unless you have something more planned to show me today?"

"Only one thing, and that is on the way," Kyrtian replied, with a slight smile. "Please, allow me to escort you. Perhaps some questions will occur to you that I can answer as we walk."

They both bowed to Lady Lydiell, who nodded gravely to both of them without speaking. Kyrtian waited while one of the servants held the door open for them; he also waited for the bodyguards to flank his guest before taking his own place beside Kyndreth. Other than that, he paid no attention to the bodyguards.

Kyndreth glanced sharply around as they passed along the hallways; for a moment, Kyrtian wondered what had caught his attention, then Kyndreth answered his question with a query of his own.

"You use no illusion here, do you?" Kyndreth asked, as if surprised.

"Very little, my lord," Kyrtian replied, and smiled slightly. "Perhaps we are somewhat conservative in nature, but we—my mother and I, that is—prefer the real to the illusory. Illusion is—" He groped for words.

"Cheap?" Kyndreth surprised him with the word he had been

trying to avoid, and the ironic lifting of his eyebrow. "I tend to agree, actually. Any halfway competent mage can cloak rotting timber and moth-eaten tapestry in illusion. To maintain a gracious and attractive home without illusion requires dedication and effort. Illusion is, I believe, the lazy man's way."

"I agree, my lord. We here prefer substance to style, one might say." Again, he ventured a smile. "Our home may be old-fashioned in style, but that is the price of preferring substance."

By this time, they had reached the area of the old nursery—which was now the new harem—and Kyrtian paused. "I would like to offer you all the comforts of our house, my lord. If you would care to pass within?"

Lord Kyndreth could easily see the shimmer of power that cloaked the door, which meant his bodyguards would not be able to follow him inside. But there was also no doubt what Kyrtian's words had implied, and he was probably curious just what sort of harem the notoriously ascetic Kyrtian had. He signaled to his bodyguards to join the two guards at the door, and followed Kyrtian within.

The three young women were waiting for them, and rose instantly to their feet, pausing just long enough for Lord Kyndreth to get a good look at them before they sank to the ground in deep curtsies.

For the very first time, Kyrtian saw the Great Lord surprised. So surprised, in fact, that his jaw dropped, just a trifle. The he recovered his composure, and turned to Kyrtian with a sly grin.

"You young dog!" he exclaimed, and clapped Kyrtian on the shoulder. "No wonder nothing tempts you to mix with the other youngsters. They haven't anything to offer that could ever match these treasures!"

Kyrtian bowed his head slightly. "So I believe, my lord." He gestured, and the young women, flushing prettily, rose again. Lord Kyndreth surveyed them again, his eyes lingering on each in turn.

"I believe I shall take up your offer," he said with a chuckle. "But after dinner. There is, as the Ancestors said, a pleasure in anticipation that the wise man learns to cherish as much as the fulfillment of that anticipation."

"Very true, my lord," Kyrtian murmured deferentially. "Very true."

Lord Kyndreth was a surprisingly good dinner-guest. He ate and drank moderately, gave praise to the cook, and took care to involve Lady Lydiell in the conversation. Kyrtian gradually relaxed. The visit was going well; if it continued in this vein, the entire expenditure of time and energy would have been well repaid.

As the dessert course was brought in, Lord Kyndreth turned to Kyrtian, and for the first time there was a hint of hesitation in his expression. "Lord Kyrtian, there is something that I have been curious about for a very long time, but I hesitate to bring up a subject that would cause you or your Lady-Mother any discomfort."

"What subject would that be?" Kyrtian asked, cautiously.

"I am—and have been—very curious about your late father," came the surprising answer. "More to the point, I am curious as to his reasons for vanishing into the wilderness. I know some have made inappropriate observations about him, but I saw nothing in your father's demeanor before he vanished to make me believe that he had anything but very good reasons for his actions."

Kyrtian glanced at his mother, who nodded slightly. The unspoken message was clear: he could go ahead and reveal some of what he already knew.

Kyrtian cleared his throat. "There is a tradition—some might call it a legend—in our family that when the Elves first came across from Evelon, the machines and most of the books they had brought with them were too burdensome to carry. More pressing concerns had to be dealt with—in the hunt for a place to live and the means to do so, ancient knowledge was of no use in such a brand new world. So all these things were more of a handicap than an advantage, and they were cached shortly after the search for more hospitable territory began. For some reason, no one ever went back for them—perhaps only because the Elvenlords were too busy subduing the natives. Those caches of ancient knowledge were what my father was hunting when he vanished."

"Interesting." Lord Kyndreth pulled at his lower lip in thought. "Assuming that there is useful knowledge there that we have lost, which is quite possible, whoever found those cached materials could have a distinct advantage."

"Since I replicated my methods of combat-training by means of research into the old books we still have, I suspect there is a great deal of knowledge that has been lost or forgotten," Kyrtian replied, somberly. "Frankly, I have no idea what might lie out there, nor did my father. We simply haven't got enough information even to make a guess."

What he did not observe was that Lady Lydiell knew something more and had told Kyrtian her family traditions as well as his father's. And it was not particularly flattering to the Great Lords of this land.

The tale of the Crossing was one that the Great Lords had probably done their best to forget. There had been a civil war in Evelon, and their side was the one that was, at the time of the Crossing, the losing side. The ancestors of the current Elvenlords decided to escape through the Gate they would build together, taking their chances on finding a hospitable land with easily cowed natives on the other side. It was either that, or face surrender, and have their power reft from them by the winners. The result would be that the losers would live on, but enslaved, and disgraced.

"Official" history said little of the war, and did not even hint that the Elvenlords might have been getting the worst of the conflict. Instead, by common consent, the Ancestors were regarded as bold, fearless pioneers, striking out on their own when life in Evelon grew wearisome through its never-changing sameness.

Lady Lydiell knew more, preserved through the female line. Even though it had been agreed that all of the Elven mages would pool their strength and magic, the more unscrupulous and selfish held back. As a result, when the Gate went up, some were drained of magic power, while others still had enough to make them the rulers on the other side.

That was the difference between the original Great Lords and the Lesser Lords, and not, as the Great Lords would have everyone believe, a matter of intelligence and inherited power.

"The machines that came over seemed to encounter difficulties, possibly due to the disruptive effect of the Gate on their spells, and may have been abandoned as a consequence. My father had found a speculative document suggesting that the war-machines they brought with them could be drained for power, even if they no longer worked correctly," Kyrtian went on. "If so, they could provide a reservoir of magic to fall back on when a mage's own powers were depleted."

Once again, he saw Lord Kyndreth's eyes narrow slightly, as he contemplated this possibility. Kyrtian's father had intended—if it could be done—to restore the magic to those Elves who lacked it. Lord Kyndreth was probably thinking in terms of keeping all that power to himself, to be doled out as he chose.

That would give him unprecedented power among his own peers, and an unprecedented tool to manipulate them. A mage with such a resource at his disposal would be what the Elvenlords had never yet had.

A King.

"At any rate, that was why Father was out hunting—looking for the machines and the books, and obviously this was not something that a rational man would have human slaves doing, because of the dangers implicit in exposing slaves to things so unknown and unpredictable," Kyrtian finished. "The humans do have their own form of magic, after all—and who knows what exposure to those machines would do? It might free them of their collars—might give them powers to match ours! No, that was a task he preferred to keep to himself."

"I can see why—and your father was a far wiser man than anyone has given him credit for being," Lord Kyndreth said gravely. "Now you have given me twice as much to think about. . . ."

Kyrtian shook his head. "But this talk of lost machines and cached books—such things surely must wait until we have dealt with the Halfbloods and our own rebellious youth." He deliberately framed the reply to include himself in the opposite party to the Young Lords, and he saw Lord Kyndreth smile in reply.

"You are correct," the Great Lord replied. "And long before we do that, there is much we must accomplish—not the least of which is to do justice to the finale of this excellent meal."

Kyrtian sighed internally, and answered Kyndreth's smile with one of his own. He had been accepted—perhaps not as an equal, but certainly as an ally. And that should put paid to Cousin Aelmarkin's plans for the near future, at least.

"Very true, my lord," he murmured. "You are entirely correct, as usual."

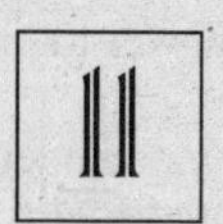

One worry, at least, was off Kyrtian's mind by the next morning. As soon as he awoke, he paid a cautious visit to the harem; if anything unpleasant had happened to the young women, *he* wanted to be the one to deal with it. He was, after all, the one responsible for them.

But as it happened, Lord Kyndreth had treated all three of the harem women very well; had, in fact, given them each a handsome gift of jewelry for pleasing him. They were excited and happy, and did not make much of an effort to disguise their hopes that there might be more such visits—and presents—from the Great Lord. Kyrtian found it rather touching, actually; they were so like three little girls in their innocent pleasure at being rewarded with baubles.

There were three other Elvenlords in Kyndreth's entourage, but none of them were of high enough status to be offered the services of the harem. They would have to put up with enforced chastity until they returned to their own homes, for house-servants, unless they actually *offered* themselves or were offered by the host, were considered off-limits. If Lord Kyndreth had shown himself to be lukewarm in his regard for Kyrtian, such a breach of etiquette could have taken place anyway, but *not* when Kyndreth had shown his favor. Kyrtian could remove at least this one minor concern from his long list of worries; the girls would not be abused by his guest, nor would his servants be mistreated by Kyndreth's underlings.

As soon as Lord Kyndreth put in an appearance and had broken his fast, the rest of the day was spent in an odd role-reversal, as Kyrtian tutored the older Lord in the magic of mock-combat.

It felt awkward. It was also dangerous work, and not from a magical standpoint. Somehow Kyrtian had to simultaneously be teacher and deferential (but not groveling) Lesser Lord to Kyndreth's Greater. Kyrtian walked a narrow line between those two extremes, and he dared not deviate from it, if he wanted Lord Kyndreth's protection.

But Lord Kyndreth wanted this knowledge badly enough to exert himself to be accommodating and charming, and slowly Kyrtian began to relax, forget about his own careful pose, and simply instruct.

He'd called in all of his fighters to act as subjects for the practice, though initially the magic was only cast on one. Kyrtian was sure enough of his own mastery that he reckoned he could counter any mistakes Lord Kyndreth made before they caused any harm, and it was a very real measure of the trust his men had in him that the fighters took that for granted, standing relaxed and unconcerned while Lord Kyndreth felt his way through the weaving of the complicated magery the first time. It took a fine touch, a delicate touch, to ensure that the fighter enspelled felt enough of a warning tingle to tell him that he'd been hit, even in the excitement of combat—yet was kept from actually being *hurt*, which would be counterproductive.

"This is the opposite of the way we train our gladiators now," Kyndreth observed, pausing to wipe his brow with a spotless scrap of white silk, which he then dropped, without thinking about it, on the ground behind him. His own man automatically retrieved the handkerchief and stepped back again. Kyndreth never even noticed. "When they practice, even with blunted weapons, the point is that they *will* be hurt if they allow a blow to fall, and so their defense-work is supposed to improve."

"Yes, but if that blow falls, even in practice, it can disable a man," Kyrtian pointed out, as the fighter waited patiently for Kyndreth to complete the spellcasting. "What's the good of learning from your mistake if you end up losing so much time in recovering from your injury that you have to go back to the beginning again? Conditioning is as important as training, or so my experience leads me to believe."

"Oh, you are arguing with the converted, young friend," Kyndreth chuckled, casually massaging his hands as if they felt stiff. "I've lost far too many fine and promising specimens *permanently* to so-called 'training accidents.' It's a costly business—too costly, when now we need fighters for *real* combat more than we need gladiators." He resumed the task before him, and the fighter began to have a faintly glowing aura.

"In the case of men who are stubborn about acknowledging hits, I do set it high enough to hurt, though," Kyrtian admitted, as he supervised Lord Kyndreth's effort. "There are some fellows who get so worked up during a fight that nothing less than real pain seems to get through to them."

"Those men I would put in the front lines," Kyndreth observed wryly, with a side glance at Kyrtian. "If they are that impervious. I've seen a few of those; they have a kind of madness in battle. It's useful if they're in the front line, but they're as much a danger to friend as to foe anywhere else. I put 'em on the point of a thrust; let them carve their way in, and take ground behind them with fighters that can keep their heads."

Kyrtian nodded, although he hated to think of *any* of his fighters being in the front lines of real combat. His eyes narrowed as he kept track of Lord Kyndreth's progress. "There—" he cautioned. "That is exactly the level you can usually set it at. That's perfect." As Kyndreth let go of his control of the field around the fighter, Kyrtian flexed his shoulders to ease some of the strain in them. "Now we build the weapon." He smiled. "That's not as difficult; it's just a little different from a truly expert illusion."

Once Kyndreth had the initial magic set, he was able to swiftly make copies upon as many fighters as Kyrtian had present. "This is amazing!" he observed, his eyes widening a little, as his total passed twenty. "The first one is difficult, but there is very little drain once the initial fighter is done! I had expected this to be quite expensive in terms of personal energy."

"I believe that is because you aren't exactly *replicating* the magic—I believe you are simply spreading it to include every subsequent fighter," Kyrtian observed, pleased with how quickly Lord Kyndreth had learned the special techniques. *The sooner he has mastered all this, the sooner he can be gone, and we can get this masquerade over with.* "I hope that makes sense to you."

"Perfect sense." Kyndreth gave him an odd look. "Do you also make a study of the mechanics and theory of magic? It's an esoteric branch of study, and one I had not associated with someone who is so clearly a—well, a *soldier,* so to speak, rather than a pure scholar."

"Only a little—I had to do a certain amount of study to replicate this—" he waved his hand vaguely at the assembled fighters. "I won't claim to be a genius, or even to have a particular knack for research, only a great deal of patience and persistence when it comes to something I'm interested in."

Lord Kyndreth's expression blanked for a moment, as if Kyrtian's attitude had taken him aback, but he said nothing.

"Well, let's have the fighters pair off, and see the magic in action, shall we?" Kyrtian continued, wondering what that look meant. *Have I been* too *modest? Have I tipped my hand? Or is it just that he isn't used to hearing someone that doesn't boast about his prowess?*

"An excellent plan." Lord Kyndreth stepped to the sidelines, and Kyrtian signaled to the fighters to begin sparring. Lord Kyndreth's pleasure in the discovery that *his* replication of the magic functioned exactly the same as Kyrtian's was obvious.

For his own part, Kyrtian was just as pleased. For once, he didn't have to hold *both* sides in the spell, and that freed up enough of his attention that he could more fully appreciate the skill of his men.

Kyrtian signaled to his men to stop, and turned to his guest, his own feeling of accomplishment matching Lord Kyndreth's. "You are a marvelously quick study, my lord, and no one would doubt your mastery of magic," he said, with no intent to flatter. "I do not think you need to learn anything else from me. You have the technique now, and all that you need is practice. In time you will probably be faster even than I at setting the magic."

"Practice is something I can get at home; I will not strain your generous hospitality longer than I have to," the Great Lord replied immediately, much to Kyrtian's veiled relief. *He wants to leave so soon! Thank the Ancestors!*

"Truly, it is a great honor to be your host," he protested anyway, for form's sake.

"And truly, it is a great inconvenience for you," Kyndreth said, with just a touch of mockery in his voice. "I am not blind, Kyrtian. For all that you and your Lady Mother live graciously, your means are limited, and I am a burden on them. This is a small and very private manor, and my folk are an intrusion and an inconvenience to your routine, no matter how you cloak that in good manners. I shall beg your forbearance for just this one night more, for there is something I would like to discuss with you, but tomorrow my folk and I will leave you and yours in peace. Meanwhile—I feel in strong need of a bath and a rest!"

Before Kyrtian had a chance to react to the first part of that statement, Lord Kyndreth had clapped him on the back like an old friend, then turned to dismiss the magic he had cast over the fighters. He strode off in the direction of the manor, presumably to return to the guest quarters, leaving Kyrtian in charge of his own people.

"You did well, men; Gel, take over the practice," was all he dared say, not knowing whether he was under some covert observation. He recast the magic, and Sergeant Gel assumed command, barking out orders to pair off and start sparring. He watched, an observer rather than a participant, as the fighters went through their usual paces, changing weapons, changing sparring-partners, until they were all drenched with sweat and exhausted. It was very difficult to remain aloof; his hands twitched to hold a sword, and several times he had to force himself to remain quiet when someone required correction. It would not do for him to correct the men himself; he must be patient and wait for Gel to spot the problem and deal with it. Kyndreth might have a man watching; he could have a magical "eye" observing them. It would not do for Kyrtian to be seen wading in as if he was of no higher estate than his own drillmaster. Only when the men were completely exhausted did he dismiss them and permit them to return to their own quarters under the supervision of Sergeant Gel. And only then could he return to his mother's office and find out what Lord Kyndreth's three underlings had been doing while he and Kyndreth were occupied with the fighters.

Lady Lydiell was waiting for him as he rose through the floor of her office; she must have seen him approaching from the practice-field. "Tenebrinth took them riding," she said immediately, knowing with that acuity that sometimes resembled a human's magic what he wanted before he even voiced the question. "They just wanted exercise; I think they were bored. Tenebrinth took them on a tour of the hunting-reserve, which is far enough away from any of our little villages to keep anything untoward from happening, and I think they may actually have done a little hunting themselves. Look—you can see them from here—"

She pointed, and he went to the western side of the office, peering into the distance until he caught sight of four brilliantly colored atomies making their way alongside a tree line that had been reduced by distance to a mere blur of green.

"What about Kyndreth's human slaves?" he asked, without taking his eyes off the distant riders.

"They remained within the guest-quarters, except for the bodyguards, who were keeping you and Kyndreth under surveillance," Lydiell told him calmly. "And some of our people were in turn watching *them.* It made me wonder how many layers of watchers-watching-watchers we could have had before people began running into each other!"

Kyrtian turned away from the window, and caught his mother's ironic smile. "It would be an interesting experiment.

That human Kaeth is a very sharp fellow; I have no doubt that he knew his people were being overlooked. I shouldn't like to have to pit Gel against him; I think that Gel might be outmatched in certain areas."

"Then let us hope we never need to." Lydiell looked at him sharply. "What is it that you have not told me? Something Kyndreth said?"

"Something he has yet to say," Kyrtian sighed, chagrined that she was able to read him so easily. *I should know better than to think I can hide anything from her.* "He learned the magic quite quickly; actually more quickly than I had anticipated. Whatever else his accomplishments may be, there is no doubt that he deserves his position as a mage and a Great Lord."

"Do not attempt to distract me; I am too old to play that game with," Lydiell responded, a touch sharply. "What was this about 'something he has yet to say'?"

"He implied that he wishes to discuss something with me, possibly at or after dinner. I have no idea what it is." Kyrtian tried to shrug it all off as of no importance, but his mother immediately looked concerned, then tried to conceal it.

"Did he say anything else?" she asked, a little too casually.

"One thing more—that he and his people will be leaving in the morning, which is not too soon for me." Feeling overly confined by the relatively formal garments he'd been buttoned into this morning, Kyrtian ruined the efforts of his body-servants by restlessly unbuttoning the collar of his tunic and running his hands distractedly through his hair.

"At least that is good news." Lady Lydiell sank into her seat behind her desk. "I knew this charade of ours would be a strain, but I hadn't expected it to be as *much* of a strain as it has been."

Kyrtian nodded in agreement, and took a quick glance back at the window. The tiny figures were no longer so tiny and were growing larger by the moment—the riders must have decided that they had exercised enough for one day. Either that, or Kyndreth sent a magical summons to them. "If I am going to continue the game, I had best get down to my quarters to dress for dinner, Lady-Mother. Since this is to be Lord Kyndreth's last night—shouldn't we do something—well—elaborate?"

"Indeed we should, and I will follow your example as soon as I've seen the cooks." She rose from her chair and moved around her desk to kiss him fondly on the cheek. "We must show him every possible honor. We need to drive it home to Lord Kyndreth that we are reclusive, but neither mad, nor barbaric."

Kyrtian was tempted to break his long-standing habit and use illusion to augment his costume, for the clothing his servants laid out for him was not the sort of thing he would have chosen for himself. It was impressive, yes, but the plush velvet tunic of a sober midnight-blue was so heavily ornamented with gold bullion and tiny beads made from sapphires and emeralds that it weighed as much as armor, and the high collar was probably going to drive him to distraction before the evening was over and he could take it off.

Nevertheless, he allowed his men to assist him into the stiff costume, and made his appearance in the grand dining room well ahead of their guest. Somehow Lady Lydiell had worked miracles among the cooks, for there was every evidence of a meal worthy of the room in the offing. The table, decked in snowy damask, was adorned with a dozen different glasses at each place, and the sideboard was laden with small dishes and a myriad of specialized knives, forks and spoons, each (by the rules of etiquette) suited only to very particular sorts of courses. Also by the rules of etiquette, there was only a single plate and no utensils at each place. The particular silverware needed for each course would be laid with the course, and whisked away again to prevent any *faux pas* in dining on the part of a guest. When Lord Kyndreth and his three underlings appeared, conducted by a household servant, even they seemed surprised and impressed by the preparations.

Lydiell arrived last, in a gown of deceptive simplicity, one that Kyrtian had never seen her wear before. It was only when she drew near that it was obvious that only the "cut" of the gown was simple; with close-fitting sleeves and a modest neckline, it was composed entirely of miniature interwoven links and plaques of silver, each no larger than a gnat, each plaque studded with diamonds no larger than the head of a pin. She seemed to be gowned in shimmering fish-scales, or that fabulous substance, dragon skin.

And I thought my *costume was uncomfortably heavy!* he thought in awe. He'd had no idea she even possessed such a thing; it couldn't be illusion, but where had it come from?

I wonder if it could turn a blade? he thought, as he waited for Lydiell to be seated. There was no telling how old such a garment might be—it might even date back to Evelon itself. If so . . . perhaps the ladies of those long-gone days had made a virtue of the necessity of wearing protective armor even to a festive meal.

They took their places, and the ceremonial meal began, course after course, until Kyrtian lost count of them. Each course was no more than a taste, a bite or two of some delicacy; then the plates and cutlery were whisked away to be replaced by a new setting, another dish. Cold dishes and hot, savory, salty, sweet, sour—fragrant noodles, lightly cooked and seasoned vegetables sculpted like flowers, flowers made into tiny salads of petals, tiny portions of barely seared meat garnished with rare herbs and sauces, soups hot and chilled—each course was accompanied with a different drink. This was not always wine; it could be a spiced juice, a tea, or delicately flavored spring water, whatever best complemented the course.

It could not be called a meal, it was an event unto itself, a thing which swiftly acquired its own momentum. If Kyrtian was amazed, Lord Kyndreth was not—although it seemed he was very, very pleased. Hours passed, the sunset faded outside the windows and was replaced by the night and stars; Kyndreth and his people exerted themselves to be charming, and Lady Lydiell was equally charming and witty. Kyrtian was awed; he'd never seen his mother quite like this before, and he had to stretch his own wits to keep pace with the others.

Finally, the last course was placed before them—and the fact that it *was* the final course was signaled by the disappearance of every human servant the moment each plate was placed before the diners. Each plate held a single delicate, gilded fruit-ice the size of Lydiell's graceful hand. Each scoop of ice had been molded into the Lion of Lord Kyndreth's House, with the details picked out in sugar-crystals and pearlescent icing.

Lord Kyndreth stood up, and raised his cup to Lady Lydiell.

"My dear hostess," he said, in a voice full of warmth and admiration. "I cannot imagine how you conjured up a Court feast on less than no notice, but allow me to declare that you are surely the equal of any Great Mage in the land, and I bow to your prowess. I drink to you, Lady Lydiell!"

The rest answered his toast, and Lydiell gracefully acknowledged the compliment with a nod of her head.

Kyndreth sat down again. "I can see by all of this that my judgment of your House was not mistaken. If you do not move in the circles of the Council, it is not because you do not merit such attention, but because you chose not to seek it."

He looked from Lydiell to Kyrtian, and back again. It was Lydiell he evidently expected to answer, and it was Lydiell who made the reply.

"My Lord Kyndreth, our family has long preferred to keep our own company, and live quietly and even reclusively," Lydiell murmured. "It is not out of unseemly pride, I beg to urge, but out of modesty and a genuine preference for a quiet and reclusive life. All of us—my late husband, his father before him, and my son as well as myself—are more of the temperament of a scholar than of a courtier, and the life of a seeming hermit suits us well. Perhaps our needs and pleasures may seem simple to you, but we find that they satisfy every wish and desire we have, for our wishes and desires are for the inner world of thought, rather than the outer world, which others might find stimulating, but we find contentious and disturbing."

Kyndreth sighed, a bit melodramatically, perhaps. "And I wish that you could continue to enjoy that quiet life, my Lady, but the times, I fear, will not permit your modesty to deny the genuine talents that lie hidden in this little haven of yours."

Now he turned to Kyrtian. "Lord Kyrtian, I do not have to tell you what your reputation is among the ignorant; you have heard it already from the mouth of your kinsman, Aelmarkin. I was prepared to discount that reputation when I accepted your invitation, but now I find that your kinsman was not only incorrect, he was—" Kyndreth shook his head. "Words fail me. Aelmarkin is either poisonously prejudiced against you, or completely blind. I have seen and heard enough in two days to convince me that, despite your own disclaimers, you, Lord Kyrtian, are nothing short of a military genius. This is no mere eccentric hobby that you have, it is a genuine vocation."

Kyrtian opened his mouth to protest, but Kyndreth silenced him with a wave of his hand.

"You have, with *no* help other than that of some ancient manuscripts, uncovered a training method that creates expert fighters in a fraction of the time we have taken heretofore and as you yourself pointed out, with none of the criminal wastage that our method entails. I have seen your strategic ability in action, I have seen your careful attention to every aspect of military life. Lord Kyrtian, you cannot remain a hermit any longer; you are desperately needed. The High Council needs you."

"I—cannot imagine why you would think that," Kyrtian stammered, taken completely by surprise. "You already hold the key to the training-magic, and you are a greater mage than I—"

"We need your *military* knowledge," Kyndreth insisted. "Between the wars with the Wizards and the revolt of our own ungrateful offspring, there are precious few with the wisdom and knowledge to command, and *none* with your talent. We need you, Lord Kyrtian. We need you to lead our armies."

Out of the corner of his eye, Kyrtian saw his mother tense, and realized that although *he* had not anticipated this demand, she had.

"You already have leaders," he protested. "Leaders of higher rank than I. I would not dare—"

"With my backing, no one would dare dispute *you,*" Kyndreth countered, grimly. "With my backing, I can easily persuade every Councilor that matters that you are the only possible Commanding General for our forces."

Kyrtian was dumbfounded; he had hoped that Kyndreth's gratitude would bring them a respite from Aelmarkin's enmity, but he had not expected Kyndreth to propose he take his place among the Greatest of the Great Lords!

"Lord Kyndreth, please do not think me ungrateful—rather, I am stunned," he managed. "And surely you realize that I have no practical experience!"

Lord Kyndreth raised his eyebrow. "All the practical experience of our current Commander has availed him nothing," he pointed out. "The situation with our young rebels has been in stalemate for the last month and more." He paused. "And *that* is to go no further than this table; only the members of the Council are aware of it."

"Stalemate—" Kyrtian bit his lip. "How much territory are they holding?"

"Roughly half of the estates are in the hands of the rebels," Kyndreth replied. "We are fortunate that none of them are vital to the economy—they were mostly estates producing little except slaves and luxuries. Nevertheless, that is a great deal of territory to be in unfriendly hands—and there are isolated estates within that territory that are still in the hands of our people, loyal folk who need and deserve succor." Now he looked shrewdly at Lydiell. "Unless I am very much mistaken, one of those is the estate of Lady Morthena, your kinswoman."

"Lady Moth?" Lydiell paled. Kyrtian bit his lip. Granted, Lady Moth had conspicuously *not* taken sides, and if the rebels had troubled her, Lydiell certainly would have heard about it by now. Still, she might be presumed to be in danger.

"Lady Morthena is encircled and certainly trapped," Kyndreth continued, his eyes flicking from Lydiell to Kyrtian. "As yet, she has held control over her slaves, so that she has prevented any incursions onto her lands. As yet, the rebels have not attempted any serious effort at capturing her. But how long will it be until they see her as a valuable bargaining tool? She is a Great Lady; the honor of the High Lords and the Council would be compromised if she were to be captured and held against her will. We would either be forced to abandon her—which is unthinkable—or make concessions to the rebels—which is also unthinkable."

It is all unthinkable. Kyrtian gritted his teeth. Kyndreth either knew or guessed that he would be extremely loyal to those members of his family—unlike Aelmarkin—who deserved loyalty. He had known that Lady Moth was close to the territory held by the rebels, for she herself had told them. The Young Lords could not block teleson messages, and did not even try; so far Lady Moth had seemed entirely unconcerned about her position in the midst of the Young Lords, even professing to a certain detached sympathy for their cause. But Lord Kyndreth *was* right; if the Young Lords cared to, they could take Lady Moth captive to use her as a bargaining-chip. A quick glance at Lydiell's face told him all he needed to know; this was no idle speculation, but a real possibility.

"You must give me time to consider all you have said, Lord Kyndreth," he managed, finally. "I am—stunned. I need time to shake my thoughts loose."

"I can sympathize," Kyndreth said gravely, but there was a smile of satisfaction in his eyes. He already knew that Kyrtian would agree, just as Kyrtian already knew he *must* agree. It was only a matter of time, and time was not his friend.

12

Lord Kyndreth retired to his guest-suite and the competent hands of his body-slaves with a feeling of total contentment. Not only had he just savored the pleasure of enjoying an exquisitely prepared, presented, and served High Court feast, but he was perfectly well aware that he was about to acquire a most useful adherent. *He* had seen young Kyrtian's reaction to the double temptations of power and the opportunity to play the hero. He had also noted Lady Lydiell's. The boy might be naive, but his mother was no fool, and she knew that the Great Lord and High Councilor Lord Kyndreth would not have made those offers if it was possible to refuse them.

She also knows that without my patronage that cousin of theirs will continue to be a thorn in their sides, at the very least, and might well find a patron powerful enough that he can take everything from them, he thought with satisfaction. *She read that implicit threat clearly enough.*

He'd mentioned Aelmarkin for just that reason. In this particular game of hounds-and-alicorns, Lord Kyndreth had herded the hounds into exactly the positions he wanted them.

His slaves undressed him and he slipped into the silk lounging-robe one of them held out for him. As always, his bodyguard Kaeth was in unobtrusive attendance, and when the last slave left the room, Kaeth remained, a faithful shadow, to be ignored—or not. Kaeth was equally receptive to either condition.

Kaeth's training must have been impeccable; Lord Kyndreth only wished that he could have gotten Kaeth's trainers along with the bodyguard. When the slave grew too old to serve, it would be difficult to replace him, and it would by necessity be with an inferior specimen.

Kyndreth turned his back on his bodyguard and took a seat beside an illusory fire burning in the very real marble fireplace—one of the few illusions in this suite. The flames danced with rainbow colors, and as the fire "burned," it gave off a pleasant scent of cedar and aloes-wood, but no heat.

"Well, Kaeth," Kyndreth said to the fire, "the boy will take the bait, I've no doubt. He doesn't dare refuse it."

"True, my Lord." As always, Kaeth was as economical with words as with everything else. "He'll accept by morning, I expect."

"He's as good as I think." That was a statement; Kyndreth didn't expect Kaeth to disagree. "The boy is going to break the deadlock for us. The only reason Aelmarkin managed to convince everyone that he was half-mad was because he stayed mewed up here. Anyone who had bothered to talk with him for more than half an hour would have known he was sane—and brilliant. If he'd been out in society, Aelmarkin wouldn't have had a chance of making a laughing-stock out of him."

"He is better than you think, my Lord."

Astonished, Lord Kyndreth swiveled his head to look at his normally laconic bodyguard. "Indeed?" he managed. *By the Ancestors, I can't remember the last time Kaeth volunteered a comment, much less an opinion! This youngster must be something truly out of the ordinary!*

"I have examined his library, his strategy-room, and some of his own writings, my lord. I also watched his men when he commanded them. It is one thing to command men; it is another to *lead* them. Lord Kyrtian is a leader. Men may not always obey a commander—or at least, they may only obey the *letter* of his commands, but not exert themselves beyond that—but they will always follow a leader." Kaeth's unreadable expression did not change by so much as a hair, but Lord Kyndreth fancied he'd heard the faintest hint of approval in the bodyguard's voice.

Interesting. Very interesting.

He turned back to the fire. It wouldn't do to give Kaeth too much direct attention. The slave was intelligent, *highly* intelligent, and Kyndreth needed to be very careful how he handled the man. Too much attention might give him a sense of self-importance that could affect his usefulness. "All the more reason to put him in charge of the army. Half the time Lord Levelis has to drive the troops into action with pain and punishment. If the troops had some other motivation, that alone might ensure our victory."

"Lord Levelis," came the surprising reply, "will be mortally offended by being replaced by a—Lesser Lord."

Again, Kaeth had volunteered an observation. Lord Kyrtian must have impressed the man so much that Kaeth's careful self-control was cracking a trifle. Kyndreth laughed mirthlessly. "By an eccentric nobody, you mean, but of course cannot say. If his *dear* cousin is to be believed, a half-mad nobody. Lord Levelis will have to survive being offended; he has done nothing to endear himself to me, he has bungled every attempt at putting down the rebels, and he is not one of *my* adherents. I can afford to offend him; let *his* patron find a way to console him."

There was no reply; the human really couldn't reply to the statements without being insolent, and Lord Kyndreth would not tolerate insolence, even from a slave as trusted as his bodyguard.

"The boy's position will be safe enough when it is clear that I am his patron," Kyndreth continued for Kaeth's benefit. "I could have him installed tomorrow, if I chose. Levelis has bungled too many times, and he will not dare move against me or anyone I choose to replace him with."

"Perhaps not against you—but out on the battlefield, Lord Kyrtian will no longer be under your direct supervision or protection. Lord Levelis may move against him there; my Lord, the battlefield is a chance-ridden place, and accidents do happen to even the most careful."

Well, well! I do believe that is another opinion!

Kyndreth could not resist the temptation to see what else he could draw out of Kaeth—further observations, even suggestions? This was more than the bodyguard had shown of himself in years!

"Perhaps I should send you to watch out for his welfare," he half-jested.

"I will do whatever you direct, my Lord," came the expressionless reply, and Kyndreth sighed with disappointment. Kaeth had revealed all that he was going to—and probably would not venture so much as a bland comment for the next year.

Kyndreth had no intention of assigning Kaeth—who was *far* too valuable where he was—to the task of seeing to Kyrtian's well-being. *The boy will either be able to protect himself, or not. And if he cannot, then he does not deserve my patronage.* There was that bodyguard of his own, after all—a man who had come very close to defeating Kaeth in combat. Having that particular slave in his train showed a certain amount of self-preserving sense.

Levelis wouldn't be able to eliminate him until after he'd broken the stalemate, anyway, and by then the real work would be done, and Levelis could have his old position back if he really wanted it. By that point, Kyndreth would have what he wanted; credit for breaking the backs of the rebels, and when the rebels were defeated, Kyrtian would be—

—expendable. Still useful, perhaps, but expendable.

Gel had stood silent watch throughout the long meal, listening to the conversation with a face as impassive as that of the bodyguard Kaeth—and when the servants vanished he did the same.

But he didn't go far. Like every public room in this manor, there was a spy-hole where a trusted confederate could listen to the Elvenlords when they thought they were speaking among themselves.

He didn't trust Lord Kyndreth. No matter how that particular Elvenlord acted, he would never do *anything* that wasn't in his own interest; solely and *completely* in his own interest. He might lull others into believing that he acted out of—say—friendship, or even the altruistic wish to do someone who might deserve help a favor, but there would always be a hidden reason for such actions, and either a later cost, or a current benefit.

It was moderately interesting to hear Kyndreth speaking so openly in front of, and to, his bodyguard Kaeth. It wasn't unheard of or out-of-character, though; after all, what was the use of having a fully-trained and intelligent bodyguard if you didn't make use of all of his skills?

The spy-hole was a clever little construction, built where the chimney would have actually been had the fireplace been real and functional. There was enough room to sit comfortably with one ear to the wall, forehead resting against a padded projection, in the utter darkness—not a single peep-hole, not even a thin little crack to betray the possible presence of a spy here.

So, the current commander is going to be an enemy. That was no surprise, though it was a good thing to have the man's name. Tenebrinth could put some time into investigating the fellow. It might well be possible to compensate him in some way for the loss of his important post.

It might be possible to placate him with no more than a simple visit. Kyrtian plays the humble soul very well.

The murmur of voices in the other room continued, and he strained to hear every nuance, wishing he also had some way to read Lord Kyndreth's thoughts.

The current commander isn't Kyndreth's? That's good to know; Kyndreth probably knows next to nothing about him, and if Kaeth does, he's only said that the fellow is going to be insulted. Well, insults can be negated with a purging dose of humility. If Kyrtian paid an immediate call on Levelis, after accepting the appointment but before it became generally known, and groveled . . .

Must ask Tenebrinth. That can be a two-edged sword.

Assuming that the current commander could *not* be placated or bought off, there was a possibility that Levelis would revert to the ancient ways of Evelon. The Elvenlord was not likely to act openly—after the display at the challenge-duel hosted by Aelmarkin, no one was going to issue a challenge that they knew they were going to lose. A challenge to a duel-by-magic was possible, and there were several potential ways of dealing with it. Kyndreth and the Council *could* forbid it. Kyrtian could accept and the duel could go on, and he could either win or lose—and in either case, Gel would have to be certain that the stakes weren't too high to lose. *What is the limit on stakes in these things? Must ask Tenebrinth. If it's pretty much a token, it might pay Kyrtian to lose anyway.*

But if the Council forbade a duel altogether on the grounds that the challenge was specious and made purely out of pique, Levelis could decide to take matters into his own hands. That left the possibility—if Levelis had or could purchase a properly-trained slave—of assassination. He wished very strongly that he had Kaeth at his disposal about now—an assassin would be the best possible expert at spotting another.

But he didn't. *And I spotted Kaeth, so I suppose I could spot another. Provided he was operating in the open, and not making an attempt at sniping from a distance. Damn.* He made another note; make sure that Kyrtian's tent and person were always out of bow shot of any cover. Fine, provided that the current battlefield site wasn't in the middle of a forest.

But he knew that there was no use in trying to persuade Kyrtian not to go; he didn't even consider the option. It was too dangerous to try and decline the invitation, at least in the short-term. So long as Kyndreth was Kyrtian's sponsor, Aelmarkin would keep his distance.

Damn them all for a nest of twisty snakes, anyway! Why couldn't anyone among these pointy-eared bastards ever do anything in a straightforward manner?

But the subject had changed, and Gel shoved his ear even tighter against the wall, hoping for more insights.

Kara and Gianna were fussing with their clothing again, hoping for a second visit from the Great Lord and a second present of jewels, no doubt. What good jewels were, with only their master to see them, Rennati had no idea. Rennati sighed, but quietly; Kara had gone through three changes of costume already, and still she wasn't satisfied with the impression she was going to make.

She looked back at the window; a doe and fawn appeared at the very edge of the lawn, but quickly darted back out of view before she got more than a glimpse of them.

I would like a fawn, more than jewels. Or a kitten of my own, like the one that slipped in when we first came here. Any kind of pet. Kara and Gianna wouldn't want to share the harem with an animal, though.

Kara tried another gown, and rejected it immediately—not that there was anything wrong with it, but because she had worn it two days ago.

Well, maybe Lady Lydiell shouldn't have given us such extensive wardrobes when she bought us and installed us here, Rennati thought. *Half of all this costume-changing is only because Kara's got an excuse to try on everything in her closet.*

Kara and Gianna twittered at each other; what did Rennati need with a bird when she had them? "The black," she said, in the first available moment of silence. "Wear the black. It's at the right end of the closet."

Two heads swiveled on two swan-like necks to peer in her direction, both sets of eyes, blue and brown, equally uncertain. "Black?" Kara said doubtfully. "But—" she shuddered. "He'll think—"

"Black's not for mourning, not with *them,*" Rennati said, anticipating Kara's objection. "I know it's not a color you usually wear, but Lady Lydiell has perfect taste, and she wouldn't have put the black in your wardrobe if she didn't think you'd look good in it."

The fair and deceptively fragile Kara pursed her lips in thought. "I could try it, I suppose—"

The thought was mother to the act; in a mere moment, the gown of seventeen overdresses made of sheerest silk was in a heap on the floor, and Kara slid the heavy satin black over her head while Gianna picked up the discarded gown, shook it out, and put it back in the wardrobe. Gianna, fortunately, had a mania for neatness. Kara smoothed the bias-cut gown over her flat stomach, settled the pointed neckline, and twitched the long sleeves so that the points of the cuffs came down precisely over the backs of her hands, then turned to gaze at her reflection.

Gianna was already staring in awe, her lips pursed. "Oooh, Kara!" she enthused. "It's perfect, Ren's right! Wear it!"

And it was perfect; Kara's misty-blue eyes in the reflection were wide with surprise as she pulled her long hair over one shoulder to fall in a silver-gilt cascade along the shining black satin. Rennati smothered a smile. "Remember those silver-and-jet ornaments that puzzled you in the jewel-chest?" she prompted. "I would bet that they're meant to go with the black." As the other two women dove for the jewel-chest, Rennati went back to her own thoughts. She and Gianna were more than ready for any potential call for their services; it was only Kara who'd been indecisive. Kara could never make up her mind about anything, and preferred to be led by the other two.

Which was fine with Rennati. Gianna was the natural leader of the harem, if one could be called a "leader" in a group of three. Rennati was indifferent to who took the lead in such pressing questions as what to eat, what music to play, or what to wear. Even now Kara sat passively while Gianna decided what to do with her hair and the wealth of silver and black ornaments that were obviously supposed to go into a coiffure.

Gianna had been ready hours ago; last night she had worn a close-cut scarlet velvet gown with a cleavage so low and tight that she nearly popped out of it—not that, with her generous features, she wasn't perilously close to popping out of anything she wore. Tonight she favored a dusty rose that was not tight-fitting at all, but plunged so low in the back that there was not a single one of her perfectly-sculptured vertebrae that was not on show, and as usual, she had made up her mind after swiftly rifling through her closet. Rennati had been ready even earlier; last night she had worn an emerald-green sheath that matched her eyes, slit to the hips on either side, and tonight it was a pale green tunic with an asymmetrical hem and no shoes. She didn't expect Lord Kyndreth to get to her, anyway; she expected to dance while the other two worked their wiles on him. Lord Kyndreth had expressed pleasure with her dancing last night, and she hadn't even begun to show off her talent. If the other two occupied his bed, that would give *her* a rare moment alone to activate her teleson-ring to speak with her real Mistress.

She hadn't learned much—except that Kyndreth was pleased, very pleased, with Lord Kyrtian, and intended to become his patron—but she remembered Lady Triana's instructions to report *everything*. They hadn't yet been allowed out of the tiny harem, though neither Kara nor Gianna particularly cared. Rennati would have liked the chance to get out, rare though it might be for a concubine to have that chance, but she had to admit that, although the suite was relatively small, it was sumptuously appointed and should satisfy most cravings.

It even had windows gazing out on the world; from the look of things, their suite was in a tower, for the window-seat where Rennati lounged was at some height above a wide, green lawn. There were trees in the far distance, although with twilight darkening the sky it was hard to distinguish anything but a vague, bluish blur at the end of the lawn. This was a novelty; Rennati had never been in a harem that had a view of the world she had last seen as a young child, and she spent as much time as possible in the windows, watching the rest of Lord Kyrtian's slaves walking from here to there with purpose in their steps, or even working on that plushy grass.

Anything they might possibly have wanted had been supplied to them. There were the usual lutes and harps to play on, if they desired, or they could leave the instruments to play by themselves with a touch of the hand on a little silver stud in the neck. If they chose the latter, the instruments somehow also supplied an accompaniment of drums, bells, and flutes. There were materials for embroidery and beadwork, scents, cosmetics of every sort, hair-dressing instruments, and even books, though Rennati was the only one of the three of them who could read with any proficiency. The bathroom was small, but one didn't necessarily need a bath one could swim in, and the food invariably pleasant, if not sumptuous. Still, one didn't particularly *want* a feast presented to one every day in a harem; it was altogether too easy to overeat, and that would be a disaster for the figure.

The door-chime sent the other two into a flutter, and Rennati rose from the window seat to join them as they flew into the reception-chamber together.

Lord Kyndreth, tall, broad-shouldered, and handsome enough for any two humans, strode unaccompanied into the room. All three of them dropped to the floor in a profoundly deep curtsy the moment his foot crossed the threshold. He laughed at Kara's eager face as she looked up at him.

"Well, last night you were a lily, so what are you tonight, hmm?" he teased. "A black narcissus, perhaps?"

"I am whatever your lordship pleases to call me," Kara replied, rising first, with an expression of adoration.

She probably didn't *feel* adoration, but she was adept at assuming any expression she thought might be met with pleasure.

"As it should be," he responded, gesturing to Kara and Gianna, and gathering each into an arm. "Come now, last night I had but a brief introduction to flame-hair's dancing, and I am eager to see more."

He took a seat on a couch piled high with silk and velvet pillows, still with a girl on either side to minister to him. Rennati made the rounds of the room, touching each of the waiting instruments in turn, then set the time for the dance by clapping her hands for a measure. The instruments, in concert, struck up a lively piece; she let it play through for four measures before leaping out into the room and setting her flying feet into motion.

This, if anything, was what she lived for. She would rather have died than not dance. Her first owner, a Lord of discriminating tastes (so he styled himself) and limited means, had grown bored with her passion, and had decided to dispose of her in a private sale to finance the purchase of a new girl to train.

"There's nothing at all *wrong* with her," he'd told Lady Triana, "It's just that she's *always* dancing. I'd really like to find a new girl who has talents that are a little more restful. One doesn't always *want* prancing about; it's very fatiguing to watch after a while."

For Lord Kyndreth, however, Rennati's passion apparently had the virtue of novelty, even if he was so busy with Kara and Gianna that he paid scant attention to the nuances of Rennati's performance. And long before *she* was weary, *he* was fully involved with them. Ornaments had been removed and set carefully aside, along with a few bits of clothing, and when Rennati signaled the instruments to play quietly to themselves and stole out of the room, none of the three even noticed. That was fair enough; she'd been Lord Kyndreth's first last night, which had left Kara out. Kara no doubt wanted a chance for a better present tonight.

Rennati stole up the stairs to the uppermost story of the tower where their bedrooms were—not so much bedrooms, as curtained-off alcoves of a room meant never to be seen by the eyes of a Lord. Here they could practice with cosmetics, sometimes to hilarious effect; here they kept the litter of their previous lives, personal belongings too shabby for a Lord to see. Kara had a battered old doll, much loved and worn, and every bit of "jewelry" she ever owned, going right back to a string of pierced sea-shells some little boy-child had once given her, up to her own efforts with needle and beads. There were a dozen works-in-progress on a table, along with a doll being costumed with beads and bits. Gianna had managed to keep hold of all of her attempts at artwork and kept her supplies and easel up here. She was making an attempt at a still-life of Kara's work-table, but Kara kept moving things around, much to her frustration.

Rennati had books—not the pretty leather-bound volumes of poetry downstairs, but dirty old things with torn covers or no covers at all on every subject under the sun, rescued from the

Lord's trash-heaps. And, of course, she had Lady Triana's teleson-ring.

With a few hesitant words, she activated it.

It was too small to allow a picture; it sent and received voices only. As she had been told to expect, the first voice was unfamiliar.

"Who calls?" the voice asked.

"Rennati," she replied breathlessly, a little astonished and a little fearful to be holding a thing of such great magic in her hand.

"Ah—wait one moment. Lady Triana will wish to speak with you herself."

The ring, a beryl like the one in her collar, fell silent. Rennati waited patiently; so long as no one came up here to interrupt her, she would wait for as long as she was told to. Elvenlords were busy, and it was not reasonable to expect one to drop whatever she was doing simply to come and hear what a mere concubine had to say.

Finally, "Speak," said an imperious female voice from the ring.

"I have been here since your agent sent me to Lady Lydiell," Rennati said instantly. "I am with two other concubines, in a tower, in a small harem. I can see outside from the windows, but I have not yet been allowed to venture past the door. Lord Kyrtian has been here once only. He is entertaining Lyon Lord Kyndreth, who was here last night and is here now. Lord Kyndreth is going to become Lord Kyrtian's patron. He told Kara tonight that Lord Kyrtian has pleased him and that we must not expect to see very much of our master for some time, since he is going to go away to take charge of an army."

There was an odd laugh. "Well, that rather puts a kink in my plans; if he won't be there, you won't be able to learn much from him. On the other hand, if you do manage to get out, you can see a great deal more when the lord himself is away. And this other news—more than interesting. I take it that this is all you have for me for now?"

Rennati nodded, forgetting for a moment that she could not be seen, then hastily said, "I am sorry, but that is indeed all I have learned."

"It is not a great deal, but the quality is good, and I am pleased. Notify me the moment you learn anything more. You may deactivate the ring now."

Obediently, Rennati passed her hand over the ring, shutting out the light from the room for a moment, which turned it into an ordinary beryl again. Then she placed the ring in the darkest corner of her jewel-box, and hurried back downstairs.

After all, it was not too late to earn another generous present from Lord Kyndreth—and more importantly, he might be inclined to talk afterwards. Elvenlord or human, if they didn't sleep, they were all often inclined to talk—afterwards.

The sun shining down on the top of the highest tower of the lady-keep imparted a drowsy warmth to Lady Moth's back that she was thoroughly enjoying. She had always liked the gentle heat of the sun; her late husband had once scornfully accused her of being half-lizard for the way she enjoyed basking in the garden. But even if it had been the dead of winter, she would have been up here, for this was the only place on the entire estate that gave an unrestricted view down into the valley below. And what she watched through the eyepiece of her bit of antique equipment was fascinating indeed. There was no breeze to stir the silken, silvery-blue folds of her dress, or disturb the simple, straight fall of her hair, nor to make breezes wave distant branches between her and the interesting scene so far away in the valley. She felt sorry for the tiny little figures that she knew by their drab tunics were human slaves. First one brightly-colored creature in scarlet paraded them out and set them to work in the kitchen-garden. Then a second appeared, clad in a violent blue, far too soon for them to have accomplished much, and marched them off to drill with weapons.

Then a *third* emerged from the stables, this one in bronze satin, and ran them off into the farm-fields. What those poor bewildered slaves must be thinking now, she could not even begin to guess.

"Lady Morthena?" said a diffident voice from behind the Elven lady. "What are you doing?"

Lady Moth took her eye away from the eyepiece of the old-fashioned, gold-and-bronze telescope, and turned to smile at her most recent guest.

"I am using an old device, my dear," she said to the younger woman in a kindly voice, knowing that Lady Viridina would never have seen such a thing as a telescope. "In fact, it dates quite back to Evelon—or at least, the lenses in it do. It is called a *telescope,* and although I normally use it to examine stars, at the moment I am using it to spy upon our neighbors." She patted the long cylinder of bronze, with ornate curlicues chased into the metal and inlaid with gold wire, for it was a very old friend and long-time companion.

Lady Viridina's pale brow wrinkled with puzzlement, with a faint frown on a face that was attenuated by long illness. "Why are you bothering to do that?" she wondered. "They already tell you everything, don't they?"

"That, my dear, is what I am ascertaining for myself." Lady Moth put her eye back to the eyepiece, and continued to make mental notes on the movements of the Young Lords' slaves outside the Great House. "In point of fact, I rather doubt that they *are* telling me everything. For instance, there seems to be some disagreement down there about just who is in charge of what. Just during the time I have been sitting here, I have seen one hapless group of slaves herded from one uncompleted task to another by three different Young Lords." She chuckled, and her laughter was echoed faintly by her companion, who patted the knot of long, silver hair at the back of her head self-consciously. "That is what comes with age, Viridina; suspicion. I stopped taking things at face value a very, very long time ago."

"So did I—but the difference between us, I think, is that *you* found other ways of finding out what you needed to know, and I didn't even try," Viridina said ruefully, twisting her hands in the fine silk of her flowing and many-layered violet gown. "If I had, perhaps—"

She didn't finish the sentence, but Lady Moth was not about to allow her to sink into self-recrimination. "If you had, I doubt that it would have materially changed anything. You and I were firmly under the thumbs of our unlamented Lords, and no knowledge or even foreknowledge would have allowed us to change what happened to us. Knowledge is not always power." She smiled again. "If it was, fond as I am of my Tower, it would be Lady Moth who ruled the manor down there, and not that rabble of Young Lords."

Lady Moth had known very well that there was going to be a slave revolt when the Young Lords staged their own revolution against their elders. Her own slaves had told her. *She* had already taken herself out of her disagreeable husband's home; she had made a bargain with him—if he gave her the lady-keep, which had been the Dowager-House attached to his estate, *she* would make no trouble for him when he filed a divorcement with the Council. He had his eye on a very young Elven girl—his tastes had begun to run to the barely-pubescent in the past few years—and he was heartily tired of the wife who could not or would not take him as seriously as he thought he should be taken.

"I wish you had managed to take the Manor," Lady Viridina sighed wistfully. "I hate to think what damage those careless boys are wreaking to your beautiful home."

Lady Moth only shrugged. "I have an equally beautiful home here—and much more manageable," she pointed out. "It's probably just as well that I didn't try."

For her part, she had been so heartily tired of *her lord* that—given that she would not be required to remarry and could have an establishment, however small, of her own—she was prepared to allow him to say whatever he pleased about her in order to obtain his freedom. She suspected that he would claim she was pleasuring herself with human slaves—but as it fell out, he never got the chance, so her reputation survived intact.

"May I look?" Viridina finally asked, allowing her curiosity to overcome her reticence. Moth just laughed, showed her how to focus the instrument, and rose so that Dina could take her seat.

Moth's husband had not even lived to encounter the revolt, though without a doubt, if he had, he and his son would have been on opposite sides of the conflict. Her son, who had suddenly become as conservative as his father once *he* was in the ruling seat, had managed to be slaughtered almost immediately, and her daughter had fled after an abortive attempt to rule the manor herself had failed miserably. Lady Moth, as was the tradition in her family, had always treated her slaves with consideration and respect, entirely as if they were servants, not slaves, and as if they were free to leave her service if they chose to. She had taken all her slaves with her to the Tower, every slave for which she could concoct even the remotest excuse to have with her—a fact which probably would have provided ample fodder for her husband's accusations. Once there, she had deactivated the elfstones in all of their collars, making them merely decorative shams, and told them frankly that they now *were* free to go or stay. They all, to a man and woman, chose to stay. When the revolt was at the breaking-point, her slaves had told her. They had fortified the place, she had armed those who knew how to use weapons. Together, they had outfaced rebellious ex-slaves and Young Lords. In fact, her burly young guards called her "little mother," and took as much care of her as if she had truly given birth to them—unlike her own offspring.

"Why not use scrying instead of this device?" Dina asked, moving the telescope to gaze at another part of the valley.

"Because, my dear, the place is adequately shielded against scrying—oh, not by magic, by all that iron and steel they've managed to collect." She stared down at the valley, one finger tapping her lips thoughtfully. "Very clever of them, actually; there aren't three of them together that are a match for a single one of the Old Lords, but the metal does their work for them."

Needless to say, her son's magic had not been enough to save him from enraged and mistreated humans who came in the middle of the night to beat him to death in his own bed—especially not when *they* arrived bedecked in thin iron armbands.

During the chaos of the revolt itself, some of her son's slaves had escaped to her; the rest fled to the Wizards and the wilderness. When more armed bands of escaped slaves had come upon the Tower, her people protected and guarded her while she stood ready to use deadly war-magics if it became necessary. She knew about the effects of iron and steel; she would not have made any attempt to blast attackers, unlike those foolish Elvenlords like Dina's husband. *She* planned to blast holes into the earth beneath their feet—or to use her magic to launch large and heavy objects at them. Most of her anxiety had not been for herself, but for her people, if they could not convince their fellow humans to go away peaceably. She didn't want them hurt on her behalf, and she didn't want them to have to witness what *she* might have to do to protect them all.

Dina stood, and relinquished her seat with a smile. "Very clever of you to know the things that can't be interfered with by that metal," she said, as Moth took her seat again.

"Not clever, dear, only resourceful. If I were *clever,* I'd have managed to find a way to eavesdrop on them." That irritated her; she still hadn't managed to insinuate a reliable spy into their slave-stock.

She was not entirely certain what her people had told marauders during those first weeks of the Revolt to dissuade them from attacking the Tower; there probably had been several different stories, specifically tailored to each group. It was true enough that a few, select escapees had decided to swell the ranks of her own folk—no doubt, because they were unwilling or unable to make the strenuous journey over the mountains to an uncertain and probably uncomfortably barbaric existence in the wilderness.

Not that she blamed them in the least. She had always had an ample portion of "Lady-magic," and although her husband had not been aware of the fact, she was his equal in the realms of Elven magic usually taught only to men. Had it been necessary, she could have defended the Tower as well as many Elvenlords, and probably better than most. Now, her magic went to ensuring the continued survival of her diminished estate. She did everything needed to ensure exactly the right weather for the farm-fields, she went over the fields and gardens daily to monitor and encourage growth and health in plants and animals. *She* had the knowledge and the long memory to tell *them* what they needed to do, and when. They trusted her, her learning, her judgment, her experience. That was what *she* had brought to the table; they had brought their labor. Returning to the grand tradition of *her* family, they had worked together to make sure that Elven-blood and human-blood prospered.

"Is there anything you'd like me to do this afternoon?" Dina asked, diffidently.

Moth examined her friend carefully. There had been moments, in those first days after Viridina took refuge with her, that she truly felt that Viridina would never be entirely sane again. But Dina was stronger than Moth had first thought; even after escaping murder at her Lord's hands and seeing her Lord incinerated virtually at her feet, she had not truly had a breakdown of her senses. It took time and careful tending, but she *had* recovered. Moth decided that it was time for her to help do her part here.

"Would you make the rounds of the kitchen-gardens for me, dear? I would really appreciate it, and I know you must have tended your own gardens thousands of times. I needn't tell *you* what to do." Moth felt herself both justified and rewarded when Dina's face lit up.

"Gladly! I have been feeling so—" she gestured frustration with both hands "—so useless. And a burden on you."

"You have *never* been a burden," Moth lied gracefully. Dina only smiled, recognizing the lie, and the graciousness behind it, and turned to go back down the stairs, her sleeves and trailing hem fluttering behind her.

After most of the escaping slaves were gone, but before Moth had a chance to move herself and her people back to the Great House, the Young Lords had moved in. Occasionally, even now, she cursed herself for hesitating—but on the other hand, the Great House was much less defensible, and even with her new followers, she still had really not enough people to adequately staff and run a property that was ten times the size of that attached to the Tower.

The Young Lords had taken over the abandoned estate; they had brought their own slaves with them. Lady Moth was not entirely certain where they had gotten those slaves; many of them seemed terribly young for the work they were required to do. She suspected that the Young Lords had raided the breeding-farms of some of the Old Lords while the latter were occupied with the fighting, carrying off hordes of confused and frightened creatures barely out of childhood.

Poor, poor things, she thought, taking one last look through the telescope, her lips tightening. *Well, at least there are enough of them to do the work they are ordered to do, and they are saved one horror. Their masters are too busy with their own concerns to abuse them; confusion is the worst they have to face.*

The reason she had asked Dina to take her place in "working" the garden was that she had an appointment with the Young Lords quite soon, and it was bound to be stressful. She had come up here in the first place to get a little more information before she faced them; now it was time to change into a riding-habit and make the short journey over to their stronghold.

She chose her clothing carefully: a tailored, severe habit of stark black, with only the barest hints of silver at the cuffs and throat. She dressed to intimidate; the last thing she wished to be thought was "feminine." Her groom brought her horse around, along with her guards, and she mounted and made the short journey to what had once been her home.

She was accompanied by four burly young men—humans, not Elves, and humans that wore scale-armor of iron, not bronze, and had ostentatiously bare necks. Moth had played the game of wits and treachery for centuries before these striplings had ever been born.

They were, one and all, less than a century old; when she swept into the meeting-chamber in her trim sable-silk riding habit, her hair in an uncompromising knot bound in a black silk snood, with all four of her escorts flanking her, they found themselves rising from their seats despite whatever their original intentions had been in the way of greeting.

She paused at her seat, looked gravely up and down the table with an unreadable expression, and only then did she sit—which in turn, allowed them to resume their seats. She might not be the leader here, but in their hearts, they all acknowledged her power.

Which is more than their fathers would. Then again, she probably wouldn't ever use tactics this crude with their fathers.

She listened without comment to the reports of their progress—or lack of it—against their fathers. The situation was clearly at stalemate, and had been for some time now. This was not necessarily bad, and had they asked her opinion, she would have advised patience. When there is stalemate, it is often possible for frustration to drive one side or the other to make a crucial mistake.

But, of course, they didn't ask her opinion, and she didn't offer it—since it was clear that they would not believe a mere female would have any experience relevant to the "man's work" of warfare.

As if they *have any!* she thought, without amusement. But warfare was not why she had come to this meeting. Eventually they got around to the topic she wished to cover, in the form of a single casual comment by one of the least intelligent (to her mind) of the lot, occasioned by one of her bodyguards stifling a cough at one of the more fatuous suggestions.

"Lady Morthena," said Lord Alrethane, with a frown on his face, "I really do not know what you are thinking, allowing armed and uncontrolled slaves to continue in your service."

"They are not slaves, they are my willing servants," she countered smoothly. "I find that I sleep better, knowing that my sleep is guarded by faithful people who serve me from loyalty and not because they are forced to."

"Loyalty? Loyalty?" Alrethane exploded. "Are you actually ascribing a civilized emotion to these simple-minded barbarians? They're a bare step above the beasts!"

Another discreet cough reminded him that he was insulting people who *were* freemen, armed, and protected with armor that would stop both magic and blades. He stopped, abruptly, and averted his eyes.

"He has a point—" someone said.

Morthena looked up and down the table again, examining expressions, and was disappointed.

So. Nothing has changed. She had hoped that some, at least, of the Young Lords would have started to see sense. Insofar as the humans were concerned, the Young Lords were of two camps; the majority—a scant majority, but enough—held humans and halfbloods in the same contempt as did their elders. The minority, led and coached by Lady Moth, wanted to see humans and halfbloods given equal status with Elves. So far, none of those she considered to be "wavering" had changed their minds. She had hoped that this particular display, showing just how far she trusted *her* people, would have had some effect.

At least the minority saw to it that the human slaves owned by the rest were not mistreated.

And there have been enough chances already that those who had the courage and initiative to escape to the Wizards have already done so.

The slaves they now had probably served out of the usual mix of fear of the collar, an inability to imagine that anything could be different, and an inability to get *their* hands on any iron or steel which would render a slave-collar useless. She suspected that it was the former two reasons that were the strongest, since anyone who really wanted the metal rings that would negate the collars could have one from Moth's people just by asking. Pity would only take her so far; if the slaves here couldn't look beyond their fear, if they didn't have the basic intelligence to imagine something different from their current life, she couldn't help them.

I won't press the issue any further; if I do, I'll only weaken my own party, and if the rest of these young fools turn on me, I will have to barricade myself within my own lands and hope they grow bored with me. There would be no point in trying to flee; I am not at all sanguine about the likelihood of a full Elvenlord finding a welcome among the Wizards, even if Dina's children are among them.

Her thoughts were momentarily distracted by that reminder of Dina's children. Poor Dina; she hadn't heard anything from them since they parted from her on Moth's doorstep. It was, after all, just as likely they were in hiding somewhere other than among the halfblooded Wizards. Only one of them was a halfblood anyway—Lorryn, the boy. Sheyrena was of full elven blood, and she could not imagine the girl being welcomed by the Wizards.

It's likely that although Lorryn might have been able to convince the Wizards that Sheyrena was not actually an immediate danger to them when he first encountered them, he would never be able to convince them that Rena is completely harmless. And if he couldn't convince them that his own sister wasn't going to bring disaster on them, he'd never be able to make them believe that an ancient Elven lady like Moth was on their side.

Poor, poor Dina; she worried so much about them, although she tried not to show it. The one regret that Moth had was that there was no way for her to discover if Dina's two children were all right, or even where they were.

It is the most likely, actually, that Rena is ensconced somewhere off in the wilderness, far from Elvenlord, human, or halfblood. She has magic enough to keep herself safe—well, according to Dina, she has magic enough to control alicorns! And Lorryn would never allow her to come to harm or suffer any want—if he's with the Wizards, he'll see to it that she's got food enough and shelter. In a way, she envied the two youngsters. *If I'd had the youth and the opportunity, I'd have gone right off the map. The world is wide, after all; wide enough to hide dragons from us for all these centuries, it can certainly hide a few Elves who don't wish to be found.*

The conversation had made a wide detour around the question of the slaves, and was back on the topic of the war. Someone wished aloud for some secret that would allow the select elimination of some of the leaders. "That would throw a good fright into them," the callow youngster said, with a savagery worthy of any "barbarian and bestial human." "Let a few more of them die the way Lord Dyran died, and they'll give us whatever we want!"

Moth held her tongue. It was just as well that the Young Lords were not aware that Dina and her daughter managed to incinerate Dina's husband, the Lord Treves, in a way very similar to the way Lord Dyran's son slew him. Her own trusted servants knew, and they had kept it a strict secret, and she was quite grateful to them for preserving that secret. *These young hotheads should never learn something that dangerous. They'd probably manage to kill each other with it.*

Eventually the meeting ground down to its inevitable conclusion, and Moth rose. "With your permission, gentlemen, I should like to go tend to the library until sunset, if I may?" she asked politely.

They didn't even take a second thought about her request—young Lord Ketaliarn waved vaguely at her, and she took that as permission and left, trailed faithfully by her escort.

Of all the things that showed how callow they were, this was by far the most blatant. *They* considered the library to be useless, fit only for the concern of silly old ladies half living in the past. They thought all she was doing was cleaning and preserving the books—removing a few, now and then, for her own amusement in her bower.

Oh, the young fools.

The room she now entered, one of the finest libraries ever assembled in this world, was (had they only had the wit to realize it) *full* of information the Young Lords could use to help their own cause. She breathed deeply of the scent of leather, vellum, parchment and paper, took a long look around the shelves that her husband had only seldom permitted her to access while he was alive, and set to work.

Many of the oldest books had not been tended in far too long; she would not permit *any* book, however trivial, to suffer from the worm's tooth or the decay of age. Whenever she was here, she spent a few hours in cleaning and restoring those ancient books—no matter how trivial they seemed to be, there was no telling when some scrap of knowledge in them might prove useful.

Most of her time, however, was spent in looking for the ones that she would rather not leave to the curious eyes of the Young Lords.

Lady Moth had helped young Kyrtian's father with his research in this very library once or twice before his disappearance, and she was well aware that he had known better than she what lay here. She only knew within her own books was a set of very, very ancient works that Kyrtian's father had consulted in his searches for ancient secrets; she did not know which books they were, nor what they held.

Nevertheless, since she had been forced to quit the place, she had been determined that at the first chance she would get in here and find them again. Since the Young Lords got here, she had been using her visits to find each and every one of those precious volumes and take them back to the Tower, a few at a time. Whatever was *in* them had led to the death of one Elven-lord; she suspected that what he had gone seeking had somehow killed him. Which implied that the secrets to be found in those books could be very, very dangerous indeed.

None of the Young Lords cared what she did in there. So as she worked on the task of keeping the library cleaned and preserved, and she ferreted out those precious few books so that one day, perhaps, she could present them to Kyrtian, they were completely oblivious to the value of what she was taking out right underneath their very noses.

I shall have to do some research of my own, I'm afraid, she reflected. A dangerous secret was exactly what she was looking for, after all; there were a few old half-remembered stories of things that had been abandoned right after the Crossing, and techniques that had been forgotten in the haste to find and build a secure haven.

For her part, at the moment, she would be happy to find some way to communicate with her nephew other than by teleson or messenger.

She had just been informed this morning of a very disturbing rumor—as yet unconfirmed, but she had been hoping to hear something either to confirm or deny it at today's meeting. One of her servants took periodic and very risky ventures into the lands still held by the Old Lords, coming back just after dawn with the situation as viewed from the Enemy's vantage—and he had told her that there was a report that *Kyrtian* had taken command of the Old Lords' army.

If that was true—

If that is true, then the other side has made a desperate gamble, and all unknowing has hit upon the one thing that will probably give them victory. And the thing is, these young fools will be dead certain that putting Kyrtian in command of the Enemy is going to be the one thing that will ensure the Old Lords' defeat. Young idiots.

If only she could speak to him, and persuade him that *she* was one of the rebels, surely he would think twice about his current allegiance!

I don't dare use a teleson—those are too easily monitored. And none of my humans have the human type of magic that lets them talk mind-to-mind with each other. And I won't send one of my people where he might be captured or conscripted into the army. It is a terrible position to be in.

She was going to have to start studying these old tomes herself.

After all, it was a far better idea than sitting with her hands folded, waiting for disaster to overtake all of them.

Besides, she decided firmly, shoving another ancient volume into the saddlebag for her guard to take with him. *I will* never *sit by with folded hands while things fall to pieces.*

—not even if someone ties me into the chair and binds my hands together!

14

In the heart of the Citadel, the home of the halfblooded Wizards, Lorryn ignored the drone of voices around the table and took just a moment to marvel at his surroundings. *It seems so strange, even now, to finally be* myself. *No illusions, no carefully hiding what I am—* In spite of everything, all the hardships, all the danger, even the silly aggravations, Lorryn was not sorry to be here, among Halfbloods like himself, at last.

This most spacious of caverns in their new home that the Wizards used as a meeting-hall was a pleasant place in which to find oneself—so long as no one was meeting in it. A peculiarity of the caverns allowed a wonderful flow of fresh air through here, so long as certain openings that served as doors and windows were left open to catch the summer breezes. Last winter things had gotten a little stale in this room, and with such a high ceiling it tended to be dank and chill.

Unfortunately for his sheer pleasure, there *was* a meeting going on, and Lorryn was glad that he had ample experience in keeping a pleasant expression plastered on his face while he himself was not feeling in the least pleasant. He had a headache like a tight band around his head, and he had inserted his tongue a trifle between his teeth to keep from grinding them and making the headache worse.

How is it that Caellach Gwain has managed to find the precise nasal whine best calculated to set my nerves on edge? he asked himself, as he nodded affably at the elder Wizard. He actually couldn't make out more than half of what the man said, thanks to the weird acoustics in the place, but then he didn't have to listen to Caellach to know what he was going to say. *The man is like a teleson stuck on endless repetition of the last thing it sent.*

This was supposed to be a meeting about the progress made in setting up the sheep and cattle farm below the Citadel, but Caellach had taken it over as usual. He was intent only on recreating as much of the old comfort of the first Citadel in their new home as he could manage, and he had taken the opportunity of a brief allusion to the old Citadel to air his usual grievance.

Which is, of course, that the Wizards are not treated like Elvenlords of the High Council. Old fool. Hasn't he figured out yet that when one group lords it over another, the underlings are going to want to strike back?

The old man's litany of complaints was as familiar to Lorryn as the texture of the wooden table he stared at as he controlled his temper and his expression. The beginning, middle, and end of Caellach's troubles were seated in his own greed. He wanted all the effort of the younger Wizards and the humans to go into making him as cossetted as he had been before the second Halfblood War. He didn't care that they had to be self-sufficient now, and couldn't steal magically from the Elvenlords anymore. He didn't trouble himself to think that it was far more important to see to the raising of sheep, goats and cattle, the cultivation of fields, than to scrub an old wizard's floor on a daily basis.

And he absolutely hated that the majority of the Halfbloods, voting down Caellach and his cronies, had made treaties of alliance with the Iron People and with the Trader clans, giving them the status of full equals and honored partners. These were fullblooded *humans* who had the status of full equals and honored partners. Though he did not dare come out and say so directly, this attitude incensed Caellach and his ilk, for to their minds, the halfblooded Wizards were clearly superior in every way to mere humans, and thus, should be treated as such.

And we should all be running and fetching for them, tending to their comfort, giving them of ourselves and the first fruits of our labors, so as to reward them for the fatiguing effort of their magics on our behalf. Lorryn, who was not only halfblooded himself, but had been brought up as an Elvenlord with all of the attendant privileges, found Caellach's attitude just as insulting and absurd as any of the highly independent Iron People or Trader clan folk did. There was nothing inherently superior about a wizard. Yes, they had magics, but so did the humans. And since they had been settled here in the new Citadel, the older wizards had not exerted themselves *once* for the common good—except, rarely, to teach some of the children how to use their powers.

Rather than listening to Caellach's words, Lorryn listened to the tone behind the words. He'd discovered he possessed an interesting knack for ferreting out the emotions and motives behind what people said, provided that they weren't as skilled at covering themselves as he was. He heard injured self-esteem and affront—that was expected—but he also heard fear, and that was interesting. He had not anticipated that.

I should have, though, he thought, raising his eyes and studying Caellach's expression as the man shifted his eyes away from Lorryn's direct gaze. Caellach was looking a bit unkempt, now that there was no one to wait on him. His clothing, the usual long robe affected by most of the older Wizards, was a bit stained and frayed about the hem. His grey hair was brushed, but no longer hung about his shoulders in a kind of thick mantle—instead, it was held back untidily in a tail, and it seemed to Lorryn that it had gotten a bit thin at the temples. *People do tend to react to new things either with interest or fear, and really, I think Caellach Gwain is too hidebound to react with interest to anything new.*

Lorryn already knew that Caellach was afraid of the dragons; that was abundantly clear to anyone with half an eye. The old Wizard wouldn't set foot outside when there were dragons about in their natural form, and as for the ones shifted into half-blood or human shape—well. If *they* took seats on one side of the table, it was a safe bet that Caellach would place himself as far from them as physically possible while still remaining at the table.

His dislike of the Traders and the Iron People was a little more complicated, and harder to understand. Lorryn let a few of the old wizard's actual words—laden with anger and apprehension—sift in past his own thoughts. What in the world had the old man's trews in a wad?

"—and how *dare* they demand payment in advance, much less *at all,* for—"

Ah. That was enough to get the key. Lorryn had the tail of the tree-snake now. Caellach wasn't incensed that he was expected to pay in advance for the goods that the Traders brought here—he was angry that he was expected to pay *at all.* Possibly because Caellach's only available coin was, quite frankly, debased. He wasn't the most powerful Wizard anymore, he wasn't the most skilled, and his greed had led him to expend most of his energies on his own comforts, leaving him with little that he could use to barter for things he wanted.

"And as for those—barbarians—"

Third leg to the stool; he was incensed that the Iron People showed him no deference at all—and *didn't need his magic.*

Though why Caellach should think that a mob of ill-regulated cave-dwelling refugees should consider themselves more civilized than a well-regulated nomadic people was beyond Lorryn's imagination. *But prejudice has nothing to do with logic.* Perhaps it was because the Iron People were completely unimpressed by the Wizards. *They* didn't need Wizards to defend themselves from the Elvenlords; they had their iron ornaments and a powerful warrior class. Not to put too fine a point on it, *they* had actually held two Elvenlords as enslaved prisoners for the purposes of their own amusement. The most that Caellach Gwain had ever managed was to escape relatively unscathed from them.

That had been a near thing, too. Caellach and his cronies either did not realize, or would not admit, that it wasn't the Elvenbane's fault entirely that the old Citadel and its dwellers had been discovered. The Wizards had been dancing on the edge of a knife for a very long time, what with their pilferings from the Elvenlords and all. So far as the Elves were concerned, there was only one kind of good halfblood—a dead one. Halfbloods weren't even supposed to exist, and most of the Elvenlords were utterly devoted to making certain that they didn't. Lashana's actions had only triggered the avalanche of Elven retribution, not *caused* it.

And if it hadn't been for her quick thinking, and her draconic friends, the wizards wouldn't have survived it.

What was more, they weren't out of the woods yet. As long as the halfblooded wizards lived, the Elvenlords would try to eliminated them, treaty or no treaty. If Caellach Gwain and his circle thought any differently, they were deluding themselves.

Not that there was anything new in the notion of Caellach Gwain deluding himself. . . .

Finally, Caellach ran out of things to say, and sat down. Lorryn had very quickly figured out that allowing the old Wizard to rant and whine, while unpleasant to listen to, generally had the salubrious effect of making him silent for the rest of any meeting of which he was a part. "Thank you, Caellach; your experience is, as always, apparent to all of us," he said, graciously. Caellach began to preen. "Your observations are continuously fascinating." He ignored the grimace that one of the younger halfbloods made at him from behind the shelter of one hand, and the spasms that crossed several other faces in an effort to keep from bursting out into laughter. "Now—I'd like to put the matter of the proposed upper pasture for the goats to a vote. All in favor?"

Even Caellach raised his hand, seduced, no doubt, into thinking that the goats would look after themselves, and not require shepherds, now that they had some of the huge cattle-dogs raised by the Iron People at their disposal. Lorryn made certain that there were no dissenters, and nodded. "Good. We're all agreed. Halfden, would you see about finding some volunteers for the job and getting them to me to be interviewed?" He needed humans for this task, preferably children with the ability to speak mind-to-mind, so that they could call for help if they saw anything, or if there was something out there that neither they nor the dogs could handle.

More of the servants that Caellach Gwain thinks are his personal property.

Halfden, one of the older ex-slaves, nodded, and Lorryn called the meeting to a close.

But like it or not, he wasn't quite done with Caellach—at least so far as Caellach was concerned.

"I really need to talk with you about the quality of my quarters, Lorryn," the wizard said, grabbing him by the elbow before he could make his escape. Lorryn leveled a blank gaze at him.

"My good sir," he said, with the kind of polite tone in which a specious warmth and charm were mixed with utter calm, "if you think you are being slighted, I invite you to come and inspect *my* quarters—or Shana's for that matter. I think you will find that they are by no means superior to yours. In fact, given that neither of us chose our rooms until everyone else had gotten their pick, you'll find them far inferior to yours."

"Yes, but—" Caellach protested—although weakly, since he had been in the little nook of a cave that Lorryn used, and knew that it was scarcely larger than the closet in his own suite of linked cavelets.

"I know that it is trying to you to be in such primitive surroundings, after having to abandon such a wonderful and comfortable place as your old home," Lorryn said, now interjecting a soothing note into his voice. "Who could know better than I? Do think what *I* left behind; I was the only male heir to a powerful lord! But you will soon find this life as exhilarating as I do if you regard it as an *opportunity* rather than a loss! Think of it! You now have the chance to design your very own quarters in precisely the way you'd most like them—rather than be forced to endure inconveniences and awkwardnesses that countless generations of wizards before you created! With a little effort, you can, for the first time, have everything *perfect!*"

"Yes—but—" Caellach faltered.

"There, you see?" Lorryn slapped him lightly on the back. "That seems better already, doesn't it? I knew I could rely on you!"

And with that, he strolled away, leaving Caellach to go over the conversation in his mind and try to determine what could possibly have gone wrong.

As he rounded a corner, someone jumped at him from the shadows. Instinctively he sidestepped and drew his hidden dagger, with a defensive magic meant deflect a levin-bolt already in place.

"You're getting better," Shana laughed, leaning against the rock wall with her arms crossed over her chest, looking quite as if she had *not* been catapulting herself across the hallway from a natural niche just at the level of his head a moment before.

"I should hope so," he retorted. "You certainly give me enough practice. Were you listening in on the meeting?"

"I was—and *you* are a genius. And some sort of mage that I haven't quite figured out." She tilted her head to the side, quizzically. "How you manage Caellach—and how you manage to *not* strangle Caellach—is quite beyond me."

Lorryn laughed and offered her his hand, which she took. "No magic—just politics," he told her. "Verbal self-defense. I didn't spend *much* time among the schemers and plotters, but I did hob-nob with some of them and, of course, I always had to be able to placate my father. I learned early how to say nothing while seeming to say everything."

She squeezed his hand. "It's still sheer genius. No matter how hard I try, I can't manage people half as well as you do."

He glanced aside at the young woman called "the Elvenbane." She didn't look like the stuff of legends; her scarlet tresses were tied up onto the top of her head in a very practical tail, which she often tossed like an impatient horse plagued with flies. Her handsome face was nothing in beauty compared to the homeliest of elven ladies, and her figure was so well-muscled that most of them would have recoiled in horror at the notion of looking like her. Today she had on a sleeveless tunic of leather and a pair of coarse slaves'-cloth trews—but to his eyes, she couldn't have looked better if she'd been enrobed in his sister Sheyrena's presentation-gown.

"I hope you aren't—bothered by me taking on all these meetings like this," he said, hesitantly. "You're supposed to be the leader, I know, but—"

"Am I jealous? Oh, Fire and Rain, get *that* idea out of your head this moment!" she replied with a laugh. "I never asked to be the Elvenbane, you know—and the only reason besides that stupid legend that people pay any attention to what I think is that I think quicker than they do. Handling the old goats is *not* a job that requires quick thinking—and you have the—" She considered for a moment, head tilted to one side. "—the 'manner born' is how I'd put it. You say things, and people *do* them, instead of arguing with you about it."

He thought that if she was dissembling in any way, he would be able to tell; he was getting pretty sensitive to *her* nuances—not that she had many, for she was a strikingly open person. No, she seemed to be happy with him taking *her* leadership role.

"If I could find a double to play Elvenbane for me, I'd do *that* in a heartbeat," she continued onwards, oblivious of his scrutiny, "And then I could just be Shana again."

"Speaking of just being Shana—oh crafty one—" he led her down a side passage that brought them out onto the top of the Citadel, into the warm air and sunshine, where they could sit and talk without being overheard.

She didn't fling herself down onto the grass as she usually did when brought outside. "Crafty one, hmm? I know what that means." She sauntered casually up the hill a little ways to a grassy knoll with a shade-tree atop it—downwind of the half-hidden entrance. Now they could speak without being overheard. Only then did she drop down into the grass in the sun, with all of the pleasure of her foster-mother dragon in basking.

"Ask away," she said, as he plopped down beside her. "I've just spent the better part of the morning talking to Keman but I need your help to reach Shadow."

Shana, freed from the responsibilities of the day-to-day running of the Citadel, was concentrating on the vastly more important project of collecting intelligence reports, by means of amplified telepathy, from Keman and some of the other people she and Lorryn had out in the greater world. Although it would not be possible to send either a human or a halfblood into the midst of Elves to spy under a spell of illusion, the halfbloods were not limited to illusion as long as they had dragons with them, for the dragons could actually shift their shape to appear like anyone or anything they liked. Shana's foster-brother Keman and his probable mate Dora were Shana's shapechanged spies among both camps of Elves.

"Your mother is not only doing well, so far as Dora can tell, she's taking over some of Lady Moth's duties on the home-fields," Shana told him, smiling at his sigh of relief. It might not be the most important piece of information, but it was the one that was most likely to relieve his mind. "Dora thinks that she's probably well over the shock of—well, you know—by now."

"I know I do her a disservice by thinking of her as being so frail," he replied, chafing one finger against another nervously, "But that's how she *looks*. And she's my mother—"

"You can't help being protective of your mother, I know. I feel the same way about my mother." By this, she meant not her real mother, who presumably had been an Elvenlord's concubine, but her foster-mother, who was a dragon and not much in need of anyone's protection. But Lorryn refrained from saying this.

"Is there any change in the situation there?" he asked, and Shana shook her head.

"Stalemate. The Old Lords can't break in and the Young

Lords can't break out. Occasional skirmishes and feints, but nothing worth talking about. Lady Moth's no closer to getting the Young Lords to see that humans are—well—*people.* And until she does, they're going to be ignoring the one resource they have that might tip the scales in their favor." Shana sounded curiously indifferent to the situation, more as if it was a chess game that she was observing rather than playing in. Lorryn wondered how she could detach herself from it so easily. *He* couldn't.

"Now, on the other side—there's something just come up that Keman thinks is going to give the Old Lords the advantage, and a major one at that." She tossed her head, and her "tail" switched like an impatient horse's. "They've got a new commander, and from what Keman says, he's absolutely brilliant."

There was no indifference in her voice now, and he sat up a bit straighter. "A new commander? Who? I thought that there wasn't an Old Lord in the lot that could coordinate a proper attack!"

"Keman says his name is Kyrtian. Kyrtian V'dyll Lord Prastaran." She turned her head to look keenly into his emerald eyes with her own, the mark of their Elvenlord blood along with the pointed ears and Elven magics. "Heard of him?"

"Vaguely." And that, in and of itself, was interesting. It suggested that for some reason the High Council had elevated a nobody into a position of major importance, with *no* steps in between. "I think his father was supposed to be a scholar—I know there was something when I was a child about Lord Prastaran who vanished off in the Waste Lands between here and the site of the Gate that brought us from Evelon." He waved vaguely in a southerly direction. "He keeps—kept—to himself, and his son did the same. Until now. And why, one wonders?"

"Apparently, because he's brilliant. And according to Keman, because he's got a way of training slaves to be soldiers without the untidy process of having half of them cut to ribbons in order that the rest get experience in fighting." She drummed her fingers silently on the side of her leg. "And you realize, of course, that this is not good news for us."

"No." That was clear enough; if this Kyrtian was as brilliant as Shana said, he wasn't bound by tradition—he would use what worked. Being encased in tradition like a chrysalis never meant to be opened was the only thing that kept the Old Lords from hammering their less-experienced offspring.

"A good commander with the resources of the Old Lords behind him can take the defenses of the Young Lords to pieces," she continued, turning her gaze in the direction of Elven-held lands.

"When he does that, he'll have proved himself to his masters," Lorryn agreed. "And it won't take them any time at all to break the treaty and send him after us." He felt his stomach turn over uneasily. "I don't suppose you have any good news for me, do you?" he asked plaintively.

She shook off her own somber mood. "I know what you're thinking, and you're right; until we know something about this Kyrtian, there is no point in imagining all the things he might—or might not—do. Besides, Mero and Rena are doing very well for us, and the Iron People seem to like them a great deal."

"The Iron People helped us hold off the Elvenlords the last time without actually getting involved—" Lorryn mused, feeling a bit less hag-ridden at the thought of another conflict with the Elvenlords. "If they joined us this time—between them and the dragons—"

"It might be the Elvenlords doing the retreating," Shana finished for him. "One of Dora's lair is helping them to find grazing and ore—and lately there have been small groups of 'wild' humans turning up who speak some dialect that the Iron People understand."

"Do you suppose they could be what is left of the Corn People?" Lorryn asked, *his* curiosity now piqued.

Shana shrugged. "They could just be Traders—we knew already that the Iron People have had some contact with Traders. Keman says they are slowly bringing in their families and dependents to join the encampment, and some of them have been saying it's safer than hiding in the wilderness. They *do* know farming, though—"

"Grazing—and farmers to help with crops." Lorryn pulled a grass stem to chew on it. "That would suit the Iron People down to the bone. They'd prefer to make a settlement, if they can. It's hard to run proper forges unless you're settled. Did you tell Mero about this new Elven commander?"

She nodded. "I told him to pass the information on, as he sees fit. There's been a complication; we *really* need to find a reliable source of iron. Mero and Rena can't do anything about finding some, and if we're going to keep the Iron People as allies, we have to get a dragon to find us a mine."

"That reminds me—we've got an iron-related problem of our own." Lorryn wished profoundly that Caellach Gwain wasn't at the heart of so many of his problems. "There is another problem among the wizards so far as Caellach Gwain and his cronies are concerned."

"The magic-twisting." Shana made a face. "Well, we've known about that for as long as we've had any amount of iron around us; you just increase your focus to get around the way the magic warps. Or you *use* the warp—I've seen Orien actually lob a levin-bolt around a corner! What's the problem?"

"Younger wizards can learn how to deal with it, because they're used to using semi-precious stones as focuses. Caellach just doesn't want the iron around, at all. So far as he's concerned, it's one more Change in the Way Things Were, and that's what he wants to go back to." Lorryn sighed, and felt his headache coming back. Why was it that so many of the problems seemed to begin and end in Caellach Gwain?

"He's just lazy," Shana snorted.

"Well—I agree, he is, but not *all* of the older wizards are, and they're having the same problems adjusting. And *they* aren't complaining, they're just suffering quietly."

"Suffering?" Shana raised a skeptical eyebrow.

"Well, not *suffering* then, but it's hard for the old ones. They *aren't* as fit, they *aren't* as healthy, and it's harder for them to learn new things. None of it's out of stubbornness." He felt very sorry for them—he'd seen some of them struggling to use a focus-stone to do things that pre-adolescents were accomplishing without a thought. He'd watched them suffer with aching joints and coughs and colds from living in caverns rather than the comfortable rooms of the old Citadel. Most importantly, he'd seen them disheartened and frustrated, thinking that after all of their years in hiding, they were now considered to be little better than useless.

"I know." It was her turn to sigh. "It's not fair, is it? If it wasn't for them, *I* wouldn't be here. But I don't know what to do about it. We can't stop things from changing—"

"No, but—let me think about this one." He offered her a shy smile. "You've said it yourself; you're the one that's good with plans and strategy, I'm the one that's good with people. Maybe we can find a way to turn all this to our advantage."

"How?" That skeptical look again—but this time he had just the glimmering of an idea, and he met her gaze firmly.

"I don't know—but there's always possibilities, as long as you keep your eyes open for them." And on that positive note, he got to his feet and offered her his hand. "Let's go take a walk and blow the cobwebs out of our brains before we go back to work."

"Cobwebs do get in the way of clear sight," she agreed, to his great pleasure. "And I could use a walk—with you."

And those last two words increased his pleasure tenfold.

15

Rena had been working hard most of yesterday, changing grasses and leaves with her elven magic into sweet treats with which the Iron People could lure in the young bulls for their first lessons in being accustomed to saddles and being ridden. Horses could be broken to saddle—it was not the best way to teach them, but it was successful—but bulls, never. Their stubborn natures and the great courage bred into their line made it impossible to break their spirit, so the only way to train them for their duties as war-bulls was to begin by tempting them, gently, into captivity, and rewarding them for every sign of cooperation with the one thing they always responded to—

food. More specifically, a treat, a taste they couldn't find on their own. Like people, cattle had a sweet tooth, and now that Rena was acting as an envoy to these people, she was determined to do everything that she could to bring the weight of debt over to the wizards' side of the scales. If that meant that she spent half a day changing grass into the goodies with which the bull-trainers could reward their animals, so be it.

The magic that elven ladies were traditionally trained in was a gentle art of transformation, which they usually used to tailor garments seamlessly to fit like silken skins, to sculpt flowers into gossamer and fantastic shapes, or to make other cosmetic changes. Rena had learned to use it to turn the relatively inedible into edible and tasty—and, at need, to stop a beating heart. It had lately occurred to her that she could also use it to start a heart that had stopped, or perhaps to cure disease or mend a wound, but she had not yet had the opportunity (or the courage) to try.

The normal noise of the camp woke her just after dawn; the sounds of voices and cooking, the far-off lowing of the cattle herds. She lived with the Iron Priest, Diric, and his wife Kala. The great friend of the Elvenbane Lashana, halfblooded Mero, who was openly courting Rena, also lived with them, but Kala watched over both of them with as stern an eye to propriety as if Rena was their own child. Diric and Kala had given them separate sleeping-chambers on opposite sides of the family tent. Rena found that reassuring; raised as a sheltered elven maiden, isolated, for the most part, from all males but her brother and father, she enjoyed Mero's attentions but she was also uncomfortably shy about being courted. Not that she wanted him to stop! By no means. But she was not yet prepared to go any further than a hesitant kiss or two.

Still, waking up in the cool of the dawn, with the bustle of the camp around her and a breath of breeze carrying the scents of grass and the smoke from dung-fires wafting under the skirts of the tent, she felt just a little lonely in her solitary bed.

Lorryn isn't so shy—but then, Lorryn isn't a girl. She sighed. *I wish I was like Shana. Shana is always so strong, so brave, and she never worries about what people will think.* She wondered if Shana and Lorryn shared a bed; she wondered, in the freedom of thought that being only half-awake lent to her, just what went on when one *did* share a bed. Mero's careful kisses and caresses sent strange sensations through her; pleasant, oh my yes, but strange. Surely it wasn't—well—like the cattle, or the birds of her garden. . . .

Her thoughts drifted; she listened to the cheerful voices of women preparing the morning meal outside. She liked the sound of their voices; they were deeper than those of the women she was used to, even the human slaves. Lovely! Instead of that annoying bird-like twitter, this was a melodious murmur.

Then, of course, the mood was broken as a child did something wrong, its mother raised her voice in a scold, and another child began to cry in sympathy. Rena woke entirely at that, and laughed at herself and her notions; how typical of an elven girl to try and cast a specious glamorie over something rich and satisfying in and of itself, if less than perfect and not at all tranquil.

She stretched, yawned, and wriggled out of her blankets, giving herself a quick wash in the leather bucket of water that stood just inside the flap that connected her portion of the tent with that of Diric's wife. The Iron People wore loose and comfortable clothing perfectly suited to their nomadic way of life. Kala had fitted Rena out with the outgrown clothing of her eldest daughter—well suited to the slim build of an elven female. Women of these people either wore a similar outfit to the men—loose trousers with a drawstring waist and a sleeveless, V-necked shirt—or long, embroidered gowns fitted to the waist with a pair of ties in the back. In either case, the colors were earthy and bold. Rena could not imagine anything less like the gowns she had once worn in the bower, with their trailing hems and sleeves, tightly-laced waists, and pastel colors, all in the most delicate silks and satins.

Today she slipped into one of the dresses, a warm brown linen that would have made her look like a bleached-out little wax doll if she still looked like the pallid, timid girl who had escaped from her father's manor. But although she still had the pale silver-gilt hair of that girl, her skin was a warm ivory, sun-kissed and glowing with health, and there was nothing that was bleached about her anymore.

She sighed, though, as she pulled the dress on over her head and tied the straps behind her back. Her first duty, today as ever, was to see if she could do anything with the captive Elvenlord, Haldor.

As if there was anything lord-like about him now!

Neither Haldor, nor his fellow-captive Kelyan, were entirely sane anymore, but Haldor was worse. When she and Mero had come back to the camp of the Iron People, one of the first things that Diric had requested of her was to see if anything could be done about the two captives, who had been taken by the great-grandsires of the current Iron People and pressed into service as entertainers, using their magic to create illusions. They clearly couldn't release either of the Elves, for even if they weren't mentally competent anymore, they still knew too much—and they couldn't give them over to the Wizards either, at least not in Rena's opinion. In the time they'd been gone, Haldor had lapsed into a stupor or torpor and could scarcely be roused enough to eat. It had fallen upon his fellow captive Kelyan to take care of him, but at least they were no longer forced to entertain the Iron People, and thanks to Rena's transformative magics their diet was something other than curds, milk, and meat.

She hated going near them, to tell the truth. She wasn't afraid of them, but there wasn't anything she could really do for them either. She had the rather sick feeling that they were both too far gone to help. If only there was some way to wipe their minds clean of everything that had happened to them since they'd been captured! Then they could be put to sleep and set down by a dragon somewhere—perhaps where one of the Elvenlords' trading-caravans crossed—

She paused, one hand on the tent-flap. *That's no bad idea,* she thought, struck by the notion. *And maybe Mero is the one who could do just that!* Mero, like all the halfbloods, had both the magics of his human mother, and those of his Elven father. The human magics included the ability to understand the thoughts of others—could Mero change them as well?

She lifted the partition-flap, intending to ask him as soon as she saw him, but to her disappointment, he was nowhere to be found. Neither was Diric, for that matter; only Kala was in the part of the tent that served as a common area for eating and social functions. The Iron Priest's ample wife was bent over her breakfast-preparations, and looked up at Rena's entrance, her teeth shining in a startlingly white smile against her dark brown skin.

The Iron People were unlike any humans that Rena had ever seen; their skins were a black-bronze (nearer to black than to bronze) and their ebony hair curled more tightly than sheep's fleece. Nomads, though not by nature, they descended from a long line of cattle-, goat-, and grel-breeders whose religion and lives centered around their forges. In the long-ago when the Elvenlords first came to this world, they had a close alliance with another human race of farmers, now vanished, called the Corn People. The Iron People provided the "meaty" side of the dietary equation, the Corn People the grains and vegetables. The Iron People worked in leather and metal, the Corn People in pottery and fabric. Then the Elvenlords had descended, and drove the more-mobile Iron People into the south, presumably adding the Corn People to their long list of slave-nations.

"There is another group of Corn People come," Kala said cheerfully. "Diric and Mero have gone to speak with them. I expect them back before too long; they went off without any food, and I have never yet seen a man who can do without his morning meal without becoming cross."

Rena laughed, and went outside to their little fire to help Kala with her meal-preparations.

Ever since the Iron People had arrived in what now appeared to be their ancient pasturage, this plain below the mountains where the Wizards and Traderkin lived, small groups of people with flax-colored hair had been drifting into their camp, claiming the right of ancient alliance. They resembled the descriptions that Lorryn had read in the old histories, and they certainly spoke a language similar to that of the Iron People, so there was every reason to think that they *were* the remnants of the Corn People.

Certainly Diric's folk believed it and welcomed them as long-lost kin. Mero was perfectly pleased to see them coming to the Iron Folk; if the old alliance could be re-established, with the Corn People farming part of the plains for grain, the fiber-crops of hemp and flax, and vegetables as they once had, the Iron People would have one more reason to settle. There was plenty of good grazing here; all they needed to be perfectly happy was a steady supply of iron ore.

If we can induce them to settle—if we could just work out a way to find them enough iron! she thought, helping Kala by spreading the thin batter for morning cakes on the hot stone that served her as an oven. All of the families had such a stone, flat and black, polished smooth, which served as a cooking surface or to keep foods or liquids warm, and they were cherished as the important objects they were. The thin, tough pancakes that they used for bread were cooked on these stones, eggs could be fried atop them, pots of tea or soup kept warm on them. They were buried in coals to heat them for cooking, the coals and ashes brushed to one side when the surface was needed.

Rena spread the batter atop the stone with circular motions of a horn spoon; Kala performed the trickier task of judging when the thin cakes were done enough to peel off and flip, and she did it with fingers toughened by many years of working at her own jewelry-forge. Rena wouldn't have dared to try; she'd have come up with blisters on the tips of every finger.

The finished cakes, paper-thin and tasty, were tossed into a basket to wait. Breakfast was always cakes, milk, a little cheese or meat, and whatever fruit could be found. There were brambles out here, and the berries were just coming ripe. Rena herself had gathered some yesterday, after cheating a bit by softening the thorns with her magic so that they wouldn't stick her while she gathered the fruit.

Just as they finished the last of the batter, they heard the voices of the two men: Diric's a low, cheerful rumble like the wheels of a heavy cart on a bumpy road, Mero's a clear tenor.

"—I haven't any idea where this 'Lord Kyrtian' came from," Mero was saying as they came around the side of the round tent. "There certainly wasn't any Elvenlord commander by that name when I had any regular contact with the Elvenlords."

By that, Rena realized that Mero had been catching the Iron Priest up on what he'd been told last night when Shana had finally been able to reach him with her thoughts.

"But this can mean very little to us," Diric objected, then paused to bend and give his wife a morning-kiss by way of a greeting. He was a tall, round-faced human, heavily muscled—not surprising, given that he was the chief Priest of a religion that centered around the forge. Rena was no good at judging the ages of humans, but Mero said he guessed that both Diric and Kala were probably in their fifties. "Kala, my rock-dove, the young one tells me that the Demons have a new War-Captain in their battle with their own rebellious youth. This one seems to have rather more sense than the last, and is making progress in his campaign to bring them to heel. Mero is concerned that this could mean trouble for us."

"This can have very little to do with us," Kala agreed complacently. "Except, perhaps, good. Let them concentrate on each other and forget that we are here."

"But that's just what won't happen if this Kyrtian is successful, don't you see?" Mero objected, as Rena nodded vigorously.

But the gray-haired Iron Priest only shook his head. "Time enough to be concerned *if* it happens," he responded with a shrug. "My people will be more fretful that their forges are dark than that some war among Demons has *possibly* taken another turn."

Mero bit his lip and looked to Rena for help, but she couldn't offer him any. Diric was right; the Iron People hadn't had to engage the Elvenlords in combat for generations, and legends were unlikely to arouse any anxiety in their hearts at this point. But the lack of iron for their forges *was* a problem, and a current, even urgent one.

It was a concern for the Wizards, as well—the Young Lords' Rebellion had been grounded on the foundation of the iron jewelry that the Iron People had made and the Wizards had distributed. Wearing this jewelry, the rebels—not just younger sons, but the abused and reviled Lesser Lords with very little magic, who often were treated as badly as any human slave—were protected from the Great Lords' magic. For the first time, they were able to act without fear of levin-bolt and paralyzing pain, and act they had.

But that had used up the scant store of raw iron, and the Iron People were grumbling about the lack of material to work with and wondering if their sacrifice to help save the Wizards by giving the Great Lords a new threat to worry about had been worth it. So far, the only bits of iron that the dragons had been able to find had been coaxed out of the ground and dropped as raw lumps between the territory claimed by the Wizards and the strongholds of the Elves. They formed a barrier of protection, difficult to find and disruptive far out of proportion to their small size, and the Wizards were very reluctant to remove them, however badly the Iron People wanted them.

The plain fact was that the Iron People were not going to make any more of their jewelry for the Wizards unless and until the Wizards came up with more iron. And the supply of jewelry to sneak in among the rebels had long ago run out. How much more disruption could be accomplished if simple iron torques could be sent in among the human slaves? Those iron bands could negate the magic that controlled the slaves through their collars—with them, escapes could be successful, and even the takeover of an entire estate. Without them—nothing would change. If this Lord Kyrtian managed to conquer the Young Lords by power of arms alone, the Wizards would desperately need another diversion to keep the Elvenlords occupied, and the human slaves could only look forward to more abuse, more repression.

Diric ate his breakfast with a placid face, oblivious to the concerns of his guests. "The Trader-people are to come, also, at last," he offered, between bites. "One of the new Corn People told me that they were following no more than a few days behind, with burdens of trade-goods. I am eager to see them, and I think the rest will be also."

Rena smiled, despite her concerns. "I have no doubt," she replied, thinking of the excitement that each new boatload of Traders caused among the Wizards.

"They are good people," Mero offered. "You won't be sorry that you decided to open full trade with them."

"So you said in council, though there are still those of my folk who think we should simply take them as slaves and have them *and* their goods." The gleam in Diric's eye reminded Rena that the Iron People were quite used to thc idca of having other humans as slaves. There weren't many slaves among the tents, mostly Iron People who had been sold by their parents or who had sold themselves to repay debts, but they did exist. Mero had been rather taken aback when he discovered their existence.

"And *I* pointed out then, as I will repeat, that it will be far more profitable to trade honorably. If you take them and their goods," Mero reminded the Iron Priest shrewdly, "you will only have a few slaves and the goods they carried. No more will come to you. But if you trade—more will pour into your camp, and you will likely be able to barter what is common to you for what is worth a great deal to you."

"Eh, now, did I say that I did not feel the same way?" Diric asked, ingenuously, pretending that he had never even entertained the notion, although both Rena and Mero knew how hard they had argued to sway him to their way of thinking. This would be one more hold on the Iron People, one more reason for them to stay here instead of looking for another spot to settle. Right now, with a growing number of voices calling for another move to some place that might have more to offer than just water and grazing, the Traders could provide what Mero and Rena needed until somehow, somewhere, they could come up with a source for the all-important iron.

The Traders arrived riding on—of all improbable things—pack-grels. These incredibly ugly animals, long-legged, long-necked, with bulging eyes and blubbery lips, served the trading-caravans into the desert commanded by the Elvenlords, but Mero had hardly expected that the Trader-clans would have any. Up until this point, he had thought that they traveled exclusively afoot or on water.

The Iron People were just as surprised, and even more excited to see a half-dozen of the creatures they themselves had once depended on. In the oldest chronicles, the Iron People had even been referred to as the "grel-riders." It was only when they had been driven south that they had lost the grels, which had not survived the arduous journey and the new pests that the cattle had shrugged off.

The grels were less enthused to see these new dark-skinned humans—*they* had no long tradition of association, and they shied and bellowed at the unfamiliar dark faces, much to the Iron People's disappointment.

"I'm sorry, but they aren't very bright, and they think anything they don't recognize is going to eat them," the grel-handler kept saying, over and over, stumbling a little over the unfamiliar syllables of the Iron Peoples' tongue. Eventually, when the beasts refused to cooperate, the curious got over their disappointment and settled down to serious trading.

Each side laid out the goods that they had brought. The Iron People offered hides, dried meat, baskets, ornamental beadwork, skilled leather work, horn bows, and weaving. They had linen—flax grew abundantly on the plains, and outriders made sure that the cattle didn't devour it before the women had a chance to gather it. They did not have sheep, although they did have goats and were skilled at spinning and weaving goat-hair. The Traders had raw wool, glass, stone, and pottery objects, flour and salt, some very specific wood products—like longbows of yew, which the warriors were very impressed with—and arrowheads, which were always in short supply. They also had some copper trinkets, copper pots, and a few ingots of copper. But most of all, of course, the Iron People really wanted iron more than anything else, and at the initial trading session it was clear to Rena that they were disappointed not to see any.

Still, they covered their disappointment well, and trading on the first day proceeded briskly. At the end of the day, Halkan, the spokesman and leader of this particular group, invited the important members of the tribe to dinner in his tent, and included Mero and Rena in on the invitation more out of politeness than anything else. The Trader clans had a set of firm agreements with the Wizards, and it wasn't as if he could have expected anything new out of two envoys to these odd, ebony-skinned folk.

Mero had never seen an actual camp of the Trader clans before, and looked around with lively interest as they accompanied Diric and Kala to the modest feast. The Iron People lived in round tents constructed of hides and felt; the Traders had square and rectangular pavilions of sturdy heavily-waxed cloth. Beneath the wax, random patterns of blotches of green and brown had been painted on the canvas, and he thought that it would be difficult to spot such tents in the middle of a forest. Out here, of course, they looked a bit odd.

All around the outskirts of the camp were wicker cages on poles; they weren't torches or lamps, and Mero couldn't even guess what function they were supposed to serve. As they all took their places beneath an ornamental pavilion to enjoy their hosts' hospitality, he found that the Traders had elected to place their guests on flat cushions around a central serving area, with Traders alternating with their guests. That put one of the Traders (a nervous, thin fellow) between him and Rena, which was a little annoying. He was worried that she might be uncomfortable with the seating arrangements, but he hadn't reckoned with her early training—*if* she was uncomfortable between two strangers, she didn't show it.

Mero mostly stuck to small-talk with his two neighbors, allowing Diric and his fellow chiefs to monopolize the conversation. But just as they were served a dessert of honey-drenched fruits (from the Traders' stores) and beaten cream (supplied by the Iron People), something reminded him of those curious wicker cages and he asked about them.

Out of courtesy, so that the Iron People could understand everything that was said around the circle, they both spoke in the Iron Peoples' tongue. "Ah! Those are to protect us from the Demons and their magic," said the young Trader whose name Mero hadn't caught. "We put fool's gold in them, and it works as the iron jewelry does."

Heads snapped in their direction from all around the circle the moment that the word "iron" was spoken. "What is this?" Diric demanded.

The Clan-chief explained, and tried to describe the contents of the ward-baskets in such a way that the Iron People would understand, but Diric was baffled. "Wait—" he said, finally, and sent one of the younger Traders to fetch one of the baskets.

In front of Diric's interested gaze, he opened the top of the basket and poured out about three fistfulls worth of glittering, gold-colored stones with rough surfaces. "Fool's gold," the Trader-chief said dismissively. "Fools think it is real gold; it is good only for keeping the—"

He stopped, his face a study in bewilderment, as Diric uttered a cry of triumph and scooped up two handfuls of the stones, brandishing them over his head.

"Tell him!" the red-haired Trader-chief said, whirling and addressing Mero frantically. "Tell him it is not gold! Tell him that it is worthless!"

But what Diric and the others were shouting was *not* gold—nor would they have been half so excited over a basketful of true gold nuggets.

"Iron!" Diric bellowed with joy, *"Iron!"*

And he and the others ran out of the camp, leaving Mero and Rena to try to explain.

"We call these things 'iron pyrites,' and there are things we can do with them that we cannot with other iron," Kala said to Rena, as she bent, gloating, over her precious pile of rocks. Once the Traders realized how much their "fool's gold" was valued by the Iron People, it didn't take long for them to trade away all they had, trusting to their own skills and a promised escort of bull-riders to make it back to the cover of forested lands safely. They didn't have much, but at least they knew where there was more, and the Iron People were no longer threatening to take their herds and the Corn People and go elsewhere.

"It is the women who will most value these," Kala continued. "The men would only wish to melt them down. There are better things to be done with these stones."

Rena watched in fascination as Kala made good her words, her plump, stubby fingers moving with great skill and surprising delicacy, as she cut and faceted tiny "gemstones" from the iron pyrites, little things that glittered like black diamonds. It took unbelievable patience.

"What are you going to do with these?" Rena asked, stirring a finished one in the palm of her hand with one finger.

"Oh, I shall melt down the waste and cast it into a setting for it," Kala responded absently. "It will be a different style than you have seen heretofore, but I think you will like it. We have agreed to exchange it for the raw pyrites, so that the Traders need no longer waste these precious things in baskets on poles in order to protect themselves. One weight of jewelry to ten weights of pyrites."

There was no doubt in Rena's mind that Kala thought she was getting the better part of the bargain. Rena continued to watch her for a while, but Kala became so involved in her work that it seemed an intrusion to stay, and she got up and went to look for Mero.

"We have a problem," she said to him, worriedly, as soon as she caught sight of him hurrying towards her through the tents.

"I know; Diric told me the trade-agreement," he replied, just as worried. "I mean, it's a good thing that they've got *some* iron, but this cuts us right out of everything. They can get most of what they need from either the Corn People or the Traders—"

"—so what use are the Wizards to them?" Rena concluded for him. "If the Elvenlords *do* manage to defeat the Young Lords and come after us, why should the Iron People bother to help now? There's nothing in the alliance for them!"

Mero nodded. "They're nothing if not practical." He set his chin. "Right. First of all, we need to get in touch with Shana and let her know what's happened. Maybe she'll have some ideas."

"And next?" Rena asked, hopefully. Mero was resourceful—surely he could think of something they could do!

"I can't think of a 'next,' " he replied, dashing her hopes. "I only wish I could. . . ."

16

Kyrtian sat wearily on his horse beneath the broiling sun, and waited for his scout to come report to him. Ahead of him—somewhere—were the retreating forces of the Young Lords. They were far enough ahead of his troops that there wasn't even the tell-tale sign of a dust-cloud on the horizon.

It was uncanny, it was indeed. The moment, the very *moment* that the Council agreed—reluctantly—to put him in charge of their forces, someone must have alerted the rebels. And that same someone must have told them that in Lord Kyrtian they were going to face a trained commander and trained troops. Because he never even got a chance to face an army in the field, only a few skirmishers meant to delay him while the army itself retreated.

That was what his scouts were out looking for now—skirmishers, traps, false trails. And, just *possibly,* signs that the Young Lords had chosen a place to make a stand. But he didn't really expect that, not for some time yet. They were too far from areas they held secure, nor was the ground particularly good for turning at bay.

Meanwhile—

The scout—one of his own people—came running up; the man stopped at his stirrup and saluted.

"Report," Kyrtian commanded.

"My lord—all's clear, and the others have marked out a secure campsite," the man said crisply. "No sign of the enemy, other than the marks of retreat."

"Very good." Kyrtian saluted in dismissal, and the scout trotted off to return to his own group. He looked over at Gel, who was also mounted, and waiting just beside him.

"Well?" he asked.

Gel barked a laugh. "It's making your reputation easily enough," he said. "But I wouldn't count on it to last."

"I'm not." He sighed. "Let's get them moving. If we camp early enough, I can drill them some more."

"Good plan." Gel wheeled his horse away and headed towards the main body of the army, paused for a rest, to relay Kyrtian's orders. Kyrtian stared at the horizon—and wondered when the inevitable blow was going to fall.

Rennati sighed, brushed her hair back over her shoulders, and bent to look out of the window in her sleeping-alcove, craning her neck to see as much of the view below her as possible. Since Lord Kyrtian had left—and she did not know *why*, only that their servants said that he had gone—there had been nothing to report to Lady Triana, and nothing whatsoever had happened here in the harem. No more visitors had come, and nothing had been told to the concubines. Rennati had assiduously practiced her dancing, but one couldn't fill every hour of the day with dancing. It had been her one passion, but now she had all the leisure she could ever have dreamed of to practice and perfect her art, and she realized that without an audience to appreciate what she did, simply practicing and perfecting no longer was enough for her.

The other two concubines were happily occupied with the contents of several chests that Lady Lydiell had thoughtfully sent up. Somehow she had known that the last batch of dressmaking materials was exhausted, and she had supplied a true horde of precious things—swaths of silks, satins, and velvets, yards of trim, buckets of glittering glass, shell and stone beads, gold and silver and silken embroidery threads, and everything the heart could desire for the making of dresses and ornaments. A thoughtful gift that had rather surprised Rennati, actually; nothing in her life would have led her to expect any such attentions from the chatelaine and mother of a young lord. And if Rennati had been just a little more like the other two slaves of Lord Kyrtian's harem, she would have been right down there beside Gianna and Kara, planning dresses, sewing, and making delicate little amulet-necklaces with the wealth of beads.

She *had* done some of that, but like her dancing, there was only so much puttering with trinkets that she could do before she lost interest. Concubines were supposed to be obsessed with clothing and self-ornamentation; Rennati *liked* clothing well enough, and she enjoyed looking pretty, but she had always felt frustrated and confined by life in the harem, though she had taken very great care never to show it. The alternative to the harem was the life of a field- or house-slave, and *they* were not treated nearly as well as the concubines.

The view from her window, though restricted, was more interesting than anything inside the harem. At least there was something going on out there, something different from the interior of the harem tower. Weather changed, slaves walked past, birds flew by. And she was, frankly, putting off reporting to Lady Triana. The Lady had been increasingly impatient with Rennati's lack of information and, the last time, had threatened to revoke her bargain unless Rennati had more to report the next time she called.

At last, with a grimace, she decided that she couldn't put it off any longer. She picked up the little box of personal jewelry, and dug the teleson-ring out from its hiding-place among her tiny treasures. Carefully she put it on, spoke the few words that activated it, and stared into the dark green murk of the beryl, waiting for a voice to call to her thinly across the vast distance between this manor and Lady Triana's.

"Well. So this is where the disturbance has been coming from."

Rennati started, and looked up, for the voice did not come from the ring, nor was it Lady Triana's.

Lady Lydiell stood in the doorway, and in her shock, Rennati could only stare at her dumbly. Elven ladies *never* entered the harem, much less came into the concubines' private quarters! She had feared discovery by Gianna or Kara, or perhaps even Lord Kyrtian himself, but never, ever by his mother!

The lady was not dressed in the same fashion that she had

been when Rennati first met with her; in fact, she looked very little like the sheltered Lady of the manor that Rennati knew her to be. With her long, silver hair bound into a severe knot at the nape of her neck, no cosmetics on her face, and no jewels—wearing a soft brown divided skirt and matching long-sleeved tunic—only her air of authority betrayed her rank.

Her eyes were quiet, unreadable pools of murky green, exactly like the beryl in Rennati's ring; her face as expressionless as a statue.

Lady Lydiell calmly took the few steps needed to cross the distance between the doorway and Rennati, and held out her hand.

"Whomever you have been reporting to won't answer you, child," the Lady said, with no sign of anger or any other emotion that Rennati could detect. "I've taken care of that. You might as well give that teleson-ring to me."

Numbly, Rennati took the ring off and handed it to her—then automatically dropped to her knees beside the couch she had been seated on, and bowed her head, clasping her hands behind her back, waiting for the Lady to punish her.

Her vivid imagination painted a dozen pictures for her of what to expect in the next few moments, as her heart beat so rapidly she had trouble breathing, and she shivered with fear. Her mouth dried, her throat closed, and she felt as if she was about to faint. She *would* be punished, of course. She had betrayed her Master—at the behest of another Elvenlord, true, but that was no excuse. No slave could betray her master and be caught, and expect to escape without punishment. At the least, she would be sent out into the fields. At the worst—

"What on *earth* are you doing, child?" Lady Lydiell asked, in an astonished voice, which turned exasperated as Rennati remained where she was. "Oh, for—get *up* little fool! I'm not going to hurt you! And look at me!"

Automatically Rennati leapt obediently to her feet, turning her astonished eyes to the Lady's face as her heart skipped beats and her chest tightened along with her throat. For a moment, she thought she would faint.

Lady Lydiell frowned, but not in such a way as [illegible] say—Lady

Triana had frowned. This frown was just annoyance, not something that would freeze the blood. It was an impersonal frown—there was no real anger in it. Though Rennati's skin felt cold and clammy, her heart slowed, just a little, and the tension in her chest eased.

"Sit down," Lady Lydiell said shortly, and Rennati obeyed, her eyes fixed on the Lady's face. "And tell me about this ring. Who gave it to you? Why? And what have you been telling him?"

"Her," Rennati corrected automatically, and clapped her hand to her mouth in renewed alarm. But when no slap, sting of the collar, or indeed, any other correction came, she took her courage in both hands, and began her tale.

There was no reason to lie; if Lady Lydiell cared to, she could have it all out of her in a moment, either under the influence of drugs or by application of pain through the collar. And at this point there was no chance that Lady Triana would keep her side of the bargain, which had specified that Rennati remain undetected. So Rennati told everything, from the moment that Lady Triana picked her out of a slave-sale to the last thing that she had reported. As she spoke, Lady Lydiell's frown softened, until when at last Rennati fell silent, the elven lady's expression was no worse than thoughtful and slightly disapproving.

As she spoke, and Lydiell's expression eased, so, too, did the feeling of panic and fear, the awful sick feeling in her stomach. As she finished her last words, Lydiell nodded.

"It could have been worse," she said when Rennati fell silent. "You haven't given that *creature* much that's going to be of any use to her, and forewarned is forearmed as they say." She watched Rennati for a few moments, then appeared to make up her mind about something. "Stand up, child," she said. "I want you to come with me."

The fear returned, redoubled, and her heart raced again, her breath coming quickly as she tried to get air past the terrible tightness of her throat and chest. *Now it comes,* Rennati thought, heart sinking with dread. But, of course, she couldn't disobey. She followed Lady Lydiell down the stairs, past Gianna and Kara—

And out past the barrier at the door that kept unauthorized

slaves from getting into the harem—and the concubines from leaving it. There was a faint tingle on her skin as she passed through the shimmering curtain of magic power, and she shivered. Now she was outside, and away from the scant protection of the presence of the other two. What was Lady Lydiell going to do with her? Hand her over to the gladiators?

"You're intelligent, and I don't think you're a bad child at heart," Lydiell said, as if to herself, then looked over her shoulder at Rennati, who shrank inside herself when those penetrating green eyes met hers. "I'm usually considered a good judge of character, by the way."

"Yes, my lady," Rennati whispered, since it seemed that Lady Lydiell was waiting for an answer as they walked down a marble-faced hallway.

"I'm going to take a chance with you," Lydiell continued, still holding her with that sharp gaze. "I'm going to do something that has never been done with a human from outside our own circle, born and raised among us. I'm going to show you *exactly* what you've jeopardized with your actions."

And for the next several hours, Rennati found herself hauled all over Lord Kyrtian's estate, seeing things that left her gaping, too overwhelmed to speak. This—this place was *nothing* like anywhere *she* had ever been before!

At first, it only seemed as if this was just an ordinary estate, although the Master and Mistress of it were unusually kind to their slaves and treated them extraordinarily well. First, the Lady took her to every nook and cranny of the Great House—not only through the rooms that she and her son and the other Elvenlords of the household used, but into the kitchen, the still-room, the laundry, the sewing and weaving room. Everywhere the Lady was greeted with respect, though not servility; more importantly, she didn't expect or seem to demand servility. In every other household Rennati had been in, slaves were expected never to speak unless directly addressed, never to raise their eyes to the mistress's face unless given permission, and never, ever, to do as these slaves did, and actually approach the mistress with a report or a query. But Rennati quickly began to realize that Lady Lydiell not only was incredibly approachable, she was also greeted with actual affection by her slaves.

Affection? From *slaves?* How was that possible?

"What do you think of our home so far?" Lydiell asked, as they moved outside and headed for a long, low building. This was a question that would have been appropriate if asked of an equal or one only slightly inferior, but *not* of a concubine. Concubines were not supposed to have opinions. They were barely supposed to think.

The question surprised her into honesty, not the least because the slaves in the kitchen had actually called cheerful and welcoming greetings when the Lady had first entered, leaving Rennati dumbfounded. "I don't understand," she said. "They *like* you! How can slaves *like* you?"

She hadn't really expected a reply, unless it came as a reproof. But what Lady Lydiell said in response to the impulsive exclamation shocked her to the core and left her speechless.

"They like me because they are not slaves," Lydiell said. "Neither they, nor their ancestors, were ever slaves; here, in this one manor, no Elvenlord has ever enslaved a human."

What? Rennati felt her heart actually stop for a moment.

"They are in my employ," Lady Lydiell continued. "They are my helpers, and we respect each other. Kyrtian and I protect them from the outside world, as his father did for their ancestors, and his grandfather for *theirs,* and for that protection, they and their families serve us," the Lady said quietly. "We have never had slaves here, and never shall, if we are left alone by the Lady Trianas of the world."

It was such an astonishing statement that it had to be a lie. It was simply not possible that there was a family of the Elvenlords that hadn't enslaved humans!

And yet—how could it be a lie? Why should the Lady make up such an astonishing story? What purpose would it serve? And how could she have gotten all of her slaves to act in such a natural way, unless it was true and not a lie?

As Rennati continued to follow Lady Lydiell out into the fields, to the cottages of the farm-laborers, to the barracks of the fighters, she had been protected by a core of utter disbelief, but the more she saw, the more that core eroded. If the Lady had only shown her the household servants, she would not have trusted what she saw, but here were people who should never have set eyes on the lady, who, if they ever by some chance *had* seen her should never recognize the plainly-dressed Lady for the authority that she was. But time after time, the Lady was met with welcome and greeting, with the kind of common talk that *might* be shared with a trusted human overseer, but never with an Elvenlord, and she herself asked questions about the farming, training, or the slaves themselves and their families *(families? Impossible!)* that showed she was intimately familiar with the minutiae of their lives.

Even so, Rennati clung to her stubborn refusal to believe in this miracle of Elven kindness, right up until the two of them approached a set of small buildings constructed around a garden. Rennati could not imagine what they could be, but to her incredulous ears came the sound of high, shrill voices—the voices of children—

As Lady Lydiell came into view of the garden, the children playing there caught sight of her, and ran toward her, shrieking greetings at the tops of their lungs.

"Lady Lidi! Lady Lidi!" "Come see my puppy!" "Will you make us sweeties?" "Lady Lidi, Jordy found a frog!"

Lady Lydiell only smiled serenely as the horde of small children (some of them very grubby indeed) swarmed all around her, holding up flowers, a frog, a puppy, dolls, and toy bows and arrows for her approval. As Rennati stared, her mouth dropping completely open, the Lady gave each of the children her gravest attention.

Now she knew why there were no breeding pens, no mass nurseries, no other signs that human slaves were bred here with the same care to selection and carelessness as to feelings as were cattle and horses. The cluster of small buildings were—houses. Houses for families. Families who were allowed to keep their children with them. And since there were no breeding pens, this must be the *norm* here, not the exception, as it was on the estate that had bred Rennati.

These children were utterly fearless in the presence of the chatelaine of the manor. They must never have received so much as an unkindness from an Elvenlord.

And look at the Lady herself! She couldn't have been more patient with this horde of exuberant children if she had been their nursemaid or beloved relative!

Rennati let fall the last of her disbelief, and felt the world whirling around her, turned utterly upside down.

"Will you please make us sweeties, Lady Lidi?" asked one of the boys, polite, but bold as a young rooster.

Lady Lydiell laughed. "All right. *One* flower each. Go pick fresh ones." She turned to Rennati, who clutched a beam embedded in the corner of the house beside her, feeling actually dizzy. "Elven women are trained to use their magic in small ways rather than large—you'll find most of them making foolish sculptures out of flowers, but that's a bastardization of what we originally did in Evelon. We healed wounds and sometimes sickness—but most important of all, we made the inedible edible. Lady Moth taught me that little trick, which she learned from her mother. I still use it to make honey-sweets from flowers for the children—ah, here they come!"

There were plenty of flowers in the little gardens that Rennati now noticed around the houses, and it hadn't taken the children long to pick out which flower they wished made into a treat. She noticed that the girls generally chose roses; well, *she* was partial to rose-petal candies herself. Many of them sucked thorn-wounded fingers, but none of them complained. The boys seemed to prefer sunflowers, dahlias, anything large. But one little girl at the rear of the group came up holding a single violet, and looked to Lady Lydiell with eyes filled with disappointment.

"Sahshi, what's the matter?" Lydiell asked, seeing her and her distress at once, and motioning for the others to let her through.

"You said only one," Sahshi whispered imploringly. "But I like vi'lets—"

"Oh dear—children, do *you* think it's fair for Sahshi only to have one tiny violet?" Lydiell applied to the rest of the children—and had they been pen-born and nursery-raised, where it was every child for himself, Rennati knew what the answer would have been. But not here.

"No!" came the clamor, instantly, and without prompting, several of them ran to nearby gardens, bringing back bunches of violets that they pressed into Sahshi's hands until the child couldn't hold any more.

Her face glowing with happiness, Sahshi held up the violets for Lady Lydiell to transmute—and *then* gave Rennati a further surprise (as if she needed one at this point) by sharing out her sweets with the others as they waited in their turn for Lady Lydiell to get to them. This was probably just as well, for had she eaten them all herself she would surely have earned herself a bellyache, but never before had Rennati seen a child of the lowest, field worker class who would not have immediately shoveled a treat into her mouth with both hands and devoured it as fast as she could, stuffing herself until she was sick because it would be ages before she might taste any other good thing.

It was all, in a word, impossible.

When Lydiell had finished with the last flower, the children thanked her and streamed back to their playground, a small square surrounded by rough-hewn logs enclosing an area of soft sand that held stumps and bars to climb on, a board with seats on either end poised on a hewn block of wood that allowed the ends to rise and fall with children balanced on seats there, and other things that the children seemed to enjoy swarming over.

These things all showed signs of a great deal of wear; they hadn't been placed there recently. This was no artificial setting made for her benefit, to sway her opinion.

As if my opinion, the attitude of a mortal, actually means something! But to Lady Lydiell it did, it patently did.

Lydiell turned back to face Rennati with a quizzical smile on her face. "Well?" she said, pointedly.

Rennati felt cold and hot at the same time, and there was a faint buzzing in her ears. "What—is—this—place?" she asked, thickly.

"Ah. That is a very good question." Lady Lydiell took Rennati's arm, as if she was Rennati's oldest friend. "Come back to the manor with me. I think, when you have had something to drink to steady you, you will have a great many more questions, and I will try to answer them."

In the end, Rennati thought she would never come to an end of her questions. Lydiell answered each and every one, with infinite patience as they sat in elegant chairs on either side of a little table on one of the outdoor terraces. Here she was—eating dainties that, in her excitement, she did not truly taste; drinking something that might just as well have been water for all the attention she paid to it; and arranged across from a highborn elven lady on one of the private terraces as if she, too, was Elvenborn. The sun shone down on the gardens below them, although they were shaded by a fine cloth canopy of tapestried linen. A few women worked in the gardens below, the very picture of bucolic contentment—well-clothed in practical leggings and long, loose linen tunics, protected from the sun by broad-brimmed straw hats, and no supervisor in sight.

Slowly she began to really understand just what it was that Lord Kyrtian's family protected here. That was when the enormity of her own treachery dawned on her, hitting her with the force of a blow. If she had still been able to weep, she would have, then; she'd have broken down and howled with the pain of what she had done to these amazing Elvenlords and their human charges. She *wanted* to; her throat closed and she nearly choked on her unshed tears, but weeping had long since been trained out of her, and she could not cry, not even for this. Concubines did not weep; it spoiled their looks, and only annoyed their masters.

But the depth of her despair could not be measured, and she could not simply sit there and bear it invisibly.

She slipped from her seat and sank down to her knees, then prostrated herself on the stone of the terrace, not daring to look at the Lady lest she crack into a thousand pieces.

"Ah," said the lady softly. "*Now* you understand."

It was hard, hard to speak; hard to get words around that lump of guilt and pain in her throat. "Yes." It was all she could manage.

"Now I have questions for you," Lady Lydiell said, in a voice that warned she would insist on answers.

Rennati could not bear to look into the face of the one she had so vilely betrayed, and she remained where she was, prostrated on the stone of the terrace, speaking brokenly to the soft grey slab just below her nose. The lady's questions went on as long as Rennati's had, every detail of her life, of her bargain with Lady Triana, pulled from her gently, but inexorably.

It seemed to go on forever, and when she was done, she felt drained of everything except pain. There was nothing that Lady Lydiell did not know about her now, and surely, surely, the punishment she so richly deserved would be forthcoming.

The lady finally made a sound—a weary sigh. "Get up, child, and sit down so that I can talk to you properly."

Rennati couldn't move—but a moment later, she found herself *being* moved, as Lady Lydiell took her elbows, lifted her to her feet and replaced her in her seat, as effortlessly as if she weighed nothing. Perhaps, for the Lady, she *was* near-weightless; she was clearly a past mistress of Elven magic, and how could Rennati know what was and was not possible in magic?

"Now," the Lady said, her eyes boring into Rennati's as if to stare into her very thoughts. "You understand what you have done to us. Are you prepared to make amends?"

By now Rennati had exhausted all emotions but one—hope. And underneath all that heavy, black despair, hope stirred and eased the constriction of her throat enough to let her breathe a little. Numbly, she nodded.

Speaking carefully and exactly, Lady Lydiell outlined what Rennati was to do. And Rennati agreed to it, without ever once making a single objection or asking what would happen to her when the inevitable moment came when she was no longer useful.

It had been a long, very hard day, most of it spent in the saddle, and Kyrtian was already wearied when his mother called him.

So far, the campaign against the Young Lords was turning into something other than the hard-slogging battle he'd been led to believe it would be. In fact, if it wasn't for the evidence of the devastated estates he'd seen, with manors half-burned and fields left to weeds, it would have been something of a farce.

Because the moment he took command of the army—quite *literally* from the moment he took command of the army—the Young Lords' direct opposition melted away. Quite simply, they turned and ran.

Now, as a commander, he had to agree with their tactics. He brought with him his *own* people, who would have strengthened the line as nothing else could have. The next pitched battle would have been a conclusive one. The Young Lords' army was not near any area that could be used as a secure base, and supplies had to be problematic, even with the use of magic. If he had been in their situation, he'd have done the same.

But now he was in pursuit, which meant that when they *did* take a stand, it would come as a surprise to him, and would be on ground of *their* choosing. And very probably he would be facing their rested force with his own weary one.

Kyrtian stared down at the tiny image of his mother in the teleson-screen set into his campaign-desk, with Gel watching over his shoulder making interested noises.

"Triana?" he said, finally. "Aelmarkin I could understand, but why would Triana want an agent in our household?"

Gel snorted, before Lydiell could answer. "That's simple enough. They're working together. Or Aelmarkin thinks they are. From all I've heard, that b—" he coughed. "—ah, *female* is an even nastier piece of work than your cousin, if that's possible. Sneakier, anyway. What do you think about this girl? Can you trust what she says? Can you trust what she'll *do,* now that you—"

Lydiell smiled. "Oh, come now, Gel. This is the Lady you're talking to. *How* many of our people have the human magic? And *how* many do you think were keeping watch on the girl's thoughts while I questioned her *besides* the ones I asked to—just to make sure that the others didn't miss something?"

Gel had the grace to blush. "Shouldn't try and teach my grandam what mushrooms to pick, you mean. Sorry, m'lady. So she's safe?"

"More than safe. I think we should keep her," came the rather surprising reply. "She's very intelligent, she's clever—which is not at all the same thing as being intelligent—and she's got a kind nature. I'd be very happy to see her make her home with our people. She could be very useful to us—we haven't got many people who've been raised in the slave-pens; she gives us a look into that world that is beyond price."

"*Not* as my concubine—" Kyrtian blurted, and flushed when Gel chuckled.

"I rather doubt that by the time she's learned to take her place among our people she'd be willing to be anyone's concubine," Lydiell replied dryly. "And after all, that would be the point, wouldn't it?"

"I take it that your plan is to have her send dearest Triana as much disinformation as you think she'll swallow?" Kyrtian said, hastily changing the subject.

"It seems a pity to waste the opportunity," Lydiell agreed, her eyes twinkling a little, or so Kyrtian thought, although the image was so small it was difficult to tell. "If it seems that the ploy is working, perhaps *you* might want to have her with you. I understand that many officers have a concubine or two with them—"

Before Kyrtian could object, Gel replied. "That's a good idea, when you're sure beyond a shadow of a doubt that we can trust her, Lady," he enthused. "If Triana *is* reporting back to Aelmarkin, we can feed her nonsense leavened with just enough truth to make it seem that the girl is doing more than the b—woman ever expected."

"I wouldn't call Triana a 'bitch,' Gel," Lydiell said mildly. "It's a terrible insult to all female canines, which are, on the whole, rather nice creatures."

Gel nearly choked on his laughter, and Kyrtian felt his face grow hot. What had gotten into his mother lately?

Or was it only that now his mother considered him enough of an adult not to mince words around him?

"In the abstract, it sounds like a good idea to me, provided that bringing her out here doesn't put her in any danger," he temporized. "And I don't mean danger from the fighting; that's turning out to be rather—well—tamer than I thought. For now, anyway. Someone's convinced the Young Lords to run, rather than stand and fight. I can't say I'm unhappy about that—it certainly makes me look like a brilliant commander. But while this girl is within the walls of our estate, she's safe enough from Triana—if she comes out here, and Triana decides that she wants more than a few words over a teleson-ring, it would be no great chore to find some way to kidnap her. Human slaves and Elvenlords are coming and going from my quarters all the time, Gel is the only person I'd trust to keep her safe, and he and I can't have her on the battlefield with us."

And I really don't want a female complicating things around here, he added, but only in thought. He really did *not* want his mother worrying about the danger. There was, of course, a great deal more of that than he was going to tell her about. When the inevitable happened, and the Young Lords turned at bay—

Lydiell pursed her lips in thought. "That hadn't occurred to me," she admitted. "For that matter, it wouldn't take a great deal of effort on Triana's part to send someone to your quarters to intimidate the girl, and we can't have that. Well, let's hold that ploy in reserve for a while, in case Triana starts urging it on her. It may be that concocting a story that I've made her into my private maid while you're gone and she can 'overhear' my conversations with you will be enough."

"I should think," Kyrtian said firmly. "Ancestors! For once, *you* have been the one with all the interesting news! All I can tell you is what I have before; that, and I'm nearer to Lady Moth's estate and I think I can push the lines back far enough to put her in our hands again within the week."

"Assuming she *wants* to be," came the thoughtful reply. "All things considered—do you think you might be able to push just far enough that she can send a message or come to you herself, without cutting her off from the Young Lords?"

Again, Kyrtian was surprised by the question, but he saw immediately why his mother had asked it. "No one is likely to question me as long as I push them back somewhere," he responded. "You think she has worked her way into their confidence, don't you?"

"Yes. And I'm not entirely sure *you* should be working so hard to defeat them." Lady Lydiell frowned slightly. "There is this: while the Great Lords are concentrating on the rebels, they aren't paying any attention to us."

"Or the Wizards," Gel added.

"Or the Wizards," she agreed. "But if you defeat the Young Lords, they are certain to want you to lead an army against the Wizards next."

The very idea made Kyrtian's heart sink, and he felt a little sick for not thinking of that himself. Of course they would! And while he didn't in the least mind bringing the young pups to heel for the old dogs, the very idea of pitting an army of slaves against their fellow humans—

"I'll resign first," he said hurriedly. "I'll find an excuse. Or Gel can break my leg."

"Or your skull," Gel growled, but there was approval in his voice. "We'll worry about that when the time comes. In the meantime—"

"In the meantime, I'll say goodbye, and you can think about what to do about Moth," Lydiell said firmly. "If we talk any longer, someone is bound to try and mirror this sending. Watch your back, my love."

"I will," Kyrtian promised, and the teleson winked out, leaving both him and Gel with far too much to think about—

—and far too little time for thinking.

17

The plight of one young woman could not hold Kyrtian's attention for long. So long as she was no longer a threat, he didn't particularly care what his mother did with her. Truthfully, he couldn't even remember which of the three girls she was; she was Lydiell's problem now, and he would just as soon that things stayed that way. Within a few moments, he had even forgotten her name as his attention turned to the more urgent task of changing his strategy to deal with Moth and the Young Lords in light of this new information.

It was just a good thing that they had already settled at their evening campsite. Outside the tent was the usual cacophony of hundreds of humans setting up campfires and bedrolls, getting fed at the mess-wagons, and being ordered about by their elven officers. The mellow golden light of near-sunset made the western wall of Kyrtian's tent glow; the air was full of dust and the scent of trampled grass and wood smoke. There was food on a tray on his camp-bed, virtually the same sort of food that the human fighters would be eating, but Kyrtian ignored it. Gel would probably nag him into eating it eventually.

"Well, we need to rethink our battle-plan," he said to Gel, spreading his terrain-map out over the blank black glass of the teleson-screen set into the top of his campaign-desk. "The question is, what can we push towards now that will allow us to get close enough to Moth that she can send someone out to us if she wants, without making straight for her estate or look as if we're trying to avoid that estate?"

"Good question." Gel pulled at his chin while he studied the map, frowning. "Damn good question. What about here—" his finger stabbed down at a spot on the map where they had noted a possible slave-camp, one full of former gladiators. "We can let it out that we think this is a training-camp for the Young Lords' soldiers. That ought to be reason enough for anyone."

Taking the army in that direction would allow them to skirt Moth's estate without actually taking it—and would give them a corridor for a strike deeper into Young Lords' territory. Kyrtian nodded, and reached absently for his mug of water, taking a sip to ease a throat tickling with inhaled dust. "Let's make a report to Lord Kyndreth and suggest the change of plan. I want him to argue against me for a little."

"Why?" Gel gave him a quizzical glance, brows knitted.

Kyrtian refolded the map carefully and set it aside. "Because this is going to serve us in more ways than one. He's going to point out that with a very little effort I can rescue Moth. I'm going to counter that Moth is probably safe where she is, that the Young Lords probably haven't even thought about one old woman in a tiny estate, and pushing towards the Young Lords at that point will make them think that Moth is valuable to us. I want him to see that it's possible some of the old retainers held behind the lines that have been ignored until now could be used as hostages. It doesn't seem to have occurred to the Young Lords to do that *yet,* but I want Kyndreth to realize he doesn't want to give them the idea. I *do* want Kyndreth to focus on that and not look for other reasons why I might not want to push at that point."

"That'll give him something more to think about," Gel said, pulling on his chin until Kyrtian wondered if he was going to stretch it out of shape somehow. "Aye, and that'll give him one more thing to warn the others about."

"Which will give the Council something else to think about besides the Wizards. It might even give them a reason to order me to hold back until they can find ways to get the people they want out of harms' way." Kyrtian nodded as Gel's eyes widened. "You see. You know, I never thought I'd be trying to think up ways to get Kyndreth to pull our forces back—but that could be the best strategy at the moment." The back of his neck ached with tension, and he rubbed it, hoping that a headache wasn't coming on. "I never thought this would be so complicated," he said plaintively, to no one at all. "If I had known—"

"If you'd known, you still wouldn't have been able to escape this," Gel pointed out bluntly. "Kyndreth wanted you; what Kyndreth wants, happens."

There was no real answer to that, and Gel knew it. Kyrtian just shook his head, and winced a little at the start of that headache he'd hoped to avoid.

He keyed the teleson with Kyndreth's seal, placing it face-down in the little round depression made for receiving such seals in the upper right-hand corner, and with a touch and a word, activated the spell. As he expected, he contacted, not Kyndreth directly, but one of the Great Lord's many underlings.

The plainly-clad Elvenlord stared up at him with a solemn and expectant expression on his long face. "Would you please consult with Lyon Lord Kyndreth?" Kyrtian asked politely. "Please inform him that I believe we need to change our battle-plans." He explained his new plans carefully and the reasons for them, while the underling took detailed and copious notes, occasionally stopping and asking him politely to repeat or elaborate on something. Kyrtian was impressed; he'd encountered no few of Lord Kyrtian's flunkies who had been utterly bored with him and his campaign since he'd been put in charge of the army, but *this* fellow was not of that ilk.

"I'm to be your liaison with Lord Kyndreth for the foreseeable future, Lord Kyrtian," the underling said solemnly. "Lord Kyndreth has made it very clear that your reports are to be given his first consideration, and I have the authority to break in upon him at any time—including in his sleep, if *you* should deem your report to be sufficiently urgent."

Well, well, well. Kyrtian blinked. "It's not urgent, since we'll still be moving through territory that the Young Lords have abandoned for at least two more days, but I should like to hear his opinion before we break camp and move at dawn tomorrow."

The underling gave a slight bow of his head. "I shall see to it that he reads this report and communicate your request to him within the hour, Lord Kyrtian."

The teleson-screen went blank again, and Gel, who had stayed carefully out of range for the duration of the conversation, chuckled. "It seems that your value has gone up in the world, Kyrtian."

"So it does," Kyrtian replied, and put a thin, flat plate of bespelled bronze over the teleson-screen, fitting it into the slight depression where the glass had been inset there, to prevent it from being inadvertently activated. Should someone—Lord Kyndreth, hopefully—wish to contact him while the plate was in place, the plate itself would glow and emit a pleasant repeating chime to alert him. Kyrtian always "plated" his teleson when he wasn't using it himself; it was possible for outsiders to activate one's screen and spy on what was going on within its range if they had a key to it—like the ones he had to Lord Kyndreth's teleson and his mother's. And keys could be duplicated by even the weakest of mages.

With the plate in place, he turned to Gel. "Interesting, don't you think?" he asked. "Are you thinking what I'm thinking?"

"That Lord Kyndreth's own status is going up because of what you've managed to do out here?" Gel countered. At Kyrtian's nod, he pursed his lips. "If that's the case, he may want you to press ahead to Moth's estate anyway."

"So we have to think of an alternate plan." The more Kyrtian thought about it, the less he wanted to press the Young Lords now holding the estate that Moth's husband had once owned. "We've got to give him a richer victory. Not just the *possibility,* but the real thing."

"Ah, horse turds," Gel said sourly. "You don't ask much, do you? Let me get some scouts out; maybe they can find us a juicy prize."

He stalked out of the tent to round up a few of the scouts who had, in all likelihood, settled in at their campfire and would not be pleased to be sent out again. The scouts were all Elvenlords, of course—the previous commander had not trusted humans to run free and act as scouts, and Kyrtian was not going to risk any of his own people in this situation. None of them had more than the bare minimum of magic; they were Elven only by benefit of birth and blood. In the world of the Great Lords they were useful only as overseers and supervisors of humans and breeders of possible mates for unmarried sons or themselves. They were expendable, and often treated worse than slaves deemed to be more valuable, such as treasured concubines or skilled gladiators.

From the beginning, Kyrtian treated them with respect, and as a consequence, had gradually won their loyalty to the point where they had accepted Gel as Kyrtian's second-in-command, something no Great Lord would ever do. He took pains never to show them that he felt sorry for them, but he did. In the long story of the Elvenlords in this place, next to the history of the enslaved and abused humans, theirs was the saddest.

A chiming from the bronze plate at his elbow broke into his thoughts, and he hastily uncovered the teleson.

The craggily handsome face of Lord Kyndreth himself stared up at him, and Kyrtian made a sketchy salute. "Hrotheran passed on your request, and the reason for it," Kyndreth rumbled. "My first thought was that the young pups wouldn't dare threaten harm to another Elvenlord or lady but—" he chuckled harshly "—my next thought was that they already have."

"Well," Kyrtian replied, "yes. Frankly, we've no way of knowing if the deaths of some of the Lesser Lords on their estates were at the hands of revolting slaves, or of the Young Lords. They wouldn't admit it if they *had* killed one of us, not when they know very well how harsh the penalties will be when we defeat them."

Kyndreth smiled without any humor. "You show a fine grasp of reality for such a young man. I'd expected a little more idealism from you until this last message of yours."

"My lord, I have studied our history since Evelon well enough to realize that honor is only for those who can afford it," Kyrtian replied, without any expression in his voice. "*We* have the all the advantages and can afford to be honorable; they cannot, and the only reason they haven't taken such a step before this is probably because it hasn't occurred to them." He paused and added judiciously, "I am afraid that I have not yet detected much in the way of imagination in their tactics. I should not like to be the one to give them ideas that would not have arisen on their own."

"Well said. Now, I'll handle the Council; you go on as you have." Kyndreth chuckled dryly, this time with just a touch of real amusement. "Given their past performance, it's entirely possible that the puppies will panic and just abandon their stronghold anyway when you've flanked them. Keep me informed."

"Yes, my lord," Kyrtian said, but the Great Lord had already broken his spell and the connection; the teleson-plate reflected only Kyrtian's own face.

It was Moth's own people, and not the Young Lords headquartered on her old estate, who gave her the astonishing news that Kyrtian's forces were inexplicably turning aside without trying to take the Young Lords' stronghold. She'd had the cleverest of her "boys" out shadowing the army, and it was one of these who had come back in the dawn to report that the army was up and away at right angles to their previous line of march. They were not merely clever, four of them had the "human magic," the knack of listening to the thoughts of others. When they were close enough, they were able to hear what the common fighters and even some of the officers knew, and that was invaluable.

The army was now headed, presumably, for the training-camp that the Young Lords had set up to retrain some of the gladiators that they had taken as soldiers.

"They just up and changed march, Little Mother," the swarthy, squat young human told her, as she kept refilling his glass and his plate. The "boys" tended to forget about eating and drinking while they were out there, and came back starved and ready to drink a lake. "It's as if they got different orders last night."

Lady Moth considered this information for a moment, then made up her mind. "Lasen, on a fast horse, how long do you think it would take me to catch up to the army?" she asked. The man stared at her, understanding slowly coming into his brown eyes; his brow wrinkled with concern so that he looked like a worried hound.

He knew her; he knew better than to try and dissuade her. He didn't have to read her thoughts to know what they were—although, if he had cared to, he probably could have, since he was one of the four with wizard-powers.

He won't though; those boys think it's impolite to hear thoughts without permission, if you're a friend. He probably wouldn't even think of doing it unless my life or his was at stake, the dear child. There was nothing in her thoughts she cared to hide from anyone these days—though when she'd been younger . . .

"You could catch them by sundown," he told her, slowly. "But the question is, can you come at Lord Kyrtian through all of his army and come away again back to us?" A fleeting ghost of fear traveled across his face then, and it was that fear she answered before she addressed the spoken question.

"I have no intention of abandoning all of you, my lad," she said fondly, and tapped his shoulder in mock-admonition with the book she was holding. "Never fear that; you and the rest are all the family I have now, and all the family I want. I want to talk to Kyrtian, that's all; I think I can do a lot for all of us if I can just talk to him."

Lasen looked skeptical, and Lady Moth smiled. "Little Mother, this is the Army Commander, not one of your Young Lords."

"He's no older than the Young Lords, my lad, and what's more, if you think *I'm* good to my people, you should see his! I pledge you my word for it."

Lasen nodded slowly. Moth didn't often pledge her word; all her humans knew that when she did, she was beyond certain of what she promised. A little of the concern cleared from his face.

"As for getting in and out—" she chuckled "—no fear there, either. So long as there isn't another Elvenlord I have to outwit, I'll get in and out again."

"I'll have Starfoot saddled and waiting—and it's myself that will come with you, then," Lasen said, in a voice that told her that he would be just as stubborn as she on that point. She inclined her head in tacit agreement, and went off to tell Viridina what she intended, and to change her gown for something more suited to the task at hand.

Lasen waited at the door of the stable, Starfoot and another horse saddled and ready, when she arrived, clad in breeches and somber tunic of brown doeskin. Starfoot was a mare so named, not because she was lovely (for in actual fact she was as ugly as a mud-pie and scrawny as a sapling), but because she was fleet as any shooting-star. She was perfect for such a task; her mud-color would hide her, just as the brown of Moth's clothing would serve the same purpose. Lasen had chosen another mud-colored, swift horse, a gelding that was Starfoot's half-brother, and already wore dust-grey tunic and breeches for the same camouflaging purpose.

And Lasen had one other advantage as her guide and guard; he had the human magic of speaking and hearing in thoughts. No one would get near to them without him knowing, and they could avoid the army's own scouts and sentries easily. *That was the one thing that idiot Elvenlords always forget,* Moth thought sourly, as she mounted Starfoot a little stiffly. *Human magic makes it possible for them to know long before an enemy arrives.*

It was a long, hard ride, even for Moth, who was used to riding the bounds of her own estate every day. They did not stop except to rest the horses and allow them to drink and snatch a mouthful of oats. And it was after sunset when they finally saw the campfires of Kyrtian's army from the top of a hill, like strange, yellow stars sprinkled across the hillside opposite them.

Lasen stared at the encampment. "The password is 'A fine satin sheep,' " he said, after a moment's pause.

"Sheep? Not sheet?" she asked, nonplused.

"Definitely sheep," he replied. "They're using nonsense phrases just to make things a bit more secure."

Moth dismounted; no need to order Lasen to watch the horses and lie concealed while she made her way into the army. He vanished into the darkness behind her; she worked her magic on herself.

She was already as thin and bony as many human men, and her loose tunic concealed what there was of her figure. With her long hair knotted on the top of her head and hidden beneath a cap, she needed only to alter her appearance a trifle to pass as a slave: round her ears, darken her skin, and so long as she kept her head down, simply darkening her eyes would suffice to hide what she was.

And the magic of elven women, after all, was to alter small things. . . .

It hurt; that was the worst of it. Her ears burned as if she had dipped them in boiling water as she rounded the points, and she bit her nether lip until it bled to keep from crying out. Then it was the turn of her eyes—not so difficult, this, to change the color, and not as painful.

Then, following the whispered conversation that Lasen had given her before he vanished, she walked into the army encampment. Thanks to Lasen she had the password she needed to pass the sentries quite as if she was part of the army herself. No one even gave her a second glance.

As she strode stiffly among the campfires, in the flickering light from fire and torch that made it possible to pull off the next part of her ruse, she kept a sharp eye out for something she could use to get up as far as, and even into, Kyrtian's tent. One piece at a time, she managed to pilfer a tray, a plate, and a rough-hewn wooden cup; with a breath of her own magic, they acquired a patina of silver. Water took on the rosy hue of wine, and a couple of chunks of wood became meat, cheese and bread, at least on the surface. A snatched handful of weeds transformed into tasty-looking "garden" greens put the final touches on. This all looked edible (although it wasn't) but by no means more than a scant touch above the ordinary soldiers' rations. She knew her nephew; knew that was what he would eat by choice. She didn't want her excuse for entrance to be snatched away by the officious servant of some lesser Elvenlord just because it looked tasty enough to be appetizing to *his* master!

By this time she was well up to the cluster of tents of the commanders; the larger size of Kyrtian's made it obvious which was his. There were guards on the tent, but her age, size, and burden made her status and errand obvious, and they gave her the merest of cursory once-overs to ensure that she wasn't armed before holding the flap aside and sending her in.

Kyrtian and his human shadow Gel were bent over maps, seemingly oblivious to anything else. She cleared her throat ostentatiously.

Neither of them turned around, or even so much as started. "We know you're there," Gel said crossly—which relieved her somewhat, since she'd been a little alarmed at how easily she had gotten close to her nephew, unchallenged. "Put it down and get out."

"That's a fine way to talk to your Lord's aunt," she replied, loudly enough so they could hear her, but softly enough that her voice shouldn't carry to the guards outside.

They pivoted so fast to look at her, their eyes so wide and shocked, that she chuckled.

"Moth? *Moth?*" Kyrtian squeaked.

"Voice just now starting to break, boy?" Moth replied with a grin, putting down her inedible burden. "Always knew everything about you was slow to grow but your mind, but isn't that a bit much?"

"So, that's the situation, then," Kyrtian finished. The arrival of his aunt on his very doorstep—and disguised as a human slave, no less!—had been something of a shock. A pleasant shock, however. "And I don't mind telling you that I've been scrambling to find some excuse not to rescue you." He and Moth had been talking nonstop for so long that they were both hoarse, and once he got over his surprise, he had never been so glad to see anyone in his life.

"Well," she ruminated. "You can see why I was in no great hurry to *be* rescued. These young rebels are still not the best answer to our troubles, but they're a damn sight better than their fathers."

He reached for a pitcher of something she had conjured up out of water, a handful of blossoms and a bit of magic and poured cups of the stuff for both of them. Whatever it was, it had as good an effect on a hoarse throat as honeyed tea. "I don't know what to do," he admitted. "I *can't* stop commanding the army—it will just mean humans slaughtering humans. At least this way I'm keeping bloodshed to a minimum. But if I defeat the Young Lords, mother thinks the Great Lords will turn the army against the Wizards, and never mind the treaty."

"Your mother's right," Moth said sourly, her mouth twisted up into a scowl. "There was never an agreement reached by any of the Great Lords that wasn't broken as soon as one or the other of them could manage it, and that's a fact you'd better get used to. There's no honor among them; your cousin is just a bit more open about his treachery than most of them are. If he was *good,* he'd have had your estate years ago."

Kyrtian could only shake his head. Since taking command, he had gotten one example after another of the duplicity of his own race, and he was still having a hard time getting used to it. What was the point of all this double-and triple-crossing, anyway? Wasn't the world wide enough for everyone to prosper?

Evidently not, or at least, not so far as the Great Lords were concerned.

Gel's sardonic expression and occasional sarcastic comments had made it very clear that *he* was not anywhere near as innocent as Kyrtian had been. And, all things considered, Lady Lydiell probably wasn't either.

"Look," Gel said, breaking into his thoughts. "We need a plan, and I think I have one, but it depends on Moth's ability to scare the whey out of these pet rebels of hers." He raised an eyebrow at her. "Can you?"

"Depends on what you and this army of yours can do," she temporized. "What's the plan?"

"You can go as yourself to this training-camp. The gladiators will trust your humans, I suspect; fighters tend to trust other fighters. *Whatever* it takes, see if you can get them to listen to you and agree to what you want to do."

She smiled. "It won't take much," she told them both, wearing an expression that told them she was mightily pleased with herself. "I can negate their collars; I've enough bits of iron to do that. We've done some experimenting, and all it takes is a thin sheet of it slipped in behind and around the lock and beryl, and you can pry the collar off without hurting the slave. I always carry a few pieces with me now, just in case."

"Hah!" Gel hit the table with his fist, greatly pleased. "Good! You tell 'em that when we attack, if they scatter instead of fighting, we'll open up our lines at a particular point inside the forest to let 'em through, then swallow them up into the army." Kyrtian immediately saw what Gel had in mind—they had a cadre of fighters that Gel trusted trained up now, who were actually *loyal* to Kyrtian. So even if, say, Lord Kyndreth was watching via magic, all he would see was that the enemy gladiators scattered and nothing more. He also had a good idea what Gel was going to suggest next.

"Then," he took over, "Moth, *you* go to your rebels, and suggest that they break up and get out of the estates; take to the hills with small groups to avoid being captured, and start a guerrilla war."

His aunt absorbed all this for a moment, then a smile broke out on her face. "I see! I scare the youngsters, by telling them what I personally witnessed of the slaughter of their best troops, and convince them that they can't possibly hold out directly. They abandon the estates, or at least the ones that still have older relatives among the Great Lords to claim them—which is half of what their fathers want. *I* can be 'rescued' and serve as their eyes and ears into what their fathers are up to—which gives *you* eyes and ears into what they're doing, so you can arrange things to your liking. You still have a war that you can fight in tiny skirmishes, without ever coming to a conclusion." Her grin widened. "I can even offer to hide the ringleaders and some of the rest on the property I hold now, and they can run their fight from there."

Kyrtian gave her a little bow of respect. *She should have been a general.* "Which means the Great Lords won't send me against the Wizards, at least, not for a while." He considered the next move in the plan. "We can delay things for a while, while I try and come up with a better solution."

Lady Moth laughed mockingly. "And my reward is to get my husband's estate back, which is no bad bribe for my complicity, boy."

"There has to be something in this bargain for you, my Lady," he demurred. She shook her head at him.

"I think this will work for a while, anyway," Gel voiced his own opinion. "I like it. And I've got no particular objection to patching together temporary solutions for the next two decades."

Lady Moth stood up. "Time for me to go. Boy, when you have the time, find an excuse to come to the estate—I've found some things in the library I think will interest you."

She didn't waste time on farewells; Lady Moth was not one to waste time on anything, as Kyrtian recalled. A brief embrace for him, and a sketchy salute for Gel was all she gave, then she was out of the tent and back on her way to her waiting human escort.

Gel followed her out, to be sure she got back safely through the lines. While he was gone, Kyrtian folded the maps, tidied the tent, and removed the bronze plaque from the teleson. He wanted to talk to Lady Lydiell about this while it was all still fresh in his mind. It was worth the chance of being "overheard," although given that this was a very odd hour to be talking to her, that was less likely this time.

Lydiell listened to his brief summary with her eyes alight. "If this had been anyone other than Moth, I would have said it was too good to be true," she said when he was finished. "But it *is* Moth, and frankly, it's exactly the sort of thing I would expect out of her. Well—look what she's done on her own, discovering how to negate the collar-spells and get them off without hurting the slaves!"

"Useful bit of information, that," Kyrtian murmured, thinking out loud. "It would have to be a human that did it, though; I wouldn't want to chance either poisoning by the metal or magical backlash. Mother, how am I going to keep Lord Kyndreth from suspecting that something is up when all resistance suddenly melts away?"

"By staging more of a rout at this next mock-battle than you're likely to get from the handful of former gladiators there," she said instantly. "You and I will create a Gate from here to there, and we'll send through all of our people that can fight. They'll pose as slaves of the Young Lords—they'll hold a line, then break and rout—straight back to the Gate and home. *That* will give you something to convince Kyndreth that you've won a conclusive victory."

"A Gate? Can I do that?" he asked doubtfully. "Am I strong enough?"

"Not by yourself—but remember what you discovered about combining magic from several people?" she countered. "You have me and the others here; together we will have quite enough to create a Gate."

He nodded, and began to feel more confident. "Perhaps I should invite Lord Kyndreth to observe?"

"At a distance," she answered. "With the Council. There's an old viewing-teleson in the Council Chamber; they probably haven't used it since the disastrous debacle with Lord Dyran."

"But if I choose where to put the teleson-sender, they'll see what *I* want them to see." This was coming out better and better. "And with all of the Great Lords jostling about, they aren't going to notice the Gate—"

"They won't notice it anyway," Lydiell said with confidence. "It's very noisy, but they won't be expecting it and they'll be too far away. They'd have to know something like that was going on."

"Oh, I can cover it with some levin-bolts anyway," Kyrtian decided. "They'd be expecting something of the sort. Mother—I think this is going to work—"

"I never doubted that you would find a way," she said serenely.

When they ended their conversation, and he had covered the teleson-screen again, he waited impatiently for Gel to return so that he could work out all the details of this addition to the plan.

For the first time since he had taken over the command of the Great Lords' army, he began to hope he could save, not only his own people, but everyone involved. Or at least, almost everyone. And that was so much more than he had ever thought he'd be able to do, that he felt as if he had just drunk an entire bottle of sparkling wine.

Now, let's hope all this doesn't prove to be as ephemeral as wine-joy!

The ears outside Lord Kyrtian's tent are a lot keener than he has any reason to guess, Keman thought with glee, as he heard Kyrtian concluding the second conversation of the day with Lady Lydiell. *So, Elvenlord, why haven't you figured out that you have dragons on your doorstep—literally?*

Keman, Shana's foster-brother, was, of course, that dragon. So was his partner in this spying endeavor, although she came from a Lair that had never known there were other dragons in the world until she met him. Dragons, with their ability to shapechange into virtually anything they chose, were uniquely suited to spying on the Elves, who could easily crack any disguise wrought with illusions. In spite of the fact that in his real form he was easily forty or fifty times the bulk of even the strongest and tallest male human (or Elf) he'd ever seen, the draconic gift of being able to push mass and weight elsewhere—they called it, "into the Out"—made it possible for him to masquerade as even a small child.

He and Dora had shapechanged themselves into human fighters and insinuated themselves into the Great Lords' army as soon as it became obvious that this new commander was just as brilliant as the old one had been incompetent. When they first began this task on Shana's behalf, they had gone from one Great Lord's household to another in the forms of various slaves—since no Great Lord ever bothered to take note of a mere human so long as he didn't disobey and had no hint of magic as an Elf understood it about him. They had actually been in Lord Kyndreth's household as a pair of pages when the first news of Lord Kyrtian's victories came in. From there it had been a matter of simplicity to insinuate themselves into the company of fighters the Great Lord sent to augment the army.

The only hard part had been slipping away at night every so often to hunt, for a dragon needed vastly more food than a human. Even that hadn't been too horribly difficult, and they had been keeping Shana informed faithfully of all that this new commander was doing. It had taken him a little time to get used to his partner's outward appearance, however; having a grizzled, muscle-bound, surly *male* look at him while he was *hearing* Dora's voice in his mind was a little unsettling. And it hardly needed to be said that while they were in these guises, they could not even make the most casual of affectionate gestures towards one another, not even the sorts of things that had been possible as pages. Only when they flew in their own shapes could he court her as she deserved.

Keman and Dora *weren't* the guards just outside the tent flaps of Lord Kyrtian's tent—that position was reserved for the handful of men that Sergeant Gel had tested and tried and found trustworthy. For one thing, although both dragons might *look* like fighters, they didn't have any real skill with the formidable weapons that they held—skill did not come with the shape, alas. They hadn't even been among the volunteers hoping for such a position. No, they were guarding the wagons holding the possessions of the other Elvenlords serving as Kyrtian's officers, possessions which had not been unpacked for days (much to the disgruntlement of their owners) since the speed of march had not permitted the kind of leisurely camping with luxuries that the previous commander had allowed.

It was a good thing that darkness cloaked any faint signs of his impatience, for Keman could hardly contain himself. They had known for some time that Lord Kyrtian was very unlike Lord Levelis, the previous commander, in more ways than simple competence. For one thing, his method of training was astounding—using magic to counterfeit blades and other weapons, so that it was possible to acquire real skill without ever getting hurt! For the first time, a human slave delegated to the position of "fighter" stood a decent chance of surviving—and *would* manage to get through his training period without being killed or maimed.

That in and of itself had brought excitement among the ranks to a fever pitch, but there was soon more to rejoice in. Rumor in the ranks had soon been proved truth—that Lord Kyrtian actually cared about the humans who served in the ranks and was not inclined to throw them into combat and use them up the way his predecessor had. But until tonight they had not realized how wildly different his attitudes toward humans were from those of other Elvenlords!

It seemed that Lady Moth and the late and lamented Lord Valyn were not the only ones of their kind to regard humans as something other than objects of possession, creatures destined by birth to serve and be consumed and tossed away at the whims of their Elven masters. Even the rebellious Young Lords had proved something of a disappointment once they had a modicum of power—the humans under their control might not have to fear the terrible punishments inflicted on them by magic anymore, but they were still slaves, and treated as such. Not so with Lord Kyrtian, whose very second-in-command was a human, much to the further disgruntlement of the Elvenlords serving as officers.

Wait until Shana hears all this! he thought, hardly able to contain himself and wait for the next shift of guards to come and relieve them.

It was clear to Keman at least that someone from the Wizards was going to have to approach Lord Kyrtian. They couldn't afford not to, now. It was clear from his two conversations that he did not want to find himself forced to hunt down the Wizards, which he would, if he managed to defeat the Young Lords.

What was more, it was entirely likely that he could find them and beat them in combat. The one thing that had saved them in the past was that the Elvenlords had used mostly magic against the Wizards—and the Wizards had used mostly magic against their foes. The problem was that the Wizards' main defense *now* was the use of iron—which was brilliant, but did prevent them from using magic offensively. The dragons could help, but they were as vulnerable to real weapons as humans and halfbloods were—and Lord Kyrtian could field an army of slaves that would have no difficulty in defeating any Wizard army.

Unless, of course, the Iron People could be convinced to help. Ah, but why should they? Why should they actually *fight,* when they themselves were in no real danger from the Elvenlords and they could always go back to the south and safety? Their leader, the Iron Priest Diric, certainly liked Shana and her friends, but he was a pragmatic sort, and he could lose his position if he advocated something that would bring danger to the Iron People with little or no reward.

Ah, but now they knew that Lord Kyrtian didn't want to fight the Wizards. True, he might find himself in the position where he had to *appear* to fight them, but if the Wizards were in secret partnership with Lord Kyrtian, he could obey the orders to do so with every appearance of obedience to the Council. If, for instance, he knew where the Wizards actually *were,* he could hunt unsuccessfully, but dutifully, everywhere that they *weren't* until the Council got tired of it all and disbanded the army.

Sooner or later they would do just that; especially if the Wizards were able to help in that direction. It wouldn't be difficult to stage scenes of abandoned camps and great desolation, to make it look as if, once chased from the haven of the Citadel, the Wizards had found it impossible to survive in the wilderness.

Keman's thoughts filled with contempt for the "Old Whiners." *They would have had that very problem if it hadn't been for Shana and the dragons.* Caellach Gwain and the others like him were no more equipped to take care of themselves than the pampered Elvenlords themselves would have been if stripped of magical powers. Put some forlorn "settlements" together, made of mud huts with crumbling walls and caved-in roofs, and scatter a few bones about, and leave them for Lord Kyrtian to "discover" and the Elvenlords might be convinced that if any halfbloods *did* survive they were not worth pursuing.

And then, Keman thought, *when we're secure again, we might even be able to secretly trade with Lord Kyrtian for things that we need.* Although he liked Diric and the Iron People, and the folk of the Trader clans, enormously, it made him very uneasy that the Wizards now depended on these two sets of relative strangers (who after all had agendas of their own) for the things they couldn't produce themselves. Keman could never forget that the Iron People had once held him, Shana, Mero, and Father Dragon captive—Iron Priest Diric had nearly been toppled from his seat of power once, and it could happen again. Keman would rather that his friends and foster-sister had one more layer to their net of survival.

The Wizards had once stolen what they wanted from the supply-wagons of the Elvenlords themselves, but that had all come to an end when the Elvenlords realized that they still existed and *were* pilfering supplies. Such thefts were too dangerous now and, in fact, had been forbidden by the tenuous treaty that the Elvenlords had agreed to with them—but the Wizards were not craftsfolk or terribly successful farmers. Hunters—oh my, yes—they merely had to magically transport an animal from the forest or fields by magic to kill it, and even the least skilled of them could do that, for magic was one stalker that no beast could scent. Meat of all sorts they had in abundance, and hides, and the rather lovely horns of alicorns, but the best they were able to do in the way of agriculture was a bit of vegetable-gardening. Shana, one of the few Wizards to manage the transportation spell that enabled her to move living creatures intact, had been able to bring the flock of sheep that had been at the old Citadel, and had purloined some chickens that had strayed and so were *technically* not Elvenlord property. Keman and Kalamadea had brought them goats, and even horses, but the terrain around the caves they had taken to live in was simply unsuited for cultivating grain.

And as for crafts, well, at some point they were going to run out of cloth, and there weren't more than a dozen of the fully-human ex-slaves among them that knew how to spin and weave. There was one single potter, and no glassmakers. As for metal-smiths, well, the less said, the better. True, the Iron People had smiths in plenty, but they were down in the plain, and thus far there hadn't been a great deal that the Wizards could provide that the Iron People wanted in trade.

At least three quarters of that lack of skilled workers was due to the attitudes of Caellach Gwain and his cronies. What sensible wild human or even a former slave, especially one with skills and a trade, would care to settle among people who regarded him as an inferior peon who should be happy to serve his "betters" with no thought for compensation? No few of the slaves that had escaped during the Young Lord's initial revolt had settled briefly with the Wizards then drifted off with the Traders to settle elsewhere.

They're as bad as the Elvenlords, Keman thought, not for the first time.

For now they were relying on the things that had once been stockpiled in the Citadel; they hadn't been able to carry those things away with them, but the Citadel had somehow remained unpenetrated—or at least, no one had bothered to loot it or destroy what was in it. Shana had teams of the younger wizards working together to transport everything possible out of there and into the hands of those who actually owned the things or into the storage-rooms of their new home. Some things were in surplus—anything that didn't get used up or suffer much from wear and tear. Nevertheless, they had more—many more—bodies to clothe and mouths to feed than they'd had back when only halfblooded Wizards lived in the old Citadel.

But if they could set up a trading-agreement with a real Elven estate . . . well, then their transportation magics could be used to swap hides and meat, raw lumber, even the gems and precious metals that were so easy for the dragons to coax up out of the earth, for most of those things that they now depended on the Traders and Iron People for.

Don't depend on that egg to hatch just yet, Keman, he warned himself. *Report to Shana first. It's more important to get to the point where we've got an agreement with this Kyrtian that will prevent him and the army from coming after us!*

Their relief party arrived just then, two stripling humans that had been recruited from the ranks of the gladiators and looked it—muscled everywhere, including between their ears. They presented themselves with the proper password, and he and Dora gratefully surrendered their arms to the new sentries and plodded down the hill to their own campsite. They had managed to make themselves unpopular, not by unpleasant behavior, but simply by being unfriendly and taciturn. No one disliked them, but no one wanted to associate with them either. Humans, in Keman's experience, when away from their familiar surroundings, needed to socialize. When any particular human offered a cold shoulder, he was generally shut out tacitly.

So Keman and Dora had a little fire to themselves; they undertook their duties in silence, and now they collected their rations from the common camp-kitchen without comment beyond a grunt or a nod. They brought their food back to their camp, and to all appearances settled down to their belated dinners.

Ah, but beneath the surface, thoughts were flying between them. They were, in fact, mostly finished with that rather meager (by draconic standards) meal, before the exchanges got beyond incredulous *:Can you believe what he said?:* and similar exclamations of astonishment.

:How soon tonight do you think Shana will try and make contact with us?: Dora asked at last. *:We have to tell her about*

this! If we can somehow get this Kyrtian on our side, it will make all the difference!:

Keman's face showed no expression, but there was nothing but glee in his thoughts. *:It's what we've needed all along, really—what Shana has needed—:* he amended.

:Oh, we dragons have thrown our lot in with the Wizards now, no matter what some of us think,: Dora said cheerfully. *:It's what* we *need, an ally and a person inside the ranks of the Elvenlords.:*

Keman thought a chuckle. *:It wouldn't hurt the Trader clans to discover they've got some competition, either.:* He was beginning to resent the casual way in which the Traders had assumed that the Wizards were totally at their mercy now when it came to things that the Wizards couldn't produce. His persistent fear was that the Traders would learn that the Iron Folk most valued and needed the metal that gave them their name, and would find a way to supply it in quantity, thereby giving the Iron People no reason to continue their alliance with the Wizards. That could be a disaster; without the Iron People, the Wizards didn't have a lot of fighting-types if it came to real combat.

:But if we can get this new commander on our side, we won't need any fighters!: Dora reminded him excitedly.

:I wouldn't want to abandon the alliance, though,: he replied with caution, as he took her tin plate and his own, and scraped coals into both of them to burn off the remains of their stew—the most common way any of these humans here cleaned their dishes when they were done with them. Even the cooks cleaned their great pots this way sometimes. Especially lately, with Kyrtian moving the army from dawn to just before dark, chasing the Young Lords' army.

:Well, do you think you've sufficiently calmed down enough to help me reach Shana?: he teased, as he sat down across the fire from her.

Her reply was not translatable, but *was* rude. He *almost* cracked his disguise with a grin, then they settled into their task—looking from the outside as if they were two middle-aged, weary men dozing by their fire.

Shana had hardly been able to believe what Keman told her; in fact, the moment he'd told her what Lord Kyrtian was plotting with his aunt Morthena, she'd asked him to wait for a moment. Then, her blood singing with excitement, she ran to get Lorryn so that *he* could hear and verify it before it actually sank in as truth.

She pounded down the rough stone corridors, red hair streaming behind her, from her chambers to the common-room, where he was sitting with Zed and one or two others, practicing working in concert and using gemstones to focus and amplify their powers. These were the skills that the younger wizards had developed that enabled them to do so much more than their elders—abilities which Caellach Gwain and his cronies resented without actually troubling themselves to learn.

"Keman has some news," she said breathlessly, as the little group looked up with some surprise at her hasty entrance. "I'd like to hear what you think about it, if you can spare the time, Lorryn."

"Certainly; we were just about finished anyway." Lorryn stood up, and handed the basket-full of baby chicks he'd been cradling in his lap to Zed with a grin. "I never thought that I'd find myself purloining chickens with magic when I ran off to join the Wizards!"

"Hah. Can you think of any better way to practice the 'safe' transportation spell?" Zed countered, with his own wide grin splitting his tanned and swarthy face. "If you flatten a chick or two, it's no great loss."

"But they're so—well, *cute*—I'd feel guilty," Lorryn protested, looking down at the yellow balls of fluff while they cheeped sleepily.

Zed only grinned wider. "All the more incentive, then," he pointed out.

"Let's take a walk," Shana suggested—a good excuse to get away from the others. She didn't want to raise hopes that might be crushed; Lorryn could be trusted to consider all possible outcomes and not just the most desired. Together they could discuss possibilities—grim as well as hopeful.

Which is just another reason why I'm glad he's with me. She'd fallen into the habit of considering him as a partner so quickly it was almost as magical as any spell. How not? She *knew* she could depend on him to do something when she asked him to, but even more importantly, she knew she could depend on him to do something he saw needed doing even if she didn't ask.

After a quick walk up to one of the concealed exits on the top of the hill covering their cave-complex, the two of them were out under the stars. It wasn't likely that they'd be overheard, but Shana related what Keman had told her mind-to-mind anyway. Just because something wasn't *likely* that was no reason to assume it wouldn't happen.

And the Old Whiners are just as like to set someone to spy on us as not, she thought resentfully. *The fat* would *be in the fire if they even thought that I was going to open negotiations with an Elvenlord!*

:Ancestors!: Lorryn exclaimed, *:This is fantastic news! I would never, ever have anticipated this!:*

While Shana went to get Lorryn, Keman had been waiting patiently; now she sat down on a rock and concentrated on the focus-stone in her hand, contacting him once again.

:I have Lorryn,: she told him, opening her thoughts slightly so that Lorryn could sense what Keman was telling her. *:Can you go through all that again for both of us?:*

Keman was only too willing to; Shana sensed both Lorryn's growing excitement and that of Dora behind Keman's carefully controlled thoughts. But Lorryn sobered immediately after the first burst of incredulous enthusiasm, and didn't interrupt anymore while Keman concluded his report to Shana. It was difficult enough for them to maintain contact at such extreme distance, and Shana appreciated that he kept his own thoughts quiet while she and her foster-brother finished their business.

But Keman had an idea of his own for *their* situation, that he voiced before they broke off contact. *:Shana, why don't you ask Mother and Kalamadea to find iron for you? Oh, I know it interferes too much even with* our *magic for them to bring it to the surface, but surely they can* find *it, and once it's been found, you can work out how to mine it. Surely the Iron People know how!:*

:I can ask,: she replied.

:Good! The more claws we have sharpened, the better,: was his final reply.

"That's not a bad thought," Shana said aloud, as a mental silence filled the place where Keman's word-thoughts had been. She headed back down into the caverns, with Lorryn following beside her. "But I thought the dragons didn't much like being around iron—"

"They don't," Lorryn agreed, "But Father Dragon and your foster-mother Alara are likely to agree to do just about anything within reason that you ask them to, don't you think?"

"Hmm. Somehow I can't believe that it's going to be that easy," Shana told him, skeptically. "Still, there's no harm in asking."

"And no time like the present," Lorryn agreed. She was not at all displeased when he took her hand and squeezed it encouragingly, then didn't bother to let it go as they descended once again into the Citadel corridors.

And when they found the two dragons who (next to Keman) had most closely aligned themselves with the Wizards, she put the question to them.

They had made themselves real lairs here, which was no great difficulty for a dragon, a creature who could shape rock and earth to its will. The two of them were in Alara's lair, reclining in their natural forms in smooth hollows filled with the soft sand that dragons preferred to rest in. Father Dragon—Kalamadea by actual name—was not at his full size in here, for dragons never really stopped growing as long as they lived, and Father Dragon was very, very old and his size was immense. He would hardly have fit in one of Alara's hollows if he hadn't shifted part of his bulk into the Out first.

Even so, both of them were huge, dwarfing the two half-bloods next to them. Alara's scarlet-scaled torso could have served as a hut if it were hollow.

"I thought what you needed were gemstones and precious metals to trade with," Alara responded to Shana's question, her bobbing head indicating her confusion. "That's what we've all been looking for. That's what you *asked* us to find."

Shana grimaced. "I know; that was my mistake. I thought so, too—actually, I didn't really *think,* not even when Shadow told us how nervy the Iron People were getting without any new source of metal for their forges. Two mistakes, then. I suppose, if I had thought about it at all, I just assumed that now that the Iron People were settling, they'd find their own iron. So, *can* you find it?"

"More or less," Kalamadea rumbled, lifting his head from his foreclaws. "Remember, after all, that we use *magic* to find things, and since the Rotten Metal interferes with magic, its very presence is going to interfere with locating it. We'll actually have to do some roundabout reckoning on where the interference is strongest to find veins of ore."

"I knew it couldn't be all that easy," Shana muttered to herself, but at least Father Dragon seemed to think that there was a way to work around the problem, and that was more than she had expected.

"We also won't be able to bring it to the surface the way we can the silver and gold," Alara sighed regretfully. "So once we find it, *you'll* still have to dig for it, and it'll be ore rather than the nice, pure nuggets of other things we can bring up."

"Oh, Ancestors—" Lorryn said in mock dismay. "Think of it—one more reason for able-bodied folks to have to leave the Citadel, which means fewer servants to attend to the whims of the Old Whiners! They *might* actually have to learn to clean up after themselves once in a while!"

Shana had noticed that Lorryn had, if anything, less patience with Caellach Gwain than she did, although you would never have known it by the way he acted with the old wizard and his cronies. She smiled. "I wouldn't mind taking my turn on the end of a shovel," she volunteered. "Especially if it meant that *you* would take over dealing with them instead of me."

He groaned and shook his head. "Oh, Shana—all right. I suppose that among the three of us, Parth Agon, Denelor and I can handle them. I've noticed a distinct improvement in Parth's attitude ever since he's seen just what an idiot Caellach is being."

"And Denelor always was a dear," Shana said, speaking fondly of her former teacher and the "master" to her "apprentice."

Kalamadea snorted. "I would not have used that description," he said. "But he certainly is far more willing to adapt, accommodate, and change than any of the other older wizards. Well, I would say that we have something of a plan, then. Alara and one or two of the others should be the ones to go looking for Rotten Metal; when they find some that is not too far beneath the surface, you and a few hardy souls, Shana, can see about digging some up. Meanwhile Lorryn will advise Parth Agon, with the help of Denelor—and me."

Shana almost laughed aloud at that last. If Caellach was afraid of anything, it was of the dragons, and Kalamadea was the most imposing of his kind. Caellach had tried—and nearly succeeded—in undoing all of the reforms of the younger wizards once, when Shana had been away from the Citadel. As it happened, she had been the captive, at the time, of the Iron People, as had Kalamadea and Keman. So there had been no one in place to keep Caellach Gwain in check.

"You or I, Shana, will always have a presence here, and Lorryn, too, I think," Father Dragon rumbled, confirming her thought. "At least, until the day when Caellach Gwain swells up with indignation and explodes."

They all laughed so hard at the images conjured up by *that* statement that a sleepy older wizard padded grumbling into the lair to lodge a protest at having her sleep disturbed, and went away muttering under her breath.

19

Kyrtian sat uneasily on his horse in the chill darkness just before dawn. He had brought in his troops just after midnight, positioning them as if this was going to be a real fight and not the sham thing that he and Moth had arranged. After all, the only people that knew it was a sham were his own people on both sides of the coming battle, all of Moth's people, and he and Gel. It was a given that some of his commanders (if not all of them) were reporting to one or more of the Great Lords. Kyrtian wanted them to report the most impressive victory yet—and the most decisive.

This would be enjoyable only if he was down there with his troops; he would have given a great deal to be able to leap out of his saddle and head up the men he knew so well. *Well, the only reason it would be* enjoyable *is because I know how much of this attack is sham.*

Ancestors, but it was cold! Armor and padded gambeson weren't doing a lot against the dankness, which penetrated everything. In fact, the armor was only making things worse; it sucked heat away from him instead of holding it in.

And—was there actually dew condensing on it?

A cold droplet sparkled for a moment just before his eyes, then dropped off the tip of his helm to splash onto his nose.

There was. He shivered and tried to stop himself; it only made his ridiculous, useless, over-ornamented armor rattle.

Not possible for him to join his men where they waited for the signal to attack, of course. The Great Lords who were his ultimate masters here would, one and all, have had him hauled up in front of them for recklessness and blatant disregard for his position.

So he had to sit on a horse on a hill—making an excellent target, incidentally, had his magic not been so strong—and direct his fighters from afar. Never once dirtying his hands with actual combat, oh, no. That was beneath his dignity as a commander, and damaging to the authority of Elves in general and the Great Council in the person of its designated commander in particular.

At least this time he would have something to do besides sit and watch and issue an occasional order. Moth's young rebels were going to be very visibly in the field today; they were also going to be wearing some of that bizarre jewelry she'd told him about. They couldn't work any magic while wearing it, but that didn't matter, since most of them didn't have that much in the first place. It *would* protect them from his levin-bolts; they wanted to demonstrate in the most public forum possible that their fathers could no longer threaten to strike them down in that particular fashion.

I cannot imagine that. I just can't. I know intellectually that there are men out there who think of their sons as possessions, and are perfectly willing to destroy them and try begetting a son again if their "possessions" offend them, but I still cannot fathom it in my heart.

Since their fathers didn't know it was only sets of gold-plated cuffs and torques that protected the rebellious Young Lords, and not some new sort of magic, this demonstration was going to set the Council rather well aback.

The rebels aren't just Young Lords either, though most of them here are. Moth had given him a brief summary of the rebellion—and to say that he'd been shocked was an understatement. *There's a considerable number of the ones who are Lords only because they aren't human, the scornfully disregarded Elvenlords no one talks about—the ones with little magic.* Moth had introduced him to two of those bitter rebels, men Lord Kyndreth's age if not older. *I wonder if the Great Lords have any idea how cordially they are hated by so many of their "inferiors"?*

Mind, this invulnerability to levin-bolts wasn't going to do the rebels any practical good, in the planned scenario. Kyrtian's army was too large and well-organized, and when the rebels fled, their army would fall apart. Kyrtian's men had orders to take anyone who surrendered as a prisoner; the rebels had no illusions about the loyalty of their slave-fighters. When *they* fled, their army would drop weapons and capitulate. Kyrtian's victory was a certainty—as finely scripted as a Court dance and as predictable.

It was definitely getting lighter. When he'd first brought his reluctant mount up here beneath these trees, it had been too dark to see. Now the horizon had lightened, and he could make out the dark shapes of trees and undergrowth beneath him, and in the distance, the square and rectangular bulks of the buildings where their quarry waited—supposedly asleep and unaware of the army about to descend on them.

Good thing we aren't going to have to besiege this place; we'd be here for months. Before battles, or even the practices he and Gel had held on the estate, he usually got a tightening in his stomach, a dry mouth, and his skin felt hypersensitive. Not today; in fact, if anything, he was bored and he wanted it over with. The conclusion here was foregone; the only question was whether or not any of Moth's people would be injured before they could surrender.

The Young Lords had actually chosen their supposed stronghold well—although there wasn't a man on the Great Council who would have valued it properly. For the last couple of centuries it had been the very minor holding of a very minor Elvenlord who had not been swallowed up by some greater Lord only because he never quarreled with anyone, never gave offense to anyone, and raised nothing more desirable than herbs and spices. This was finicky work, far more than any Great Lord had any interest in undertaking, so V'trayn Ildren Lord Jeremin and his wife, daughter and slaves had been left in peace. Until the rebellion, that is. At the moment, Lord Ildren and his household were safely waiting out the conflict in their caravanserie in one of the cities.

So much for him; what was of interest was his manor, which in the far past had been one of the original fortified manors of this region, built back when humans had armies and were considered at least a threat to Elvenkind. It had been further fortified at the beginning of the first Wizard War, making it quite a snug little retreat. It was Kyrtian's opinion that its former owner would have done better to remain buttoned up inside it rather than fleeing to the city and the cramped discomfort of his tiny caravanserie.

But he hadn't, and the rebels had appropriated it as a place to house and train their human fighters.

It had been, therefore, of minor strategic importance until this moment. But he and Moth had decided that for today's purpose it would play the role of the rebel's headquarters, so that when the Young Lords all went to ground on *Moth's* estate after a spectacular rout, no one would be looking for them there.

It was a given that no one on the Council would wonder why people who had been clever enough to choose a defensible structure like this one as their headquarters would also leave it for a pitched battle *outside* the walls of the structure. Analyzing the enemy's strategy was not a skill that the Great Lords of the Council exercised. So long as things went their way, they were not inclined to ask why or look the situation over very closely.

Which is why they are in this particular quandary in the first place.

Birds twittered softly and sleepily overhead. They had begun to wake; it wouldn't be much longer before the attack.

Light seeped into the landscape, revealing it in shades of blue-grey. Rounded shapes were bushes, trees. Pointed ones, rocky outcrops. And in the far distance, leagues below his hill, the squares and rectangles were the fortified manor.

The light strengthened, although the only sign of the sunrise to come was the steady brightening in the east. A single figure stood sentry on the walls below; those of the Great Lords observing this in their telesons must be laughing now. One sentry! And the gates wide open!

The gates were wide open so that the army within could boil out easily—which, in a moment, when the sentry "spotted" the first of his troops attempting to approach by stealth and sounded the "alert", they would.

The distant figure suddenly moved, and the thin wail of a trumpet carried up to Kyrtian's ears, and the peace of the morning shattered like brittle glass as fighters erupted from every gate, shouting, their voices rising to Kyrtian in a confused babble.

Time to give the signal.

Kyrtian stood up in his stirrups, pointed his right hand skyward, and launched a bolt of magic up to the deep blue-grey bowl of the pre-dawn sky: not a levin-bolt, but one of the harmless illusion-bolts often used to enliven evening entertainments, a soundless shower of colored sparks of light high in the air. And now it was the turn of *his* army to emerge from the places where the men had lain hidden half the night, not shouting, but eerily silent, like an army of spirits. . . .

But they didn't stay silent for long; that was too much to expect of flesh and blood. Halfway down the hill their nerves or their excitement got the better of them, and their own throats opened with a collective roar. Beneath his horse's hooves, the ground shook, and the terrified birds burst out of the tree above him.

At that moment, before the two armies had even met, Kyrtian spotted the Young Lords coming out of the gates of their fortress. He knew them by their colorful armor, riding out through the flood of their own fighters, their horses carried along like flotsam in a stream.

Ha!

He had been told not to hold back, and he didn't. As soon as the foremost of the riders got free of the human sea about him, Kyrtian aimed—gathered his power from the depths of his soul—clasped both hands above his head, and let loose a levin-bolt at the nearest.

The levin-bolt streaked from his clasped hands across the space between them, a fire-streaming comet, and those who saw it and had the time to react flung themselves screaming out of its path. Anyone with any experience of levin-bolts would see that *this* one was deadly—and strong.

It hit—it hit! Kyrtian's throat closed for a moment—what if Moth was wrong? But in the same moment, he knew, he *knew* that Moth had not been wrong, for his fatal levin-bolt in the moment of striking fragmented into a thousand shards of light, blinding his view of his target for just a moment. In the next moment, there was his target, unharmed—though the poor horse was frozen in place, all four hooves planted.

Yes! It works! Now sure that he would not kill someone, Kyrtian didn't hesitate, and at last he had a little of the thrill of battle, the exultation of success; bolt after bolt flew down the hill and into the chests of the Young Lords; bolt after bolt shattered on their defenses just as the first had.

By now the fighters of both sides had cleared out of the way of the bolts, which meant that aside from a few scattered pairs locked in combat, the main body of troops weren't actually fighting anyone. That, too, was part of the plan.

But instead of taking heart from the failure of his levin-bolts to kill—as any sane commander would have—the Young Lords apparently "panicked" when confronted by a mage of superior power.

They turned tail and fled; not in a body, but breaking from their army, sending fighters tumbling out of the way of the hooves of their bolting steeds, and scattering in every possible direction except towards the enemy, whipping their horses in a frenzy of feigned fear. And at the sight of their leaders in a rout (which was, of course, the signal to certain of the human fighters to move into the next phase of the plan), the rebel army itself suddenly broke off combat before it had even begun. Leaderless, it was every man for himself, and the humans were under no obligation to carry out the orders of masters who had abandoned them. Most surrendered or fled within moments. The lion's share of the ones who fled were Kyrtian's—brought to augment the Young Lords' troops and make the army look formidable enough to have been a real threat. Kyrtian's men, throwing down their weapons the better to flee unencumbered, were heading for a Gate that would take them home.

The rest dropped their weapons as well, but threw themselves on their faces to surrender—Kyrtian had counted on that, and he had the satisfaction of seeing that the surrendering fighters managed to impede those who might have followed the ones who fled.

Now there was some pleasure, the thrill of seeing a plan unfold perfectly, though there was and would not be any of the excitement and triumph of a real victory.

The Great Lords' fighters pursued—but the vanguard was composed of more of his *own* men, and they managed to obstruct the passage of the men behind them by getting tangled up with those who were surrendering. This managed to impede the rest of the fighters, slowing them and permitting the vanquished to get a head start. By the time real pursuit got underway, the enemy was already too far ahead to pursue effectively afoot. So, given that Kyrtian gave no orders to urge them on from his hilltop command-post, they began the easier task of taking charge of those who surrendered. Moth and Lady Viridina had taken the precaution of tampering with every slave-collar to make it seem that the Young Lords had found a way to override the rightful owners' compulsions. Gladiatorial slaves—the only ones that were reasonable candidates for combat—weren't so plentiful these days that anyone would even consider killing or punishing these men for something they could not help; if their original owners couldn't be determined, they'd probably be allotted among the Great Lords as booty.

Further enrichening the coffers of those who don't need it. Kyrtian felt almost depressed, as he watched the chaos of the battlefield sort itself into tidy groups of prisoners and captors. There didn't seem to be many dead or seriously wounded; there were a few distant figures still on the ground, but they were moving in a way that suggested injury but not serious trauma.

I should be glad of that. And he *was*—but he also felt as if he'd been cheated, somehow; all of the preparation for a battle—*more,* far more, in the way of planning and organization—but none of the excitement. The most he felt was gratitude that it was done with and there were so few casualties.

The sun was only just cresting the eastern horizon, the merest fingernail-paring of hot rose, and the battle was over; so far as the Great Lords were concerned, the war with their rebel offspring was over, too. Now would come the hard part; hunting them down individually, or waiting for them to come crawling back, looking for forgiveness. That was what *they* would be thinking, anyway, and Kyrtian was not about to allow them to discover any part of the truth.

He signaled to his horse, and let it plod back down the hill to his tent. Time to prepare himself for Lord Kyndreth's congratulations, and pretend to an elation he didn't feel.

The subcommanders milled about in the background, not daring to approach such exalted personages as Lords of the Council without being summoned, but clearly hoping to be noticed.

Kyrtian, on the other hand, was very much the center of attention, and not feeling particularly comfortable in that position.

"Brilliant!" Kyndreth boomed, as Kyrtian ducked his head

modestly. "Brilliant! Clearly they never guessed you would force a march after dark to get into place before sunrise."

"I had made a point of always bivouacking before sunset until I knew where they had made their headquarters, my lord," Kyrtian said, as Lord Kyndreth accepted a glass of wine from one of the slaves. "I wanted them to see a pattern and become uscd to it."

Kyrtian's tent had been cleared of everything except tables and chairs borrowed from those of his underlings who insisted on traveling with suites of furniture; with carpets on the floor and slaves holding trays of refreshments, it could not have looked less like his campaign headquarters. But Lord Kyndreth had insisted on Gating here ("with a select few of the Council, nothing to trouble yourself about") to tender his congratulations in person. "Nothing to trouble yourself about" had entailed non-stop, frantic work on the part of his staff up until the very moment that the temporary Gate opened and Kyndreth and entourage marched through.

"Ha—of course, you'd never done such a thing before, so they lacked the imagination to suppose that you would do it now," Kyndreth laughed, as the other three Great Lords he had brought with him nodded wisely. "Of course, old Levelis never did such a thing either."

"Levelis," said one long-faced Lord sourly, "never exerted himself to travel more than a league or two at a time."

"Levelis is an old fool," Lady Moth snapped, joining the discussion, wineglass in hand, "and if it had been left up to him, I'd still be penned up on my estate next Midwinter."

Moth rode over, escorted by her bodyguards, soon enough to welcome the Councilors along with Kyrtian and to serve as his hostess. This was not the first time in the conversation that she had made a point of mentioning that Kyrtian had rescued her from the rebels, and it probably would not be the last.

"Entirely possible, my lady," the sour-face Councilor said, with a slight bow. "And now what do you plan, young commander?" he continued, turning to Kyrtian.

Kyrtian sighed. "Now, my lord, comes the most tedious, most time-consuming, and least-rewarding part of this campaign," he replied. "We hunt down the fugitives one at a time and bring them back to the Council for judgment. I'd calculated that something like this would occur, and planned for it from the beginning; this is a task for smaller parties of men, and if you will permit me, my lords, I would prefer to use my own men if possible. I can count on them not to damage the fugitives when they are caught. As for the rest of the force—well, if it were my decision to make, I would disband it. An army is essentially a great beast that is all mouth and stomach out of which no useful work can be gotten when it is not engaged in a campaign."

"We will—take that under consideration," Lord Kyndreth replied, with a glance at his fellow Council members. "It does make sense, however."

He's thinking about the Wizards. Kyrtian took a sip of wine and tried to look unconcerned.

"Oh, come now, Kyndreth, the boy's right," said the sour one, appropriating a tidbit from one of the trays and examining it as if he expected to find a bug on it before putting it cautiously in his mouth. "There's no point in keeping these men sitting about doing nothing more useful than military maneuvers when we could have them all back on our estates doing some meaningful work, even if it's only in the breeding pens."

He's not. And he might not be in favor of another Wizard War if the subject were broached at the moment.

"And Levelis," pointed out a Council member in midnight blue and deep green, who was making steady inroads on the wine without showing the least sign of intoxication, "would immediately advise to keep these men out here under his command."

"And you know how I feel about Levelis," Kyndreth acknowledged with a faint smile. "Another salient point, but one that is better discussed in Council, don't you think?"

"Hmmm," said the fellow in blue, but didn't add anything more.

How is he drinking so much and staying sober?

Kyndreth immediately changed the subject back to the current victory, but Kyrtian couldn't help but notice that there was an aspect of it that he did *not* touch on—the rebels' ability to counteract his own levin-bolts. It was the fourth member of Kyndreth's party who brought it up.

"I had no notion that you had so much magic of your own—and *how* were those brats managing to dodge your levin-bolts, Kyrtian?" he asked, incredulously. "I thought they hadn't but driblets of magic of their own!"

He shrugged. "I never saw anything like it," he admitted. "Even if they had been using shields as I know them, the levin-bolts wouldn't have acted in that way when contacting a shield. I'm baffled."

"Huh. I wonder if they found anything in my library. . . ." Moth mused, as if thinking aloud—but her sly glance at Kyrtian alerted him that she was about to present him with an opportunity for something.

But what?

"Your library, my lady?" Kyrtian asked, obeying her prompting. "What do you mean?"

"Oh, when I got into the Great House on the estate, the library was in a right mess," she replied promptly, "books down off the shelves, piled up on the tables, left lying open—something on the order of the huggle-muggle your father used to create in there when he was doing his research, Kyrtian, but on a larger scale. My household is cleaning up the chaos now, but to tell you the truth, it's as if they were following his lead and looking for something."

"Perhaps they found it—" Kyndreth said slowly, speculation creeping into his gaze as he looked from Moth to Kyrtian and back again. "Perhaps—having discovered that the son's little eccentric hobby was so deadly to their cause, they thought to counter it by following the father's example."

Kyrtian did his best not to stare at Moth with his mouth open in shock, gathered his wits, and seized the opportunity he'd been given with both hands. "If that is true—and I do recall my father being very enthusiastic over something he found in Lady Morthena's books—then the rebels might have done just that, and we need to discover what it is that they found!"

"Agreed!" said the Councilor in blue, instantly. "Someone should begin immediately!"

I wish mother could hear that. My father has just gone in an instant from crazed eccentric to vindicated.

He turned to Lord Kyndreth. "My lord, if I may be so bold—anyone can track down fugitives; it's only a matter of having good hunters and endless patience—but I know the direction of my father's research as no one else could. Would the Council be pleased to permit *me* to course this particular hare?"

Lord Kyndreth's speculative expression gave Kyrtian the thrill of excitement that the sham battle had not. "What, precisely, was he looking for?"

"A way, or perhaps a device," Kyrtian said, very slowly, "for those with little magic to amplify that magic." Even as he said that, he realized that this would not be pleasant hearing for those whose powerful magic kept them at the top of the hierarchy. "Presumably it would do the same for those with great magic as well," he added quickly. "I would assume it would work for anyone who used it, whether 'it' is a device, an object, or a method."

"What sent your father into Lady Morthena's library, Lord Kyrtian?" asked the wine-loving Lord, with every evidence of interest.

"He was a student of our history, and could not fathom why we were unable to replicate some of the feats of the Ancestors, when according to the fragments of chronicles he found, even the least of the Ancestors could accomplish what the Great Lords could," Kyrtian replied carefully, looking earnestly into the older Lord's intent eyes. "And he could see no reason why magic should be thinning in our bloodlines."

"A good point." Kyndreth mulled that one over, as the other Councilors looked interested, even eager. Even the sour-faced one lost some of his dour look.

Kyrtian thought about saying more, thought again, and held his peace. It was Moth who dropped another tidbit into the pool for the shining carp to gobble.

"It was all of the oldest books that were left lying about," she observed innocently. "The same sorts of chronicles exactly that Kyrtian's father used to look at. And my word—the dust was unbelievable!"

"Kyndreth, I think we ought to let the boy investigate this," the sour-faced Councilor said decisively. "Let him keep his own fighting slaves in case he finds nothing and elects to hunt down our fugitives, while you take the rest of the army back to the mustering-barracks. We can decide what to do with it after Kyrtian determines if there's anything to this hunting about in the old chronicles or not. Meanwhile, we've got men and arms ready to send out on the chance that one of our puppies manages to scrape together another force and mounts an attack on one of the outlying manors."

"Good plan!" seconded the one in blue, and drained his wineglass. "Personally, I think they're going to crawl back to us begging for mercy, but I'd rather be ready for the treacherous young dogs just in case."

Lord Kyndreth looked in bemusement from one to another of his fellow Councilors—evidently *he* was the one who normally concocted all the plans in Council of late, and he was somewhat taken aback that these three had suddenly devised a solution of their own.

"We don't need a majority vote for this, Kyndreth," the wine-lover pointed out. "Kyrtian won't actually be *doing* anything, not unless he decides that there's nothing to be found in that library, and by then the whole Council will have had a chance to sit."

Lord Kyndreth laughed. "I see that you have already made up your minds," he said, genially—though Kyrtian wondered if there was a hint of annoyance, and even anger, under his smooth words. "As it happens, I am entirely in agreement with you, if for no other reason than that it gives our fine young commander an opportunity for some well-earned leisure before we lay any further burdens on his shoulders." He cocked an eyebrow at Kyrtian. "I *am* correct in recalling that you consider delving into mountains of musty old books to be an enjoyable leisure activity?"

Kyrtian laughed. "You are correct, my lord," he agreed, smiling a genuine smile for the first time that afternoon. "Like father, like son, you see."

"Well then." The smile Lord Kyndreth returned never reached his eyes, but there was no sign of disapproval that Kyrtian could detect in it.

I suspect his annoyance is reserved at this moment for his fellow Councilors.

Kyndreth spun, and fixed one of Kyrtian's subordinates with a steely gaze. "You've heard the plan, Astolan. You're in charge of everything but Kyrtian's slaves. Give the lot a good feed and good rest, then march them and the prisoners back to mustering-barracks. We'll sort out the prisoners there. And see to it that you make as good time coming back as Lord Kyrtian did going out."

Lord Astolan went flushed, then pale, and drew himself up straight as any of Gel's recruits. "My Lord!" he responded, with a crisp salute, followed by a bow, just for good measure.

Kyndreth transferred his gaze to the others. "The rest of you see that he succeeds in making good time," he concluded, making it perfectly clear that the penalty for failure would land on *all* of their shoulders.

Before they could make any reply, Kyndreth's attention had already gone back to the other Councilors. "Shall we make our departures, my lords?" he asked, making it very clear that *he* was leaving, and if the others wanted to remain, they would have to find their own ways back. And since *he* held the key to the temporary Gate . . .

There was no dissension.

Kyrtian escorted them to the Gate, and watched the strangely shining structure fade and disappear after they passed through it. He returned to his tent to find Lady Moth entertaining his subordinates with scandal.

"Well, Astolan!" he said cheerfully as he pushed the tent-flap aside. "*My* things are already packed up and out of the way, and yours are here—well, part of them anyway—so why don't I just round up my slaves and escort Lady Moth back to her estate and leave you free to follow Lord Kyndreth's orders?"

Astolan swelled with pride and self-importance. Clearly he hadn't expected to be confirmed in his new—if temporary—command so soon. "Certainly, my lord, if that is your wish—"

"It is; if we start now, we will all be at Lady Moth's estate well before sundown," he said firmly, and offered Lady Moth his arm. "My Lady?"

She swept him a curtsy, and allowed him to see a glimpse of the wicked amusement in her eyes before accepting his arm. "My lord," she replied. "Let us go in search of that so-admirable chief of your slaves, that so-stern fellow Gel, and be on our way. I cannot wait to be home, now that I know that my home is safe again."

How is she managing to keep a straight face? "I shall be at pains to keep it ever so, my lady," he replied, deadpan, and was rewarded by the shaking of her shoulders as she tried to keep from laughing as they swept out.

20

Her guide paused at the edge of the mining-pit, and Shana surveyed the activity below her with an intense feeling of satisfaction. The dragons had, incredibly, found a place not that far from the New Citadel where iron ore lay near to the surface of the earth, making it possible to extract the precious substance without having to dig dangerous underground tunnels.

The dragons, however, had given some strict orders regarding mining operations. The fertile topsoil was to be carefully removed before true mining began, and set aside; when a spot had been played out, the harvested soil was to be returned and replanted with saplings culled from the forest, or clumps of meadow-flowers. Although this made very little sense to most of the Wizards and all of the humans, the dragons were so adamant about this that no one argued.

Shana, however, fully agreed with this injunction. She had lived among dragons for too long not to think in terms of centuries rather than years—and the scars left on the land by unconsidered mining would last for centuries. In the desert and the mountains, resources were not inexhaustible; to scar the land and leave it that much less able to support the humans and Wizards of the Citadel was unthinkably stupid. No matter what else she was, she hoped that even her own worst enemies would never think of her as that stupid.

A great deal of work was required to produce a few ingots of iron. In the pit below her, twenty or thirty quite burly men, broad shoulders and backs pouring sweat, labored with picks and shovels to fill crude wheelbarrows. The barrows were in their turn trundled up a dirt ramp to the rim of the pit by less burly men, some women, and even a few adolescent boys with the muscle to make the grueling trip over and over.

At the opposite rim of the pit stood their primitive smelter, the mysteries of which were of no interest to Shana. That was Zed's purview, and so far as Shana was concerned, as long as his fuel-cutters and charcoal-burners cut their timber selectively and replanted where they cut, she didn't care. Her concern was for the iron to trade with and the land it came out of, not for how the iron was produced.

It was the number of people at work here that surprised her—and their ages. *She* had sent Zed and his would-be miners off with the young dragon who'd found this place, and there hadn't been a single one of them much over the age of twenty—nor were any of them particularly muscular. But down there in the pit were men that could have been labor-slaves for an Elvenlord—

"What do you think of my crew?" called Zed, as he waved at her from across the pit. The miners looked up, glanced from him to Shana, and grinned broadly. Fire and Rain! They looked like labor-slaves and were scarred like gladiators!

Not a familiar face among them. . . .

"I think they're very impressive," she called back, as she and her guide made their way around the edge of the pit. "But what I'd really like to know," she continued, as she came closer and didn't have to shout, "is where they came from—"

Zed laughed. "They're slaves—ex-slaves actually. The same ex-slaves that old Caellach drove away from the New Citadel by treating them as slaves rather than our fellow-creatures."

"But . . ." She wrinkled her brow, puzzled. "They're working just as hard—harder—than they would have if they'd stayed at the Citadel."

"But I'm *not* treating them as slaves," Zed pointed out. "I don't expect them to work here for the sheer gratitude of serving a wizard and getting nothing more generous than food and shelter. They each get a fair share of the iron we smelt; they can trade it back to me for whatever we Wizards have that they want, or for what I've gotten from the Traders or the Iron People. That way the actual iron stays in our control, but *they* get a fair wage for their work." He raised an eyebrow. "We're great believers in wages here."

She shook her head in admiration. "Zed, that's brilliant! Are they settled here? Do they want to stay? Can they build a village or something?" It would be wonderful to have these strong folk nearby—there was so much they needed simple laborers for, and Shana didn't in the least object to bartering for work done.

"They want to know whether Caellach is likely to poke his nose in here first, before they actually build a settlement," Zed replied with a grimace.

Shana glanced down, and saw that all work had stopped, while the former slaves all listened for her reply.

She was not at all loath to give it, pitching her voice so that the workers could hear it as well as Zed.

"Caellach Gwain is about as likely to appear here as I am to be welcomed into the ranks of the Elvenlords," she said, with a touch of acidic humor. "He's gotten so bad about having the tiniest bit of iron near him that we've taken to wearing the false-gold pendants when we aren't working magic. Lorryn calls them 'Caellach-chasers.' "

Zed's guffaw drowned anything from the workers, but Shana saw plenty of grins as they bent back to their work.

"I think you can count on a settlement going up here, then," Zed replied. "There's enough iron ore here to keep the smelter going for years and years, and more than enough work for everyone. Whoever isn't mining, smelting or hauling can be put to work on the replanting and restoration of played-out areas."

"I was afraid, after I saw that first load of ingots, that I was pushing you too hard over here," she said in tones aimed only for his ears, once he stopped speaking. "I'm glad to see that I was mistaken."

Zed patted her shoulder. "Anything but," he replied. "Ah—would you like to see the smelter? Or not—"

"Not," she said firmly. "I'm no Caellach, but this much iron kind of makes the inside of my head itch."

Zed shrugged. "Doesn't bother me as much, but then I've never had as much of the elven magic as you do. Here, I'll show you where we want to put a settlement instead. I think you'll be surprised."

He turned away from the smelter and headed into the woods. Shana followed him, glad to get out of the hot sun, away from the smelter and under the tree-shadows.

"How did the Iron People react to our first delivery?" Zed asked, with acute—and thoroughly understandable—interest.

"By throwing a festival, or so Mero tells me," she was happy to tell him. "I'm afraid that the Traders are a bit disappointed, though."

"The Traders can learn to live with their disappointment," Zed said smugly. "Now *we* can start doing more to protect ourselves—and we can send out the jewelry again."

"That can't happen too soon for me," Shana said fervently. "It's not just the Young Lords who need it, though the more jewelry we can get into *their* hands, the more disruption they'll make with the Great Lords. No, I want to get pieces to the Ladies, and I especially want to get it into the hands of the slaves."

Want was too mild a word; ever since she had last heard from

Keman and Dora, she was positively wild to get the jewelry moving out into the Elven lands again. If they could get Lord Kyrtian on their side—

The jewelry might *put* Lord Kyrtian on their side. If he had a way to protect his own people from Elven magic, to protect his lands from the magical attacks of other Elvenlords, there was no doubt in Shana's mind that Lord Kyrtian's own intensely loyal fighters would be more than a match for any physical force that the Great Lords could bring against him. It was only attack—magical attack—that he needed to fear.

And treachery. There was that. And the Great Lords were past masters at treachery.

"You think it might nullify the collars?" Zed asked with interest. "Remember, if we can't do that, we might as well not give the stuff to them."

"I think I know how." Eagerly she outlined her idea, which had come to her just that morning. "If we make a sort of clamshell device that closes over the beryl in the collar, back and front—" she mimed the idea with her hands "—something that will lock in place, tight, even if we can't get the collar off, we keep commands from getting to the elf-stones and the stone from actually doing anything to the wearer."

Zed considered the idea. "Interesting. It doesn't help someone like a concubine, who might have a collar studded with beryls, but a common worker won't have more than one. So unless the Lords start replacing all the collars on all their slaves, which would be expensive, even for them, we could free whole groups at a time!"

Shana grinned with glee. "That was my idea—the clamshells wouldn't be big, and it wouldn't be hard to distribute them. For instance, we could smuggle a whole bagful out to the workers in a field, the slave taking the water-bucket around could pass them out, and the whole group could bolt at once."

Or the shells could be passed around an army, at night, under cover of darkness. And when the morning comes, and coercion no longer works on the fighters and they are safe from magical attack, how many of them will remain to fight for their masters?

"Tricky," Zed said with admiration. "It's too bad that collars are usually metal, not leather; we could incorporate cutters into the edges of the clamshell, and nullify the beryl and remove the collar all in one go. Well, this is where the camp is, and where the men would like to put in a permanent settlement."

There wasn't much there at the moment, and it was a good thing that not only was it high summer but there had been remarkably good weather, for the shelters were barely enough to keep off the rain. Shana could see how it would make a perfect spot for a settlement, however, and she made all the right sounds of enthusiasm for Zed and his people. There was no doubt in her mind that she and Lorryn had made the right decision in putting Zed in charge of mining, smelter, and crews to man both operations, although she would not have pictured him as a leader. And Caellach Gwain had, of course, argued against the mere thought of putting someone as young as Zed in charge of anything.

She completed her inspection—if that was not too official a word for merely looking the situation over—in short order. Things could not possibly be better; at the moment, she really didn't want production going any faster. It wouldn't hurt trade to keep the Iron People waiting for their ingots just a little between each shipment; she didn't want them to start thinking that the supply was unlimited, and she had a long talk with Zed on just that subject. He was disappointed in one way, and relieved in another. He wouldn't have been unhappy to be asked to find more ex-slaves to recruit, but on the other hand, he didn't want his workforce growing past the point where he could handle everything himself.

In the end, Shana and the latest load of crude iron ingots returned overland to the New Citadel by pack-mule, arriving just about sunset.

Just in time for Caellach Gwain to run straight into them.

He stared; he began to shake with anger. In a matter of moments, he was practically beside himself with rage.

"*What* are you *doing*, girl?" he screamed at the top of his lungs, drawing everyone within hearing distance to the mouth of the cavern where the unloading was taking place.

"I should think that was perfectly obvious," she retorted. After the long walk—for she was not going to ride when she had two perfectly good legs, and her weight-equivalent in iron bars could be loaded on a mule in her place—she was hot and tired, and not in the mood for the temper-tantrums of irascible old men.

"You *idiot!*" he shrieked. "Bringing that—filthy stuff *here?* Bringing it inside the caves? You're mad! You're crazed! How is anybody supposed to work magic with that foul garbage practically on top of us?"

There were some grumbles and mutterings from the older wizards in the crowd that had gathered around them, but this time Shana stood her ground. It was about time that the recalcitrant wizards adapted to the situation, instead of expecting someone to work around their reluctance to change.

"You'll work magic around it the same way we youngsters do," she said firmly, hands on hips, glaring at him. "I should think you'd be grateful to me! The more iron there is around here, the safer you are! Haven't you at least figured that out by now?"

Usually she made some pretense of politeness to the old man, but she was in no mood for him at the moment, and her attitude sent him into an incoherent frenzy.

That was just about the last straw.

"Shut up, you stupid old man!" she screamed—and since her soprano was considerably more piercing than his hoarse howls, even *he* heard her, and stared at her, mouth agape.

"Ever since we arrived here, all you've done is complain!" she shouted, her face flushed. *"We've* fed you, clothed you, seen to it that you got your creature comforts, and you have done nothing, *nothing* to help the rest of us! You're a parasite, Caellach Gwain, you're as useless as a second nose and you aren't even half as entertaining! Now *shut up* and learn to work magic around iron like everyone else, or—or—"

"Or what?" Gwain sneered. "You'll turn me over to the Elvenlords? That's just what you would do, isn't it? *Elvenbane?"*

As hot as she had been the moment before, now she was cold. "No," she said flatly. "But only *you* would think that I could. No. If you won't learn to adapt to our new life here,

Caellach Gwain, I will see to it that no one else will cosset you from this moment on. You will find your own food or starve, clean your own clothing or go dirty, cut your own firewood or freeze. Sooner or later, you'll figure out how to live like a responsible adult, and high time, too."

And with that, she turned on her heel and stalked off, pushing her way through the surrounding crowd of mingled young and old wizards.

Someone grabbed her elbow; she started to pull away blindly, when she realized it was Lorryn. "Don't run off," he muttered. "Not now. This isn't over yet." He turned her back to face the crowd.

"I've heard the mutters and the complaints," he said loudly. "I've heard them from the moment that I arrived here. I couldn't help but notice that most of them came from the same set of mouths—so let's just address this situation once and for all. I'm calling a convocation of all Wizards."

"Here?" someone gasped. "Now?"

"Here and now," Lorryn agreed. "I give you all a quarter-candle to get everyone assembled; whoever isn't here by then I'll assume has no interest in the way things are run in the New Citadel, and doesn't feel the need to have his voice heard."

About half of those present shot or lumbered off in every direction to gather friends and enemies from every part of the Citadel. Shana looked askance at Lorryn.

"Is this a good idea?" she asked doubtfully.

"It had to happen sometime soon," Lorryn replied. "Better that it comes as a surprise to both sides; Caellach and his cronies won't have a chance to prepare themselves."

"And we're prepared?" she replied, staring at him incredulously.

"More than they are—and what's the besetting sin of every one of the Whiners?" he asked, and answered himself triumphantly. "Laziness! That's why I only gave them a quarter-candle. How many will think it's too much trouble to drag themselves away from whatever they'd planned or were in the middle of?"

"Maybe enough to make a real difference," she said slowly—

for already the young wizards were coming up to the clearing at the entrance, brought in by the youngsters who had scattered like quail to bring the message to everyone within reach of a pair of fleet feet.

With the help of a couple of their friends, Lorryn prepared the area. This was also the spot where firewood was chopped and stored, and the young wizards got to work, rolling in some logs for the less-than-healthy to sit on down in front, and setting up sawn sections of trunk for himself, Shana, and presumably Caellach to stand on so everyone could see them. Caellach, of course, merely stood about and observed them sourly. More and more people were arriving with every passing moment, and by the time the allotted span was gone, the only Wizards not present were a scant handful of the oldest or laziest. The biggest surprise was the number of pure humans who had come as well; virtually every full human in the Citadel.

With a great deal of overacted infirmity, Caellach bullied a couple of human youngsters into helping him up onto one trunk-section, as Shana and Lorryn took the other two.

"Now, settle down!" Lorryn shouted, very loudly, so that those who were chattering and milling about obediently stopped talking aloud and turned their attention to where the three of them stood. "All right, then. I am going to moderate this convocation since I'm the one who called it."

"But you're Shana's lover!" Caellach sputtered, red-faced.

Shana was going to protest, but Lorryn beat her to it. The furious look that Lorryn turned on him sent him from red to white, and he even shrank back a little. No one had ever seen Lorryn angry before—and he looked positively murderous.

"I am *not,*" he replied into the silence, "Lashana's lover. We are friends, and she has been relying upon my experience on my father's estate to help her handle you unruly lot. Even if that were true, it would have nothing to do with this situation and it would be none of *your* business so long as her foster mother approves. I am offended, Caellach Gwain. I do suggest that you confine your words to the issues at hand, or I will be tempted to challenge you."

Challenge him? What on earth does he mean by that? Shana

thought, bewildered. Caellach Gwain evidently knew, though, for he turned even whiter, and stammered an apology.

"The primary issue at hand," Lorryn said, when the old wizard was done, "is a greater one than just the presence of iron within the Citadel, or the number of people who are attending to tasks other than . . . housekeeping." His bland expression gave no hint as to his own feelings on the subject, and although they were no secret to Shana, from the looks on the faces of Caellach's cronies, they were not sure if he *was* Shana's partisan or not. He might be courting her, but he was also an aristocrat, used to the attentions of hundreds of slaves, so shouldn't he be on their side? For that matter, he might only be using her to get the power of leadership himself—she saw that in the new speculation with which Caellach regarded him.

"Caellach Gwain," Lorryn continued, turning to the old wizard, "you have voiced your opinions often enough for the ears of your friends and supporters—I must insist that you allow *everyone* in the Citadel to hear them."

Caellach stared at him; tried without success to stare him down. His expression remained inscrutable. "As moderator, I will *not* be questioning either of you. Instead, you will answer questions from everyone *except* me. I will see to it that there are no interruptions and that you both have a fair chance to be heard."

What? That took Shana completely by surprise, and she felt seriously shaken. What on earth was he after? Surely the Old Whiners would try to make her look a fool—

But it was too late to back out now, for either of them, as Lorryn fielded those who wanted a chance and selected one of Caellach's cronies for the first question.

"You were the one that brought the Elvenlords down on us in the first place, girl, so what've you got to say for yourself?" shouted the old man, who practically trembled with eagerness to finally have a chance to confront her in front of witnesses. "If it hadn't been for you and your pretensions of being some mythical Elvenbane, we'd still all be back in the Citadel and comfortable!"

Think! Don't react, think! "*I* never called myself the Elvenbane," she retorted, throttling down panic and irritation that mingled uncomfortably, setting her insides topsy-turvy. "I never even heard of the Elvenbane until after I was brought to the Citadel. And besides, it was the dragons that made the Elvenbane up in the first place, not me!" She caught sight of Father Dragon back in the crowd, in his halfblood-shape. "Right, Kalamadea?"

Gazes followed hers, and several of the more wary, elderly wizards who found the dragons as uncanny as Caellach did cleared away from him. Father Dragon cleared his throat modestly. "Well, it was mostly my doing," he admitted. "But yes. We dragons created the legend of the Elvenbane, and we were just as surprised as the rest of you when the legend came to life." He warmed to his subject. "We believe, we dragonkin, that certain creatures are endowed at birth with great *hamenleai,* which is the power to become Fate rather than to be steered by it, and I tell you all now, Lashana, even as an infant, showed such tremendous *hamenleai* that even if she had been raised by alicorns in the wilderness, the legend would have fitted itself around her. Every dragon acknowledges that now, whether or not they count her as a friend. Where she walks, great change will follow."

That was not what Shana had hoped he would say—nothing like it, in fact—but she gamely took up where she had left off. "As for all of you still being in the Citadel, I don't think you would have lasted undetected for much longer. You were taking too many risks. Someone would have found out why goods and supplies were vanishing and where they were going, if nothing else. The Elvenlords were already starting to wonder about that even before I joined you."

"Didn't I say that was too risky?" said a wizened old scrap of a wizard, before he was hushed. Lorryn had already signaled someone else to ask a question, and Shana felt her heart sink as she surveyed the faces around her. She had felt, and sounded, weak and uncertain. She hadn't convinced anyone, and Father Dragon hadn't helped.

"What makes you think you're better than any of the rest of us at leading?" shouted someone from the back. "*Both* of you!"

"I don't," Shana replied promptly, but Caellach was already swelling with self-importance and ran right over the top of her.

"I have decades of experience, not to mention intelligence and wisdom," he boasted, "which is far more than this impudent little girl can claim. I do *not* make impetuous decisions, and I do *not* rush to embrace something just because it is novel and new. There is no doubt in my mind that the situation here is well on the way to becoming intolerable, between these foolish innovations in magic and dangerous liaisons with barbaric wild humans, not to mention creatures that aren't even human. The young should serve their elders, not dictate absurd rules to them! They should be thrilled to trade their service for the wisdom that we have gathered!" He warmed to his subject, surrounded as he was by his own nodding supporters, paying no attention at all to the expressions of some of those who were farthest away. "What should we Wizards have to do with humans, anyway—except in that they, too, should be eager to serve us! We are more powerful, we are longer-lived and have the opportunity to garner *far* more experience than what can be learned in the few years these mayfly humans enjoy. It is clear that we are far superior in every way—and this *girl,* this *child,* thinks that we are to treat them as equals! Never! I will never tolerate treating such debased creatures, creatures who should be competing in devotion to me, as my equals!"

An actual growl arose from the humans who made up the bulk of the crowd—perhaps few of them had ever realized just how deeply Caellach's prejudices went, nor how poisonous they were. At that moment Shana realized Lorryn's tactics in allowing this convocation to take place in the way it had, for he had permitted Caellach full freedom to say whatever he chose with his followers around him, and the old wizard's mouth had run away with him.

"Debased creatures, are we?" came an angry shout from one of the carters who had brought the last batch of iron ingots up from the mine. "I'd like to see *you* try your hand at a little honest work, you soft white worm!"

"You can just fetch and carry for yourself from now on!" came another, disgusted voice, along with a chorus of similar sentiments. Even some of the children that Caellach had cowed into obeying his demands took heart from the sentiments of their elders, and added their shrill voices to the rest.

Caellach and the others woke to their danger, but considerably too late for any retraction. They gathered in a knot around Caellach and it became painfully clear to them how tiny a minority they formed, as a sea of angry faces surrounded them. Shana and her shortcomings were quite forgotten.

Lorryn allowed them enough time to really begin to frighten Caellach, before using a little touch of magic to amplify his voice so that it carried over the noise of what was fast becoming a mob.

"Friends!" he boomed. *"Quiet! Please!"*

Surprise silenced all the voices for the moment—just long enough for one single voice, the voice of her foster mother Alara, to be heard.

"Shana, the objections seem to be to all of the changes," Alara said, in the first reasoned voice Shana had heard in the last few moments. "And you really were the author of most of them. So what have you to say about the objections?"

"If you don't change," she said, very slowly, choosing each word as carefully as if she picked her way across a treacherous swamp. "I think you become just like the Elvenlords."

That brought true silence, in which even the sighing of the breeze in their clearing seemed loud. It was a silence that begged for an explanation and drew further words, however unwillingly, out of her.

"*They* haven't changed, not since they conquered this place, and maybe not even in longer than that," she continued. "*They* assume that they're the proper lords of the universe and that nothing they want or think or do can be wrong—no matter how many times things happen that prove that they *are* wrong. When you don't change, you get brittle, and the next thing that hits you will break you."

She looked past the faces of her own friends, out to the humans, in whose eyes smoldered resentment for all Wizards now, even her. "Changing means that we can't sit in our Citadel and think we're superior to *anything* just because we can do some things well. Don't you see?" She fumbled a little. "We all need each other. Oh, I can bring in a live sheep from the hills with magic, but I don't have the first idea of how to take clay and make a watertight cup, and let's face it, if I'm thirsty, I need that cup, and the person who can make it is superior to *me* at that moment! Don't you see?" she pleaded. "I never wanted to be a leader, but—I don't know, maybe Kalamadea is right and *hamenleai* has something to do with it and I just can see that we all need to change and we all need each other if we are going to survive—and maybe, if they'll learn to change a little, we even need—them—"

She gestured helplessly at Caellach and his friends, unable to put what she wanted to show them into words—the great puzzle that *she* saw in her mind that somehow had places for all of them to fit into.

But evidently, although there was some puzzlement out there, she got part of her point across. The resentment and anger had faded, and although there were grimaces at the thought of including Caellach and his ilk back into the fold, there seemed to be acceptance of the idea, too.

Then came the thing she hadn't expected—

"It's hard on an old man, all this changing," said one of Caellach's cronies plaintively. "It's hard, girl. You go along with your life all even, then suddenly it's all upset—but—"

He took a deep breath, and shuffled across the space between Caellach's crowd and the rest of the convocation. He looked up at her, and heaved a sigh. "I *hate* all of this uncomfortableness and having to do without," he continued, half in complaint, half in resignation, "but I'd rather stand with you than against you. Just don't ask too much all at once of an old, tired man, will you?"

She got down off her slice of tree-trunk and offered her hand. He took it, and that was the beginning of the end. In ones and twos, the rest of Caellach's followers came over to her side, although most of them just tried to blend back into the crowd and didn't actually come to stand with her. It didn't matter; they'd abandoned Caellach. Even if they didn't entirely agree with her, even if they were still going to argue and grumble, they'd abandoned their leader and they had opened themselves up to the possibility of change.

It was enough. For now, it was enough.

21

Rena took her place on the carpet next to Mero in Diric's tent. The flaps were rolled knee-high, and scrims of loosely woven linen kept bugs out while allowing a breeze to flow through. It was dinnertime, a meal much enlivened these days by the addition of vegetables supplied by trading and the gardens that the Corn People were growing, as well as by the changed herbs provided by Rena herself. Dinner, shared with Diric and Kala, was a more-than-pleasant meal, now that the first lot of crude iron ingots had arrived from the Citadel. Once again, Diric's star was in the ascendant, so far as his people were concerned; and he had lost that worried frown. Kala was just as pleased and far more open about it. After all, the Iron People now had everything they needed—iron, good grazing and water, and even the remains of their old allies, the Corn People, to settle in somewhere nearby and commence the farming that they would not or could not do.

Rena and Mero were reaping the benefits as well; as the representatives of the Wizards, everyone with a forge wanted to know what *they* knew about possible future production, and there were no few folks who wanted to see if they could somehow ease to the head of the queue waiting for the next shipment. The Trader clans were a little discomfited to find that they were no longer the only source of iron, but they'd gotten over it, particularly now that the women among the Iron People had begun to experiment with faceting the fool's gold and polishing yet another form of mineral with a high iron content that the Traders had brought in. Both made fine "gems" for setting, the new "oil-iron" in particular having a lovely liquid-black sheen to it that looked wonderful in blackened-iron filigree. So now the women had more material for their tiny jewelry workshops than they'd ever had before and the new materials had brought on a spate of creativity that had even the men intrigued and hovering over the women's work, trying to reckon how they could coax their mates, mothers, sisters, and friends to produce some of the new work for *them.* Diric already sported leather arm-guards inlaid with iron settings that held large oil-iron cabochons, courtesy of Kala's hands, and she was working on a matching collar as well. He was setting something of a fashion, much to Rena's silent amusement and Kala's open glee.

It seemed an auspicious time for Rena to see about something *she* had been planning for a while.

Kala brought in plates of flatbread, broiled meat, thinly sliced vegetables, and bowls of soured cream. The Iron People could now enjoy one of their favorite meals—flatbread rolled around spiced meat strips and vegetables, garnished with dollops of cream. Rena and Mero had come to enjoy these as much as their hosts, and Mero quickly made himself a roll as soon as Kala set the platters on the carpet before them.

"How badly do you want to keep your two Elvenlords, Diric? They don't look very healthy to me," Rena asked, as Diric reached for a piece of flatbread.

He didn't even pause in his motion. "They haven't been a lot of use for some time," he admitted, laying a paper-thin slice of cucun-pod and some of Rena's sweetened and tenderized grasses on the flatbread, following it with strips of meat and a dollop of soured cream. "Out of respect for your wishes they haven't been entertaining us, but I don't think they would now even if we tried to force them into it with beatings. I think they're going mad, actually. Their keeper can barely get them to eat and drink; I'm told all they do is stare at whatever they're pointed at."

"I think they've *gone* mad," Rena replied, relieved to hear the matter-of-fact tone in his voice. "You can still get Kelyan to talk if you try hard enough, but Haldor—your keepers are having to feed him by hand. I want them, if you don't."

"Tell me what you want to do with them, first," Diric replied cautiously.

Rena took a deep breath and looked to Mero, who gave her an encouraging smile. She looked back into Diric's sable-brown eyes, and told herself what a fundamentally reasonable man he was. "I want—I want to try something. I want to see if my magics can change people's memories. There have been rumors, oh forever, that some of the Old Lords can do that, and I should think that since women's magics among my people are used delicately, it should be easier for a woman to do that than a man. Since Kelyan and his friend are already mad, I can't hurt them further, and I may be able to help them." She steeled herself. "If I can—help them, that is—there are several things I want to do with them. The *first* thing is to find out how the elf-stones of the slaves' controlling collars are made and how the slaves are controlled by them."

"Shana's got this idea that would take less iron than the jewelry," Mero put in helpfully, his green eyes alight with enthusiasm for his friend's plans. "Sort of a clamshell arrangement to close around the beryl like this—" he demonstrated with his two hands snapping together "—and cut it off from magic getting out or in. Those would be easy to get in to the slaves in sackfuls, and if everyone who was ready to escape all snapped their iron-clamshells over their stones at once, they could make a run for it. The Elvenlords wouldn't be able to pursue any single individual or track him either, and by the time someone with enough magic to cast levin-bolts was summoned, the slaves would be long gone."

"But we have to know how the elf-stones work so we can see if the plan would work," Rena continued, as Diric set down his half-eaten flatbread and leaned forward, intrigued by the idea. "I never learned how, and I don't think Lorryn ever did, either, but Kelyan probably did. So I want to see if I can get him to show me. If I can't trick him into doing it, maybe Mero can get the memory straight out of his mind. Once we know how to make the elf-stones, we can test the clamshells."

"But that is not all you plan, I gather?" Diric asked, with heavy eyebrows raised. He looked more than intrigued now, he looked enthusiastic.

"Um—no." She decided to go ahead and tell him her entire plan while he still was open to it. "I want to wipe away every trace in their minds of being captured, of the Iron People, and replace it with something else."

"What else?" Diric wanted to know. "Why?"

"I thought—" she faltered for a moment, then went on. "I thought I'd construct some new memories—illusions really—out of the way Lorryn and I wandered around in the wilderness. Or maybe Mero can help me *put* things in their minds, when I've blanked out the old memories. And once I knew that they weren't going to remember anything about the Iron People or the Wizards or dragons or anything, I'd put them to sleep and get Keman or one of the other dragons to drop them somewhere near enough to an estate for them to find their way back." She bit her lip and waited for the inevitable reaction.

"You mean that you intend to free them?" Diric's eyebrows had crawled all the way up to the top of his forehead. "You think we should let them go to join the rest of our enemies?"

"Well, we can't *kill* them!" she said, a little desperately.

For a moment she feared that Diric would respond with, "And why *can't* we?" But he regarded her thoughtfully, pulling on his lower lip, and said nothing for a very long time.

"If that was your plan," he replied, pitching his voice low, "it seems a waste of a perfectly good resource for deception that we can further use against the Demons that you call Elvenlords. Rather than giving the prisoners memories of wandering about in the wilderness, why not give them memories that are *completely* erroneous?"

"Such as—?" Rena asked, her heart lifting. He was going to let her do this! Finally she was going to be able to do something that would help poor Kelyan and Haldor, but maybe help out Shana as well!

"Oh—I think we can work out something. Make them think that they were held captive by the Wizards, more Wizards than the Elvenlords have any notion exist." Diric grinned in that sudden way that made him look like a boy full of mischief. "And in their minds we can locate their prison in some impregnable fortress somewhere in the opposite direction from the real Citadel." He winked wickedly. "For that matter, concoct a set of Wizards that have never even *heard* of our set! Make the Demons think that they have an enemy that until that moment they had known nothing about! Make them waste time and warriors trying to find this *new* set of Wizards!"

Mero uttered a whoop of laughter. "Ancestors! What an idea! It'll have them *scrambling* to guard their rear, it'll have them fighting over which set of Wizards are the most dangerous, and best of all, it will buy us more time to get stronger!"

"Exactly so." Diric picked up his forgotten meal, and waved his free hand at Rena. "If that is your plan, child, take them and welcome. They are nothing but a burden now, and if you can succeed in your plan, you will convert them to an asset."

He said nothing about what would happen to them if she couldn't wipe their memories clean, but she decided that she would deal with that if the occasion arose. She thanked the Iron Priest and turned to her own untouched meal with a good appetite.

Diric had something he wanted to discuss with Mero after dinner, and Rena decided that she might as well tackle the first part of her plan straight off. Not being a halfblood was something of a handicap, as she couldn't read the minds of the two Elvenlords directly—so what she planned to do was to try and coax the information out of them using words, illusion, her own sex, and gentle prodding. She'd had the Traders bring her an old, deactivated collar from one of the escaped slaves working with Shana; she brought this with her as she entered their tent.

"Kelyan?" she called; she'd put on the illusion of one of the fine gossamer gowns she'd worn in her old life, and as Kelyan roused from his apathetic trance and slowly raised dull eyes to look at her, she created a second illusion, that they were in a typical room that one would find in an Elven manor. She used as her model one of the rooms in which her father would informally entertain guests, but kept the place shrouded in shadows.

Kelyan looked terrible; his emerald eyes were clouded, his

pale hair hung lank and brittle, the only time he changed his clothing was when his keepers stripped him of the soiled clothing. Rena wasn't sure what had triggered this dive into insanity—perhaps he'd just snapped when he'd first seen Keman in dragon-form, or perhaps he had just given up when it became obvious that even though the Wizards had been accepted as allies, there was no way that two Elvenlords were going to be released. But his current confusion, and the way in which he drifted in and out of a world of his own making, would help her. She hoped that in his current mental state he would either believe that he was back among his own people, or was dreaming; either would serve her equally well. It was unlikely that he would recognize the Rena he knew in the Elven lady-guise she had just created for herself; she'd even done herself up in High-Fete fashion with exaggerated cosmetics.

His eyes brightened as he took in her and her surroundings; there still wasn't a great deal of sanity in them, but there was more sense. To reinforce the illusion she had created, she hid Kelyan's companion in captivity in the shadows so that he wouldn't see Haldor's motionless form and have his illusion broken. He didn't seem to notice or care.

"My lady—?" his head tilted inquiringly, showing that he really didn't recognize her.

"Sheyrena," she supplied. "Welcome to my fete, Lord Kelyan."

"My Lady Sheyrena." He nodded his head. "Do I know you?"

Good. He doesn't remember or recognize me, or something deep in his mind doesn't want to. He'd much rather live in dreams than in the world he's in now.

"I am the daughter of a friend of your mother's," she replied, aping as best she could her own mother's manner when with a guest. "Thank you for coming with your mother to my little entertainment. I wondered if I could impose upon your good nature for a trifling task?"

"I am at your command," he responded, with a hand over his heart and a slight bow.

"I have taken a new body-slave, a little girl who has not yet been fitted with a collar," she lied glibly. "As you know, my father will not return from his meetings with the Council for several days, and I wondered—could you—help me with clearing and setting this so that I can use it on the child?" she held out the collar, and he took it from her fingers.

And frowned, slightly. "This is hardly a fit collar for the neck of a lady's slave," he pointed out.

She pouted. "It is the only one I could find that has not been set and placed on the neck of a living slave, and I don't want to wait for someone to construct one for me," she said with just a hint of petulance. "Besides, I've taken a particular fancy to this one child. She's quite pretty, and I don't want Father to decide to give her to someone. If she's sealed to *me,* he shan't be able to."

Kelyan smiled, and she smiled back, instantly forming a conspiracy of two against their greedy elders. "In that case, I shall be happy to set it to you on your behalf," he replied easily.

He bent over the collar and went immediately to work on it—

And she followed the slightest nuance of that work with an intensity that surely would have startled him, had he not been concentrating on the collar to the exclusion of all else.

She had been doubly-prepared; in case she needed to use this ploy again, she didn't want him to think it was anything other than a dream.

When he finished his magics, she thanked him prettily. "You have done me a great good turn, Lord Kelyan," she said, flirting subtly with him in a way that would probably have had Mero wild with suppressed jealousy. "How can I properly thank you?"

She plied him with drugged wine as she fluttered her eyelashes at him, perfectly aware that he wouldn't actually *do* anything other than flirt back. There was a rhythm to this sort of courtship; until he had her father's tacit permission to approach her, he would only indicate gallant interest. He wouldn't want to find himself called into a challenge that he might not have the trained slaves to meet. Leasing gladiators to meet a challenge was possible, but expensive, since some of them would almost certainly die in the combat. Better to be cautious.

"Performing any service for a fair lady is a privilege, not a burden," he replied, downing the wine in a single gulp. As she had planned; she'd doctored the wine to make its taste smoother than honey and disguise its nature. She refilled his glass, and he downed that as well. She passed him a little bowl of highly-salted, toasted bits of root—also manipulated by her magic. The more he ate, the thirstier he would become.

"Thank you," he said after his first taste, and when she left the plate there beside his hand, he didn't object. "I do not have the company of a lovely lady often enough that I see it as less than a reward in and of itself," he continued, now sipping from his glass and nibbling at the snacks.

She laughed softly, producing a tinkling little sound that surprised her and made his eyes widen with approval.

"I do not have the company of fine young lords often enough to think it less than a treat," she replied in the same vein. "Tell me something of yourself."

He was not at all loath to do so, and she continued to ply him with wine as well as conversation until his eyes drooped, his head dropped, and he collapsed limply down onto the pallet he'd been sitting on all this time. With a thought and a flick of her fingers, she banished all the illusions she had created, leaving him again in the felt-walled tent. When he woke the next morning, if he recalled the incident at all, it would probably be as a dream.

Then she blew out the lights, and left him in the darkness, turning the collar over triumphantly in her hands.

Now it was Kala's turn on the new project to liberate the slaves; she examined the collar and the stone, and set about making the clamshell clasp that would lock the stone away from wearer and mage. She was certain she could make such a mechanism; the trick would be to create one that was small enough to conceal, but large enough and sturdy enough to have an effective seal.

Meanwhile, dropping her guise and coming as herself, Rena attempted to engage the two Elves in conversations every day while Mero "eavesdropped" on their minds. As she talked to them—or, as often as not, *at* them—she played, delicately, with her magic inside their heads.

When the Great Lords removed memories, they did so

wholesale, leaving behind a blank. She had delved into the mysterious workings of the brain as well as she could, and now she suspected their crude efforts, difficult as they were, created a mental infant. Probably afterwards their victim had to be re-taught even the simplest of things, which was why she—it was usually a rebellious girl who was so cavalierly treated—wouldn't make a reappearance for a year or more after she was subjected to the treatment. Rena wanted to be more subtle.

So while she talked and spied upon the physical workings inside their heads, she did so on the same minute level that she worked when making the leaves and plants sweet and tasty—or just plain edible. When Mero "saw" a memory that he knew they needed to expunge—which would be when one of the Elves actually thought about it—he signaled Rena. She would know then where it physically resided, and that, she could change. After a few days, she began doing just that. Gently, she broke the connections that made the memories, then erased them altogether with the tiniest of shocks—much, *much* smaller and more subtle than those that caused brainstorms. When she was done, those particular memories were gone. Ask Kelyan about them, and he would look at her blankly.

She had hoped that she would be able to remove the memories sequentially, but alas, that was not possible. Memory, it seemed, was a peculiar thing. It wasn't sequential; memory chains led oddly to incidents that seemed to have nothing whatsoever to do with the triggering recollection.

But one thing was absolutely certain, and that was the more she erased, the more normal Kelyan—and in particular Haldor, since he was the most withdrawn—became.

When that happened, memories were easier to trigger and thus, to remove. Rena's progress with them came in leaps and bounds, and soon they were both as active and alert as they'd been when first captured. That was promising, since it would have been the next thing to murder to drop the two of them unconscious somewhere if Haldor was still near-catatonic, but it created a new problem.

As they regressed into the past, they no longer had the memories that told them that resistance was of no use, that escape was not possible. By having their evening food drugged, building illusions, and interrogating them separately, Rena was able to convince them that she and her questions were no more than an intriguing dream. She didn't even have to convince them that they were in the midst of a dream *sequence,* since she was able to erase the memory of each night before she left them drugged and sleeping.

"But what are we going to do with them?" she asked Mero desperately, three days after she had begun this task, when Haldor had announced his intention to escape from their current captivity the next day. She dropped down beside him on the grass outside their tent, both of them staring up at the star-begemmed sky over their heads. Her hand reached for his, only to find his reaching for hers. She took comfort from the touch. "Sooner or later, they're going to *try* to make a run, and that's only going to make a terrible amount of trouble."

"Keep 'em drugged by day," Mero advised, squeezing her hand. "We have to figure out how to give them a new past, and I haven't worked that one out yet." Moonlight flooded the camp, almost bright enough to read by. He shook his head at her. "I don't know. Illusions? But that would take as much time to *show* them as it would for them to live it? I might be able to stick new memories right in their heads where the old ones were, but for one person to create all that—"

"Does it have to be *one* person?" Rena interrupted. "What if there were several?" She flushed with the excitement of suddenly seeing a possible solution. "*We* don't have to be the ones to make the new memories! We could ask Kalamadea and Alara to come get them, and Shana and Zed and some of the other Wizards could all pitch together and do it!"

Mero shook his head. "I don't know," he replied dubiously. "Wouldn't those memories get awfully confusing with so many people meddling?"

"Isn't it better for us if they are confusing?" Rena countered, feeling even more certain that this was the right way to handle the problem. "We don't want them to have a whole picture, we just want them to have fragments, don't we? Let them think they were drugged most of the time, or enspelled, but the more confusing their memories are, the more confused the Old Lords will be."

"And the more confused the Old Lords are, the more likely that they'll be alarmed—I see where you're going with this." Mero chuckled unexpectedly, and hugged her. "You're right, Rena, you're right! I'll try and reach Shana and explain all this and see if she falls in with the plan. I'll *keep* trying until I reach her."

"And I'll wipe their memories back to their capture," she said happily, secure now that her plan would work exactly as she had hoped.

In a few days, the dragons arrived—but quietly, without fanfare, in the guise of Wizards. Rena had never seen Alara in that form; Shana's foster-mother had chosen to resemble a very sturdy woman of indeterminate age, with high cheekbones and hair of deep brown. Kalamadea, of course, wore the guise with which the Iron People were already familiar, and when he and she walked into the camp at dawn, Diric and the other leaders of the group welcomed him—though the welcome was tempered with the memory of the last time they had seen him, in his real shape of a huge, blue-black dragon.

"We've come to carry off your inconvenient guests," Father Dragon said genially, beaming as if he'd had the greatest of treats bestowed upon him. No matter that the last time anyone of the Iron People had seen him, it was as a dragon; he behaved so normally, and looked so harmless, so inoffensive, that it was hard for anyone to think of the menacing dragon with those guileless green eyes peering at them out of a sea of wrinkles. Father Dragon played the part of an eccentric little old man to perfection, and soon had Diric chatting with him like the old friend he was. With Diric acting so normally, the rest of his people relaxed as well.

"And what have you done with Myre?" he asked, at last.

"We gave her over to the keeping of the Corn People for

now; they do not trust her in the least, for I told them only that she had nearly betrayed us and her own people to the Demons." Diric looked smug, and Rena had to smile. That was at least partly true, after all! "They give her field tasks to do, and no food if she will not work. She has quickly learned the value of carrying out what she is told to do."

"Obviously, you aren't concerned about her escaping?" Alara made that a question; she couldn't quite control the pain she felt at this position her second-born found herself in, but Diric misinterpreted it.

"Oh, no, lady! If she wishes to run off, we will let her! She is not so great a help to us that we would miss her, and she cannot remove the collar that keeps her looking as one of the Demons' slaves. She cannot go back to the Demons, so—the Wizards, we, the Corn People and the Traders all know of her treachery and would not remove it." He smiled. "If she wishes to wander the plains, alone and unaided, in preference to remaining with the Corn Folk where she has food and shelter, well, let her savor her freedom."

Alara sighed, but said nothing; Kalamadea covered her silence with chatter. Rena gave her a look of sympathy; for all that Myre had been a miserably thankless child, Myre *was* her daughter. It must have torn poor Alara's heart to have to side with one child—or children, counting Shana as Alara's foster-daughter—against another.

"We'll wait until dark to take them, so we don't distress your people unduly," Kalamadea was saying quietly, as the other Elders of the tribe made their cautious greetings, lost interest, and went back to their usual tasks.

"That is well," Diric said judiciously, then brightened. "But you must also see the progress my Kala has made upon your other need! And you must see the new jewels my lady-smiths have made! Come!"

Rena and Mero spent the rest of the day in the company of Diric and the two dragons. Diric must have shown them every jewelry forge in the camp, and although Alara did not once ask to see her wayward daughter, Rena had to wonder if Diric was trying to distract the dragon to keep her from making that very request.

At last—at long last, for even Rena was beginning to tire of watching jewelers at work, a task she normally found fascinating—the sun set, and darkness fell.

She left then, to see to the two she now considered "her" charges. She found them insensible, so thoroughly drugged that not even a hearty shaking could wake them. Nothing less would do; obviously they couldn't ride out of here as she and Mero had done, a-dragonback. They would have to be carried.

She and four of the younger Iron Priests bundled the unconscious Elves into the same kind of swaddlings that the Iron People used for their infants, only adult-sized, complete with a rigid board very like a cradle-board. The swaddlings would prevent them from moving, the board would ensure that they wouldn't bend in the middle; now they could be put in a net sling, to be carried in dragon-claws back to the Citadel.

Once packaged up like a pair of parcels for delivery, the Iron Priests each took an end and unceremoniously carried the motionless bundles out into the darkness.

Rena followed behind, as the young Priests in their peculiar cloth headresses and leather aprons carried the bundles as far as the open grasslands outside of the camp, put them down in the waiting nets, and hurried off. They didn't look back and Rena didn't blame them; if she herself hadn't spent so much time with Keman in all of his forms, *she* would have been nervous around the dragons.

And Kalamadea and Alara would be back from feeding at any moment. . . .

The sudden "wind" that came up all around her, the thunder of unseen wings overhead, warned her that they were here.

Silvered by the moonlight, casting black shadows that stretched across the frantically-waving grasses in front of them, they backwinged in beside their charges. Rena stepped back involuntarily; she had somehow forgotten how *big* the fully adult dragons were in their true forms. Father Dragon usually reduced his, to fit in with the others, and to be able to use the lairs inside the Citadel—but dragons never stopped growing entirely, and he easily dwarfed Alara, and Alara was twice the size of her son, Keman.

They were like forces of nature, too big, too powerful to really comprehend; she put her hands out in an unconscious gesture of warding. She might not even have been there for all the notice that they took of her.

They had eaten well among the herds, and they had a long way to go, all of it this very night, before the two Elves woke. There was no time for farewells, and in her heart, Rena couldn't blame Alara for wanting to be gone from the place where her youngest languished in her prison of iron collar and human flesh.

Instead, each paused on the ground only long enough to seize a net and hook it into claws as long as Rena's arm. Then, with a leap for the sky and a tremendous booming of wings, they were off.

In moments, they were only dark shadows, beating slow wings against the silver moon. Then, gone.

Rena strained her eyes, but couldn't see them—and jumped when Mero touched her arm.

"Well," he said quietly, "it's out of our hands now. You've given Shana a tremendous weapon, my love, and now it's up to *her* to make the best use of it. You've done your part; you can relax."

Only when he said that did she realize that she *could.* And that Mero had said that she had, at last, given Shana material help unaided by anyone. She glowed with pleasure at the mere thought, and laughed a little.

"I suppose I can, can't I?" she replied, and turned so that his arm went around her shoulders. "Well, then—" she continued, playfully, feeling strong and emboldened by her success, "Don't you have some—ah—courting to catch up on?"

For a moment he stared at her, as if unsure of how to react. "I do?" he said, a little stupidly.

—then he grinned, broadly. "I suppose I do," he said with far more sense . . .

. . . then proceeded to make a very good start on all that catching-up.

Lady Triana supervised the preparation of her reception chamber with the same care a good general would have given to the preparation of battle-plans. Things were beginning to move, at last, although not entirely in the direction she had wanted. Aelmarkin was on his way to her manor—she knew this, of course, because she had *not* given him an access-key to her Portal, and as a consequence he had to make the last leg of his journey the hard way, overland from the manor where Aelmarkin had a friend willing to allow him the use of *his* Portal. He probably didn't even know that she had a Portal. There weren't many who she trusted with keys to it, so it wasn't common knowledge.

She'd had plenty of time to prepare for him by now, and he knew that. Already she had an advantage over him.

She had been expecting this visit for some time; in fact, she was surprised that he hadn't turned up before this. Aelmarkin's cousin Lord Kyrtian, rather than disgracing himself, was distinguishing himself on the battlefield against the rebellious Young Lords. After that last rout of the Young Lords, his star was particularly high with the Council. Aelmarkin must be furious.

She only wished that she had nearly as much of an advantage over Aelmarkin as she was going to pretend she had. Her little spy in the household, kept as she was in the harem and with no access to young Kyrtian when he was away on his martial business, had proved of little use. The domestic details that the slave had been sending were only of interest in that they showed how thoroughly Kyrtian's mother held the reins of the manor. A pity, that. It appeared that Triana was going to have to do most of the work of subverting Lord Kyrtian herself.

But it was, of course, not to her advantage to allow Aelmarkin to know any of this, and she didn't intend to. She would probably let him know that she *had* the spy; that would be useful without giving away too much.

When Aelmarkin arrived, what she *did* intend was that Aelmarkin would see a side of her that he would never have expected. All he had ever seen was the temptress, and that was all he was ready for. He probably expected that she would try to use her wiles on him.

Men were so predictable.

She had two different reception chambers, for two very different purposes; this one also served as the office from which she ran her own little estate, and as such, it was both totally "like" her and completely unlike any of the faces she presented to the outside world. It was not spare and ascetic by any means; the desk behind which she sat was a work of art, fitted together from massive pieces of hand-carved, petrified wood polished to a mirror-gleam, and fitted around her so that she could keep every bit of work near at hand without having to reach for it. The charcoal-colored, leather-upholstered chair that cradled her was as comfortable as any sybaritic couch, and glided on rails into and out of the niche within the curve of the desk. There was a matching couch across from the desk; it matched superficially, that is, but it had been made so that, although it was extremely comfortable, it was treacherous. Be the occupant ever so tall, whoever sat there would find that his head was lower than hers, and getting up created some awkward moments. For the rest, the chamber exuded a restrained opulence; soft, dark grey carpet with subtle grey-on-grey pattern, silver-grey satin draperies covering the walls, lighter in color than the carpet but with the same pattern. The only color in the room lay in the stone of the desk, which drew the eye like a magnet, away from Triana. Which was the point; it was difficult for a beautiful elven lady to appear intimidating, but the desk managed to overwhelm simply by *being.*

Aelmarkin had reached the gates of her estate and been admitted not long ago. He would arrive at any moment, and she was perfectly ready for him.

Meanwhile she busied herself with the accounts. With the

fall in her fortunes, her little estate had to be self-supporting, for there were no more gifts—well, call them what they were, *bribes*—forthcoming from those who wished to attach themselves to a rising star. She supposed she *could* have improved her fortunes by marrying, but that was hardly a solution that was to her taste. There wasn't anyone free among the Old Lords who wasn't a close match for her wits and who wouldn't hedge her around with so many constraints that it would take all of her energy just to continue to enjoy herself as she had. And as for the Young Lords still loyal to their sires—

—well, she was not minded to wet-nurse a callow youth, who had no inclination to *work*, no interests but his own amusement, and no ambitions except to indulge in sex and games. She'd be better off adopting such a young fool than wedding him; at least then she could treat the fellow like the child he was.

So, following her fall from grace, she had applied herself to the business of raising and training very special slaves, exquisite creatures much in demand for their beauty and skills. There was always a waiting-list for her pretty boys and decorative men—she was an expert, after all, in the things that made males both ornamental and useful. There were plenty of Elvenlords—Aelmarkin for one—who bred and trained lovely female slaves for the luxury trade, but Triana was the only supplier of males for the same purpose. Some were bought by Elvenlords, but not nearly as many as were bought by the ladies—not that the lords these ladies answered to were ever made aware of the existence of these special slaves. Ladies might well be hedged about by rule and custom and kept close in the harem—but nothing prevented the visits of another Lady.

Triana, say, with a small entourage of her special slaves.

Now, once Triana and her slaves were within the walls of an estate, it was child's play for the lady she visited to purchase one or more; unless she was totally hedged about, she had simply to order that the requisite price be sent to Triana's steward by her own household steward, who would not gainsay her. The slaves then vanished into the household, assigned to the lady's personal service, never to be seen—oh, most certainly never!—

by the master of the house. It was easy enough to do, for even on estates that bred their own slaves there were always more being purchased—a special skill might be needed, or the slaves themselves disobliged by presenting one with too many of one sex and not enough of the other. The purchase of a great many of these male slaves that Triana so carefully trained was concealed under the bland heading "household expenses."

One of Triana's own slaves, sleek in her livery of dark silver and midnight, came to the door of the chamber, and Triana looked up and nodded acknowledgment of his silent signal. A moment later, a second arrived, Aelmarkin in tow.

"V'kel Aelmarkin el-Lord Tornal, my Lady," he intoned, as Aelmarkin sauntered past him into the office. Both slaves vanished as soon as Triana nodded to them.

"Aelmarkin, it is a pleasure to see you," she said, exuding subdued warmth. "Forgive me for not rising to greet you properly, but as you see, you have caught me in the midst of my little chores."

Now, Aelmarkin knew very well that she had gotten ample enough warning of his imminent arrival to have set her "little chores" aside, and she knew that he knew, and he knew that she knew that he knew, so they were most comfortable in their mutual knowledge. He looked the visitors' couch over before sitting in it, and was probably not surprised to discover what a disadvantage it put him at.

"My cursed cousin has covered himself with glory," he grumbled, as a slave appeared at the door, offered him wine, and disappeared again. "I hope you've been making better progress than I. It will be worth it to me to lose this bet if you can bring him down."

She smiled enigmatically. "You are aware that the key to all this is to either get rid of his mother or encourage him to put her in her—appropriate—place?"

Aelmarkin wasn't stupid; she had to grant him that. He sat up—or did so as much as the couch would allow him. "So it's Lady Lydiell who rules that roost, does she? I'd suspected as much. That's hardly surprising, given how long she has been the sole authority on that estate." He looked sour, and would probably have added his disapproval of a lady assuming such authority, but that was hardly politic in Triana's presence.

"But it's high time that Lord Kyrtian assumed his proper role as head of the estate, I should think," Triana replied, carefully examining her flawlessly polished nails. "And I expect, after all of his victories in the field, he's not going to be content to sit back and let somcone else manage his property anymore."

Aelmarkin relaxed back in his seat and produced a thin smile. "And the right woman could—would!—certainly encourage him in that direction, wouldn't she? The only question in my mind is, to what effect?" The smile hardened. "It is not going to please me particularly to find that the mother has been supplanted by the equally—competent—wife."

She left off examining her nails and gave him a chill look. How very like a male to assume that *she* intended to take the mother's place! "I do assure you, Aelmarkin, that *wedding* that child is no part of my plans. There is nothing about his estates or his person that could tempt me to the folly of putting *my* estates and *my* person into his legal control."

"See that you remain of that mind," Aelmarkin responded shortly. There was no mistake; he fully expected her to be that foolish! Did he think that every female in existence lived only to wed?

"The thought would never have crossed my mind, and is no part of my plans." She allowed a tinge of contempt to color her gaze. "Did you come all this way to fence with me, or have you another purpose you haven't yet revealed?"

He had come to discover what, if anything, she knew or had done, of course—but she suspected that he had also come to keep an eye on her. *Of course* he had begun to think her plans might include wedding Kyrtian as well as seducing him—he was a male, after all, and he was blinded by the automatic assumption that every female wanted ultimately to be someone's lady—as if the only possible identity a female had was through her male relatives.

Idiot.

But she could use him. This little exercise that had begun as a bet had taken on a life and a purpose for her far beyond its original. No, she did not want Kyrtian or his estates—but she *did* want that seat on the Council that had been denied her for so long. She wanted to be counted as the equal of any Great *Lord.* She knew—how not?—that Lord Kyndreth only intended to support Kyrtian for as long as it took to destroy the Young Lords' Revolt and possibly the Wizards. Once that was over, Kyrtian had the potential to become a dangerous rival for Lord Kyndreth's ascendancy in the Council. He would be altogether pleased to find someone willing to help and placed to eliminate Kyrtian when the time came. Not by assassination, no—that was too crude, and besides, there was the small problem of getting away with murder once it had been committed. That altogether-too-efficient bodyguard of Kyrtian's was another problem.

But elimination by *other* means—that was another covey of quail altogether. Once Triana was close to Kyrtian, trusted by him, there were any number of options open to her. She could arrange for him to do something that would disgrace him entirely—something to do with slaves, perhaps. He treated that bodyguard with suspicious softness, and Lydiell's family was known for its ridiculous cosseting of humans. Perhaps something could be concocted linking him to the Wizards as a sympathizer. Or if none of that seemed possible, a female, allowed closer than any male, could do things that were not open to men. She could administer drugs that would enfeeble mind or body, but gradually—and most important of all, irreversibly. She could leak important financial or other details of the estate that would allow someone like Kyndreth to work the magic that would ruin it—its main source of income lay in foodstuffs, after all, and properly manipulated weather or insect-plagues for several years in a row could bring the family to its knees. She could and would encourage infatuation on Kyrtian's part, along with the giving of very expensive gifts and reckless behavior to impress her. It was possible that she could arrange him to bankrupt himself, in games of chance and the like—or to break his own neck in sport and the hunt.

Or, even, to emulate his father and vanish into the wilderness, never to be seen again. That, in particular, appealed to her.

Encouraging him in that direction had great potential, and shouldn't be all that difficult. The wilderness had killed the father, so why not the son?

There were so many options open to her, once she got close to Kyrtian, that she had no intention of limiting herself to any one plan for the moment.

Meanwhile, it was actually possible for Aelmarkin to prove useful.

"If you would care to stay for a visit, I think we can accommodate you," she said, smiling, and surprising him. "Have you come prepared to remain?"

She knew he had, of course; although she might not know the contents of his baggage, she certainly knew the weight and volume. He'd brought a cart-full and only two personal slaves, so he'd been intending to inflict himself on her for a good fortnight at least.

"I confess I was hoping that you would tender the invitation," he replied cautiously. Clearly he had hoped to trick or bully her into the invitation, and had not thought for a moment that it would be offered freely.

"Then why don't you settle in," she said airily, waving a hand at the door, where at her invisible signal, the slave who had brought him here arrived, having responded to that summons. "I'll deal with my little household affairs, and we can discuss plans over luncheon."

She kept invisible her amusement at his struggles to extricate himself from the couch, and responded to his none-too-gracious bow with a nod of her head. As he accompanied the slave to the guest quarters she went back to her accounts. While not of spellbinding interest, they were important after all, and needed to be attended to. These days she didn't trust that anything had been done properly unless she herself had run a critical eye over it.

Now—luncheon was certainly going to be interesting. She was quite looking forward to it, after all.

She counted on the fact that she had welcomed Aelmarkin, and that there wasn't a great deal for him to amuse himself with on her estate, to ensure that as soon as he had convinced himself that she wasn't playing a deeper game than he thought, he would leave.

And, in fact, that was precisely what happened. Although he had clearly come prepared to remain for a week or more, within three days he was gone.

She had speeded his departure by being ridiculously virtuous for the duration of his visit. She held no parties, entertained no other guests, and although he did have access to some attractive female slaves she made it politely clear that if he damaged them, he could consider them purchases. His finances were not so secure that he could contemplate the purchase of one of *her* slaves at the uxorious valuation she would make, that pretty much put paid to *that* possible amusement.

That left hunting (which he detested), landscape-viewing (which bored him), and gaming (which he was ill-equipped for, either mentally or physically—nor would he have enjoyed either losing to a human slave or winning over one who was allowing him to win. No indeed.

So, off he went, liberating her from his unwelcome company and allowing her the freedom to find out just what Kyrtian was up to.

That meant a select dinner-party. Not one of the libertine affairs that she threw for those of the Young Lords who were still loyal to their fathers, but a sedate, yet very luxurious dinner for those few of the Great Lords who found her amusing and could afford to be seen with her.

Which included, of course, Lord Kyndreth.

First, she spent a profitable hour in the kitchens, informing the staff of her plans and terrifying them with casually dropped tales of what had happened to slaves whose food and service displeased the Great Lords who would be her guests. Of course, one thing that separated her establishment from that of other Elvenlords was that her meals relied on the skills of her kitchen-slaves and not on illusion—now her servants would exert themselves to the utmost to please.

She did not trouble herself about the menu; her chief cook would determine that. He knew what was best, freshest, at its peak of ripeness; he knew what fowl, fish, and meats were at perfection. She could leave all that to him, and set about delivering the invitations via teleson to her select Great Lords—six of them altogether, including Lord Kyndreth and his son Gildor. Gildor was a bore, but she would see that his simple needs were taken care of.

All male, of course; there would be one female, but only a human slave, Gildor's favorite concubine. He was absurdly faithful to the creature, but when Lord Kyndreth issued a delicate hint that Gildor would probably want to bring her, she laughed lightly.

"Children must have their toys, mustn't they?" she said, with just a hint of mockery. "No matter, my lord. I shall supply the rest of you with comely companions, so she will not be conspicuous. I may not *specialize* in such slaves, but I promise that you will be contented with what I supply."

"That will suit me very well," Lord Kyndreth replied, from the depths of the teleson embedded in the wall across from her desk, which was normally hidden behind the draperies there. He seemed just as amused by his offspring's dogged infatuation as Triana was. "Your hospitality will be gracious, as always."

"Then I can expect you tomorrow night." She smiled at him, exerting all her charm. "Good. You still have my teleson-key I assume?"

"I never let it out of my keeping," he assured her, as all of the others had. "Till tomorrow night, then?"

"Till tomorrow night." She allowed him to break the connection, and sat back in her chair, well-content for just a moment.

But only for a moment, for she had a decision to make. Should she display her expertise in magic, by creating a fantastical setting for her party, or distinguish herself by hosting the dinner with no magic whatsoever?

With magic, she decided after long consideration. But it must be subtle. These men were experts in powerful magic, and it would be far more impressive to caress them with surroundings that had a calm depth than to bombard them with—say—an enchanted exhibition of song and dance.

Subtlety would take time to produce; she had better start on it now.

She let the chair glide back on its rails, and took herself to her dining room, walking around it to study every angle.

Should she attempt an illusion of space, or create an atmosphere of intimate enclosure?

The aura of intimacy would be better for her purposes.

She called in her servants, and set them to removing the dining table and chairs from her last party and replacing them with two-person dining couches with attendant tables. By the time they returned with the moss-green, velvety drapes she wanted for the couches, she had decided on the theme.

Overhead, stars. As a backdrop, moss-covered stones, as if this place was a deep and narrow, secret valley. Slowly, and with great care, Triana built up the illusion as she sat on one of the couches, spinning it out of air and energy. She placed, and re-placed each stone, each graceful tree, each tiny violet, until she was satisfied with the balance and harmony. Tendrils of energy formed into branches and dissolved again until she was happy with the effect.

A waterfall? No. Everyone had waterfalls lately; they'd been done to death. Instead, she simulated the calls of frogs and crickets, and a single nightingale.

She called for refreshments and real trees in tubs that would be masked with draped vines, supervising the slaves as they moved the real trees into position around the six couches. It was already past sundown, but her guests would arrive well before dinner tomorrow, and she must have the dining room ready long before then.

She overlaid an illusion of moss on the carpet, visual only, as the carpet itself was soft enough to the tread to please. That left only scent—easily taken care of with no illusion at all. She left orders for garlands of flowers and leaves to be draped between the tubbed trees and wreathed around the couches.

She sat down on one of the couches and surveyed her work with a critical eye, making minute changes here and there so that the grotto appeared random, entirely natural. Even the sky overhead was a clever variation; she had keyed the stars to follow the movements of the real sky. By the time she declared herself finished, she was exhausted with the unaccustomed labor.

But it would all be worth it, tomorrow.

Triana surveyed her guests and smiled openly. Gildor and his favorite concubine were installed on the most private of the couches, at the rear of the grotto. Gildor clearly considered this to be a favor, not an insult—and so, evidently, did his father.

Each of the other five guests shared his couch with an attractive female slave, too, but these men were all powerful and probably had concubines that made these girls look like field-slaves. For them these slaves were nothing more than sentient furniture that served them silently without needing direction—pleasant accoutrements, which demonstrated the thoroughness and thoughtfulness of their hostess, but nothing more. They ate and talked as if the girls weren't even there. And the girls had been well-schooled, if not given the kind of intensive training that Triana lavished on her male slaves; they acted on the needs of their temporary masters before those masters even knew they had a need. Cups were refilled after a single sip, plates replaced with ones filled with new dainties the moment the hot foods began to cool or the cool ones to warm.

Triana herself had no companion, and ate very little. Her guests had loosened up enough to begin to speak of Council business, and she waited for the subject of Lord Kyrtian to come up, as Gildor dallied with his concubine, completely oblivious to his elders.

It was Lord Kyndreth who broached the subject, launching into a description of the aftermath of the climactic battle that routed the Young Lords.

"So where are the wretches?" asked Lord Wendrelith, his brow wrinkled with suppressed anger. "All that's been captured are slaves."

"Scattered like flushed quail—but unlike quail, they aren't regathering," Lord Kyndreth replied. "I suspect that they've each concocted bolt-holes during the time they were holding us off, and now they've gone to ground. How much time and effort are you willing to spend in tracking them to their lairs?"

"Not nearly as much as it will take, I suspect," said Lord Vandrien dryly.

"It will be a massive effort," Lord Kyndreth agreed. "Every tracking team will have to have a lord with it—one whose loyalty is unquestioned and cannot be subverted. Human slaves can be deceived or corrupted."

Lord Wendrelith shook his head in disgust. "Ancestors! We'd either have to track them down one at a time—"

"Which would take forever, even by *our* standards—" Triana interjected softly.

"—or strip our estates of supervisors. Neither is a viable option," Kyndreth said, nodding.

Triana, seeing that she had not been rebuffed, put in another of her observations. "Aren't they now crafting their own punishment?"

Another of the Great Lords turned his full attention to Triana. "That is a very interesting idea, my Lady," Lord Arentiellan said, with an intensely alert expression in his eyes. "Could you elaborate?"

"They cannot have more than one or two slaves apiece; they dare not collect in groups of more than three. They will not have anything that *we* think of as decent housing—not so much as a hunting lodge. They are likely to be living in caves or other crude shelters. None of them are truly powerful magicians; if they wish to eat, they must steal, hunt, gather—with their own hands and those of the one or two slaves they still retain." She laughed, in a voice low and husky. "It is entirely possible that many of them are out there, burning their dinners over smoking fires, only to shiver through the night in scant shelter, even as we speak." She smiled sweetly. "I cannot imagine a punishment worse than that—living like a wild human, and knowing that the only way to rectify the situation is to come groveling back to us."

All five of the Great Lords stared at her for a long time; then Lord Kyndreth broke out in unexpectedly loud laughter, in which he was joined by the rest. Gildor looked up at them for a moment without interest, then went back to his concubine.

"By the Ancestors, my Lady, I think you have the right of it!" said Lord Arentiellan with admiration. "My miserable brat is certainly welcome to all the burned rabbit and rain he can stand."

"What of the army, Kyndreth?" asked Vandrien. "If it were up to me, I'd disband them."

To Triana's veiled joy, the rest murmured agreement.

"It's up to the full Council, of course," Kyndreth demurred. "And there are the Wizards to think of."

"True . . ." Vandrien mused.

"Who we will, inevitably, outlive," Triana pointed out quietly. "With half their blood coming from slave-stock, I cannot see that they would have our years. With no more of the full blood, they will dilute their stock to the point that they are no more long-lived than mere slaves. Assuming that they don't kill each other off in their own quarrels."

"Once again, my Lady, you surprise and delight me." Lord Vandrien sat up enough to give her the full bow of respect. "I am in your debt for such reasoned observations."

"Thank you." She lowered her gaze modestly.

"Still, the Wizards . . . the question is, whether it is possible that they could pose a threat to us, simply by existing and serving as a temptation to the slaves to revolt." Kyndreth raised an eyebrow. "After all, our own offspring did."

"And slaves would have no difficulty with the notion of—of—living like wild humans." Arentiellan nodded. "Still, I don't know—"

"If you disbanded the army, there is a question of what Lord Kyrtian would do with himself," Triana suggested gently.

"If you ask me, he ought to be on the Council!" Arentiellan said immediately—but Triana saw Lord Kyndreth exchange a pointed glance with one of the others. *She* strove to catch his eye, and nodded slightly.

Lord Kyndreth looked surprised, then speculative, then returned her nod.

She leaned back into her couch, secure in the certainty that her message had been read and understood.

When the last honeyed grape had been eaten, and the last pleasantry exchanged, the Great Lords took their leave of their hostess, one by one. Lord Kyndreth sent his son and the concubine back through the Portal and made as if to follow, but found a sudden excuse to remain until all of the others had left *but* himself. Triana had accompanied them to the Portal herself to bid them a polite farewell, and now found herself, as she had hoped, alone with the Great Lord.

"So, my lady," Kyndreth said, when the last haze of energy had died from the Portal mouth. "You seem to have some notions about Lord Kyrtian."

"You are coming to the point with unaccustomed abruptness, if I may say so, Lord Kyndreth," Triana demurred.

"I am—somewhat concerned about Lord Kyrtian," the Great Lord replied, shifting his weight restlessly from his left foot to his right. "I may have awakened sleeping ambition in him, and if now he finds no outlet for it, he may be—distressed."

"He *may* use his new-won reputation within the Council to the disadvantage of others," Triana retorted, coming to the point just as directly as Lord Kyndreth had. "The strategies of war and politics are not unalike. On the other hand—"

"Yes?" Kyndreth prompted.

"His energies could be turned elsewhere, by someone who is clever enough to devise a channel for them." She looked up at him from beneath her long lashes, and smiled.

"And what would this distraction cost me, if I may ask, my lady?" Kyndreth was wasting *no* time; it occurred to Triana that he might be more worried about Kyrtian's ambitions than she had thought.

She decided to risk all on a single throw of the dice. "The Council Seat once held by my father."

His mouth pursed, but he didn't look as if he particularly objected to the notion. "It could be done . . . there have been females on the Council before now."

But he hadn't committed to the bargain either. "The same

clever person who found one outlet for his energies could turn them back to a more—unfortunate—direction, if bargains made are not kept."

Now he smiled, wryly. "You have a way with words, my lady. The bargain will be kept—and I believe that you will find our young Commander at the estate of his Aunt, the Lady Morthena."

She smiled radiantly at him. "Thank you, my lord. That is all I need."

He gave her a full court bow. "And all I require, as well." He stepped towards the Portal, which began to glow with energy in response to his proximity. Then he paused on the threshold, to look back over his shoulder at her. "Good hunting, my Lady," he said.

"And to you, my lord—" she replied. And he was gone.

23

Shana hadn't seen Kelyan and Haldor in ages—and she would have been hard-pressed to recognize them now. Rena had been right to take action; perhaps the change in the two "young" Elvenlords had been so gradual that it had passed relatively unnoticed by the people who saw them every day, but to Shana's eyes the change was something of a shock. Elvenlords were rarely "robust" by human or halfblood standards, but Kelyan and Haldor were wraith-thin, bones showing through skin gone quite translucent. Their silver-gilt hair was lank and brittle, and they bruised badly and easily. The dragons had brought them to the Citadel in a stupor induced by Mero; after waking them only enough to stuff them full of food and drink and clean them up after their journey, Shana had put them back to sleep again.

Two elven captives summarily dumped on their doorstep—one more problem to try and fix.

This time she was at a loss; this was *not* her area of expertise! If it hadn't been for Lorryn coming in and volunteering to find a group to help her with them, she wouldn't have known where to start.

Now Shana and the group of young wizards Lorryn had called together stared down at their pair of captives as they slept in a magic-induced fog, illuminated by a pair of mage-lights. And it wasn't just *wizards* that Lorryn had asked for help, either; the group included some of the strongest of the human mages that Shana had ever met as well.

I wouldn't have thought of that—stupid of me. Humans are the ones with the magic that works on thoughts. There were several of them now, living among the Wizards, drawn down out of the hills by the promise of a place where they could live without fear of being captured by elven-led slave-hunting expeditions. They stayed because Caellach had been very quiet ever since he had been defeated in the war of words with Shana. She was not altogether certain just how long he would remain quiet, but for now she was going to take the gift and not worry about him.

One of these human magicians was a middle-aged man called Narshy, whose ability to create illusions *within* the minds of those who were not adept at the Iron Peoples' mind-wall technique was nothing short of boggling. It was he, evidently, that Lorryn had first thought of when Mero had first suggested that the Wizards take over where Mero and Rena had been forced to leave off. Narshy could sometimes even get past the mind-wall—and because of that, Shana considered it a good thing he was on *their* side.

It made Shana wonder—before she dismissed the idea, appalled that she'd even considered it—if Narshy could be used to manipulate Caellach Gwain. A base and immoral idea—but oh, so tempting! It had taken a distinct effort of will to put the idea firmly aside.

It was just a good thing that Caellach regarded the full humans with so much disdain, though. She wouldn't have put it past *him* to use the weapon that she discarded as immoral.

For that matter, was it immoral to be tinkering with the minds of the two Elvenlords?

Probably. But they were already mad. We'd either have to kill them or fix them in such a way that they can't either betray us or the Iron People. She was caught between two equally distasteful solutions but had no real choice, since Mero and Rena had already meddled with the situation past mending.

Both Elvenlords lay on pallets in the middle of a small, disused room, with their human and halfblooded—"physicians"—clustered around them. "Well, it shouldn't be too difficult for ten or twenty of us together to concoct whatever memories of being held you want us to," Narshy told Shana with such supreme self-confidence that Shana felt a kind of grudging admiration. Whether he was right or wrong here, it would be nice to be able to feel, just once, that same sort of self-confidence. "With that many of us working at once, we can just—*engrave* the new memories in place within a few days. So, where do you want these two to have been held?"

"Umm—" she hadn't thought that far, to tell the truth, but if she admitted that, would she lose authority in their eyes? They were all looking at her as if they expected her to present them with everything they needed, ready to go. "What about the old Citadel?" she suggested, unable to think of anything more clever on such non-existent notice. "That way we won't have to make anything up—wouldn't real memories be better than ones we concocted?"

"But the Elvenlords know about the old Citadel," someone protested. "Wouldn't they have found these two?"

Before Shana could answer that, someone else did it for her, with glee in their voice. "No! Because we can use our memories of the old Citadel, but we don't have to have them think that the place they were kept *was* the old Citadel. If we don't leave these two where the old Citadel actually is, whoever finds them will think that their prison was somewhere near where they were found! Let the Elvenlords think that there's another hidden Citadel somewhere."

"What about the forest on the edge of Lord Cheynar's estate?" Lorryn suggested, from the rear of the group. "It's got a bad reputation anyway. Ancestors only know what's in there; plenty of hunters have gone in and never come out again. Cheynar won't even send his own men in there after escaped slaves anymore."

"That's true enough," Shana said thoughtfully. "I remember that Mero told me about some spooky sort of invisible thing that got his horse in there and nearly got him, when he and Valyn were escaping." She couldn't help it; she caught herself smiling grimly. There were plenty of things in those hills that were more than a match for Elvenlords.

"Good enough," Narshy said, taking the decision as made. "That's what we'll do—the lot of you that lived in the old Citadel, let's pry some of those memories out of your skulls and get them shared around so we can stuff these two full of them."

Shana was pleased and amazed at the way he managed to take control of the little group and herd them off to a corner where they could work undisturbed. With a sense of relief that was quite palpable, she realized that this time, for once, someone else was going to take care of a problem.

Unbelievable. "Where did you find him?" she asked Lorryn. "He acts as if he's been in charge of people, mages even, before this—"

"He has been—that's why I asked him to take charge of this group of yours," Lorryn replied, then suddenly looked anxious. "You don't mind—I hope—here I've gone and usurped your authority and now so has Narshy. Please tell me you aren't upset!"

"Mind? I should think not!" She shook her head and smiled, tiredly. "I don't know how you just *do* this, find the right people and get them to take over this or that job—I can't seem to find the right way to get people to think for themselves—or find the ones that can take the initiative on their own." She bit her lip as the all-too-familiar frustration arose.

"Maybe it's because you can't believe that *you* don't have to do everything," Lorryn said gently. "That's all I do; I find the people who are good at something, I ask them to do the job—

and I believe that they can. Then I get out of the way and let them do it, in their own way, at their own pace."

There was no graceful way to reply to that, and she just sat down on a stone ledge, feeling totally inadequate and utterly deflated. "I never wanted to be a leader," she said, forlornly. "If anybody had asked me, I could have had the chance to say no."

"I know." He sat down beside her. "I'd rather you were free to do what you're good at; planning, thinking, coming up with solutions. You're all bogged down with trying to get people to see that your solutions are sensible—or to come up with better ones. You spend half your time trying to convince people, and the other half trying to herd them into working on the solution rather than sitting around and arguing about it. I'd rather you didn't have to worry about all that."

"So would I." Suddenly she felt like weeping, and swallowed the lump in her throat, blinking rapidly. "But—"

He interrupted her. "Would you trust me to take what you aren't good at off your plate?" he asked, looking earnestly into her eyes. "I'm beginning to think that I am a leader, that it's in my nature—people listen to me, and I'm good at getting them to cooperate. But would you trust me to do what I'm good at so that you can do what *you're* good at?"

It took her a moment to work out what he was getting at, and he probably wasn't entirely certain of it himself. *Would* she put him in the position that Caellach Gwain wanted so badly, trust him to carry out what she could see were the right plans and decisions for her? Shouldn't she have someone older, someone from the original Wizards of the Citadel?

But neither Denelor nor Parth Agon—who *should* have been the leaders, and who Shana had expected would act as the leaders—seemed to be up to the job. Instead they had been delegating more and more authority to her, regardless of how she felt about it. Denelor never had cared to stir himself more than he had to, after all—she already knew that his besetting sin was sloth—and Parth—

Parth, she suddenly realized, was *old.* How old, she didn't actually know, not in years—but once they had gotten settled here and it seemed that she and her young wizards had the situation well in hand, he'd started taking a back seat, letting *her* fight with Caellach and his cronies, waiting for *her* to make the decisions. From vague hints over the years, she realized that he must be at least a century old, and perhaps more.

He's too old and tired to lead anymore, especially now that the Wizards are doing things and not just hiding. He doesn't want the leadership position either. It's too much for him now.

Maybe that was the case with Denelor, too.

But could she hand over that much authority to Lorryn? It would make her terribly vulnerable.

As vulnerable as if he truly is *my lover, the way everyone seems to think he is—and this is the sort of thing they'd expect me to do, start making him my—my—ruling consort. This will only make them more certain that we're lovers even though we're not—even though I—*

She flushed as that thought came, unbidden, and she must have forgotten to shield it, for suddenly he flushed, too. "I can't help what other people think," he said, defensively. "I can't help it that we—that I—"

She flushed again, fumbled for words, and couldn't find any.

"This isn't a very nice position for you," he said at last. "Even my own sister thinks we're—you know. No matter what we do, people are going to make up their own minds about your personal life and there's nothing you can say or do that will change what they think. But that doesn't make things easy for you, when there's nothing going on between us."

"Nor for you," she managed. "I mean, here I've been dumping all these things on you, and people are making all these assumptions, and you aren't even getting—" Now her face reddened so it felt as if she were inches from a fire.

"Assumptions! *I* don't mind, but I'm not in the same position that you are. It's got to be intolerable for you!" he exclaimed. "I—Shana—I wish—"

Suddenly, everything fell beautifully into place, as if the broken shards of a vase flew back together again before her eyes. She *knew* what he wished; he didn't need to say it, he was projecting it so forcefully that he was almost shouting the words in her head. He wanted those assumptions to be true, but he had been afraid that if he tried to push himself onto her, she would react by sending him away. He—he loved her. He really did! And—

Fire and Rain! I feel the same way!

Lorryn wasn't just a supportive and clever friend anymore. It wasn't *just* his friendship she needed and wanted. How long had she been feeling this about him? When did she stop feeling mere attraction, just enjoying his company, and suddenly start needing his presence the way she needed to breathe?

"I didn't—I *don't* want to force you into anything," he was saying, a little wildly. "I knew how you'd felt about Valyn and I didn't want you to think I thought I could replace him! I wanted us to be friends, really good friends, and I wanted it to be that we could *depend* on each other, and then after a while, when things started to get calmed down, and we had the leisure to think about ourselves we could—I mean I know that—I don't know—"

"Oh, hush," she said, suddenly full of a half-mad joy, and kissed him, putting everything *she* felt behind it just so she could get it all past the wild tide of *his* feelings.

:oh: she heard in her mind.

And then, for some timeless time, there was no room in either of their minds for words at all. Finally, for that one moment, no matter what would come after, everything was perfectly, completely, *right.* And she knew that she could trust Lorryn more than she could even trust herself.

"This isn't exactly the choicest spot—" he said, finally, into her hair. "We're rather out in public, not to mention our audience."

"I suppose they could wake up." Shana sighed and reluctantly broke the embrace.

She smoothed down her hair, self-consciously. He brushed a strand or two out of her eyes and tucked it behind her ear for her. "Have you any time to spare?" he asked wistfully.

No—there's this, and the forges, and the slave-collars, and the defenses and—

"I'll make some," she replied.

* * *

The irony of the situation was that the only people affected by this sea-change in their relationship were Lorryn and Shana themselves. But oh, the difference for them!

No one seemed to have noticed that Lorryn's quarters had been stripped and converted into a storage area. Spiteful comments from Caellach Gwain as reported by Shana's sharp-eared observers among the children were in no wise changed. And yet—the difference to her!

But the world outside their chamber was not going to go away.

A plan—a large and complicated plan to safeguard the Citadel forever—was beginning to take shape between the two of them. When news came from Keman that Lord Kyrtian had either given or been ordered to give the command of the army to someone else while the Council debated its future, the need for that plan took on a new sense of urgency.

The old Citadel had defenses that this one didn't; it was time to put them in place. Alara and Kalamadea were the chief architects of the Citadel, and it was time to consult with them.

She and Lorryn, Alara and Father Dragon sat together over a three-dimensional "map" of the Citadel, sculpted in removable layers, trying to plan what next needed to be molded out of the rocks of their mountain. One grim consideration—escape tunnels. Just in case the Great Lords decided to send the formidable Lord Kyrtian after them. Another, a duplicate of the Citadel far enough away to flee to, but near enough that an evacuation could take place by means of the transportation spell. There were enough Wizards able to use it now that the entire population could be evacuated within hours, and the advantage of the spell was that there would be no tracks to trace them by.

The existence of this duplicate—which was near enough to Zed's iron-mines to provide extra protection, but at this point hardly more than a few chambers molded out of the rock by some of the youngest dragons—was for now a closely-kept secret. Even from the dragons working on it. Alara had told them it was nothing more than a new set of lairs.

Which we also need, Shana thought, wondering just how

thin their resources could be stretched before things started snapping.

"The prisoners—how goes the memory-making?" Father Dragon asked. He and Alara were in halfblood form at the moment, or they would never have fit into the map-chamber. "I do not wish to alarm you unduly, but the sooner we can drop those two where they can be found, the better."

"Narshy's sorted out who's the best at planting the new memories, and he's got them stuffed with about a year's worth," Shana replied, tracing a possible exit tunnel from the lowest storage chamber onto the model with a wax pencil. "We decided to make the memories confused and foggy, as if they'd been kept drugged."

"We nominated Caellach as the Chief Wizard of this imaginary lot," Lorryn put in, getting a grin from Father Dragon and a head shake from Alara. "We had to have *somebody,* and at least he's memorable."

"Narshy says we should be able to plant them in a few days. He took the real memories of being captured, put new faces on the people doing the capture, then took it from there." Shana brooded over the model. "He's using as much of their real memories as he can, just changing the faces to Wizards, the tents to rock walls—and eliminating the iron collars. He's making those into something like slave-collars, so that the Elvenlords will think that this new lot of concocted Wizards are actually better at using elven magic than the Elvenlords themselves are."

"A good touch," Father Dragon said, admiringly.

"Now if only I could figure out a way to be in two places at the same time," Shana said, staring down at the map.

Keman and Dora had not been able to get any nearer to Lord Kyrtian without revealing themselves, thanks in no small part to the suspicious Sargeant Gel. Shana had not dared ask them to take that final, irrevocable step. *I need desperately to see Lord Kyrtian for myself!* Only then would she know whether or not he was truly to be trusted—and if trusted, to be approached. But if she was gone from here, there was no telling what mischief Caellach might not get up to. If she was delayed—if something happened—could Lorryn control the old troublemaker for long? Or would Caellach manage to regain his hold over his old faction and set this entire warren seething with so many quarrels and bad feelings that it would all fall to pieces?

"Your mind or your body?" Kalamadea asked, suddenly, with an odd birdlike twist of his head.

"What do you mean?" she replied, wondering what had prompted *that* sort of reply.

"Well—if it's your *mind* that needs to be in two places at once—that is, if you feel that you have to be able to see and make decisions yourself about things going on in two different places at the same time, then we can't help you," Kalamadea said. "But if it's your *body* that needs to be *seen* in two places—if, for instance, you wanted to leave, and had confidence in someone enough to let him make decisions for you but you needed a sort of figurehead or puppet of yourself so that certain people wouldn't decide to make trouble while you were gone—

"A certain person whose name rhymes with *drain,*" Alara put in, with a sly wink.

"Exactly—and if that's what's concerning you, well, that's entirely different. And it's something Alara and I can help you with." Father Dragon looked particularly smug, and it didn't take long for Shana to realize why, what he meant, and she wanted to smack herself in the head for not thinking of it sooner.

"Of course!" she exclaimed. "Oh, Mother—there's no reason why you can't shape-shift into *me,* is there? You know me well enough to counterfeit me for everybody—" She flushed, as Lorryn laughed and made a face. "—well, *practically* everybody!"

"No reason at all," Alara said agreeably. "And I don't know why we didn't think of this before, when You-Know-Who became so interfering and disagreeable. Unless it was because we were too worried about what had happened to you to think of it."

Already her mind was racing; if Alara could do this, and was willing, then *she* could go in person to see this Lord Kyrtian and make a decision about whether or not she should try to make an ally of him.

She exchanged a glance with Lorryn. "Lord Kyrtian," he said simply, their minds following the same track.

"I can't make a decision about him without seeing him myself," she replied, nodding.

"Nor should you," Kalamadea said firmly. "Keman and Dora are good children, but if they make a poor choice, they have the option of flying away from Wizards and Citadel and all. Not—" he added hastily "—that I believe that they *would,* but the option is there, lurking behind their thoughts, and it could make them a bit less cautious." He rubbed his chin thoughtfully. "I believe that same option might have made me too cavalier in my own decisions at the time of the First War."

Since Shana had occasionally wondered that herself, there was no good answer she could make to that.

Since she couldn't, she held her tongue. "Lorryn can control Caellach better than I can," she said, with complete confidence and a wink to him. "And Lorryn is someone the rest will listen to."

They listen to him more than they do to me, actually. Maybe because he never was a wizard's apprentice. There were some profound disadvantages to having been the rawest of raw beginners within the old Citadel and the old regime itself, and that was one of them. "There's only one difficulty, and that's—well, if anyone looks into Alara's mind, they're going to know she isn't me."

"But the troublemakers are not the ones who are at all adept with the powers of human magic," Lorryn pointed out logically.

Alara just shrugged off the difficulty. "How often is anyone likely to snoop on the thoughts of the Elvenbane anyway?" she asked. "I shouldn't think it happens often, and besides, I can probably learn mind-wall well enough to keep them out."

Perhaps. Perhaps not. Dragon minds aren't like ours. But Alara was right that in all this time, Shana had very seldom felt the touch of another's mind on hers, and even then it was someone wanting to communicate, not snoop.

"I can take you to where Keman and Dora are," Kalamadea continued serenely. "Now that Lord Kyrtian has taken leave of his command while the Great Lords debate whether or not to disband the greater part of the army, Keman and Dora have just today followed him to Lady Morthena's estate."

"Lady Moth?" Lorryn's exclamation made them all turn to look at him—and this news must have come as a surprise to him. "But that's where my mother is! Lady Moth is one of her oldest friends!"

"Really?" That was interesting, but not overly so, and it didn't seem particularly important to their current situation. But Lorryn was continuing.

"You remember, we've been getting some communications from mother—irregular letters," he continued. "Lady Moth isn't just any elven lady. She has *never* mistreated her humans—they're servants, not slaves, to her. In fact, when we left mother with her, just at the start of the revolt, she was riding the bounds of her estate with armed human men who called her 'Little Mother' and treated her—well, with *affection.*"

That got her attention. The only Elvenlord that she had ever seen treated with affection by humans had been Valyn. "Really?" And Lord Kyrtian had gone there—why? "I wonder—"

"Don't wonder, go and find out," Father Dragon urged her. "Do it before the Great Lords make up their minds what to do about him. Because if they don't decide to use him, you can be sure that they'll try to destroy him."

"Would that be so bad?" Shana countered, knowing that she sounded heartless—but she had to bring up the point, because others would. If it came down to it, her authority rested on one thing, and that was the ability of the rest to trust her decisions. With some rare exceptions, the humans and Wizards of the Citadel would see Elvenlords taking down other Elvenlords as a step in the right direction, and not trouble themselves as to what might follow.

"It could be." That was Lorryn, looking troubled. "For one thing, Shana, *if* we can make him an ally, he'd be better than anyone here at the art of war. For another—he *has* to be one of the rare ones, like Lady Moth. If he's removed, all the humans on his estate will be in deadly danger from whoever they put in his place. You can't want that!"

She groaned, but had to agree; if all that was true, even if they managed to rescue all of Lord Kyrtian's slaves, it would strain the capacity of the Citadel to support them. Why was it that every turn of fate brought more and more people for whom she had to be responsible into her purview?

"He may not realize just how treacherous the Great Lords are, Shana," Kalamadea said quietly. "He may not dream he's *in* danger. If nothing else, he deserves to be warned."

"And the best person to warn him is me, I suppose." She tried to sound resigned, but aside from the pressure and burden of apparently additional responsibilities, she didn't really feel resigned at all. She felt excited—*this* was the sort of thing she was good at.

But Lorryn—to separate, even temporarily, now that they were *together*—

Once again, he read her feelings as well as her thoughts.

"You go," he said, softly, before she even looked at him. "You have to go. I'll see no one makes trouble here, and you'll be there and back again before you know it. It can't take more than a few days at most, can it?"

"I wouldn't think so, but—" Now she looked at him.

:I'll miss you every moment, but this is something only you can do. He might not trust a dragon. He won't trust that some strange wizard has the authority to speak for all of us. Rena can't get here soon enough to talk to him, even if she'd be willing to leave Mero. But you're the Elvenbane. If you make him an offer, he'll believe you.:

And there, after all, was the heart of the matter. She was distinctive; no one could mistake her for anything other than what she was. Her description had circulated to every part of the Elvenlords' domain now, and once Lord Kyrtian set eyes on her, he would know who she was.

:Just promise to come back to me.:

That was the easiest promise she had ever made.

24

Kyrtian's nose tickled, and he rubbed it absently. *Why is it that in spite of decades of practice, the Ancestors had handwriting that was uniformly atrocious?* The tiny words not only looked as though they had been written with the aid of a lens, they conformed to no school of calligraphy *he'd* ever seen.

Kyrtian labored his way through yet another personal journal, making notes on sheets of foolscap for later transcription in his own neat (and extremely legible) hand. This business of concocting a "personal" script-style must have been a common affectation among the bored. But why they should choose to also write as if paper was more valuable than gold was beyond his comprehension.

Here in Lady Moth's library, it was so quiet he could almost hear dust motes falling out of the air to add to the accumulation on the books. Lady Moth had brought back all the volumes that she had extracted during the time that the Young Lords were using the place as their headquarters. The situation was reversed now, and she commanded her late husband's estate and holdings as she should have done some time past. With no army to command and no war to fight, the Young Lords were hardly in need of a command-post, although they were still full of an impotent defiance.

Kyrtian reached for a glass of water and absently took a sip.

For the moment, the Young Lords were living on the grounds of the dowager-estate, Lady Moth's Tower, hiding in the one place where no one was likely to come looking for them. Wearing illusory disguises to make them look like human slaves, it was unlikely that even if a search was made there for them that they would be found.

As long as they can hold together, and not have someone get a change of heart and defect, they should do all right.

He'd talked to them all, and at the moment, he didn't think that likely. Not while they were safe and not having to suffer any serious hardships.

Not even Moth's own slaves knew who they were—the story was that they had been part of the Young Lord's army, and that Moth was sheltering them to keep them from being punished for having been conscripted in the first place.

It was a situation that made it hard for Kyrtian to keep a straight face whenever he thought about it. Living among the slaves was going to do them a world of good.

Already he'd seen signs of a change in attitude towards the humans from some of them. He had every confidence that if—or when—the Revolt started again, it would be on a very different footing.

If it happened, they already counted on it having a very different ending. *Their* plans called for him to either join them openly or permit the Great Lords to place him back in command of the army and proceed to actually do as little as possible. Then, at the right moment, he could turn the Council's army against the Great Lords themselves.

But I don't want to do that if I can help it. Such a war—because it *would* be a war, and not a revolt—would be bloody. Most of the casualties would be human; there was just no getting around that. And although—if the Young Lords had changed their attitude towards slave-owning by then—the humans on their side would have an active stake in the outcome, they would still be the ones taking the full force of the fighting. There were far more of them than there were Elves, and as physical fighters—well, the Young Lords were not very good.

Kyrtian's plan, which he hoped to talk the Young Lords into, was more subtle. He wanted them to creep back to their august fathers one at a time, in secret, and grovel. They would still have the iron jewelry that kept their fathers from working magic on them; that was key.

After they returned, and once they managed to regain some freedom of movement, he hoped they could work their own way back up through the hierarchy, and attrition among the Great Lords would eventually put *them* in the seats of power.

Such a plan, however, did have a number of drawbacks, not the least of which was that there were plenty of the Great Lords who would quite readily slay their rebellious sons and underlings out of hand if they ever so much as showed their faces. And once back in a father's good graces, there was always the chance that someone would turn traitor. That would be . . . awkward.

So for now, they were in hiding, and if they weren't accomplishing anything, at least they weren't getting into trouble either.

Meanwhile—as the Council debated the next use they were going to make of him, and his erstwhile enemies cooled their heels in circumstances he hoped would teach them some empathy, *he* was using his enforced leisure to get back to the search for his father.

The answer to his father's whereabouts was in this room, somewhere, he was sure. The trouble was that there was so *much* to wade through, and none of it had ever been properly cataloged. Personal journals were crammed in next to the sort of romantic novels considered appropriate for ladies to while away their hours with—books on flora and fauna were piled atop maps and volumes on magic.

His nose tickled again, and he unsuccessfully tried to suppress a sneeze. Moth or her friend Viridina were in here a dozen times a day, trying to clean out the dust magically, but every time he opened a volume more of it flew up into the air in clouds.

Moth's family had a mania of their own—for collecting. Most of this library had come to her from various family members. They were, however, indiscriminate in their mania. In the case of the ones who'd acquired books and manuscripts, the definition of a "book" seemed to be "any collection of paper with covers on it" and the definition of "manuscript" was "any collection of handwritten paper." As far as he could tell, there was no method in what they'd selected, no categories, no attempt to place a value on anything.

Perhaps, if he'd been in here *before* the Young Lords took residence, he'd have been able to find the things his father had studied that had given him his real clue. But they had simply shoveled everything they found to the side in heaps so that they could use the room for their own purposes, and Moth hadn't helped when she extracted the books that *she* thought were important. Moth, bless her, had been under the impression that she had kept some order and cleanliness to the library.

Yes, well, that was before *we found the boxes in the storage-chamber.* Moth's husband had maintained a "show" library, with things he thought worth keeping attractively shelved. The rest—which amounted to four or five times the volume of works on show—had gotten packed into boxes and stacked up in a storeroom behind the library itself. Moth had thought that the storeroom was empty until they'd opened the door. In their search for maps they could use to plan their campaign and the plans of manors and estate-houses, the Young Lords had rummaged through it all, bringing some things into the library and leaving them, removing other things to make room for what they brought in. Whatever order had once been here was gone completely. Now the storeroom had shelves, and so did the unused office next to it, and the unused reception-room next to *that,* and Kyrtian was trying to bring some order to the chaos.

Kyrtian, however, was fast becoming convinced that his answer lay, not in printed books or illuminated manuscripts, interesting as those might be, but in the personal journals kept often by elven ladies, and infrequently by their lords.

His father had almost certainly divined the location of the Portal from *something* in here. That location was lost, and what was more, there seemed to be evidence that the Ancestors who had built the thing had engaged in an active effort to *hide* that location from their descendants—and even from some of their own who had come through the Portal.

Why? That was a good question. Perhaps they feared a traitor in their midst who would re-open the Portal to their enemies. The Portal itself had cooperated in erasing memories; it was fairly clear that the Crossing was such a traumatic ordeal in and of itself that a substantial number of those who Crossed *could not* remember a great deal of what happened immediately thereafter.

And perhaps some of those folk were "helped" to forget.

None, not one, of the Great Lords that had created the Portal and survived the Crossing left any substantive records about it. That much was fact. Nor did any of the historians—another fact. So with no official records, he was left with only one other source, the unofficial ones—and of those, the best would be the records of those who were considered too insignificant to matter.

The ladies . . . ah yes, the ladies.

And the eccentrics.

Some of those journals were attractively bound and might at one time have been shelved in the main room—and that might be where Kyrtian's father had gotten his information.

Or he might have found something in official records that Kyrtian had somehow completely overlooked.

Kyrtian ran a dusty hand through his hair in frustration, then told himself sternly not to get so impatient. After all, his father had been hunting for the Portal for decades before Kyrtian was born; by the time he found what he was looking for, he had probably gotten to the point that he was *so* familiar with the Ancestors and the way their minds worked that he was able to intuit things that weren't obvious.

So he was wading through everything handwritten that Moth had in this library, with the Great Book of Ancestors beside him. Before he could eliminate any manuscript or journal, he first had to figure out who wrote it, or at least who the author's contemporaries were, then discover whether or not the author lived far enough back to have made the Crossing.

Since it was almost a guarantee that most of the manuscripts he found would be from too late a period to mention the Crossing except in passing, he would then try to find every *other* manuscript that could be attributed to that person. Most people who were addicted to journal-writing had produced multiple volumes over the course of their very long lives. If the author was of too late a period, well, it helped to be able to weed out everything that could be attributed to her pen.

It was a painfully logical and methodical plan of dealing with the situation. It was also very tedious, very time-consuming, and very, very dusty.

Kyrtian had two helpers at least—Gel, and that little female concubine that Lady Triana had been so considerate in planting on him. He'd sent for her a-purpose once he'd turned over his commission to Lord Kyndreth while the Council debated. If Triana was so interested in what he was doing, he was inclined to allow her more information than she could comfortably digest. He had a notion that she was working with Aelmarkin, at least for the moment. Lady Moth had been very helpful in presenting him with a summary of her past behavior, and from that he'd formed the opinion that whatever game she played, whatever alliances she made, her ultimate goal would serve no one but herself.

Now, to his mind, the best possible way to handle her was to give her the information he *wanted* her to have. Gel had examined the girl himself, interrogating her to the point of exhaustion and even tears, and it was *his* opinion that Lydiell had succeeded in "turning" her. Whenever she reported to Triana—and Triana had been *very* interested to learn just where he was and what he was doing right now—Gel was there, making certain she stuck to the script they'd agreed on.

Nevertheless, she didn't know exactly what it was he was doing in Moth's library; what she didn't know, she couldn't be forced to reveal if Triana or Aelmarkin ever got their hands on her. She knew only what she *saw*—which was that he had ordered all the books down off the shelves to be sorted—that Moth's slaves had then reshelved and cataloged all of the printed material. While they worked, he examined the handwritten stuff, creating a second catalog, and she and Gel shelved what he was done with. She couldn't read elven hand-script; she didn't know what he was keeping and what he was rejecting. So although she now had a wealth of information about his movements, none of it was likely to do Triana any good.

He actually expected the infamous Triana to put in an appearance before too very much longer. He couldn't see how she could possibly resist trying to pry into his affairs in person. She would probably also try to seduce him; that was her pattern in the past. He had heard, even from Moth, that she *was* a great beauty, and not a passive, statuesque creature either, but lively, witty, aggressive, and not afraid to show her intelligence. Such a woman had learned how to turn her looks and fascination into a weapon long ago. She might even have approached Lord Kyndreth as well as Aelmarkin, prepared to use anyone and anything in her quest for personal power. If that was the case, she might well have met her match in Lord Kyndreth, who had been playing deep games for far longer than little Lady Triana.

Ancestors—I've turned into such a cynic—

There were times when he longed for what he had been—when the worst of his worries was working out little battle-plans and conspiring with Lydiell to keep Aelmarkin at a distance. To think that he had actually looked up to people like Lord Kyndreth!

Well, I know better now.

It hadn't just been his own experiences that had enlightened him, nor the night-long, acid-washed "frank talk" that Moth had had with him when he first arrived. It was the testament of these very manuscripts beneath his hands, that outlined the machinations and betrayals, the abuse of power and the use of it, from the point of view of those that the powerful considered too insignificant to monitor. Mind, some of *them* were no prizes, either, acting like chickens in the hen yard, turning, when pecked, to hammer on those beneath *them.* But it had been an enlightening, if distasteful education, wading through the pages they probably thought no one else would ever read.

Is it any better among the Wizards and free humans, I wonder? With most of his illusions gone, he had to guess that it was probably more a matter of degree. The Great Lords were *so* powerful and those who aspired to their power were *so* fixated on achieving it, that the very power they all held or craved corrupted them. It was inevitable unless, like Moth, they were acutely aware of just how dangerous that much power was. The fact that they lived such very long lives only meant that the corruption and selfishness was etched deeper than it could ever possibly go with a mere human.

But there are the others. Like Moth, Lydiell—and myself, I hope. Power didn't have to corrupt, if you knew just how dangerous it was, and were well aware that it came burdened with incredible responsibilities. He hoped that there were those among the Wizards and free humans who knew that.

Perhaps that was the key to those among the Elvenlords who did treat the humans who had come under their protection with the same consideration that they would have given an elven underling; and those elven underlings who treated humans as equals. They were the ones who had felt the boot of the Evelon overlords on their backs, and had *learned* from the experience—or who, at least, had determined never to treat one with less power as they themselves had been treated. And those Ancestors, in their turn, had passed their attitude down to their offspring.

Were there more such households as his and Lady Moth's? Possibly—for a moment, he dared to hope that there were, hiding their nature just as he and his father and grandfather had. They were probably just like his family—remaining quietly, self-sufficiently in the background, permitting the Great Lords to believe that they were hopelessly provincial and not worth troubling with. Ancestors knew that if Aelmarkin hadn't been such a thorn in their side, *their* household would never have come under the scrutiny of Kyndreth, and *he* would never have been forced into the "open" to find himself recruited as a military expert.

He realized at that moment that he'd been staring at the same page for quite some time, and hadn't deciphered a word of it.

Gah. I'm a scholar, not a philosopher! He bent over the closely-written page again.

Whispers from the rear of the library intruded on his attention—because one of the whisperers was Gel, and there was a tone in the man's voice he'd never heard before.

He took a quick glance over the top of the manuscript. Sure enough, there wasn't a great deal of shelving going on, but Gel and the pretty little concubine certainly had their heads close together.

Well, well, well! The granite crag cracks at last!

He didn't know whether to laugh or be annoyed. Not that *he* wanted the girl; oh, she was attractive and talented enough, but so were the two other girls his mother had purchased for him. But of all the times for his tough-minded partner to pick to go soft over a woman, this had to be the worst!

On the other hand, this was *Gel* he was talking about. Gel, who had taught him the business of war and fighting, Gel who stuck by his side like a faithful dog, Gel who had never asked for anything for himself. How could he possibly be annoyed that Gel had finally found someone who touched his heart?

Oh, Ancestors.

Now how was he going to juggle all this? Hidden rebels, possible treachery from his superiors, the hunt for his father—and now Gel in love? What next?

As he stared at the not-so-young lover, he felt a tap on his shoulder. Lady Moth had come into the library without his noticing, and she wore her mask-face, the one that generally meant that she was—well, up to something.

"We have a visitor that I believe you will want to meet yourself," she whispered, after a glance at Gel and the girl who were completely oblivious to anything else going on around them.

Oh no—not Triana—

"You may tell Lady Triana that—" he began.

But Moth's eyebrows shot up, and she interrupted him. "I don't know why you should be expecting *her*," Moth replied, "but it's not Lady Triana. And I do think you should put down that stupid journal written by an equally stupid blockhead and come with me. Now."

Seeing that she was not to be denied, Kyrtian sighed, marked the place where he was leaving off, and stood up.

The lovers never noticed that he was leaving. That in itself was an indication of just how hard Gel had fallen.

Oh, Ancestors, I only hope that Triana didn't place that girl with me to get at Gel rather than me. . . .

With his thoughts flitting between amusement and concern, he wasn't paying a great deal of attention when Moth brought him into a tiny chamber kitted out as a sitting-room, where a young woman waited, pacing up and down in front of the windows, displaying no great patience herself. All he noticed at first was that she was red-haired and green-eyed, clothed in the same sort of tunic, boots, and trews as a common laborer, with the physique of someone who was athletic and very much used to taking care of herself in any and all circumstances. He couldn't imagine why Moth had insisted he meet this person—unless, perhaps, she was one of Moth's human servants and had information about the Young Lords?

"Lord Kyrtian," Moth said formally, "I believe that you have many things to discuss with Lashana." She tipped her head to the side as he sighed with exasperation, still wondering what she was getting at. She pursed her lips, but her green eyes held the ghost of amusement in them. "I believe you might know her by another name. *Elvenbane.*"

WHAT?

He lost every vestige of exasperation, annoyance, impatience in that moment. He stared at the woman, who stood poised like a deer about to flee, trying to make his mind believe what his ears had just heard.

Red hair—but elven eyes. And the ears. Wizard blood, unless it's an illusion—

But Moth would never have been fooled by an illusion. Moth had met Wizards. Moth's friend Viridina—her son was a wizard.

"Lashana arrived bearing a letter from Viridina's halfblood son, verifying her identity," Moth said, as if divining his thoughts.

She probably is, the old schemer! She doesn't need to read thoughts, she knows me like her favorite sonnet!

"I am—fascinated to meet you, Lashana," he said carefully. "Or should I call you 'Elvenbane?' "

"Please *don't,*" the young woman said firmly. She was still tense and very ill-at-ease. "It's not a name I ever claimed for myself."

Both of them stood so awkwardly, so stiffly, that Moth began to chuckle. "Kyrtian, Lashana, for Ancestors' sake, sit down! You look like a pair of bad carvings, I do swear!"

Kyrtian relaxed marginally, and gestured to Lashana to take a seat on the cushioned bench nearest her. She did so, moving as if she was an old creature with frozen joints. He selected a slightly lower seat on a stool, to put his eyes a little lower than hers.

"I don't have much time," she said, finally. "And I'm not certain how to begin."

"I can tell you that," he offered, and tried a smile. "Begin with why you knew you could trust me not to kill you on sight."

As he had hoped, such a direct and blunt approach was precisely the right way to approach her, and she began telling him the most amazing story that he had ever heard in his life. He listened and had to work not to allow his mouth to fall open with shock more than once. To think that two of her people had gotten close enough to him to stand guard on his very tent so that they could spy on him! He would have to have a word with Gel about that, later.

At some point his capacity for sheer astonishment was exhausted, and he could only listen to her in a sort of trance. It was all too impossible to believe, and yet he had to believe in it. The things she told him fit too well with what he already knew.

Then, after talking until she was hoarse, she paused, and exchanged a significant look with Lady Moth. "So," she said. "Now you tell me to take myself off. Or—"

"Or I ask you if your Wizards would dare accept the Elvenlord Commander as an ally," he finished, having already come to the conclusion that this, and only this, could be the reason why she had come to him. Brilliant—audacious—and completely logical. And on the other hand, completely illogical that she should *ever* trust a fullblood.

She stared at him, and suddenly every bit of tension ran out of her, just like water running out of a cracked jar. "Fire and Rain!" she exclaimed weakly. "You're *just* as Keman claimed you are!"

He wondered if she had read his thoughts, using the same human magic that some of his own people had—and Moth's.

"Only the surface," she replied instantly. "I don't pry; none of us would. And if you want, I can teach you a method to keep even the surface thoughts private."

He looked deeply into her emerald eyes, so like and unlike a fullblood's, and saw only sincerity in them. He'd been around human mages too often to feel unnerved by her instant response to his thought. "I'd appreciate that," he replied. "But it can wait. So, now I assume you know about my own people?" A sudden, blinding idea occurred to him at that moment, the way that he could, finally, safeguard his own people and his mother no matter what happened to *him,* and he saw that *she* saw it in his thoughts by the surprise that flashed into her eyes.

"Yes!" she exclaimed. "Oh, indeed yes, Lord Kyrtian, we can, and we *will,* take your folk if they must be evacuated! Portals—the transportation magic—whatever is needed; between your people and mine we can do whatever it takes to get them to safety. And you needn't fear for your mother and the other Elves of your house, either—we have Lorryn's half-sister with us and she is as welcome now among us as he is!"

Now it was his turn to feel relief that made him sag. "Blessed Ancestors," he murmured, passing a hand over his brow. "If you knew what it meant to me to hear that—" Then he smiled weakly. "What am I saying? Of course you know."

But relief from one problem didn't help much with the others, and if this young woman did not have much time, they needed to make plans, urgently. "Bless you, Lashana. Now—let's decide between us what I can do for you and yours."

Gel was not happy with him.

"Next time—" Gel muttered under his breath. "The next time you go making hare-brained meetings without me, with women you've never seen and don't know anything about, I'll take you to the horse-trough and hold your head under till you come to your senses, I swear!"

Kyrtian sagged against the back of his chair, but was not going to back down this time. He didn't blame his old friend—but something had told him that Lashana and Gel shouldn't meet, yet. There wasn't enough time to negotiate all of Gel's suspicions, not and come to an understanding before she had to leave. Ancestors! The *danger* she had put herself in by coming to him directly! And the danger had increased with every moment that passed; there was no telling who could have discovered her there.

Gel's dinner sat uneaten in front of him; he had already stuffed *his* meal down his own throat as he'd explained the miracle that had happened in that incongruously ordinary room this afternoon. "Gel, Morthena was there the entire time—and what could one little wizard-girl possibly do to me?" he asked, reasonably.

Gel only growled. "I suppose you know she could have been talking things she's got no authority to promise?"

"Morthena says she has the authority, and that's good enough for me." His mind was too full of plans now to be put off by Gel's irritation. His old friend was mostly just annoyed that, for the first time, he had made plans and forged a pact without Gel's supervision. "I know what I'm doing, Gel," he said, with perfect conviction.

Gel looked at him with one eyebrow raised, then slowly and grudgingly nodded. And his expression changed completely. He went from anger—to defeat.

"I guess you do," he said slowly. "I guess you don't need *me* anymore."

Now it was his turn to feel exasperated, and he tossed his fork down on his plate. "Oh for—don't be ridiculous. I'd as soon cut off my right hand! Now, look—we need to try and think of all possible contingencies here, and have some sort of skeleton in place if—"

There was a tap on the door, and Lady Moth poked her head into the library. "If I didn't know better, I'd say you were a wizard, or else you somehow conjured the baggage by saying her name," she said sourly. "I seem to be attracting all manner of visitors today."

This time, Kyrtian knew that the name that sprang into his mind was the right one. "Oh, no—" he said, grimacing. "Lady Triana. Just what we need."

25

"Moth! Can you keep the b—Lady Triana occupied for a little?" Kyrtian asked, a little desperately. He ran both his hands through his hair frantically. "I *can't* see her just yet—"

"Oh, probably." Moth's annoyance was turning to amusement. "In fact, I'll take it as a challenge. Obviously you'd better talk to Gel; I'm sure he can advise you. Besides, you're in no state to entertain a lady—the least you can do is clean yourself up." Moth eyed him with disfavor. "Believe me, you'd better have your wits about you *and* present a marble facade to Lady Triana. I'll go and insist she tell me every tiny detail of every affair, quarrel, and inconsequential bit of maneuvering among the Great Households while you do so. I've been isolated for some time—and everyone knows what a terrible old busybody I am. If I can't engage her, Viridina can."

"You are not old," he protested, earning a smile. "Thank you."

Moth was right; he needed time to get his wits about him. While Lady Moth left the library to keep her visitor busy with a flood of gossip—under the excuse that she needed to be caught up on all the news she had missed while surrounded by the Young Lords—Kyrtian had a lot of work to do. And first on his list was to warn the girl that Triana was here.

But when Kyrtian got up from the table, Gel finally broke off the conversation with his young woman. Renna? Reanna? *Rennati,* that was it. Both of them looked up as he approached.

"I've been telling Rennati that you had a visitor," Gel began, and Kyrtian felt a surge of panic, which eased as Gel went on, with a lift of an eyebrow, "It's a rather good thing that those poor misused slaves that the Young Lords commandeered have realized that no blame is going to be attached to them and sent one of their number to talk to you."

Thank the Ancestors he didn't give her the real story yet! Kyrtian thought, relieved. "Yes, well, you can't blame them for wanting to send a sort of delegate to me to plead their case," he replied, mendaciously. "They can't have realized that Lady Moth would treat her human servants exactly the way we treat ours. But we've got another visitor, it seems. Lady Moth tells me that Lady Triana has come calling."

Rennati's face went dead white; that alone would have been a giveaway that she had been covertly serving Triana, even if Kyrtian hadn't already known the whole story. Triana had chosen her tool very poorly, on the whole, if she so readily betrayed herself by her mere expressions.

But Triana never really thought of humans much, except as cat's-paws. She probably never once considered that he or Gel—or anyone that mattered!—would be around to see her reaction if Triana's name was mentioned.

But Gel immediately put his weathered paw over her slim hand, and said gruffly, "Now, Rennati—she needn't even know you're here—"

"On the contrary," Kyrtian said firmly, "I *want* Triana to know she's here. In fact, I have something in mind—it might be a little humiliating for you," he continued, turning to the girl, "but if you can weather a bit of humiliation, I think we can turn her attention away from you completely and for all time, if you'll cooperate."

He explained what he wanted her to do, and although the girl flushed with embarrassment, and Gel growled over the plan, they both eventually agreed it was the only possible solution. "She'll probably corner you at some point this evening, if only to get her teleson-ring back," he cautioned. "I think we can manage to interrupt that confrontation before she can do anything to you, but you know, if she *does* take back the ring, it will effectively sever all contact with you and show that she's got no more interest in you."

And if what Lashana told me is true, we can also expect to have a device to completely neutralize the collar she placed on you in a day or so, he thought, but did not say aloud. That was a secret he wished to keep to himself until Lady Triana was long gone.

Rennati nodded, and licked her lips. "I think that would be best, my lord," she whispered, as Gel squeezed her hand comfortingly. "I'll go to my quarters and prepare."

"And I'd better go to mine," Kyrtian said, stifling a groan. He left the two of them alone; no doubt Gel, who had delivered encouraging speeches to fighters in the past, could find the words to put courage into this little dancer's heart.

He didn't have a great deal of clothing with him suitable for formal occasions but he had the run of Lady Moth's mansion, and asked her servants to rummage through the closets of her late husband's wardrobe and select something appropriate. He worked a little judicious use of magic to adjust the fit of the sober, black silk and silver outfit they brought him, and it made him presentable enough. He descended from the second-floor guest quarters to Lady Moth's drawing room looking (he hoped) like the successful, but no-nonsense, military commander he was.

The ladies broke off their conversation as he entered the spacious, pale-pink and gold chamber; Lady Viridina and Lady Moth flanked Lady Triana, perched on delicate chairs on either side of the sofa that Triana occupied.

If women's clothing served as a weapon—and given all that Kyrtian knew about Triana, there was no doubt in his mind that for her, it did—then Lady Triana had come armed to the teeth. Nothing about her costume was excessive, there was nothing about it that any other lady could take exception to—except that the flesh-colored silk of her gown, though it covered her literally from neck to knee, could not have revealed more of her unless she'd been stark naked. But the effect was oh! so subtle; the silk was heavy, not thin, and her charms were disclosed by imperceptible degrees as she moved. The color contributed to the effect, and knowing what he knew *now* about the lady, Kyrtian couldn't help but admire her tactical expertise on her own battlefield.

That did not, however, mean he intended to fall victim to it.

He half-bowed to all three ladies, then took a step forward and made a more formal bow over Triana's hand. "Lady Triana, I have heard a great deal in praise of you," he said, keeping the irony out of his voice.

"Likewise, Lord Kyrtian," she replied. "Most especially from my friend, Lord Kyndreth. So much so that when I heard you were here with Lady Morthena, I thought I would trespass on her hospitality and come to see you myself."

Very nice. Drop Kyndreth's name so that I know I can't just dismiss you out of hand, then turn on your charm. She was certainly doing all of that, and the amazing part was that it was not at all blatant. If he'd been the naive fellow he was when he'd first taken on command of the army, he probably would have fallen directly for her. Kyrtian had always been inclined to give people the benefit of the doubt until he met them himself; if he'd done that with Triana he would have been certain that she could not be as bad as she'd been painted.

So, let me think, what should my reaction be? He really didn't want very much except to see the back of her; he doubted that there was very much he could learn from her, and frankly, there was far too much that she could learn from, or about him if she stayed very long. "I do hope that I am not a bitter disappointment to you, but I fear that most people find me quite boring," he said bluntly. "And they generally tell me so to my face. I don't cultivate any interests outside of the battlefield, my lady, and at the moment, I can't afford to."

That took her aback for a moment; he watched her as she tried to think of something flattering to say that wouldn't sound like flattery. "Well, since I haven't heard you speak more than a few sentences, I'm not in any position to judge!" she replied, with a throaty laugh that probably stole the breath of many an impressionable lad.

"It won't take you very long to verify," was his reply, brusque to the point of rudeness. Then he was saved from further pleasantries by the servant come to announce dinner—to which, of course, Triana was of necessity invited. She would have to stay the night as well, since she had come the way any uninvited guest would have—overland, from the nearest point to which she had a Portal key. Possibly Kyndreth himself had gotten her as far as the army camp, which was quite near enough for an easy day's ride. If she was on any kind of terms with Kyndreth, he would have found that an easy thing to do.

Which meant that it could be Kyndreth, and not Aelmarkin, that she was working with.

Or both. Given what the Elvenbane had told him about Kyndreth, there was very little doubt in his mind that the moment his erstwhile benefactor saw him as a possible rival, he would be eliminated—and that, of course, played right into Aelmarkin's plans. So, it didn't matter whether she was working for his cousin or the Great Lord, what he had to do was to paint himself as utterly unlikely to engage in politics—the bluff soldier, happiest when on the battlefield.

Very well; now he had his course of action. Moth had ordered dinner in an intimate setting; that suited him very well. Over the course of the meal, he worked hard to establish himself as a monomaniac, obsessed with war and tactics primarily—and secondarily with discovering the whereabouts of his father, or at least, his father's fate. Every hint that he might—once the Council had decided they needed his services as a commander no longer—seek a Council seat was rebuffed. "Never!" he said at last when she stopped hinting and suggested it outright. "It'd drive me mad in a day. I'd rather take up flower-sculpting! At least the flowers wouldn't argue with me!" And that was very much to Triana's surprise, though interestingly enough, not to her discomfiture. In fact, once he established that course, *she* encouraged it.

"In that case—well, your training methods certainly work wonders with the gladiatorial slaves," she said smoothly. "Perhaps, if you aren't interested in breeding them yourself, you could establish a training school in concert with a breeder."

"I might." Then he threw her another mental puzzle to chew on. "Of course," he continued pompously, "as long as those wretched Wizards are in existence, the Council will require the army to exterminate them, and they'll need *me* to lead that army. They may have been clever tacticians compared to—well, I won't mention names—but I'm better."

Thanks to Lashana, he knew what she didn't—that two long-held Elvenlords had just been turned loose in the vicinity of Lord Cheynar's estate, with false memories of being held by a second, entirely unknown group of Wizards hidden in the strange hills and forests somewhere near there. He knew that once the Council learned of these specious Wizards so near them, there would be panic. And *he* would be called on to find them.

Especially if Triana brought word of his hubris to Kyndreth or Aelmarkin or both. For Kyndreth, sending him on a hunt for these Wizards was a winning strategy all around. If they defeated him, he would almost certainly die—in the past the Wizards had made killing the Elven commanders a key part of their strategy, and that wasn't likely to change. If he defeated them, Kyndreth would get the credit, and *he* could be deflected back into the hunt for his father's fate. For Aelmarkin, well, doubtless his cousin would hope for his defeat, and bide his time.

When Kyndreth heard his plan for finding the imaginary Wizards, he'd be doubly pleased. . . .

"Pardon, my lord," said one of Moth's "slaves" in as formal and stiff a manner as even the most protocol-obsessed Elvenlord could have wished, "but the matter you wished to attend to—the slaves you requested have been brought, and are awaiting your pleasure."

The lad almost gave himself away; Kyrtian caught the twinkle in his eye, but his own sober expression, only barely lightened with dour pleasure, kept the liveried servant from losing his composure. "I beg your pardon, my lady," he said to Triana, "but I had arranged for a certain matter to be dealt with at dinner this evening, and I didn't think to cancel my orders. I am sure you won't mind my attending to it."

"What—a chastisement?" For just a moment there was an avidity in her eyes that made him sick. *Thank the Ancestors I was warned against her—*

"No, my lady—a reward, actually." He turned to Moth's slave, stiff in his formal livery. "Have them brought in."

The lad bowed; a moment later, in came Gel, escorted by two of the fighters, followed by Rennati, escorted by a pair of Moth's handmaidens. All humans, of course—

Kyrtian allowed himself a smile. "Sargeant Gel," he said, in the most overbearing manner possible, "you have distinguished yourself in my service for years, but in this campaign against the rebels, you truly have outshone any other slave in my possession. I am loath to lose you; however, I am even more loath to lose such a patently excellent bloodline. I have decided to retire you—and to ensure that your line continues, and provides me with more outstanding fighters and tacticians in the future, I am presenting you with this handsome wench as your mate." He gestured, and the two handmaidens ushered Rennati forward. The poor child was blushing furiously, casting her eyes down. Gel had managed to contrive an expression of utter dumbfoundedness. "She's quite a little athlete in her own right—" he laughed coarsely "—which should complement your own attributes, and I'm sure that providing *me* with more of your stock will be a pleasure to *you,* given her expertise and accomplishments."

Gel dropped his eyes, and went stiffly to one knee, and from the way that his neck had reddened, Kyrtian knew that it was only the full knowledge that this insulting speech was meant for Triana's benefit alone that kept his old friend from exploding with rage. "Thank you, my gracious lord," Gel got out through clenched teeth. Fortunately, with his head bowed, it sounded sincere and humble. "I can never be worthy of this honor—"

"Well, go take the girl and see about rewarding my generosity as quickly as possible," Kyrtian said airily, waving a dismissive hand. Gel got up, took Rennati's limp and unresisting hand in his own, and rather abruptly hauled her away, followed by the rest of the "slaves."

Oh, I'm going to pay for this the next time we practice.

He turned to Triana, whose face was a study in shock. "Nice little dancer my mother bought for me," he said dismissively. "Knows her business. Perfect to make sure the old fellow can do his duty by her and by me—I can guarantee she's been well trained. On top of that, she's got a fantastic physique and reflexes. If I don't get a set of unbelievable bodyguards out of those two, I'll eat my boots without sauce." Then he pretended belatedly to see Triana's stunned expression. "Oh, your pardon, my lady—I hope I didn't shock you by being so frank, but I understood you were a breeder of some note—"

She quickly got hold of herself, and smiled falsely. "Oh, you didn't shock me in the least, my lord," she replied. "I was just contemplating what the results of that mating are likely to be. Splendid bodyguards, no doubt—but forgive me for hoping that the stock takes after *her* looks, rather than *his!*" She produced another of those low, breathy laughs. "You will recall that *I* breed for esthetics!"

"Of course, of course." He then turned the conversation to something else, and eventually the dinner ground its way to its finale.

He left the ladies, as was the custom, to conclude their evening together over sweet wines and conversation, blessing the custom for allowing him to escape the table before Triana.

She would, without a shadow of a doubt, try to get at Rennati. But it wouldn't happen tonight, and it wouldn't happen on *her* terms. It would be tomorrow—at the time and place that Kyrtian had picked.

The pale pink marble hallway outside Lady Triana's guest-suite looked, Kyrtian reflected with no little amusement, as if they had planned an ambush for the elven lady. In a sense, they had. Rennati waited in a marble-paneled niche close to the door. A little farther along, behind a second bronze door left just the tiniest bit open, Lady Viridina waited. And farther still, watching from the end of the hallway, behind the paneled door to one of the sitting-rooms, was Kyrtian himself. If Triana gave the little dancer too much trouble, Lady Viridina would appear—and if Viridina's presence didn't give Rennati a chance to escape, *he* would put in an appearance and claim "his" slave.

The doors made no sound as they opened, of course, and the only clue he had that Triana had finally emerged was the soft patter of Rennati's footsteps on the heavy carpet.

"My lady, I beg your favor!" Rennati's high, clear voice,

with a hint of desperation in it, rang down the hallway. A little judicious magic allowed him to hear every word as she approached the elven lady.

"My lady," Rennati repeated, as she flung herself to her knees beside the waiting Triana, who had paused beside the open door. "My lady, forgive me—I failed you—I know I have failed you—"

"Indeed you have," Triana said, in a level voice. "The information you gave to me was of little use. You were near Lord Kyrtian only once, and that briefly. And now he has turned you into a mere breeder, which will remove you from the household altogether and occupy your time with things of no interest to me. I am not pleased."

Kyrtian peeked through a crack where the door met the frame. Rennati bent her head, trembling with fear. The poor child wasn't acting, she really *was* afraid of Triana. It was terribly brave of her to take this step, but it was the only possible way for her to escape Triana's toils, and both she and Kyrtian knew it. "I had no choice, my lady," Rennati replied humbly. "I am only a slave; I have no control over how I am disposed of."

"Hmph." Kyrtian took another cautious peek; Triana stood over Rennati looking down at the girl with a measure of disgust. "If you'd had an ounce or two more of ambition—" She shook her head. "I do not reward incompetence, girl. A good part of your failure is your own fault. You did not make yourself indispensable to Lord Kyrtian."

"Yes, my lady." Rennati couldn't have gotten any lower to the ground without prostrating herself.

Triana prodded at the dancer with her foot. "You've managed to maneuver yourself into your own punishment, fool. You'll be nothing more than a breeder for the rest of your life. And bred to that hideous old man! You can expect to be beaten when you don't please him, and taken like an animal when you do. On the whole, I must say I couldn't have contrived anything better as chastisement." She laughed, a cruel laugh that made even Kyrtian shiver. "I trust he'll make you suitably miserable. Now, you have something of mine, I believe?" She put out her hand.

Rennati, shaking like a willow in a windstorm, pulled the

teleson-ring from her finger and managed to place it in Triana's palm. Triana slipped the ring on her own finger, spurned the dancer with her foot, pushing her off-balance so that she sprawled clumsily onto the carpet. With a final, nasty chuckle, Triana stalked off.

Rennati lay where she'd fallen, shaking violently, until Triana was out of sight; Kyrtian and Viridina remained in hiding as well. Once they were both sure she was gone, they both rushed out into the hall—

Only to find that Rennati was shaking, not with fear or in tears, but with the weak laughter of relief. Kyrtian helped her to her feet, and Viridina fussed over her for a moment—a strange sight, that; an elven lady seeing to the welfare of a mere human!

"I'm all right, really I am," Rennati protested at last. "Thank you, my lady, thank *you* for being so close—but I am all right. I was only afraid that if either of you had to intervene, *she* would sense something wasn't quite right."

"You did wonderfully well, young lady," Kyrtian told her approvingly. "Wonderfully well. I couldn't have asked for better. I must say that you've shown an ability to play-act that I hadn't expected."

"I was afraid I was going to start laughing when she described poor Gel," Rennati told him, dimpling and coloring prettily. "She couldn't have been more wrong about him—"

"And it's just as well that she doesn't know that. It's my turn to apologize for putting you through all that embarrassment now, and last night," he continued, "and I hope you'll forgive me for it."

"Only if you—" she colored more deeply. "Only if you—don't take back what you said—about me and Gel—"

"My dear child, that is between you and Gel!" he exclaimed, holding up both hands in mock-defense, as both Rennati and Viridina giggled like a pair of young girls. "I have *nothing* to do with it! If you have the audacity to collar and tame that wretched man, you may have joy of him!"

Stifling their laughter in their hands, Viridina and Rennati retreated into Viridina's suite—for some womanish reason, he had no doubt, perhaps to plan the conquest of poor Gel! *Ah,*

Gel, you wretched man, you haven't a prayer against them! Whatever it was, the important mission had been accomplished; Triana no longer had a spy in his household, and it was vanishingly likely that she'd get another in there. Now he could continue with his own library search, and wait for the two "lost" Elvenlords to be found, for the Council to learn of the "new Wizards" and for the panic to begin.

Triana left that very day, and no one, least of all Kyrtian, was sorry to see her leave, although Lady Moth managed to convey the opposite. With Triana's departure, everything went back to "normal."

Kyrtian, however, gave up trying to use Rennati and Gel as his helpers. Instead, he commandeered a couple of the slaves that had been liberated from the Young Lords, a pair of remarkably intelligent twins. Bred and trained to be household slaves, not handsome enough to be put to "front of the house" duties, they had been wasted both on the menial tasks they'd been assigned and as the fighters that the Young Lords wanted them to be. They quickly learned what he wanted of them, and as they had been taught to read and write, were soon actually helping him with his hunt for information. Once he had identified the author of journals that were too late to be of any interest to him, the boys could pick through the remaining volumes and eliminate any more by the same author. As they shelved these books, the task in front of him began to look a bit less daunting.

Meanwhile Rennati had evidently taken him at his word; *she* was the "aggressor" in this courtship, and in Kyrtian's opinion, Gel might just as well run up the flag of surrender, because he hadn't a chance in the world. Not that he seemed to be unhappy about the prospect. But it was certainly an odd thing to see tough old Gel wandering about the gardens, eyes faintly clouded with bemusement, holding a basket for the flowers Rennati was selecting to grace the vases of Lady Moth's chambers.

Three days passed, then four, and there was no sign that the two "lost Lords" had yet been discovered. On the one hand, Kyrtian was perfectly happy with this, since it gave him more time among the books.

On the other hand, he grew more anxious with every day that passed, for there was no telling what Lord Kyndreth and the Council were up to, what they were thinking, and perhaps most importantly of all, whether Triana had been convinced that *he* was not ambitious for a place on the Grand Council as a Great Lord. Only if she was convinced would she in turn convince Kyndreth.

There was no further sign from the Elvenbane, either, but Kyrtian didn't truly expect anything. It had been terribly risky for her to come to him; it would be better for the next meeting to take place somewhere in the wilderness, perhaps while he pursued the false Wizards.

Then, on the fourth day after Triana left, came the summons to the teleson that he had been waiting for. It took all of his self-control to maintain a curious, but calm expression when he greeted Lord Kyndreth's image in the flat glass.

"Something entirely unexpected has come up, my Lord," Kyndreth said, in tones of controlled urgency. "Two minor Elvenlords that we thought had somehow been killed on a hunting expedition decades ago have turned up. They were found by two of Lord Cheynar's slaves and brought straight to his manor, and their story—well, it's terrifying."

Ancestors! They managed to walk all the way from the forest to the estate? They must have been exhausted!

"Where were they all this time?" Kyrtian asked, carefully assuming an expression of concern. "I know that forest has an evil reputation, but how could they have been lost for decades?"

"They say that they were held as prisoners by Wizards," Kyndreth continued, "and the accident of a rockfall in the caves where they were held is what allowed them to escape. There is only one problem—the Wizards that held them are *not* the Wizards with whom we fought!"

"Ancestors!" Kyrtian exclaimed, falling back a little in feigned shock. "But—that's terrible!"

"It is, and the Council was in an uproar about it," Kyndreth replied with visible unhappiness. "We have to find these creatures and eliminate them. If they are laired up somewhere within striking distance of Cheynar's estate—"

"Then they are *too* close, however few in number they may be," Kyrtian said firmly. "I will deal with the matter, my Lord. This is precisely the sort of thing my personal slaves are trained for. We will take a small force into the forest to find the place, then return with a larger one and wipe them out."

"I knew I could rely on you," Kyndreth said, with evident relief, and broke the connection.

With a laugh, Kyrtian leapt to his feet, feeling very like a racehorse finally let loose—*now* he could show what he was really made of; this might have been what he had been training for all of his life.

And let Kyndreth and the others scheme as they would, for *he* was finally on the right side.

Kyrtian's own estate was roughly halfway between Moth's property and Lord Cheynar's, around the perimeter of the ragged circle defined by the outermost Elvenlord estates. Although it might have been shorter to cut through the heart of elven lands, it was quicker to take Moth's Portal to his own property, select the men he wanted, and go from there to the nearest estate with a Portal that he could get access to. In this case, it was the estate of the late unlamented Lord Dyran, which had eventually wound up in the hands of Lord Kyndreth. Dyran's estate bordered on the desert; Cheynar's, between Dyran's land and the rest of the elven-held world, was in well-watered hills that ran up to low, forested mountains that were equally well watered. So much water, in fact, that the estate spent most of the winter shrouded in grey clouds that drizzled continuously. There could not have been a greater contrast in territory, but that wasn't the most interesting part. The interesting part was, beneath those hills and mountains—caves, and a great many of them.

Going home first also allowed him to take Rennati back to the estate. That took one burden off his mind and would give him an excuse to leave Gel as well. Not that he didn't want Gel along—but this would not be a mission where Gel's expertise was needed. Given that *he* could not be at home, he wanted someone he trusted to be there. Lady Lydiell was clever and cunning, but she was no soldier. If soldiers were needed, Gel could command as well, if not better, than Kyrtian.

As for his own troops, those who were left were by this time heartily tired of real warfare and ready to go back to the farm, field, and household positions they had left. It was time to take them home, too—and by the greatest of good fortune, he would be taking *all* of them home. There had been only minor casualties among his own people, no deaths at all, and those injuries they sustained were neither crippling nor incapacitating. That was not by accident or *entirely* by good fortune alone; Kyrtian's men, with their greater expertise in fighting than the Young Lords' conscripts, had shown their clear superiority in the field in all ways.

He was terribly proud of them. The point was, they *weren't* professional, trained fighters; they were farmers, house-servants, herders. But they had applied themselves with will and enthusiasm to his training, and when called on to use that training, they had done so with all the dedication he could have asked for.

He didn't quite know how to reward them; the kind of great feast he usually held for a successful "campaign" was woefully inadequate as a recompense. And as he shepherded the last of his people through Moth's Portal, he made a mental note to ask his mother her opinion. Of all people, she surely should have some notion.

Finally there were only the three of them left to cross—himself, Gel, and Rennati. And as he watched the other two waiting patiently for the Portal to clear, with Gel's arm openly and protectively around the apprehensive little dancer, he knew with considerable amusement that there was at least one person he had had no difficulty in fitting a reward to. There had been a grain of truth in that pompous and incredibly insulting little speech he'd made in front of Lady Triana; he really did hope that Gel would have a son—or several—to train to take the father's place at Kyrtian's side. No one could have had a better bodyguard—or friend—and Kyrtian was not looking forward to the day when he would have to tell Gel to stand down and let another take his place. But like it or not, the fact was that unless something happened to him, Kyrtian would likely be served by Gel's great-great-great-great-grandchildren. Near-immortality came with its own costs.

He shook off the melancholy thought, and brought his mind back to the present. Lady Lydiell would be very amused, he was sure, when she realized what had happened between Rennati and Gel. An inveterate matchmaker, she had been trying to pair Gel off for years. She'd find the current situation entirely to her liking.

She'll have them tucked up in a little cottage or suite of their own in the manor before the two of them get a chance to turn around.

"Go on through, you two," he said, waving at them. He turned to Moth, as they stepped into the utter blackness within the Portal.

"Are you going to be all right?" he asked. "Can you keep those idiot children from trying to start the rebellion all over again, or somehow getting caught?"

She laughed. "The day I can't keep an unruly pack of puppies like that under my thumb, now that they've had a good scare, is the day you might as well start planning my funeral-games. You and your boys showed them that everything they'd won against their fathers was due to their incredible good luck, the Wizards' iron, and the Great Lords' incompetence. They're happy enough to be escaping the hounds, and I imagine they'll stay that way for some little while."

He had to smile at that. "I should have known better than to ask; I should be asking them if they think they'll be safe from *you.*"

"Indeed you should." Moth smiled, and winked. "Two or three of those lads are rather toothsome, and still young enough to train properly. I'm not too old to remarry." She grinned as he laughed. "Now, get on with you. By now, poor Lydiell is probably wondering if the Portal's broken down."

He embraced her, then stepped across the threshold.

As soon as he recovered from the shock of crossing, which was always disorienting, he saw that his mother had already sorted out the new relationship between Gel and Rennati. And much to Gel's surprise and bemusement, she had taken it all in stride and with considerable aplomb—and from the sound of things, had begun making plans for them without waiting for Kyrtian.

Heh. I wonder if he expected Mother to be shocked or outraged that Rennati has managed to capture him? He should have known better than that—given all the matchmaking she's done all over the estate! He's just lucky she never seriously took it into her head to find a woman for him, or he'd have been tied up long before this.

"Our people will expect a wedding-ceremony and a feast, of course," she was explaining to a bewildered Rennati. "Our Gel is a person of great importance here, and if we did anything less, people would feel cheated. We'll have to have all of the fighters and their families, of course—I wonder if we could have the whole thing in the open air? I can't think of any building on the estate large enough to fit everyone inside—"

"But—" Rennati said, feebly, looking alarmed.

"Oh, I know you've no idea what to do, child," Lydiell continued calmly. "But *our* people never had their traditions wrenched from them and buried past retrieval. They have their priests and their rituals exactly as they did before we came on the scene. Don't concern yourself with it; they know what to do, and if you can learn a clever dance, you can certainly learn a simple wedding ceremony. Now, this could fit in very nicely with the general homecoming; your wedding can be the start of a week of festivities and—"

"Mother, my love," Kyrtian interrupted her. "Don't forget, with all your planning, *I* have to be off with a select crew on

Lord Kyndreth's Wizard-hunt as soon as may be. This will have to look as if I consider it to be as urgent as he does."

"So Gel tells me," Lydiell said serenely. "All the more reason to have the wedding as soon as possible. I have been planning these homecoming celebrations for a fortnight, and you *will* be here for at least the first day and night of them! And if Kyndreth gets impatient, *I* will tell him that you needed the time to select exactly the right group of scouts and hunters."

Kyrtian bowed to the inevitable. "Yes, Mother," he said obediently, and beat a hasty retreat to his own suite, leaving Gel and Rennati to face his formidable mother and all her plans alone.

A coward's ploy, and he would surely hear all about it from Gel once the Sargeant got away. But in the meanwhile—

He can take care of himself. At least for a while. Once Rennati gets over being dazed, she'll probably join forces with mother, the females against the poor, helpless male. I've never seen a woman that could resist an opportunity for a celebration and a new gown. Gel won't have a chance.

But oh, the more he thought about it, the more he hoped that his own time to wed wouldn't arrive anytime soon.

I think I'll run off and have Moth take care of everything. I'll hide in her library until the very last moment, so no one can swarm over me.

He pushed open the doors to his own rooms and sighed; it seemed an age since he'd been here, and the sight of his own quarters was very welcome.

But more welcome still was the bathroom, the ready tub, and the smiling servants waiting to help him.

He didn't stop for their help; he threw off his clothes and plunged into the hot water, relaxing completely in the penetrating heat, as he had not been able to do since he left. Much as he loved and trusted Lady Moth, *she* had all those Young Lords still lurking on her premises, and Lady Triana's unexpected arrival only proved that even the formidable Lady Morthena could be surprised by unexpected visitors. Furthermore, she admitted later that she had no notion how many keys to her Portal her late husband had handed about. It could be many, it could be few, but the fact was they probably existed. And if *anyone* was likely to ferret those keys out, it would be Kyndreth, Triana, or Aelmarkin. As a result, he had not really been able to relax, even while on her estate.

And, of course, while on campaign he'd had no such luxuries as this. Just the thought of all the times he'd gone to bed aching and bruised and bathless made this all the more pleasurable.

It might be a while before I get to enjoy it again. Although his hunt for the non-existent Wizards was by its very nature a wild-goose chase, he would have to conduct it as if it was serious. The bare essentials for camping, no more than six men, and they would have to keep themselves fed off the land as much as possible. There would be no hot, soaking baths out there in the forests.

He was, however, too energetic by nature to relax for too long in a hot bath when he wasn't bone-tired and wasn't currently aching and bruised. Soon enough he was out and dressed, and went looking for his father's notes. They were still where he had left them, in the library. A quick glance through them told him everything he needed to know.

He sent his bodyservant Lynder to find Gel. Just about now, Gel should be frantic for a way to escape the two females who were planning a wedding around him, will-he, nill-he.

Sure enough, within moments Lynder and Gel were back, Lynder's eyes dancing with merriment, Gel looking distinctly harried. "Before everyone gets wrapped up in this festival business, I want you to help me pick out six of our trackers for this pseudo Wizard-hunt," he told Gel. "I want men who didn't go out as fighters, but who can still be spared. It's getting close to the first hay-harvest, and I don't want to leave Mother shorthanded even by a trifle."

"I can tell you who without even thinking about it," Gel replied immediately. "Kar, Tem, Shalvan, Resso, Halean and Noet. They're all the junior foresters; they don't help with the harvest and their da's can live without 'em for a bit. Why so many? You plan on actually *doing* anything in there?"

"It's dangerous; it isn't going to be a pleasure trip," Kyrtian warned. "Even if the new Wizards are a fabrication, there are still a lot of deadly creatures in that area. And you aren't going to be along."

Gel's face fell, but he also looked resigned. "I was afraid you were going to decide that," he grumbled. "Damn it all, Kyrtian—"

"Gel, you're a fighter, a tactician; you're neither a hunter nor a forester," Kyrtian pointed out. "You'd be of less use to me than one of those boys. You'll be of *more* user here to me—and Mother—on the bare chance that Aelmarkin tries something while I'm gone. Mother is many things—but not a soldier."

Gel's mouth tightened. "You're not thinking he'd convince Kyndreth to put this place under siege?"

"I'm not thinking anything," he lied with a straight face—because that was precisely what he was thinking. He didn't trust Aelmarkin—and he didn't trust Kyndreth, either. *Maybe* he was still useful to the Great Lord—but maybe he wasn't, anymore. "Kyndreth still needs me as long as he thinks there's a tribe of Wizards hiding right on our borders. I'm more worried about what Aelmarkin might do—or try. But between you and Mother, with Moth to feed you gossip, you'll see through *anything* he tries before he's done more than make a tentative probe." He clapped Gel on the shoulder. "I am *not* trying to put you out to stud like my favorite warhorse, although I suggest you make that charming little dancer into a very happy wife! I *am* allocating my resources where they'll do the most good. I need you and Mother here, watching for trouble, while I go into the forest and wait for the Elvenbane to contact me again—which she will, since the forest is the most logical place for that." He rubbed his chin thoughtfully. "There's one other thing—before we had to leave Moth's, I was reading some personal journals, and something I ran into reminded me of some of Father's notes that he left behind. It's possible we've been looking for the Great Portal in the wrong place. I think it's underground, and the area around Cheynar's estate has a lot in common with the forest our ancestors fled through when they first arrived."

Gel knew *exactly* what he was hinting. "Those hills are *riddled* with caves!" he exclaimed. "Come to think of it, if your ancestors found that their Portal dropped 'em into a cave, they wouldn't have been displeased about that, I wouldn't think; coming into a strange world in a protected spot."

"It's one possible place to look," Kyrtian agreed. He didn't tell Gel the one thing that concerned him deeply—the Ancestors had fled the vicinity of the Great Portal in terror, but why? That was the very last thing he wanted Gel thinking about when he was gone. "That's why I want your hunters and trackers. As long as I have to pretend I'm hunting for Wizards living in caves, I have every excuse to check every cave we come across."

"Then you don't want hunters and trackers—or, at least, not all hunters and trackers," Gel said decisively. "You'll need men that can keep all of you fed, but you'll also need men who're used to clambering around underground. Instead of Kar and Tem, I want you to take Kar's brother Hobie, and your laddy Lynder, there."

"Lynder?" Kyrtian turned to his bodyservant in surprise. *"Lynder?* Why Lynder?"

"Because Lynder and Hobie have been trying to kill themselves climbing down holes in the ground on their spare time ever since they were in their teens," Gel replied, wryly, as Lynder flushed a brilliant scarlet. "If you're going to be doing the same, I suggest you take people who've had the experience of nearly drowning when a cloudburst outside flooded the cave they were in."

"We got out ahead of the flood!" Lynder protested, turning redder. "We heard it coming!"

"And it would be useful if you had a couple of lads who'd been stuck in a passage they realized a bit too late was too small for them." Gel was clearly enjoying himself.

"It wasn't too small originally," Lynder muttered. "The rock shifted."

"I can see Lynder has plenty of experience," Kyrtian interrupted, trying not to laugh, although he also felt very sorry for the poor young man. "Haven't you told me, time and time again, that the best teacher is experience?"

"Hobie and I have been cave-exploring for three years now

without a single serious mishap," Lynder said, getting his blushing under control and trying to gather the scattered shards of his shattered dignity. "And the kinds of minor injuries we've had could happen scouting through a forest or doing some heavy work on the farm." He didn't glare at Gel, who was still clearly amused, but Kyrtian sensed that he wanted to.

Gel finally took pity on the lad. "Kyrtian, I wouldn't have recommended young Lynder if I didn't think he could guard your steps as well in *his* world as I can in mine," he said generously, and now Lynder flushed with pleasure rather than embarrassment.

Kyrtian nodded. "In that case—Lynder, I want you to get the cave-exploring gear together for seven. Gel and I will take care of the rest of the supplies we'll need. I'd like everything ready by—" He thought, and impishly decided to tease Gel a little more. "I'd *like* to leave tomorrow, but—"

Gel turned white. Lynder shook his head. "Gear for seven—we'll need some special climbing equipment and we don't have anything like that here. I'll have to get straight to the blacksmith, and he and his helpers will have to work the rest of today and all tomorrow. The rest will take a bit of hunting among the stores."

"But you can have it by the day after tomorrow?" Kyrtian persisted.

"If you *dare* leave before this wedding folderol—" Gel growled under his breath, glowering.

Kyrtian couldn't hold back his laughter—and then he had to run, for Sargeant Gel lunged for him, and he knew that if Gel got his hands on his master, the "master" would wind up in the bathtub again, but this time fully clothed.

They couldn't get away in less than three days, after all.

On the evening of the second day, Gel and Rennati were wed at sunset in an open-air ceremony, presided over by an old man wearing a long, black robe. So incredibly dignified was this individual, and so full of solemnity, Kyrtian had a difficult time in recognizing Hobie's father Rand, the manor's chief stablehand, who always had a joke for everyone, usually ribald.

Rand first wafted smoke over the couple, then, while chanting under his breath, sprinkled them with water, waved a lighted taper around them, and blew dust at them. Then he drew a wobbly circle around all three of them with the pointed end of a staff. Still droning a chant that Kyrtian couldn't make head or tail of, he conducted a long ritual that involved an amazing amount of sprinkling of herbs and water and salt on the part of the happy couple, a great deal of walking in circles and figure-eights, and the sharing of bread and salt.

Finally, at Rand's low-voiced order, they held out their conjoined hands, and Rand bound their hands together. Then, turning to the crowd, as the last wink of the sun descended below the horizon and the first stars came out, he spread his arms wide behind them.

"Hands are bound as hearts are bound; two are one!" he shouted.

A tremendous cheer arose from the huge crowd come to see the ceremony. Then, of course, came the celebration. There was a very great deal of wine and beer available, there was dancing and willing girls to build up a thirst, and all of Kyrtian's chosen party were young men with hard heads and the usual inability of young men to remember what a hangover felt like during the time that the drink was sliding smoothly down their throats. As a consequence, none of Kyrtian's six were good for much on the following day.

However, that was not so bad, because *that* was the day of some of the riskier competitions—the wrestling, the hurling of large objects, the game pitting two teams against each other in competition for an inflated bladder, with no holds barred. Nursing headaches and uncertain stomachs, it was easy to persuade the six that they should be spectators, not participants.

On the morning of the third day, a day devoted to the gentler pursuits and competitions of the women-folk—footraces, target-shooting, milking, sewing, and cooking competitions—they were in fine fettle and high spirits, and quite ready to go. So was their equipment, and Kyrtian was not going to allow the temptation of another feast, dance, and drinking soiree incapacitate them all over again. By mid-morning he had them all lined up at the Portal, fully-laden, with still more of the servants equally burdened.

Lord Kyndreth had promised horses on the other side, and Kyrtian was going to hold him to that promise. He sent his party and all of the servants through first, and waited for the servants to return before passing through the Portal himself. There were no farewells this time. He had chosen a time when Lydiell was busy supervising and judging a contest, and as for Gel—well, he hadn't seen his old friend since the ceremony, and he hoped that Rennati was teaching him a few of the tricks she'd shown him. . . .

He passed the dark and cold and disorientation of the Portal—and with a jolt, came out on the other side.

"Lord Kyrtian?"

He shook his head to clear it, and forced his eyes to focus. The person who had addressed him was a rare creature—an elderly Elvenlord, whose thinning, silver hair and faintly-lined face came as something of a shock. "Yes," he said, "I'm Lord Kyrtian."

The elderly gentleman bowed. "I am Lord Rathien. Lord Kyndreth directed me to supply whatever you require."

Well, that was pleasant. "I need enough horses to carry all of this lot," he said, waving at the supplies and equipment heaped on either side of the corridor leading to the Portal.

Lord Rathien eyed the piles with an experienced glance. "Seven riding-mounts and as many pack-mules," he said with authority. "You will find the mules can carry more than horses, and their tempers are steadier. When you camp in the forest, tether each horse to a mule before you stake out the line—should anything attack, the mules will run unfailingly away from danger, they will not plunge blindly into further danger, and they will stop when pursuit stops." He smiled then, with great charm. "I am very fond of mules, myself."

"So I see." Kyrtian smiled back, but Lord Rathien had already turned away, and was ordering a set of human slaves to pick up the piled goods and take them to the stables. All Kyrtian and his party had to do was to follow.

By noon, with the mules loaded, horses saddled, and a mule

tethered behind each rider, they were on their way. His task completed, Lord Rathien was gone by the time they rode out of the gates; Kyrtian wondered if he was one of Lord Kyndreth's underlings, or was a legacy from Lord Dyran. He was certainly efficient—and if he treated the slaves exactly as he did the mules, well, at least he didn't treat them worse. Kyrtian's own young men had been cautioned as to how to behave once they were off the estate, so they had not done anything to arouse Rathien's suspicions. Their tension had been palpable during that time; they hadn't dared to speak, lest they say something un-slavelike, or to raise their eyes above Kyrtian's knees, lest their posture or demeanor betray them.

Once they were all on the road, however, they relaxed. "Sargeant Gel told us that we were going down in caves, m'Lord," Hobie said, urging his horse up beside Kyrtian's, as Lynder did so on the other side, and the rest of the six got in as closely as they could, the better to hear what he had to say. "Why's that?"

"Well, you know that we're chasing after Wizards that don't really exist," Kyrtian began.

"Aye sir. Better than chasing ones that do!" replied Hobie. One of the men in the rear laughed.

"They're supposedly living in an underground stronghold where we're going, so we'll be exploring caves. Now, as it happens, I *think* my father may have been hunting these same caves when he disappeared, and I'm hoping we'll find some sign of him there." The man who had laughed sobered immediately, and there were some sympathetic murmurs from all of them.

"You—surely don't expect to find him after all this time, do you, m'Lord?" Hobie asked hesitantly.

Kyrtian sighed. "Not after all this time, no—not alive, at any rate," he said sadly. "But, you know—my claim to the estate is clouded as long as no one knows what became of him. And until Mother and I find out what really happened . . ."

He let the sentence trail off. Hobie dropped his eyes for a moment. "Well, m'Lord," Lynder said into the silence, "if there's a sign to be found, we'll find it. Hobie and I have found a great many strange things in caves."

"Such as?" Kyrtian asked, to change the subject and cheer the men up again. Touching as their sympathy was, he'd far rather have laughter around him than gloom.

It was, after all, a long ride to Lord Cheynar's estate, and there was no reason to make it under a cloud of depression!

There was *quite* enough that was depressing about Lord Cheynar's estate to have suited a dozen funeral processions.

The manor, surrounded by pine forest, boasted nothing in the way of magical amenities; no mage-lights to illuminate the darkness, no illusions, all work done by slaves or mechanical devices. The pines were of a variety that Kyrtian was unfamiliar with—so dark a green as to be nearly black, and inhabited by flocks of crows. Cheynar, a taciturn individual with very little magic of his own, warmed slightly to Kyrtian when the latter congratulated him on some of his mechanical devices—and when Kyrtian at darkness made cheerful use of the lanterns, rather than showing off by creating his own mage-lights.

He warmed still more over dinner, and finally came out with something entirely unexpected.

"I knew your father," Cheynar offered. "I mean, I met him—he was here just before he disappeared."

That electrified Kyrtian, and he could not conceal his shock. "What?" he exclaimed. "But—why didn't you—"

"Why didn't I say something?" Cheynar asked shrewdly. "I did, to Lord Dyran. I suppose he didn't think it important enough to pass it to your Lady Mother. But then, he wasn't at all pleased with what your father was hunting."

"The old devices the Ancestors brought with them." Kyrtian was torn between excitement and despair. If his mother had known *where* her husband had last been seen, would it have made a difference? Could they have found him still alive?

Cheynar nodded. "One of those—your father said—would put those of us with weak magic on a par with those who are stronger," he told Kyrtian. "I don't know if Lord Dyran knew that. Your father told *me,* at least in part because he saw all the mechanical devices I use around here instead of magic, but he might not have said anything to Dyran." He shrugged.

"And Lord Dyran was one of the Great Lords of the Council, anyway," Kyrtian sighed. "And my father and I—well, we're nothing like the equals of any Great Lord. I doubt that Lord Dyran even paid any heed to anything father said. *You* know." He half-smiled at Cheynar, hoping that Cheynar would warm a little further, and see himself in the same position as Kyrtian. "When we're useful, we're equals at the feast-table, but once they don't need us anymore . . ."

Cheynar took the bait. "Probably he just thought that the man was half-crazed, if he even took time for a thought at all," Cheynar said, and with some sympathy. "But I can tell you this—"

He paused significantly.

"If you are going Wizard-hunting in those caves, you'll be walking in the steps of your father. Because the last time anyone saw him—that was where he was going, too."

27

One set of items in their packs was immediately useful the moment they entered the forest: rain gear. Kyrtian had never seen so much rain in his life; he was glad that he'd checked on the climate when arranging for the supplies. And oh, the advantage of being on equal terms with one's females in an elven household! He had not realized that silk could be made so completely waterproof. Evidently that oft-derided "women's magic" used for flower-sculpting had a great many other purposes that the women themselves knew but seldom shared. He certainly didn't blame them, the "lords of creation" that Elvenlords considered themselves to be would probably greet such innovations as trivial and women kept pent up in their bowers, disregarded and discarded as toys themselves could hardly be expected to share such knowledge voluntarily. He could well imagine several disgruntled ladies sitting around in their bower, contemplating their dripping menfolk, and saying to each other with glee, "Well, why don't they just stop the rain?"

Rain-capes, with hoods snugged in around their faces, coats with an outer water-proofed surface beneath that, meant that what could have been a miserable situation was merely interesting. Provided that one could manage somehow to see past the gloom, this was a truly unique forest.

More waterproofed sheets—which would later serve as shelters for their three tents—covered the seven packs carried by the pack mules. This meant that their supplies and belongings were dry and would *stay* dry; no small consideration when, at the end of the day, they were going to be able to camp *dry.*

Too much water was, in the long run, better than too little. This could have been a hunt in the desert, and even Kyrtian was not entirely sure that magic would be enough to ensure water for everyone. Grels were the only option in the desert for transportation, but neither he nor anyone on his estate knew anything about grels. Their main problem here—and to some extent, in the caves—would be to prevent getting wet and cold with no way to get warm and dry again.

Game was certainly available, if not precisely plentiful. One would expect large game here, and yet the only animals that made an appearance were small game. Well, the advantage of traveling with foresters was that *they* didn't scorn small game in a futile search for something larger. The four foresters quickly traded their heavier bows and arrows for hand cross-bows, and took careful shots without ever seeming to aim. One by one, plump little bodies accumulated, tied to the cantles and pommels of saddles.

The rain never stopped. It let up, from time to time, decreasing to a mere drizzle, which percolated down through the trees and dripped from every limb, every needle. Then, when the rain resumed, it obscured everything in the distance, far or near, reducing visibility to a few horse-lengths ahead of the lead rider.

Which was *not* Kyrtian.

He knew very well that he was not a forester. That was why

he rode in the dead middle of the string, with Lynder in front of him and Hobie behind, two of the young foresters ahead and two behind. It surprised him, a little, that an entire train of fourteen animals could make so little noise, but the track that they followed, which led in the general direction of a purported cave-entrance, was ankle-deep in a layer of pine needles. They proceeded at an ambling walk, and not just to save the horses.

Up at the head of the string, Noet rode with his head slightly cocked, listening. Behind him, Shalvan concentrated on peering through the mist and rain. At the rear of the train, Halean and Resso shared the same duties.

Beyond the omnipresent sounds of rain plopping onto their capes, into the needle-bed, trickling down trunks, and dripping onto leaves, there *were* other sounds of life that Kyrtian took to be good signs that nothing else was stalking them. Once the crows got used to their presence, the birds stopped making alarm-calls and went back to their crow-business with only an occasional appearance as if to take note of their progress. Unexpected showers of droplets heralded the passage of small birds through the branches, and little rustles betrayed the passage of those plump little squirrels and rabbits.

By mid-afternoon, Kyrtian knew his men were looking for a place to stop and make camp for the night. Already there was a change in the quality of light under these trees, and his nerves were just a trifle on edge. He didn't know *why*, just that there was something . . . odd. . . .

Noet held up a hand, and the entire cavalcade stopped. Now Kyrtian knew what had him on edge—the absolute absence of any sound other than the dripping of water. Even the crows were gone.

"I don't like this," Noet said, in a low voice, but one that carried easily in the silence. "The horses and mules haven't noticed anything, but—"

"But maybe that's the point, if this is a hunter," Resso replied. "If it works by ambush and stealth."

"Should we turn back?" Kyrtian asked.

"Yes—but slowly and carefully. Just turn your horses and mules in place, people. Shalvan and I will become rear-guard.

We'll stop back at that stream we crossed, and try following it for a while."

"With any luck, it'll lead us to the caves anyway," Hobie opined.

One by one, they turned their horses and drew the mules behind them, the rearmost first. Shalvan and Noet already had their heavy bows out with arrows nocked to the strings. And as for Kyrtian—

His fingers tingled with power. At any moment, he could, and would, launch a levin-bolt into whatever might emerge.

"It's out there, all right," Shalvan said grimly, as Noet turned his horse and mule. "It's up the trail—off to one side, in the bushes. Every so often the bush shakes, and from the movement, I'd say that it's about the size of a haywain. It's not moving much, though. I don't know if that's because it's not certain of us, or if it's territorial."

He turned his horse as Noet stood guard and they moved at the same leisurely pace they'd maintained all along, back up the way they had come. The back of Kyrtian's neck prickled. What would—whatever it was—think of its prey moving away from it?

"Uh-oh—" That was Resso, now in the lead, and the hair on Kyrtian's head literally stood straight up. Pacing deliberately towards them was—not one—an entire herd of alicorns. Their red eyes flashed, and the black stallion in the lead tossed his head with its wicked, slightly curved, spiral horn.

"Don't move," Halean said in a strangled voice.

Kyrtian had no intention of moving. One alicorn was dangerous; what was a herd? They were trapped, between a very visible menace an invisible one.

The alicorn stallion snorted and moved towards them. Kyrtian wondered what was going on in those narrow heads. Should he fling a levin-bolt at them? But if he did, what would the thing behind them do? And wouldn't their horses spook if he did? None of them were war-trained—

None of them are war-trained. Mules will run until there's no pursuit. The mules are tethered to the horses—and vice versa.

"Give your horses free rein, and hang on," Kyrtian ordered,

feeling that sense of *presence* and *danger* at his back increasing, just a little. "And duck your heads on the count of three."

The alicorn-stallion pawed the ground and bared its fangs.

"One. Two. *Three!*"

On the count of three, Kyrtian fired a *kind* of levin-bolt—straight up over their heads. It exploded in a blinding flash and a violent *boom* that actually shattered the nearby limbs of trees. The horses, as Kyrtian had hoped, bolted—and so did the alicorns.

The horses shot forward in the direction they had been facing, along the game trail. The alicorns, foe and prey forgotten, scattered in all directions, some off into the woods to either side of the trail, some turning and fleeing, and three, following the stallion, charging head-down towards them. At the last moment, the alicorns veered a little to the left, and the hysterical horses to the right.

Kyrtian hung onto his mount with every bit of strength that arms and legs possessed, ducking low along its neck to keep from being knocked out of his saddle by low-hanging boughs. Hooves thundered all around him; even if the horses weren't sticking to the game-trail, they were at least staying together. Behind him he heard a roar, and the battle-scream of an alicorn, but whatever was going on would have to remain a mystery.

His heart raced, his hands and legs ached, and he clenched his teeth; he couldn't see what was happening or where they were going. His mount's mane lashed his face until his eyes watered.

Then, sooner than he'd thought, he felt the horse beginning to slow, felt a weight tugging at the lead-rein fastened to the saddle. The horse didn't like it; he tried to surge forward. The mule wasn't having any.

Gradually, the mule won. The headlong gallop slowed to a canter, a trot, and finally, the horse's sides heaving and sweat pouring from his neck and shoulders, a walk. Kyrtian took up the slack in the reins and brought his mount to a stop, and looked around.

The rain had slackened again, and through the mizzle, he

counted his men scattered among the trees and quickly came up with the right number of riders and pack mules.

"Ancestors!" he breathed, in profoundest relief. The men said nothing; they simply guided their weary beasts back towards him until once again they formed a coherent group.

"Everyone all right?" he asked, as their horses stood with heads hanging, and flanks a-foam with sweat. Only the mules looked unperturbed.

"I've been worse," replied Noet laconically. "Gonna kill whoever designed this saddle with a pommel right where it don't belong, though."

Noet did look a little pale, and in a certain amount of pain. Kyrtian winced, and hastily changed the subject. "Does anyone know where we are?"

"We bolted in the general direction of where we wanted to go," reported Shalvan. "So the stream should still be that way—" he pointed with his chin, rather than his hand. "We might as well get on with it, the horses aren't going to be the better for standing in the cold and rain, and they're going to need water after this."

Once again they formed up, but this time not in single file since they weren't following a trail; Halean rode on the right flank and Resso on the left. And, not too much later, they came to the stream, much to everyone's relief.

There wasn't much time before nightfall, and with the overcast skies and the forest all around, darkness would come soon. They quickly made camp, with Kyrtian tending to the firemaking chores. They pitched their three tents in a triangle, with the fire in the center. Once the tents were pitched and Resso took up the cooking, the rest gathered more firewood while Kyrtian ran a circle of mage-lights around the tents to stand between them and whatever was in the woods or across the stream. As firewood was brought in, he stacked it near enough to the fire that it stood a decent chance of drying out some before it was used.

The last thing he did was to run a string hung with small bells around the trunks of trees beyond the glow of the magelight at about ankle-height. Anything that brushed against that string would set the bells jingling.

"Do you think we need to worry about something coming in from above?" he asked Noet, with a frown of concern.

Noet glanced up. "Not through branches that thick," he replied. "I wouldn't think, anyway."

Darkness, as Kyrtian had anticipated, came quickly. They tethered the horses—and tethered the mules to the horses—within the circle of magelight. The rain actually stopped once darkness fell, and as they gathered around their fire, Kyrtian felt their mutual fear of what lurked outside that magic circle drawing them all together despite rank and race.

Resso had managed to grill the day's catch tastily, with a minimum of burning, skewered on twigs over the fire. With that and journey-cake, and sweet water from the stream at their backs, they made a satisfying meal. They had thrown the bones into the fire and were ready to divide the night into watches, when a voice from the darkness saluted them.

"Hello the camp!"

Kyrtian knew that voice, and had been hoping to hear it. He stood up eagerly and waved in the direction from which it had come. The Elvenbane walked calmly into the magelight circle without tripping over the line of bells.

"Well met, Lord Kyrtian! Good idea, those bells," she remarked cheerfully, as she joined them beside the fire and offered Kyrtian her hand. Today she was wearing a pair of breeches and a tunic of something glittering and blue, covered with jewel-like scales, a wicked-looking knife strapped over it. Her abundant auburn hair had been bound back at the nape of her neck in a severe knot.

The men were staring at this unexpected visitor with their mouths dropping wide open.

"Gentlemen," Kyrtian said solemnly, firmly repressing the urge to laugh at them as he accepted Lashana's hand. "May I present to you Lashana? Also known as the Elvenbane—"

If he had set off another of those explosive levin-bolts in their midst he couldn't have gotten a more interesting reaction.

Noet practically choked, Hobie and Shalvan let out involuntary whoops of surprise, Resso leapt to his feet wearing an expression of such utter shock that Kyrtian would not have been surprised to see him faint dead away in the next moment. Only Lynder managed to retain his composure. He got to his feet, gathered his young dignity about him, and took the hand that Kyrtian relinquished.

"My lady, this is an honor, and a privilege," he replied, bowing over the hand before releasing it.

"Oh pish," she said, blushing a little, but clearly pleased. "Didn't Lord Kyrtian tell you that I'd be intercepting you out here?"

"Lord Kyrtian didn't *know* you would, he only hoped you would," Kyrtian replied for himself. "Won't you join us?"

How she had gotten there, how long she had been out in the woods watching them, he didn't know. And, truth to tell, it didn't matter. As his men took their seats again and Lashana settled easily among them, it was very clear why this young lady wizard had become a leader. She drew all eyes towards her in a way that had nothing to do with her looks or her sex.

"Well, here's what I can tell you," she began. "We—the Wizards—have got watchers on *your* estate, my Lord, and that of Lady Morthena. If anything should threaten them, we'll know, and we'll be able to evacuate as many or as few people need to be gotten out." She dimpled. "And may I say, that is *quite* a celebration your people are putting on! I'd like to ask your mother if she would organize one for us, some day, when things are—more stable."

Kyrtian felt a great weight lift from his shoulders, but Lashana's next words made him tense again. "A certain Lady Triana—" she arched her brow at him, and he nodded grimly his acknowledgement that he knew the Lady, "—paid another, very short visit to Lady Morthena after you left. She claimed that she wished to consult Lady Morthena's favorite library, and indeed, she left again within a few hours. She arrived and departed by means of a temporary Gate set up just outside the Lady's estate. I don't suppose you can cast any light on what she was looking for?"

Kyrtian shook his head reluctantly. "I haven't a clue. But knowing Triana, it can't be for anyone's good but her own."

Lashana snorted. "Believe me, I know. I've had—some experience of the Lady myself."

"My condolences." That response startled a smile from her.

"The army—minus your contribution of troops—has moved nearer to the trade-city of Prethon, where it's easier to supply. I'm assuming that in the absence of an actual place to put them permanently, that's where they'll stay, camped just outside the city walls." Lashana's green eyes twinkled. "Which is, of course, precisely where we'd like them, as far from our new Citadel as possible, which was why we suggested this place as the location of the imaginary Wizards. Even if they decided you weren't moving fast enough for them, this is *miserable* country to try and do any hunting of invisible people in, and the place is absolutely hollow with caves. You could spend a century trying to hunt through them all!"

"Actually—I wanted to ask you about that, Lashana," Kyrtian said hesitantly. "Do you have the time to hear some history?"

When she nodded, he launched into the story—as he had puzzled it out—of the Ancestors' arrival in this world, and followed it with the more personal tale of his father's own interest in that arrival and the things that might have been left behind. "So the last place where he was doing research before he disappeared was Lady Moth's library—and that was where I found some personal journals that gave descriptions that sounded like *this* area—" He waved his hand at the dripping forest beyond the camp. "You must admit that it's pretty distinctive. And the very few passages that described the Crossing made me think that the Ancestors might have come out into a *cave,* and not aboveground as everyone has always assumed. Then when we staged at Lord Cheynar's," he concluded triumphantly, "Lord Cheynar admitted that my father *had* gone off into these forests, and that he was probably the last Elvenlord to see my father alive!"

Lashana pursed her lips thoughtfully. "That—that's interesting. You know, I discovered that Wizards, at least, can use gemstones to help concentrate and amplify their powers. I don't know if they'll work for Elvenlords that way, but it stands to reason that if *our* powers can be amplified by something, so can yours."

"I can't see any other way that the Ancestors could have built the things that they did," he admitted. She tilted her head to the side.

"It's a very good thing that I trust you, Lord Kyrtian," she said in a measured tone. "Otherwise I don't think I could allow *you* to leave these woods alive."

Lynder leapt to his feet, his hand on his dagger-hilt, and the others weren't far behind. Lashana appeared unconcerned.

And she probably has good reason to be. She'd be a fool to have come here alone, and no matter what the Elvenbane is, no one has ever suspected her of being a fool.

"Sit down, all of you," he said mildly. "Don't you realize what a horrible menace would be let loose in the world if someone like Aelmarkin got his hands on a way to make himself as strong as Lord Kyndreth? She's only speaking sense."

She made a little gesture of thanks in his direction. "Now, there's one other thing I'd like to show you, something my people will shortly be handing out to Moth's and yours, among others, then distributing covertly among the field-slaves." She held out a little object, shaped rather like an open clamshell, of a dull grey metal. He started to reach for it, and she hastily pulled it back.

"Don't touch it, Lord Kyrtian!" she warned. "At least, not with your bare hand! That's what you call Death Metal—forged iron."

He hastily drew back his fingers. He'd touched unprotected steel before, in the shape of one of the iron collars that Moth's own slaves wore under their pseudo-slave collars, and it had burned him like acid. He was in no hurry to repeat the experience.

"I brought an active slave-collar with me to show you what it does," she continued. "Watch—with your magic-senses." She took out a leather slave-collar set with a cloudy beryl, which was, indeed, active. She fitted the back half of the clamshell device behind the beryl, then snapped the top half over it, and flipped a catch to squeeze it closed and lock it.

The Elfstone went dead to his senses. He looked at her hand, with the dull-grey object locked around what *had* been an active device for the complete control of a slave, dumbfounded. Then he looked up into her knowing eyes.

"Ancestors—" he breathed. "You've done it. You've found a way—snap one of *those* over a collar-stone, and you can cut the collar right off without hurting the slave!"

"Or leave the collar on, it won't matter, and any magic that an overseer flings at a fleeing slave will simply misfire," she pointed out, barely concealing her glee. "We have the iron, we have the craftsmen, and we have the ways to get these into the hands of the slaves. Within months, your Young Lords and my Wizards will be the *last* things that the Great Lords will be worrying about!"

"Slave revolts—" murmured Shalvan, wonderingly.

"All over the estates," Lashana agreed. "Which is why I'm here with you. Every moment of time that you can buy us with your wizard-hunting will enable us to make that many more of these devices, and bring the moment of freedom for all humans that much closer."

"At which point, my lord," Lynder pointed out diffidently, "*Our* people will also be the very last thing that the Great Lords will be worrying about."

"Except that—if you and yours can pull this off, Lashana—" he bared his teeth in a feral grin, the recollection of the stories he'd heard from the mistreated slaves sheltering with Moth fresh in his mind "—you may consider *my* estate to be the training ground for a new human army!"

He held out his hand; she clasped it joyfully, as his men made the sounds of subdued cheering—even now, they didn't want to arouse the attention of things that might be out there in the darkness.

"Lord Kyrtian—" she seemed to be searching for words, then gave up altogether, and just shook her head, her face radiant with smiles. "Thank you—seems inadequate."

"It's early days yet," he warned, as the men settled down, although he could not help but feel a little intoxicated with the heady intellectual wine she had just poured for him. "We've a long way to go."

"So we have." She sobered as well, and started to stow the iron device and the collar in her belt-pouch, then evidently thought better of it and handed it to Lynder. "Here. If you've got crafters and a source of Death Metal, you might want to start duplicating these yourself."

Lynder nodded, and stowed the device away.

"Now—about the caves and your father—I think I might be able to help narrow your search a little. You see, I've run these hills myself." Lashana then began a tale of her own, about the time when she, a mere child then and not yet the Elvenbane, had rescued a band of human children—with human magic—who were going to be culled by Lord Treves's overseer.

Lord Treves—would that be Lady Viridina's Lord? Moth's friend? What an odd coincidence!

Lashana had helped them escape and flee into these very hills—and, by another odd coincidence, had run into the infamous young Lord Valyn, fleeing with his wizardling half-brother and looking for Wizards to protect them both.

The story was an absorbing one, and Lashana told it well. He could see in his mind's eye the huddle of frightened children, the drenched and miserable young Valyn and the equally miserable Mero. She described the strange monsters they had encountered, one of which sounded eerily familiar.

"I think we nearly ran into one of those—invisible lurking things back there," Noet said thoughtfully, and described being trapped between it and the alicorn herd, and how Kyrtian had solved the situation.

"Which is why *he's* the general, and we aren't," Lynder put in, as Lashana shook her head in amazed admiration.

"That certainly sounds like one of them—well, as you move deeper into the hills, more or less in *that* direction—" she pointed "—and don't worry, we can guide you tomorrow—the wierdlings get thicker, and odder. Now, suppose that this Portal of yours isn't *entirely* closed? I've heard from Sheyrena and

Lorryn that your Ancestors left a pretty nasty place to come here. . . ." She looked at him with speculation.

He nodded. "If the Portal isn't quite closed and shut down, yes, things could slip over, when enough residual power built up to let the Portal open for a moment. And what came over would be very unpleasant."

"And the area nearest where they were coming through?" she prompted.

"Would be the place nearest the Portal, of course." He felt another burst of elation—but then worry. "That would make it that much *more* dangerous. I'm not sure I should ask you fellows to share in something like this—it's pretty certain that Father is—dead—"

There. He'd said it. It couldn't be unsaid.

"—so looking for what became of him is really only my concern—"

"Balderdash! Begging your pardon, my Lord," Lynder exclaimed. "Your father, and his father, and his father before him, are the ones that allowed us to grow up in freedom. It's as much our concern as yours."

"And my people have—ways of dealing with most of these creatures, or getting you around them," Lashana added. "We've both got magic, you know, and mine's enough different from yours that they'll combine well. I'd be pleased to help you out, here."

"It's settled, then," Shalvan said, as the rest of his men nodded.

Once again, Kyrtian felt a surge of emotions—pride, gratitude, a touch of embarrassment. But most of all, the warmth of knowing that they would support him, and they knew that he would support them, through anything. And a different kind of warmth, of discovering an unexpected friend and comrade in the woman called the Elvenbane, who was so very different, and so very much *more*, than he had ever imagined her to be.

"Then in the morning—?" he made it a question. She laughed and stood up.

"In the morning you can expect me—and a friend," she promised. "And until then, sleep well. And don't worry, you're being guarded. So get a good night's sleep."

And with that, she walked off into the darkness.

And managed, again, not to trip over the bells.

"My Lord," said Shalvan, looking after her with undisguised admiration, "begging your pardon myself, but that is one *fine* woman. Not to *my* taste," he added hastily, "but one *fine* woman."

"Yes she is," Kyrtian agreed. "And not to my taste, either! But I hope she finds a man who deserves her, assuming that's what she wants! I will make no assumptions about anything the Elvenbane might want!"

That startled a laugh out of them, and on that note, they took to their tents, and to bed, knowing that the morrow would begin an entirely new and stranger quest than they had ever imagined.

28

Triana set her jaw grimly as she paced in and out of the bars of sunlight pouring through the windows of her solar—a traditional part of the bower, where she seldom spent any time. Why bother, when *she* was the mistress of the entire manse?

It looked as if she was going to have to leave her domain, for a short, but distinctly uncomfortable quest. Of all the things she would have preferred *not* to do, this was going to be right on the top of the list. She did not enjoy "the outdoors," she loathed having to camp without proper amenities, and she despised rain, damp, drizzle and cold. But she was going to have to endure all of that, because where she was going and what she needed to do required secrecy.

Her skirts swished around her ankles with a hissing sound. She *hated* this idea. But she couldn't trust Aelmarkin; she couldn't trust him to be any fitter for trailing someone in the savage forest than she, and she was pretty certain he would try to keep whatever he found all to himself. She had failed in her attempt to subvert his boring cousin for now—she was grateful that she hadn't put any term on the bet with Aelmarkin—but Kyrtian's ongoing success was making Aelmarkin impatient. Not that she cared whether she lost the bet. It wouldn't be all that difficult to train one stupid slave for Aelmarkin's use. No, the thing itself had become a challenge, an obsession. She *would not* be beaten, not in this, not when it was only her own skill and wit that stood between her and failure. For once, she didn't *have* to rely on anyone else.

It hadn't taken long in a conversation via teleson with Lord Kyndreth to discover what Kyrtian was up to and where he was going—openly. That was the key; Kyrtian might be pompous, might be deadly dull, but after his decisive victory over the Young Lords no one would ever claim that he was stupid.

She kicked the train of her skirt out of her way impatiently as she turned. No, he wasn't stupid. And just because he was dull, that didn't mean he wasn't capable of keeping some things to himself.

Triana had her own ideas of what else might be going on, when a quick check with Lord Kyndreth confirmed that Kyrtian was planning on a new expedition at the behest of the Council. What hadn't made any sense was why he would have been interested in the caves beneath those hills *before* that second batch of Wizards made an appearance. Because he had been—she knew it, because she knew some of the questions he'd been asking, and some of the maps and books he'd been requesting, before the two mind-addled captives had appeared in Lord Cheynar's forest.

It hadn't made any sense, that is, until she visited Morthena again, determined what he'd been doing there in the first place, and ferreted out just what books he'd been looking at. The two slaves who had been helping him were no challenge to her; within moments, she had them eagerly pulling volumes down for her perusal.

Now she knew. And she was, perhaps, better than any other Elvenlord, equipped to figure out what Kyrtian's ulterior motives were. There were her *own* familial traditions of the Crossing, and journals she had idly leafed through in moments of boredom. Putting Kyrtian's sudden fascination with the journals in Morthena's library together with his *father's* lifelong obsession with finding the Gate, and she knew, she *knew,* that he expected to find, at long last, some trace of his father.

But as important, given Lord Kyrtian's new-found importance as a military leader to the Great Lords, were the weapons supposedly left behind as useless. With those weapons, Lord Kyrtian would not need an army to impose the will of the Great Lords. With those weapons, he could become a Great Lord himself. Perhaps more than that. Perhaps—their first king?

Perhaps. That dull exterior might conceal a great deal of ambition.

Unless someone else got there at the same time. Someone who could bring accurate information back to—say—Lord Kyndreth.

Or someone who could use that information for herself.

Triana liked to keep her plans fluid. Which was why her slaves were putting together the gear that she and two male slaves—men who knew how to hunt and track—would take through the nearest Gate and on to the thrice-bedamned rain-soaked forest that Lord Cheynar's estate bordered.

Lord Cheynar did not approve of Triana. No matter. She didn't need his approval, and she didn't need his help. She didn't even need to get onto his lands; she had only to journey to his estate and follow the fences and walls around it, entering the forest where she pleased. Her men were good enough to find Kyrtian's track and follow it.

Even if that meant she did have to camp in a wretched forest in the constant rain. Just because Triana loved her comforts, that didn't mean she wasn't perfectly prepared to sacrifice them without hesitation for the right incentive.

Without hesitation.

Not without *complaint.* She kicked savagely at her train.

Aelmarkin brooded over the injustice of the world from the comfort of a favorite lounge, staring at a delicate stone sculpture of a dancer as if it had offended him personally.

Aelmarkin did not trust his cousin. There was more, much more, to this business of pursuing stupid Wizards in a half-inaccessible forest than appeared on the surface. Kyrtian might be dull, he might be obsessive, but he wasn't stupid.

Aelmarkin traced a circle in the upholstery with his fingernail. Kyrtian was not going on what Aelmarkin would consider a "military expedition." He wasn't taking any other Elvenlords with him, nor was he taking a very large party. In fact, he wasn't taking any slaves other than those from his own household; either he was ridiculously sure of himself, or . . .

. . . or he thought there was something in that forest that he could use for himself. What could it be?

There had to be something. There was no reason to take that sort of risk, unless there was a powerful reason for it. Something to do with the Wizards themselves? Aelmarkin hadn't heard anything that made them sound different from the ones that had already been driven out into the wilderness. Quite to the contrary, in fact, it seemed very much as if they were fewer.

Except . . .

Except that they also had that curious ability to nullify magic that the Young Lords had somehow acquired!

Aelmarkin slapped the arm of his lounge with a feeling of angry triumph. Of course that was it! So far, no one had managed to catch *any* of the ringleaders, so no one knew just what the trick was—but if Kyrtian could capture a Wizard and get the answer that way, he'd be in a position to demand, and get, anything he wanted from the Council, including a Council seat even if there were no vacancies!

And if that happened—Aelmarkin's chances of getting the estate dropped to less than zero. For all their bickering, no Council member had *ever* been known to back a move to oust another Council member from his lands, position, or seat, and not just because it "wasn't done." They guarded their primacy jealously, and when an outsider threatened one, he threatened all, and they closed ranks against him.

For a moment, Aelmarkin despaired, and began pounding the arm of his lounge with frustrated fury. He broke the underlying wooden frame with a *crack,* but his anger didn't ease until the arm of the lounge sagged, its structure reduced to fragments.

Finally his temper wore out, and he was able to think clearly. He left his study and went out into his gardens to continue thinking. The sky was overcast, but the pall over his spirit was darker than the grey sky.

He had to think . . . as he paced, his feet making no noise on the velvety sod of the paths, he ignored the murmur of fountains and artificial waterfalls he passed.

First, this all might come to nothing, but he didn't dare to take that chance. Kyrtian was too good at finding what he wanted to find. Persistent—obstinately persistent.

Second, it was just barely possible that Kyrtian would fail; either he wouldn't find a wizard or he wouldn't be able to take one captive. Aelmarkin thought sourly that *this* was not something he should count on; Kyrtian's luck had been disgustingly good. Persistence *and* good luck. It was damnably unfair.

Third—

Third . . .

It hit him, blinding as a ray of sun lancing through the clouds. He hadn't ever expected duplicity out of Kyrtian—but he hadn't expected brilliance, either. *What if all of this was a double-game?*

What if Kyrtian planned, not to capture a Wizard, but to treat with them? What if he intended to *ally* with them?

Ridiculous thought, of course but—it stopped him in his tracks. Both because of the audacity of it, and the possibilities the mere idea opened up.

If the Great Lords *thought* that was what Kyrtian had in mind, their support of him would not only collapse, they'd turn on him. Rightly so, of course; *treason* didn't even begin to cover it.

Well, there was only one way to find out, and that was to follow Kyrtian himself. Even if Kyrtian didn't mean treason, perhaps the appearance of treason could be manufactured.

For the first time in many days, Aelmarkin's spirits rose.

He even laughed out loud at the thought, his mind working busily. The first thing, of course, would be to follow Kyrtian and see if, against all probability, Kyrtian really *was* a traitor. It would be best not to have to manufacture anything out of whole cloth. If he could find even the *appearance* of duplicity, he could build on that. This, of course, meant that he could not trust this to anyone else.

Least of all Lady Triana.

He curled his lip in contempt, trying to imagine Lady Triana actually exerting herself enough to follow Kyrtian as far as Cheynar's, much less entrust herself to the privations of rough camping. She couldn't be bothered to visit her own gardens without a dozen slaves, a pavilion and cushions.

No matter. This wasn't something to be shared with anyone. And the saying was, after all, that if you wanted to be sure of something, you had better see to it yourself.

Besides, there was one last possibility, one that he doubted even Triana, as ruthless as she was, would think of. He could arrange a little "accident" to befall Kyrtian, especially if he had left that bodyguard of his behind.

Oh yes. Now he had it. Kyrtian would not leave that forest as he had entered it. When he came out, it would either be as a prisoner, or in a shroud.

For the first time that day, he smiled, and the slave walking patiently and invisibly behind him to supply whatever the master needed shuddered at the sight of that smile.

Caellach Gwain paced the uneven stone floor of his miserable excuse for a room, brow furrowed, a banked fire of anger in his gut that hadn't diminished in the least in the time since that wretched girl had debated him in front of the entire population of the Citadel. How had he let himself get drawn into *that?* A disaster, a total disaster; and he still couldn't see where it had all gone so horribly wrong. He'd only told everyone exactly the truth!

At the time, it had seemed like a stroke of the purest luck; the brat had no experience at making speeches, and she didn't know how to exude the confident authority that *he* certainly could. And over and above all of that, *he* had been the one in the right! Miserable creature! How had she managed it? How, when he had spoken nothing that was not true, had she managed to turn virtually everyone in the Citadel against him? By the time he realized that every word he spoke was turning more people away from him, it had been too late.

He kicked a shoe out of his path with a savage wish that it was the rear end of one of his so-called "friends" who had deserted him like the cowards that they were. As a consequence of that debate, he had been left utterly, completely without servants. No one would lift a finger to so much as keep him from tripping over an obstacle.

Even the humans, even the human *children,* ignored any command he gave them. If he wanted to eat, rather than enjoying a meal in quiet dignity in his room alone, he had to trudge up to the cavern used as a common dining hall, sit down at one of the common benches wherever he could find a place, and serve *himself* from a common pot. There could not possibly be anything more degrading than that—a regular punishment, thrice daily. How he hated it! He didn't know what was worse; having to starve himself until the last moment and content himself with whatever the rest had left him so that he could sit at a bench alone, or braving the crowd to get something edible, but having to bear the snickers and the way people ostentatiously spread themselves out so as to leave no room at their tables for him. At least they were still permitting him to eat. There were a growing number of loud remarks every time he appeared that there should be a rule in the *new* Citadel about having to do some work if you wanted to eat.

Ingrates! He'd show them! If they forbade him meals, he'd go back to the old ways, and steal his own food by magic from the Elvenlords' stores, and to the Netherworld with Lashana's stupid treaty! That would show them!

At least he'd have something decent then; real cheese, real bread, ham and sausage. Hah. If he even filched food from the kitchens, he could have anything he liked!

He thought sourly of his last meal; harshly-flavored goat-cheese, stringy mutton and not much of it, some nasty mess of wild greens, and bread made with coarsely-ground flour, heavy and dark. If they wanted him "punished," the quality of the food around here was punishment enough. How he longed for the good things filched from the Elvenlords, the delicately-smoked meats, the fine cheeses, sweet butter and clotted cream, the cakes made with proper flour and sweetened with white sugar! His mouth watered at the mere thought of them.

He glared at the fire in his "fireplace"—fortunately for *him,* he had secured this room before his current disgrace, so at least it had a fireplace: If you wanted to call a mere alcove in the rock wall with an open-topped shaft punched up to the surface with draconic rock-magic a "fireplace." When it rained up above, water dripped down into the fire, and when the wind blew wrong, it drove the smoke back *down* into his room. Right now it was raining, and drops sizzled and spat in the flames, threatening to put them out. If he wanted a fire, he now had to gather the wood *himself,* and if he didn't want the plaguey thing clogged with ash, he had to sweep it out and dispose of the ashes himself.

At least he was putting some things over on them all. He knew very well when firewood was delivered to other rooms; he just helped himself when the occupants were out. And as for the ashes, well, he didn't sweep them any farther away than the hall, and serve them all right. They could either sweep them up themselves or trample them everywhere; *he* didn't care.

It had finally come down to this; a job he'd spent most of the day on until the anger in his heart started to interfere with his scrying spell. Spying with his own magic on the Wizardling children teaching his former cronies the magics that they used to transport themselves without harm and magnify their own powers, so that *he* could learn to use those magics without having to humiliate himself further. And he *had* to have those lessons, because he had no choice; if he wanted something, he had to obtain it himself, and he didn't have the power he needed, alone.

And every day, new humiliations were piled atop the old. No one appeared to clean his quarters, and he, *he,* had to either do it himself, or find something one of the wretched children wanted and use it to *bribe* the little beast to do the work! And, of course, what they wanted was never some useless trinket of his own or something he could just go and appropriate from the stores, oh no—it was always something difficult, and *usually* something he had to use his own powers to fetch from the old Citadel! It made him so angry he could hardly think for hours afterwards. He longed for the days when he could drop something on the floor in the supreme confidence that whatever it was would be whisked off immediately to be discarded, put away, or cleaned as the case might be.

And it was all the fault of that overweening *female.*

She was up to something, too. No good, of course; that went without saying. He could tell that there was something in the air, something clandestine going on; from the way she acted, from the way that lover of hers acted. He'd felt the transportation spell being triggered more times than it should have been of late, now that he knew how to recognize it. A noisy magic, that; nothing subtle about it, and oh so typical of a female, to use something that only drew attention to the caster. He knew how to use it himself now, of course, no thanks to anyone's effort but his own. He'd gone back to the Old Citadel in person, to rummage through not only his own quarters, but the rooms of as many other people as he could before he grew too tired and hungry to stay there any longer. After all, if you didn't know or remember what was in a particular place, you couldn't bring it back by magic unless you did some fairly painstaking scrying. He'd piled what he wanted in his room when he could, and he'd made plenty of notes on what he couldn't pick up that he wanted in other rooms. He was getting more possessions together now, besides the armload of things he'd brought back with him.

So he knew quite enough about the transportation spell to recognize it, and there was no doubt in his mind that it was being used a great deal by Lashana herself of late. And for what? There was no need to use it to bring living things here anymore, now that they had flocks of sheep and goats and even cattle—you could bring anything you wanted here quietly, with the old magics that the Wizards had always used before, to steal what they wanted right out from beneath the noses of the Elvenlords.

In fact—that peculiar discordant feeling in the back of his

skull signaled that someone within the Citadel had used that particular magic *again.* It had to be Lashana. And in no way could it be for anyone's good except that selfish brat's.

But no one, no one would believe a single word he said against her. Not their dear *Elvenbane,* the person who had brought them the dragons (treacherous, sneaky beasts, whose minds could shift as easily as their shapes), the Trader clans (untrustworthy, wild human barbarians), and the Iron People (folly to put faith in any people who were not only wild human barbarians, but who had their own defenses against the Elvenlords and didn't need allies). Everyone so easily forgot that it was because of Lashana that they had *needed* those "allies," and *needed* to leave their comfortable, easy life in the old Citadel in the first place!

She was up to something; he knew it, he could taste it! She was up to something, and it could only mean new trouble for everyone else!

If only he could find out about it *before* everything fell apart—if he could catch her at some folly and prove she was up to something that would only drag everyone here into some new danger, they'd all believe him again!

That was it—that was it!

He kicked another shoe from his path, but this time with a triumphant cackle of laughter. That would serve the brat her just desserts! He'd use her own fancy magics to spy on her and find out exactly where she was going—then he'd use more of them to find out what she was doing! He'd catch her red-handed, and then he'd haul her back to the Citadel and make her confess in front of everyone! Oh, it would serve her *right* for her own magic to be used against her!

He turned abruptly and rummaged through the litter on his desk for the piece of smoke-quartz that served him for a magnifier of his power, then cleared a space and concentrated on the scrying spell. Lashana didn't discover *everything* about magic, after all! She hadn't been the one to learn that in scrying, you didn't have to look for a place you knew, or even a person—just a particular object or kind of object. That was how they filched provisions from the Elvenlords, back in the good old days. . . .

So rather than look for Lashana—because she might be alerted if she sensed someone scrying for *her*—he looked for an object. Something she always wore. A dragon-skin belt, made from the shed hide of her so-called "foster brother" and unique in that it had been dulled with dye so that it didn't catch the eye the way the brilliantly colored skin normally did.

When he found it, he would find her—then he would study where she was carefully—very carefully.

Then the next time she left, he would follow, a little behind. He'd find out where she was going, and what she was doing.

And the moment that he found out her secret—

He closed his hand into a fist, and smiled.

Triana lay on her stomach on the cold, hard ground beneath a bush, peering down at an encampment in the tiny valley below her. Water dripped down on the hood of her cloak from the branches above her, and although the cloak itself was waterproof, mist permeated even the cleverly-magicked fabric somewhat. It was not a comfortable position, but her sheer astonishment at the sight that lay beneath her allowed her to ignore her discomfort.

There was a campsite down there in the mizzle, with six or eight standing figures, putting the place to rights, and one sitting figure. It was the seated one that had her attention.

"You see, my lady?" murmured the human tracker in Triana's ear. "It is as I told you. There is the Elvenlord you wished to find."

Well, it was an Elvenlord, all right, but it was *not* the one she had intended to find. Not that the tracker could be blamed in this case. *He* didn't know what Lord Kyrtian looked like, especially at a distance. He couldn't know that Kyrtian, the fool, would never have sat back and watched while his slaves put up a camp. But what in the name of all the Ancestors had gotten *Aelmarkin* to stir his lazy behind and come out to this howling wilderness?

She was rather pleased to see that he didn't look very happy. Hunched over, elbows on knees, even from here she could see his frown. Ancestors! She could *feel* his frown. His slaves were trying to light a fire and not having a lot of success with the wet wood; he slumped on a stool beneath the shelter of his tent, watching them. She couldn't tell what he was thinking from here, but a moment later, he pointed his finger at the pile of wood and it roared up, causing his slaves to leap back lest they be scorched.

Could it be that he, too, was following Kyrtian? And without ever bothering to inform *her?*

She ground her teeth in a sudden flare of temper. The nerve of him! How dare he—

But just as quickly the temper subsided, because she couldn't honestly sustain it. Hadn't she expected this? And had she bothered to tell *him* what she was planning? Of course not, so why be angry with him when she was doing the same thing? And although to her this was just a wager, to him it was a great deal more than that. Enough to force him into a place that was as alien and uncomfortable to him as it was to her.

Well, if he was following Kyrtian, she would just follow him! It would save her a great deal of work, for he was by no means as woods-wise as his cousin, nor were his men. Only if he began to flounder would she have her men strike out on their own.

Meanwhile, Kyrtian was bound to go underground eventually; he had to look for Wizards, and he wanted to look for the Great Portal, and both would be in caves. If the caves were as extensive as rumor painted them, it would be child's play to get ahead of Aelmarkin.

"You've done well," she whispered back to the slave, who beamed at her, the smile of pride transforming an otherwise unhandsome face. "Watch them. I will send Kartar to you. When they leave, you both follow. Send Kartar back to fetch us to where they camp next."

"My lady," the slave bowed. He was a hard man, as were the others she had with her; forest-trackers all, they were used to the roughest of conditions. He was outfitted for the forest, in tough canvas, sturdy boots and a waterproof, hooded tunic. She wore the same, with modifications—an additional waterproof cloak, and her clothing made of materials that were just as tough, but softer to the skin. From the look of it, Aelmarkin had taken no such precautions, and she smiled grimly as she eased her way out from under the cover of the bush and back down the other side of the hill, where another of her slaves awaited her.

He led her silently down a tangle of deer-trails; only the Ancestors knew how he was finding his way, and she didn't worry about it. That was *his* job, and he'd been trained very, very well for it. She did wish, however, that the need for stealth had not required the horses be tied up quite so far from Aelmarkin's camp. The thing about deer-trails was that the deer didn't care a bit if there were branches stretched across the path, or roots to trip up the unwary.

It was dusk by the time she and her escort rode into a camp that was, thanks to *her* good sense in picking the right sort of slaves for this job, in much better state than Aelmarkin's. There was a very small fire burning beneath a clever shelter of branches that not only shielded it from most of the omnipresent rain but dissipated the smoke rising from it so there would be no plume above the trees to betray their presence.

Good men. She was glad that she had bought them from Lord Kyndreth, once she'd learned they were not only foresters, but had been trained to serve as war-scouts. They were efficient, unobtrusive, quiet—they already knew how to work together as a team, and they didn't need constant supervision.

And they already knew their reward could be very great indeed if they served her well. She'd given them a taste of it. There was a time for the lash, and a time for the velvet glove, and when you needed someone's utmost effort in a skill, the velvet glove was the only sensible choice.

Besides, they weren't *bad* looking, any of them, although they were craggy and rough-hewn—and they *were* a pleasant change from her usual pretty toys.

So despite being chilled and damp, she bestowed praise all around and made sure Kartar was well-provisioned as well as well-fed before he set off to join his fellow tracker to keep watch over Aelmarkin's camp. Dusk lingered for a long time out here, and Kartar had a clear trail to follow. He'd be in place by dark.

In spite of her dislike for this whole situation, things were becoming interesting. Definitely interesting. She smiled again as she accepted a plate of slightly-charred meat from one of the slaves and retired with it into the privacy of her tiny tent. She might never forgive Kyrtian if it turned out he had led her out here on some idiotic wild-goose chase, but if he hadn't—

If he hadn't, this might prove to be the best opportunity for upsetting the balance of power among the Great Lords that had come along in a while.

And there was always one other possibility she could pursue—one which, given the circumstances, could provide a lot of satisfaction even if this *was* a wild-goose chase.

If Aelmarkin hadn't told *her* where he was going and what he was up to, he probably hadn't told anyone else. Except possibly Cheynar, and then it wouldn't have been much. Everyone knew these were dangerous forests. *Her* forest-trackers had been trained for war. His hadn't. And *no one* knew that *she* was in these hills as well.

So if he and his men just—disappeared—no one would be surprised, nor was it likely that anyone would come looking for him once Cheynar reported where he'd gone.

She wouldn't win her bet—but she wouldn't lose it, either. And it just might be worth violating every law and compact the Great Lords had sworn just to see his face when she slit his throat.

This was the darkest forest Kyrtian had ever had the misfortune of camping in. He found himself wondering as he kept half of his concentration on the conversation around the fire, and the other half on the sounds out in the woods beyond the camp, if the overcast skies here ever lifted. Surely they had to at some point . . . it couldn't rain all the time. Could it?

And yet, there hadn't been so much as an hour since they'd entered the place when it hadn't at least misted. And it was a good thing that he and his men weren't depending on that old saw of finding north by looking for moss on a tree trunk, because moss grew *everywhere,* thick as a carpet in most places. If ever there was a spot meant by nature for ambushes, this was it. So far they'd managed to avoid any more of those invisible whatever-they-weres, but the very nature of the gloom-laden landscape had his whole group edgy.

The snap of a twig brought Kyrtian and everyone in his camp to instant alertness. The whistle of a skylark came out of the darkness, and they all relaxed again. A moment later, Shana and a young male wizard walked into the circle of light cast by the fire, the omnipresent mist sparkling like gems on the edges of their hoods.

"I don't know how you do that—getting past my sentries," Kyrtian complained good-naturedly. "I hope no one else can."

"Only humans that have their special magic, dragons, and Wizards," Shana told him, grinning, as she settled down on a bit of log that one of the men rolled to the fire for her. "Speaking of which—this is my foster-brother, Keman."

"I am pleased to make your acquaintance," Kyrtian said politely, but warily. "So, you're another wizard, then—"

"Ah, actually, I'm not," the young man said diffidently, with a glance at the Elvenbane. "Shana thinks it's time you were—ah—"

"If you're going to trust *us,* we have to give you a reason," Shana said briskly. "I've already talked this over with the other leaders, and they think it's time for you to be entrusted with the biggest secret we have."

"Which—would be what, exactly?" Kyrtian replied, wishing she would just get straight to whatever she was going to say.

"First, just indulge me and do whatever it is that you normally do to dispel an illusion or a glamor. Keman isn't exactly what he seems," Shana said, and there was a certain—tone in her voice that made him look at her with suspicion for a moment. Just what was she up to, anyway? Was this "foster brother" of hers fully Elven—or perhaps human? No, if he was human, there would be no need for all this secrecy and fiddling about.

But it was obvious that he wasn't going to get any further information out of the woman unless he did as she asked, so, with a sigh, he gathered threads of magic and wove them into a net, casting it over the two of them, just for good measure. He might as well see if the Elvenbane herself was under a glamor.

Nothing happened. The two of them remained exactly as they had been when they walked into the firelight.

Now Kyrtian was puzzled. Had the magic been countered? It couldn't have been deflected; he'd have seen that. Could they have absorbed it, then negated it? But how? "Are you carrying something new that works like iron?" he asked. "Or have you—"

He never got a chance to finish his question, because in the next moment, the young man who had been standing at the fireside, looking altogether as normal as it was possible for a wizard to look, suddenly began to . . . change. He didn't *writhe,* exactly, but he blurred and twisted in a way that induced a really violent case of dizziness and nausea. It felt as if something was wrenching Kyrtian's eyes out of their sockets and stirring up his guts at the same time, and Kyrtian clapped his hand over his mouth and turned away. He wasn't alone; the rest of his men were doing the same thing, their complexions in varying shades of green.

What in the name of—

As soon as he turned his eyes away his symptoms subsided, and he looked up, glaring at Lashana, angry accusations on his lips.

Which died, as he continued to look up—and up—and up—into the jewel-like and surprisingly mild eyes of a very large, sapphire-blue dragon.

At least, he thought it was a dragon. He couldn't think of anything *else* it could be. It was huge, scaled, winged, fanged and taloned. There weren't many other creatures that fit *that* description.

As he stared, he heard the men behind him reacting to the presence of the creature. One was praying in the ancient language of the humans, one was cursing with remarkable fluency, and he distinctly heard the *thud* of a third dropping to the ground, presumably having fainted dead away.

Not that Kyrtian blamed him in the least.

"You can cast all the illusion-breaking spells you like, but dragons can look like anything they care to and you won't know it. The dragons are shape-changers, you see," he heard the Elvenbane say, quite cheerfully, but it was as if he heard her in the far distance. His mind was still too involved with the impossibility of what he had just witnessed, and the sheer *presence* of the dragon itself. "That's our biggest secret, and that gives us undetectable spies among you Elvenlords. The dragons can go anywhere and be anything or anybody, and *you* can never tell that they're there, because they're not taking on illusions, they're taking on the real form of whatever they imitate. They've been spying on your people—oh, *forever.* From the moment the Elvenlords arrived here, the Eldest say."

"Oh," Kyrtian said, faintly. "I suppose—dragons must have been in my camp, then?"

Lashana let out a peal of laughter. "My good Lord Kyrtian, dragons were *guarding your tent.* And neither you nor your good Sargeant Gel had any notion!"

"Actually," the dragon said, with a note of apology in his deep voice, "I was one of them. Sorry. Hate to eavesdrop and all that, but we really didn't have much choice. We had to know what you *were,* you understand. Suddenly you were doing all sorts of efficient things against the Young Lords, and we calculated that you'd be coming after us, next."

Kyrtian wasn't entirely certain how the dragon was *speaking;* the voice seemed to rumble up out of the depths of that massive torso, and the mouth opened and closed, but the dragon didn't have anything like lips, and he couldn't figure out how it could shape words with that mouth. . . .

"At any rate, *this* is our biggest secret, and now you know it," Lashana continued. "So—well, you can see that we trust you."

"Ah . . . yes." Carefully, very carefully, Kyrtian felt blindly for the piece of log he'd been sitting on and lowered himself down onto it. "I . . . can see that."

The dragon lowered his head until his eyes were level with

Kyrtian's face. "You can do us as much harm, knowing this, as we could ever do to you, you know," the creature said, quietly.

"Forgive me," Kyrtian managed, finally gathering some of his wits about him, "If at this moment—with a mouth big enough to swallow me whole not an arm's-length away from me—I find that a little difficult to believe."

The dragon suddenly reared up, and for a moment, Kyrtian was certain that they were all going to *be* swallowed up—

But then an enormous, rumbling laugh started somewhere deep inside the dragon, bubbled up through the long, long throat, and emerged from the upturned snout as a trumpeting hoot.

It should have terrified him—and his men—further still. It was a completely alien sound, something that *could* have meant the thing was about to attack them. But somehow, it wasn't frightening at all, somehow, in the depths of Kyrtian's mind where the basest of instincts gibbered in terror and tried to crouch as small as possible so as not to be noticed by this monster, it translated as exactly what it was—the laughter of a fellow creature who meant no harm at all. And that primitive part of him stopped gibbering, and relaxed. . . .

"Look aside, Lord Kyrtian," the dragon said, when he'd finally done laughing. "I think I'd best come—back down to your level."

He didn't need urging, not after his previous experience.

When Keman looked again like an ordinary wizard, poor Resso had been revived, and they were all seated around the fire, Kyrtian contemplated the wizard-dragon from across the flames as Lashana and the foresters discussed which of several possible caves they ought to penetrate first. He couldn't help himself; he couldn't reconcile the apparent size of the wizard with the obvious size of the dragon he'd become. The puzzle ate at him; he couldn't explain it, couldn't rationalize it, and when he couldn't find an explanation for something, he had the bad habit (and he *knew* it was a bad habit) of worrying at it to the exclusion of everything else.

Finally the dragon himself leveled a stare across the flames and said, "What, exactly, is bothering you, Lord Kyrtian?" in a tone of irritation mixed with amusement.

"Where did it come from?" Kyrtian blurted, as conversation ceased among the others. "I mean, you're no larger than Resso right now, and you're not exactly having that log splitting under you from your weight—but when you were—" he waved his hands wildly "—that wasn't *air,* that was mass—well, look at the imprints you left! So where did it come from? And where did it go?"

Keman shrugged. "Elsewhere, Kyrtian," he said. "That's all I can tell you. We call it, 'shifting into the Out.' We move the real bulk of ourselves to and from the Out, but—well, we don't *know* what the Out is. It's here, but it's somewhere else—"

"But when you know what to look for, a dragon casts a sort of—shadow—when he's in another form," Lashana put in. "It's not the kind of shadow you get from light falling on you, but it's there, and when you've learned how to see it and look for it, you can always tell whether something is a dragon or not."

Kyrtian could only shake his head, more puzzled by the explanation than by not having one. But at least that obsessive part of his mind had it to turn inside out and examine while he set most of his attention to work on more important things. "Never mind," he said, after a moment. "What in the name of the Ancestors are those—invisible horrors that lie in wait for you on deer trails? And what can we do about them?"

Lashana and Keman exchanged a look and a nod, and the planning moved into more practical spheres.

Caellach Gwain was beside himself with rage.

He'd followed Lashana to this benighted forest once he'd scryed out her location and once she'd abandoned it, trusting to distance and preoccupation to keep her from noticing the "noise" of his arrival. Of course, just as he apported into the spot, the wretched trees delivered a load of water from their disturbed branches, creating the effect of a localized downpour for a moment or two, which was certainly enough to drench him from head to toe. Since he hadn't taken the precaution of wearing a waterproof cape, never thinking that Lashana would drop herself into the middle of a rainstorm, he was hardly prepared for such a reception.

His temper wasn't improved when he followed the clear trail that she and whoever she'd brought with her had left. It led through underbrush just thick enough to be a nuisance, catching in his soggy robes and snarling his hair. And it was *dark,* plague take it all! If he hadn't kindled a mage-light, he wouldn't be able to see where he was going!

Fortunately, he'd been on the alert for the thoughts of others, because he managed to detect the sentries before they got a glimpse of his light, and douse it. And he was able to avoid them the same way, though his command of thought-sensing wasn't the equal of someone who'd wasted his time honing it to a fine pitch. Still—he knew human thoughts when he sensed them. So what was Lashana up to? Had she found yet *another* group of wild humans to bring to the new Citadel, using up more precious resources that should have gone to support Wizards and not useless mouths?

He spotted a fire, then, and belatedly caution took over. He would far rather have scryed out what was going on, but that would have required light—so instead, he crept on hands and knees, with every bone creaking in protest, until he was close enough to see most of the figures there, if not hear what they were saying.

Sure enough, it looked like another plaguey lot of mere humans!

But then, the one that had his back to Caellach turned his head, and Caellach froze.

An Elvenlord!

And there, chatting away with him, just as bold as could be—Lashana and Keman.

He very nearly rushed out from beneath his covering bush and accosted them then and there. As it was, sheer rage held him frozen in place.

How dare she! Traitor! Unnatural, ungrateful wretched girl!

He wanted to throttle her, there and then. He wanted to blast her into a hundred thousand bits. After everything she had done to the Wizards, who had taken her in, taught her, sheltered her—

He just sat and shook for a long time, while she, oblivious, chattered on as if she was old friends with them all.

He didn't know how long it was that he sat, encompassed by anger so hot it burned away every vestige of thought. But finally, it ebbed, and when it did—

Unholy glee flooded in, replacing the anger with savage joy.

He had her now. Finally, *finally,* he had her! Let her try to deny *this!* When the others heard about it, they'd throw her into a prison she could never escape from!

He had to get back, though, before he could lay any charges. And to do that, he had to get far enough away from here that the noise of the transportation spell wouldn't be noticed.

And he mustn't get caught. Not now, not when victory was so close he could taste it.

He opened his mind as he never had before, paying obsessive attention to the whereabouts of all of the sentry-slaves. When he moved, he did so only when he knew that they were nowhere near, and the sounds of his movement would not reach them. He literally felt his way along the path that had brought him here, moving loose twigs out of the way so that he wouldn't step on them and betray himself. At least now the sodden nature of this forest worked for him rather than against him; thick moss apparently covered every surface, and the fallen leaves he encountered were too wet to crackle.

When he was finally far enough away that he felt safe in doing so, he kindled a mage-light once again, got to his feet, and shoved his way along the first clear path he spotted. He didn't particularly care where he was going—and it really didn't matter. He could get back to the Citadel from practically anywhere; what really mattered now was that he get away from *here.*

The further he got, the brighter he made his light; at first, as the light itself frightened nocturnal animals out of his path, he was afraid that the disturbances *they* made would betray him, or draw in something like an alicorn that could be a real danger to him. But the further away he got, the less wildlife he saw, until at last there didn't seem to be anything at all along the path but himself.

They must have hunted it all out on the way here, he thought vaguely, most of his attention on what he was going to say when he got back to the Citadel. He recalled some vague admonitions by the stupid dragons that one shouldn't hunt an area out, but apparently that Elvenlord paid as little heed to such things as *he* would have. And now that the trail was wide and beautifully clear, he was going to get to a point where he could transport himself back in a matter of moments, now—just as soon as he got past that cluster of bushes—

The violent shaking of the bushes was the only warning he got. Then he was engulfed in something horrid, and slimy, and his mage-light went out. There was a moment of absolute surprise, followed by an eternity of hellish pain, and in the end, only . . . nothingness.

And then there was no sound at all on the trail, except the noises of something feeding in the dark.

30

Keman and Shana elected to remain with Kyrtian and his men, but only after modifying their appearance to that of ordinary humans. That was a precautionary measure, easy to maintain, but vital just in case someone came looking for Kyrtian—or decided to scry for him.

Besides, as Keman pointed out, they'd been in these woods before. They'd helped rescue a pen full of slaves from Lord Cheynar by taking them into this forest, and even if they didn't exactly know every trail and rock, at least they knew enough about the dangers to keep Kyrtian's people from walking into trouble. Or rather, *more* trouble. Kyrtian had already had one narrow escape from the ambush beasts.

And they were both rather good at *finding* things, Keman in particular. When Kyrtian explained in detail what he thought he was looking for—the place where his father had gone hunting ancient artifacts, probably within a cave-complex—and the details he'd gleaned from the ancient journals, they both volunteered their services. Shana went with Kyrtian and his people, to act as a lookout for alicorns, ambush beasts, and other unpleasantries, while Keman went off on his own.

It didn't take Keman very long at all to come haring back to the main party with a find in his hands and a grin on his face.

"Where did you find *that?"* Kyrtian exclaimed, seizing the oddly-shaped chunk of metal that Keman had found as if it were made of begemmed gold. It had probably been flat, once, with rolled edges on two sides. Now it was twisted and crumpled, like a piece of paper that had been wadded up, then smoothed out again.

"Up that way—" Keman pointed. "You know dragons can tell where caves are—"

He could tell immediately by Kyrtian's expression that, no, he *didn't* know that, but he continued with the explanation anyway.

"—I've just been cruising at treetop level, probing for caverns. I found a place where there *had* been a big entrance that led into a huge complex, but there'd been a rock-fall that blocked the entrance, and when I landed to look it over, I found that this was caught in the rocks." He tilted his head to the side with curiosity. "What is it, anyway?"

"I haven't the vaguest clue," Kyrtian replied, turning it over in his hands with every evidence of fascination. "But feel it! Feel how light it is? Is it any metal that you recognize?"

"Well, no," Keman admitted. The lightness, and the lack of corrosion, had been what attracted him in the first place. The dull grey bit of debris, twisted and distorted, had blended very well into the fallen rocks, and only a dragon would have been able to spot it at once, by the different "feel" associated with it.

"And look at this—" Kyrtian pointed to a tiny line of engraved figures, incised deeply enough that not even the mist collecting on the surface obscured them. "You see? That's ancient script—*Elven* script!"

Keman peered at it. "What does it say?" he asked, dubiously. He couldn't begin to guess what an Elvenlord would choose to engrave on a piece of—something that looked like nothing more than a bit of shelf, but probably wasn't. It could be anything. *A bit of a poem? "Touch this who dares?"*

Kyrtian chuckled. "It says, 'Keep this edge up.' Not what you expected, is it?" But his eyes were afire with excitement. "Keman, this is—must be—a piece of one of the artifacts from the Crossing! We've found the Great Portal!"

"We have?" Keman replied with surprise. He shook water off his hood with a gesture of impatience. "I didn't know we were looking for it. I thought we were looking for your father."

"My father was looking for the Great Portal, and I'm sure he found it—but something must have happened and he couldn't get back to us." The Elvenlord's expression suddenly darkened. Kyrtian didn't say what he thought the "something" was, and Keman decided that he wasn't going to ask. "How recent was that rock-fall?"

"There have been several, I think." Now Keman was on firmer ground; if there was one thing that a dragon knew, it was rocks and caves. "I managed to get this bit out from under the bottom layer, but it looks to me as if there was one large fall quite some time ago, and several since then. There's still an opening big enough for a person to squeeze inside, but the opening used to be—well—big enough for my mother, much less me! I didn't find anything like—well, bones," he added hastily, realizing only then that he might well be describing the place where Kyrtian's father had died. His addition didn't reassure Kyrtian in the least; Kyrtian's expression darkened further.

Kyrtian handed the artifact to Shana, who examined it curiously, but paid more attention to the Elvenlord than to the piece of metal. It suddenly seemed very quiet, in their little camp under the trees. Quiet enough to hear water dripping everywhere, to hear the far off calls of bell-birds. His face shadowed now, all excitement gone, the Elvenlord stared off into the trees for a moment. "How far is this? Can we get there soon?"

"Two days, I think, over the trails," Keman told him, after a moment to try and gauge distances. "I could fly you there, one at a time—"

But both Shana and Kyrtian shook their heads. "I don't want

to divide the party," Kyrtian said first. "And Lashana, I know that you can use magic to bring us there, but—"

"But I'll fall on my nose afterwards," Shana said bluntly. "And if you need me, I won't be able to do anything. No, overland it is." She sighed, then smiled, and tried to make light of the situation. "Ah well. I haven't gotten nearly enough hard exercise lately, and you *do* have horses to help. Keman and I will be the only ones who have to walk—"

Keman burst into laughter, as she hit her head with the heel of her palm.

"I don't think you'll be *walking,* Shana," Keman told her. "If you'll just give me a chance to 'change' into something more suitable—"

Kyrtian got the hint immediately. It was only a moment of work—as Kyrtian hastily averted his eyes—and an "extra" horse stared at Shana mockingly.

"What color would you like, foster-sister?" he asked shaping the mouth and larynx a bit off the horse-form, so he could talk properly. "Roan? Bay? Black?" With each suggestion, he changed his color to match. "How about a nice buckskin? Or spots? Stripes? Checks?" The changes flashed across his hide in bewildering succession.

"Ew!" Shana wrinkled her nose at the last. "Brown. Please. Brown will do very nicely."

"Not even alicorn-white with pretty blue eyes?" he teased, fading out the checks into a uniform brown. And, for good measure, making the hair much better at shedding water. By this point he had concluded that he should have taken to the guise of a horse a lot sooner—no need for rain-capes and, in fact, the rain felt rather good! It certainly kept the biting flies away.

Their exchange had lightened Kyrtian's mood a little, but it was very clear as he gave his men their new orders to move out that he was tense. Keman didn't have to ask why; it had been clear when he'd told them of his missing father that he didn't expect to find his parent alive. After the initial burst of excitement faded, how could you possibly look forward to finding a body—or what was left of one?

He hurried them all into packing up the camp; it was interesting to Keman that even under the press of urgency, Kyrtian's people worked efficiently and without fumbling. In far less time than Keman would have thought possible, given his experience even with the Iron People, everything was packed properly, stowed on the horses, and they were ready to leave.

The others looked to Kyrtian for orders; he gestured to Keman, who obviously was the only one who knew where they were going, and Keman and Shana took the lead. Kyrtian rode behind them, and everyone in his party gave him a respectful distance. With a stony expression, and his mouth set in a grim line, it was pretty clear that he didn't want to talk to anyone, and it seemed best to leave him alone.

It was a very, very quiet ride. None of the men wanted to break the silence, and even Shana didn't talk. The rain started up again shortly after they took to the trail, obscuring the distance behind a veil of grey, but Keman wasn't worried. Dragons couldn't get lost; he knew where he was, exactly in relationship to where their goal was. The only thing standing between them and that rock-covered cave entrance was the trifling matter of several leagues.

It would have been funny, if it hadn't been so important that Triana keep the presence of her party secret, not only from Aelmarkin, but from Kyrtian as well. As it was, when everyone else suddenly packed up for no apparent reason and began to move, Triana's group had to scramble to clean out their camp and move deeper into the forest.

It was a near thing. Kyrtian's party didn't ride in on top of where Triana's camp had been, but they came closer than Triana liked, and Aelmarkin's bunch *did* just blunder on through. If his foresters had been half as good as Triana's slaves, they'd have spotted the signs of recent occupation for certain.

But after that, it was a simple enough matter to trail behind Aelmarkin. He was leaving a trail as broad as a highway and making no effort to hide it—but interestingly enough, Kyrtian wasn't going to any effort to conceal his trail either.

He *must* have found something. That was the only possible explanation. Triana wished she knew what it was.

Only when they pushed on past dark was she certain that it couldn't be Wizards—because Kyrtian kindled mage-lights and sent them up above their heads to illuminate the trail. Her own scouts reported it—and when her group was on the top of a hill, she could often catch a glimpse of the lights flitting among the branches of a valley below, like impossibly huge fireflies in the distancc.

He wouldn't have betrayed his presence this way if he thought he'd found signs of the Wizards he was supposed to be looking for. At least, she didn't think he would.

The trouble was, *he* could use lights, but neither she nor Aelmarkin dared.

That had her gritting her teeth in frustration, until it occurred to her that there was one thing, at least, that she could do. She could make mage-lights of a different sort. Not powerful enough to light their path, but tiny things that would mark where Kyrtian's horses, and Aelmarkin's, had gone by following the scent in the air. If the others saw them, they'd either assume they were ordinary fireflies or were some bizarre creature native to these forests.

It took her the better part of an hour to get the magic right, but in the end it was worth it; the trick was to set the spell to seek "horse," but with the specific exclusions of the horses she and her group rode—otherwise, all the little motes did was cluster around *her.* So even if they were stumbling down the path in the darkness now, they had something to follow. What a miserable experience, though—wet, cold, the endless mizzle in the face, and it seemed as if there were entire trees just waiting until they passed beneath to drop a load of water on their heads. They didn't have to worry about moving quietly, though—there were so many frogs calling in a dozen different tones throughout the woods that they could have blundered about thrashing through the bushes and never been heard.

Presumably Aelmarkin came up with something that worked equally well, since they didn't run right into the back of his group. Triana was dreadfully afraid for some time that Kyrtian was going to ride all night, for he showed no signs of wanting to halt. The rain poured on past dusk, and only slackened to the usual mist long after dark, but still Kyrtian road on.

By this time she was convinced that Kyrtian had gone quite mad, but her best forester assured her that no, not even someone as driven as Kyrtian was going to be foolish enough to press himself and his men *that* hard. And the slave was proved right; after what seemed like half the night, her foremost scout came back with the intelligence that both Kyrtian and Aelmarkin were settling in for the night, and with the profoundest relief, Triana directed her own men to do the same.

But the moment that the first thin light showed among the trees, the scouts who watched the camps came back and roused them, and they were out of bedrolls that had just gotten comfortable and off again into the fog of pre-dawn. Kyrtian was pushing hard, and Triana needed to make a decision. She called her best man to ride alongside her.

"Can we outflank my cousin—get ahead of him without him realizing that we're out here?" she asked. Not for the first time, she was glad she had bought these men from Lord Kyndreth. Whoever had trained them had done such a good job that she didn't have to give them exact instructions—she had only to ask for what she wanted done, and they worked out a way to accomplish it if they had the skills. Unfortunately there was one thing that they did *not* have the skills for. They weren't very good cooks. *They* didn't seem to mind eating squirrel and hare that was half raw and half burned, but she had begun eating the leathery journey-bread in preference to the game they provided.

The slave pondered her question, then nodded. "I believe so, my lady, but—" he looked uneasy, and wiped a film of moisture from his forehead that wasn't from the mist. "—it isn't the forest that's the problem. It's what's *in* the forest. We know of alicorn herds at the very least, and the outriders have seen signs of other things. Worse things, my Lady, than alicorn stallions."

"Worse things?" She wrinkled her brow. "What sorts of signs?"

"One of them came across signs that something had killed

and eaten several alicorns in the past week or so." He grimaced. "I would not care to encounter anything that could do that."

"And I suppose he didn't see it? Had no clue as to what it was?" If she knew what they needed to guard against, she could perform some specific magics—magic that would either repulse the creatures or at least give warning of their presence. But without knowing what it was she was trying to ward off—she could waste her energy and skill shooing away spiders, only to have a giant slug descend on them.

"Nothing *we've* ever seen or heard of, my lady—the scout didn't get near; he said the place looked like an ambush in the making. From what he told me, the alicorns were torn in pieces, and I wouldn't even expect one of those dragons we've heard about to do that." She gave him a suspicious glance, but he didn't look as if he was exaggerating.

Well, that did fit in with what she'd been warned about this place. Kyndreth himself had been none-too-eager to go looking for purported Wizards in these hills, and had jumped to accept Kyrtian's offer to track them down. She'd probably lose some men in this. Now she was glad she'd bought them outright from Kyndreth instead of borrowing them. When an accident happened to a borrowed slave, it was amazing how the value of that slave suddenly increased. . . .

"Do it," she ordered him. "Send the outriders ahead, find us a clear path so we can get around Aelmarkin and run alongside Kyrtian. You're supposed to be Lord Kyndreth's best, aren't you?"

He bowed. "Yes, my lady," he said. No hesitation, no excuses, no objections. Just obedience. Exactly what she had paid for.

Well, not *all* that she had paid for. She'd also invested in excellence; so far, these slaves had been most satisfactory, but now they had better well prove that they could go beyond "satisfactory."

Or when she got back, she'd be having some words with Lord Kyndreth.

But right now, she had better keep her own mind on the job at hand. If these slaves couldn't rise to the challenge, she might have to abandon them to their fate and narrow her goal to getting her own self out intact.

They'd just paused long enough to pass around rations for lunch, eating in the saddle, before the afternoon downpour arrived on schedule. By nightfall, they should be at Keman's cave-complex. As rain drummed on the hood of her cape and a few cold drops slipped around the collar and got down her neck, Shana was grateful that her "mount" was Keman, and not a real horse. She couldn't have fallen off if she'd wanted to, not even on the steep trails he was taking, and at the moment, she needed to be able to concentrate on holding the mental line of communication with Lorryn as tightly as possible. There was a lot of distance between them—and something unexpected had happened, something that made all the discomfort she felt completely irrelevant.

Caellach Gwain had vanished from the Citadel.

: . . . so when he didn't turn up for breakfast, either, Hala thought it was more than odd,: Lorryn told her. *:He's pulled sulks before, usually when he's managed to squirrel away food in his room, but missing three meals in a row was exceptional. The door was bolted from the inside; it wasn't hard to get it open, not with a half dozen Wizards working on it—but he wasn't there when we opened it.:*

Caellach Gwain gone! It was so tempting to allow herself to wallow in sheer relief, but—Caellach Gwain vanished out of his own room was a puzzle that only promised more trouble.

She wiped rain from her face and closed her eyes, concentrating. *:You don't suppose he's learned the transportation magic, do you?:* she asked, apprehensively.

:That's exactly what I'm afraid has happened,: was the grim reply.

Well, that made perfect sense. You didn't have to attend lessons to get the advantage of them. The miserable old toad could simply have sat in his room with a scrying glass and learned everything any of the other Old Whiners was learning.

:You've got a good reason, I'll bet.:

She felt Lorryn's nod. *:His room was full of things from the old Citadel—a good many of them not* his *property, so many of the Old Ones tell me. By the way, that's put him beyond the pale, if that's any comfort to you. Even the Old Whiners who were his most vocal supporters were wild with rage when they found* their *property in* his *room. There's no way he could have known where some of those things were without going back in person, because there were a lot of small, valuable trinkets that were hidden away in drawers and chests he'd never seen the inside of.:*

Her heart sank. *:So he could be anywhere.:* If he knew the transportation spell, all he had to do was be familiar with a place to go there. She supposed it was even possible to become that familiar using simple scrying.

:The old Citadel, some new hideaway of his own, even out spying on you,: Lorryn replied, and there was apprehension in his thoughts. *:You know what would happen if people found out where you are right now, what you were doing, and who you were doing it with.:*

Never mind that Lady Moth was clearly the Wizards' friend, that Lorryn's own mother and sister were fullbloods. This was different. This was consorting with the Great Lords' chosen general. She could try to explain until her face was blue, but if Caellach Gwain broke the news at an inopportune time, well—

:That's my worst fear, because there are some of the youngsters who think that there was a second burst of transportation noise right after you and Keman left.: She sensed Lorryn's worry, and she more than agreed with it.

:Fire and Rain!: she swore angrily. *:That would be just like him, wouldn't it!:* Even through her anger, she tried to think if she'd detected anything since she'd arrived. *:He might be here. He might not. If he came in far enough from us, I wouldn't have heard the arrival.:*

:Look, I'm going to do two things, and the first *is that I'm going to turn his room into an iron cage,:* Lorryn told her. *:And when he tries to transport back in—he'll get a shock. Zed tried*

it with a rock, and what happens is that you bounce back to where you came from.:

:With a demon of a headache, I can only hope,: she said sourly. *:He'll try to go to another part of the Citadel, of course—:*

:Maybe, maybe not. Because the next thing I'm going to do is start planting iron wedges all over the Citadel except in designated 'magic rooms,' and those will be brand new ones that Father Dragon is going to carve out for us.: He sounded—well, rather pleased with himself for coming up with a plan so quickly, and she didn't blame him.

:Zed can pour simple wedges for us easily enough, can't he?: she asked.

:With no problem at all; he's already pouring them, the children are planting them, and Father Dragon has the first magic room carved out. I've been wanting to do this for a while, anyway. It's one more defense against the Elvenlords, even if it is a nuisance for us to confine doing magic to those special rooms.: He sighed. *:Still, it'll be worth it, and we can have the whole Citadel protected by tomorrow. Caellach Gwain will have no way of knowing where the safe rooms to transport to are or what they look like. So to get back here, he'll have to apport to somewhere he knows.:*

Her anger faded as she considered that. *:I don't think he's set foot outside the caves more than a dozen times since we arrived. There can't be that many places where he can apport back.:*

:And I can have all of them watched by people we trust. That leaves only the old Citadel for him.: Lorryn sounded absolutely smug when he said that, and she didn't blame him.

:He can go live there and rot for all I care,: she said maliciously. *:Maybe the Great Lords will decide that our fictitious Wizards live* there. *That would serve him right, if they find him sitting there like an old toad in a hole.:*

:Well, just keep alert for any sign of him, love,: Lorryn cautioned. *:He's a twisty old beast. I'm not sure I can think of every way* he *could think of to cause us harm.:*

:I will,: she promised, and gave him a wordless, loving farewell that she hoped remained untainted with her anger at Caellach Gwain.

"Well, that's not good," Keman muttered up at her, shaking the rain from his mane. He had, of course, been listening in.

"No, it's not. Should we tell Kyrtian?" She was of two minds on the subject. It wasn't as if Kyrtian didn't already have enough on his hands—and it wasn't as if his men weren't perfectly capable of catching one old man who was anything but woods-wise if he *was* spying on them.

Unless, of course, he was using the transportation spell to get him away each time it looked as if he was going to get caught.

But she hadn't *heard* the distinctive "noise" associated with that spell!

"I wouldn't," Keman replied after a moment. "It's not his business. It's wizard business. Let Lorryn take care of things at the Citadel; you and I will just have to be very vigilant from now on."

"I hope an ambush beast gets him," she grumbled.

Keman shook his head. "I wouldn't wish that fate even on Caellach Gwain. And you shouldn't, either."

"Well—maybe not an ambush beast. But I wouldn't mind seeing him treed by an alicorn," she relented.

"Nor would I, foster sister," Keman replied. "Maybe we'll have the privilege. And maybe he'll just get into trouble he can't get out of, all on his own, without our ill-wishing him. That would be best of all."

"I suppose it would," she sighed, and left it at that.

31

Dusk—and Shana looked up through the gloom and the drizzle at the mountain of rubble marking the site that Keman swore hid a major cave-complex.

Well, if it did, the original cave-mouth must have been bigger than anything Shana had ever imagined, much less seen. It looked from this perspective as if half the side of the mountain had come down over the years, and it wasn't a small mountain. Steep, though; very steep, covered with trees and brush that clung to the slope with vegetative stubbornness, and probably kept the rest of the mountain from losing its outer skin.

The most recent fall had been quite recent indeed, and had added bulk to the pile on the left-hand side. There were trees, large trees, crushed under all that rock, with the remains of dead leaves still clinging to the branches.

Mage-lights hovered over the pile as Kyrtian's men looked on apprehensively. Keman—back to human-form—and Kyrtian climbed the rock-pile to the single opening that Keman had discovered near the top of the mound.

"Is he going to be safe?" one of the men asked dubiously, as Keman offered Kyrtian a hand-up over a tricky bit. Shana was dead-certain that he wasn't worried about Keman.

"Keman's a dragon," she reminded him. "They don't *know* rock, they *live* rock. Keman feels where each pebble is rubbing and might be loose. He'll know if something is going to slip before the rock knows."

"You'd better be right," Lynder muttered darkly. "I climb—I explore caves all the time—and *I* wouldn't go up there without spending weeks checking my path."

"You're not a dragon," she retorted, and turned her own attention to the base of the pile. There, in a place where rock had been melted and reformed to stabilize the area (the indisputable mark of dragon stone-shaping), was where Keman had found the strange piece of metal. Shana examined the spot on her hands and knees with her own little mage-light, and in a few moments, there was no doubt in her mind that what he had found was not a random bit of something that might have been dropped by a curious Elvenlord long ago. There was more of the stuff under that original rock-fall. As she brought her pin-point light in close to the ground, she saw a thin edge of some-thing squashed along the boundary of rock-pile and dirt that didn't look anything like the fractured edge of a rock. What it *did* look like was another sheet of metal.

Just what was under that pile of rock?

Just what is inside this cave? That's what I should be asking. . . .

She looked back up again. At that moment, Keman turned and waved back down at her. They must have found the en-trance. A mage-light left the formation and swung purposefully towards the two figures up on the pile, then vanished, seem-ingly into the rocks. There was some activity up there, as the two bent over something. A moment later, the first figure fol-lowed the light into the tumbled rocks. Keman remained bent over while Kyrtian's men fidgeted restlessly, then eventually started back down the pile. Clearly Kyrtian had gone down in-side the cave by rope, and Keman had remained just long enough to see that he was safely down.

"Now what's Kyrtian thinking?" the man beside Shana mur-mured, fretfully. "We ought to be making camp, not climbing around in caves."

"Kyrtian's probably seeing if we can camp *in* the cave," one of his fellows pointed out. "It would be a lot drier, and we wouldn't have to worry about—Things."

"Unless, of course, those Things have been coming *out* of the cave," Shana warned, darkly. The more Kyrtian had explained what he hoped to find, the less she'd liked the idea of crawling around in there. So far, every sign had pointed to the conclusion that Kyrtian was right, and this was the site of his race's entry into this world. What if that Great Portal hadn't quite been closed—or had been reopened? From what Lorryn had told her, Evelon was hellish at best; there was no telling what kind of horrors lived back there. The ambush beasts and the other weird things in this forest could be coming out of Evelon—or been sent by the Elvenlords' enemies, the ones they had fled *here* to escape.

Fire and Rain! If they were the losers in their fight, I don't want to meet what the Elvenlords we know thought was so bad they would risk running into an unknown world rather than face it or surrender to it.

Kyrtian's men didn't look very happy with her observation, so she didn't share any more of her thoughts. Forewarned was forearmed, but no point in making them too nervous.

Keman came down the slide a great deal faster than he had gone up; more sure-footed than any goat, since he needn't trouble himself about the stability of the surface he trod on. He looked as gleeful as only a dragon could, with the prospect of a new set of caves to explore. "The outermost cavern has a lot of things in it, but they all look like personal belongings that people dropped while they were running away. Kyrtian wants to camp in there," he told them, as he leapt down from the last boulder. "Right now, we need some ropes to get down inside."

"And just how are we going to get the horses up that mess?" one of the men demanded. "They won't go, and I don't blame them."

"Oh." Keman clearly hadn't thought of that, and obviously, neither had Kyrtian. "I could stabilize it, but that would take time—"

"And then what are you going to do? Lower them on a rope? Hobie and Lynder can go with my lord, and the rest of us will stay out here," the man replied firmly. *"They're* the ones that go mucking about in holes, not us. You just put some of those magics on our camp to keep the horrors away, and we'll be fine waiting in the open."

Keman looked at Shana, who just shrugged. These weren't

her men to command. "Go see what Lord Kyrtian has to say about that," was her only advice.

So back up the pile went Keman, and back down again, just as quickly. "He says it's all right, but camp away from the rock-fall area," he called as he leapt from rock to rock. "So we need to scout a secure area—Hobie and Lynder, though, he wants you to bring up the climbing gear he asked for."

"What about the camping stuff?" Lynder asked immediately. "How are we going to get that down?"

Keman just laughed.

"Leave that to Shana and me," he said; so the two men Kyrtian called for gathered up a pack apiece, and several coils of rope, and began the climb while Shana and Keman and the rest went to look for a good place for the others to set up.

They found it soon enough, an indentation in the side of the hill, too small to be called a valley, too large for a ravine. More of a pocket in the hillside that Shana could fence off with magic for them to keep the horses confined and screen the camp from view.

That was easy enough for her to do; an illusion of solid hill-side and vegetation, layered onto a barrier that would only let people pass. She kept the mage-lights going while they set up camp, then once they had a fire and their own lanterns going, dismissed all but one of her lights. Then she and Keman collected all of the gear they were going to need inside the cave. He had taken the form of something rather grel-like, with a broad, flat back to carry a great many packs, and four strong, limber legs ending in claws.

It was a very good thing that he *had* taken all the gear, because Shana had a hard enough time getting herself up that slope. It was as much of a scramble as a climb, testing each foothold only to find her feet skidding as loose scree dislodged, grabbing desperately for a handhold until she could get her feet firmly planted again. Fortunately, once they reached the top, Hobie and Lynder were waiting with ropes set up to bring down everything a bit at a time. Keman himself carried Shana, pick-a-back, with her arms wrapped around his neck, legs wedged under the muscles where wings met shoulder. He was in his own shape, of course, climbing down with the agility of a fly on a wall, disdaining the use of rope. She kept her eyes shut; if anything, it was a lot farther to the floor of the cave than it had been to the ground outside, and the rock-fall had piled up into a much nastier barrier on this side.

Once they were down on firm soil, though, she opened her eyes to take her first look around.

Mage-lights up near the vaulted top of the cave imparted a soft glow that was as good as daylight. There was rubbish *everywhere,* about half of it being wood, leaves, branches, and other detritus that had blown in or washed in before the cave was so totally sealed up. But the other half of the litter *wasn't.* It looked, just as Keman's brief description had suggested, as if a great many people had come through here laden down with personal belongings, and for one reason or another, had simply dropped them or left them here.

Quite clearly, the mess had been poked at, dug through, and nested in by all manner of animals over the course of several centuries. Anything of fabric or leather had long since gotten so close to the point of disintegration that all you had to do was poke it and it fell apart, leaving only bits of metal and less-identifiable substances that had been used as ornamentation or fastenings. Some of it was armor; recognizable breastplates and greaves, helms and vambraces poked up here and there among the wreckage. There were boxes that fell to bits at a touch, revealing a tantalizing glimpse of what their contents might have been before those, too, fell into piles of dust and fragmented flakes. There were swords and knives and axes, but also less recognizable objects and some that Shana couldn't make out at all.

It wasn't so much the metal objects themselves that were fascinating, it was the metals that they were made of. Living among the Elvenlords as she had, Shana was familiar with the ways in which they made bronze, brass, copper, silver, and gold serve any number of purposes—but the objects she found weren't made of any of those metals. Most were constructed of the dull grey stuff that Keman had found, very light and strong, but clearly nothing familiar. Other objects were made of something equally light and thin, and looked like ceramic or glass, but whatever it had been it was brittle and shattered when flexed. It couldn't always have been that brittle; presumably age had rendered it friable.

This sad litter lay among the leaves and sticks that had blown or been carried in over the years, the mounds of dirt, of dust and cobwebs, the bones of little animals who had lived and died here or had been brought in and eaten.

But there were other bones here as well that were not of animals—and when Shana accidentally kicked a helmet and it rolled and disgorged a skull, she decided that she'd had enough of exploring and hurried back to the spot that Hobie and Lynder had cleared of debris and were making into a camp. Kyrtian had already gathered a small pile of things there, and was going through them while the other two put together a fire and the makings of a hot meal. There was certainly no shortage of fuel for the fire, anyway.

"It's a pity nothing of the books survived," Kyrtian said, looking up, as she approached the friendly warmth of the fire. "They've all gone utterly to bits that not even Moth could reconstruct."

"I don't think it's a pity at all," she retorted. "Kyrtian, it looks as if these people were running for their lives, and *something* made sure that not all of them got out of here. That Evelon of your ancestors must have been worse than even *you* thought, and I'd rather not know *anything* about it."

"They're your ancestors, too, Lashana," Kyrtian pointed out with surprising gentleness. "Many of them were arrogant and selfish creatures who, as soon as they got away from those who were exploiting them, turned about and oppressed others—but some were like me, like my father, and like your friend Valyn. And they knew a very great deal that we would find useful, if we could rediscover it."

"All that great learning doesn't seem to have done them much good here," Lynder observed, looking around the cave, and shuddering. "Do Elvenlords leave ghosts behind when they die?"

Shana knew exactly how he was feeling. She had spent a great deal of her life in caves, and normally she felt quite comfortable in them, but this one had an atmosphere that she could only describe as "haunted." Every word they spoke whispered and echoed in a way that was quite unnerving, with bits of their own conversation lingering long past the time when Shana would have expected the sounds to die away.

And now that they were all gathered in around the fire, Kyrtian had thriftily canceled his mage-lights. She was used to the way that a fire made moving shadows on cave-walls, but here were shadows that moved *within* the shadows, and places where blots of darkness were there when she looked, but gone when she looked again. As for the smell—under the usual damp "cave" scent, there was a hint of something metallic and harsh.

It was only the first in a series of caves, as Keman had described, for in the wall opposite the rock-fall, a dark maw of a further entrance gaped. She guessed that this cavern had been water-carved at some point, but where the water had gone was anyone's guess. Perhaps it had sunk further into the depths of the hills, and they would encounter it as they got deeper into the caves. It was a half-dome now, the rock-fall covering what had been a vast entrance; the "ceiling" was a good three or four stories above their heads. Under all the debris, the floor was of sand, which at least had the virtue of being dry and softer than rock.

But this cave was not what Kyrtian had come to hunt, not really. The relics here were nothing more than the sign that this place *was* what Kyrtian's father had been looking for. There was no sign of the Elvenlord himself—unless some of those bones—

No, he would have found something to recognize his father by, I should think.

There was also no sign of his "Great Portal," or anything like it; no sign of the complex devices Kyrtian had described when he'd told Shana what he was looking for. How long before

Kyrtian decreed that it was time to move deeper into the complex? The only concession to "making camp" so far was the fire and a few rocks as seats around it.

Kyrtian saw her glancing reluctantly towards the open entrance at the rear, and caught her eye. "Whatever is in there has waited for decades," he said—sadly, she thought. "It can wait another night. We rode like fools to get here, we're tired and wet and cold. We'd be further fools to go climbing around in an unknown cave in this state. People get themselves killed doing stupid things like that."

Lynder let out his breath; clearly he'd been holding it the moment Kyrtian began to speak, dreading being told they were going to have to gather their strength and be off again once they'd eaten. "Thank you for that, my Lord," he said stoutly. "You've prevented me from having to say the same thing. I was afraid if I did, you'd be angry, and if I didn't, Sargeant Gel would have the hide off me when we got back."

"I would hope I would never be the kind of leader to put you in that sort of untenable position, Lynder," Kyrtian replied, but a weary sparkle came back into his eyes, at least for a moment. "Food and sleep, my lads—and my lady—" he added, bowing to Shana. "That's what's called for here. And perhaps a little narrative from your friend on what it was like to eavesdrop outside my tent. I *am* curious to hear about that."

Keman bowed in his turn. "The only difference between us and your usual guards, Lord Kyrtian, was that we have much sharper hearing—and one of us was a lady herself."

"Oh really?" Kyrtian leaned forward. "Please go on. . . ."

Hours later, the fire died down to coals. Keman had gone out to catch himself something of an appropriate size for a dragon's dinner. Before he left, Shana and Kyrtian had both taken the time—comparing notes the while—to fence in their little camp with protective magic. Interestingly enough, neither of them had chosen to use magic-shields. Instead, they had both opted for something that would trigger an alarm if crossed, clearing a circle that Keman could easily see so that he wouldn't trigger the alarm by tripping it when he returned. After all, *he* could simply shapeshift into a boulder, and nothing would disturb *his* rest; he didn't need alarms to warn him of danger, since danger would pass by without noticing him.

Despite those precautions, despite being weary, Shana was having a hard time getting to sleep. If conversations had echoed uncannily around the walls, the little sounds the others made as they moved or sighed or mumbled in their sleep were worse. Someone would cough a little, or turn over—moments later the sound came back, much distorted, into something that sounded like a footstep, or a whispered word. Sometimes multiple echoes came back, a breath, a murmur of not-quite-intelligible conversation.

She didn't actually fall asleep until after Keman finally returned. He entered as a dragon—a thin, snake-like dragon, the only way he could fit himself in through that tiny opening. He remained as a dragon, curled up just outside the boundary. His solid presence, bulking large so close at hand, finally made her feel safe. And in that moment, sleep came.

Triana's people had pitched a secluded camp at a discreet distance from the site that was evidently Kyrtian's goal. Rain dripped steadily on the canvas of her tent as she plied the forester with questions, a soft glow from a mage-light suspended above them shining down on his face and highlighting rough-hewn features that Triana had begun to take a liking to. The rugged looks of all of these men were beginning to grow on her; by comparison, her carefully-sculpted and trained slave-toys, though more defined and muscular, actually seemed rather boyish and immature.

"So, five of them entered, and the rest are—where?" Triana asked her scout.

"Gracious Lady, I couldn't find them." He didn't shrug, but she wondered what his impassive expression hid. Probably nervousness, fear of her anger; he was definitely sweating, just at his hairline. "I stayed to watch, then remained once they had been inside for some time and darkness had fallen. I climbed to the entrance to make certain that Lord Kyrtian and the four who accompanied him intended to set up camp there; they had gear down there enough to do so, and such seemed to be their intentions. When I went to look for the others, however, they could not be found."

"I can't believe he would have sent them back," she mused aloud. "No, I'm sure he must have created an illusion to cloak their camp—it is what I would have done in his place. Or else they themselves are taking no chances on the creatures lurking in this forest, and have hidden their camp. . . ."

"It was quite dark by that time, my lady," he said diffidently.

"And you correctly remembered your orders to keep track of Kyrtian, not his slaves." She nodded. "Did you make any effort to see what was within the cave itself?"

He shook his head. "Lord Kyrtian had mage-lights all through the place, but it is very large, and a hard climb down. The floor is littered with debris, but I could not tell you what it was at that distance. The usual trash one finds in a cave, I suppose."

So he had come straight back here; that showed a fine balance between obedience and good sense. She smiled at him, and thought that his nervousness ebbed, a little. "You've done well; I would rather that you came back here to tell me what happened than waste time in trying to discover the whereabouts of a lot of men who will probably do nothing until their master returns." She laughed, then, and her man relaxed a little further. "As I have said before, what Kyrtian can do, I can do. I have no need of you men inside that cave; I have no intention of confronting Lord Kyrtian, I only wish to discover what he is up to. I can do that being careful and using my own powers of illusion to cloak my presence once one of you has helped me climb down. *You,* meanwhile, have managed to outflank Aelmarkin and get us here only a little behind Lord Kyrtian's men. I believe you deserve a bit of a holiday."

Now the slave unbent entirely. "Thank you, my lady," was all he said, but she saw the expression in his eyes change to one of wary gratitude, rather like a somber, alert coursing-hound offered an unexpected treat. She offered him a cup of her wine; he accepted it with a profound bow and drank it off at a gulp. A pity; it was a good vintage, but likely he wouldn't know good from bad. Perhaps she would educate him.

"I will go into the cave tomorrow to follow Kyrtian. Before I do, I would like you to find a good, out-of-the-way place to camp that is unlikely to be stumbled across by Aelmarkin's men. I'll cloak it with illusion and you all can disport yourselves as you will until I return." His eyes absolutely lit, and she laughed. "And yes, this means you may help yourselves to *any* of the provisions, the wine included. I don't expect to have to spend much time in that hole, and when I return, our business will be to make all speed back. Too many provisions will only slow us down."

She would take the precaution of changing the wine so that it made anyone who drank it tranquil rather than rowdy. She could always change it back when she returned. Better that they laze a little while she was gone; it would ruin her plans entirely for Aelmarkin's people to discover hers because they were carousing and singing or fighting behind her cloak of illusion.

If something else came across them and they were incapacitated, well—there *were* other ways she could get home. If they didn't take the precaution of setting a sober sentry, they weren't worth the money she'd paid for them.

"Have another cup," she said, with a dazzling smile, refilling his goblet. "Then go and tell the others what I just told you. I'll want climbing gear ready for me first thing when I wake; you can see me safely down, then return here to the others to wait for my return."

A few hours past dawn, Aelmarkin stood looking up at a vast pile of tumbled rocks; the trail apparently ended there, according to his forester. As usual, the skies dripped. He shook rain out of his eyes with irritation; was there *never* a break from the wretched stuff here?

And Kyrtian, Ancestors curse him, had found a way out of the wretched stuff. "A cave?" Aelmarkin said incredulously. "There's a *cave* up there? And Kyrtian crawled in there?"

"Yes, my Lord," the forester said into the ground at Aelmarkin's feet. "It is a very, very large cave; the opening is near to the top of it. I could not tell how many of his men went in with him, but the main trail ends here, and I can clearly see where a number of people went up that slope and entered into a gap at the top. Without light I cannot see what is inside, but if they were still immediately inside it, I must suppose they'd have lights of their own, so I presume they've gone in dccper."

"By the Ancestors." Aelmarkin began to chuckle. "Well, it's pretty clear that, whatever *is* here, it's not Wizards. Unless this is some forgotten entrance into their lair."

"Forgotten, my lord, or no longer in use because of the rock-fall," the scout said, head still bent. "But I dropped a torch within, when I could see no signs of Lord Kyrtian or his men down below, and before it guttered out all I saw was litter. It appears that *if* this place was ever in use as an entrance, it has not been used so for a very long time."

"That's good enough for me!" Aelmarkin replied. He considered the situation. "I'll take you with me; the rest can camp here. We'll see if we can't discover what Kyrtian thinks he's up to."

"It will be very difficult to conceal ourselves in a cave, my lord," the man began.

Aelmarkin cut him off with a gesture; the water from Aelmarkin's sodden sleeve spattered him from head to toe, and Aelmarkin felt a bit of sour pleasure as the slave winced. "Not for a mage, you fool! Get whatever gear we'll need—we're already hours behind him." He looked around at the rest of his slaves. "And you! Put up a proper camp this time! When I get back, I expect to see something other than a half-pitched tent and a fire that won't start! *And get moving!*"

He put a sting of warning in his voice to remind them of the sting of his punishments, punishments that he had inflicted frequently through their collars each time they bumbled a task. It got them going, although sluggishly.

Well, no matter. In a few moments, *he* was going to be inside a dry cave. If they couldn't manage to put a camp together properly by the time he got back, on the way home he'd start crippling them and leaving them behind on the trail to attract the horrors that seemed to stalk these forests. That would give his dear cousin something to have to deal with on *his* way back to civilization. At the least, Kyrtian would be delayed in returning to his patron, Lord Kyndreth.

And at the most—Aelmarkin would no longer have anything standing between himself and everything he wanted.

This must be that fabled Portal to Evelon, with all of the things that had been left behind scattered about. The Wizards, if they existed at all, certainly weren't here. Opportunity waited and Fate smiled on Aelmarkin at last. And depending on what he found in that cave—well, by the time he returned home, Aelmarkin might even be able to give Lord Kyndreth himself a little healthy competition for ascendancy on the Great Council.

Triana looked up at the dim, uneven oval of grey light that marked the opening to the outer world, and absently kicked something dry and crackling from beneath her feet. There was no sign of her slave, but she hadn't expected him to linger once she was safely down. She wondered if she had surprised her forester by getting down into the cave rather handily with nothing more in the way of help than one of the ropes that Kyrtian's people had left behind; she certainly surprised herself.

Then again, it was very interesting what sorts of things one could do with magic when one was terrified out of one's wits. It *had* been a very long way down to the floor of the cave from that tiny entrance above; fortunately Kyrtian's own people had left all their ropes behind, ready to climb out when they returned, so at least she had had the comfort of knowing her lifeline was tested and tried.

Ah, but Kyrtian had never been taught the subtle art of Elven *female* magic, and if he came back he'd have the benefit of her passage. She'd had no notion she could make a rope stronger—or herself briefly stronger as well. By the time her feet touched the floor of the cave, she had imparted the transitory strength of one of her foresters to her arms and legs—and she could have used the rope she dangled from to lower a horse and wagon without worrying about it snapping.

So at a guess, she ought to be able to get herself back *up* the tumble of rock without mishap and no assistance; it was admittedly easier to climb when one had magic to help.

It *was* tempting to think about blasting her way out with levin-bolts, though; she'd been practicing for years now in secret and she was getting quite proficient. It would mean less exertion. However, there were drawbacks as well—in the glimpses she'd gotten of the ceiling, she wasn't altogether sure of how stable it was, and it wouldn't do her a great deal of good to bring the ceiling down on herself instead of blasting her way out.

Not subtle, my dear. Not your style.

Besides, unless Kyrtian came to grief in there, she didn't intend to leave any trace of her own passing, so she would probably have to get out the hard way.

Meanwhile, in the gleam of her mage-light, the only sign that Kyrtian had been here was a dead campfire and a cleared circle among the rubbish littering the floor. He must have gone off long before she even woke, and had gotten a good deal ahead of her. So if she was to discover what he was up to, she had better get moving.

She paused long enough to recover her breath and her power—she'd been hot and sweaty as well, but in the cold, dank cave-air she'd cooled down quickly and was glad of the cloak she'd brought with her, tied in a bundle about her waist.

Now for a little magic. She smiled to herself as she wove

power around her; *this* was subtle, and not something a mere male would ever appreciate. The illusion she cast upon herself was a rather clever one; it wasn't precisely *invisibility,* since that wasn't strictly possible. Instead, she cloaked herself in the image of what was behind her, so that anyone looking at her would see only what her body ordinarily would have obscured—a kind of reflection, but not exactly. The illusion wasn't perfect; it couldn't be. Anyone looking closely might well see a faint outline of her body, or notice her shadow on the floor. That was why she wore a light cloak that covered her from head to toe, for a bulky irregular outline against the rough rock of the cave was less likely to be noticed than one with arms, legs, and a head.

She had a rather clever device with her as well, a cone of mirror-finished metal with a handle at its point. She brought her mage-light down and coaxed it into the cone. Now she could direct all of the light where she chose without half-blinding herself, or setting the stupid thing to hover above her head. She cast the beam of light reflected out of the cone around herself, and used it to pick a path across the debris to an opening at the rear of this enormous cavern.

She began to wish that the light wasn't showing her way quite so clearly. As the light picked out this or that object amidst the sticks and leaves and trash, she'd have had to have been blind not to spot the bits of armor—and the bones.

Bones which were not all the bones of animals, nor of human slaves, even if the armor could have been mistaken for anything but elven-made.

Her skin crawled as the empty eye-sockets of an elven skull glared at her on the edge of her circle of light. She had already known that something terrible had happened here, but it was one thing to know that intellectually, and quite another to be confronted with the evidence of utter disaster.

A chill that had nothing to do with the temperature of this place settled over her, and she resisted the urge to flee back up that rope into the open. Whatever had happened here had occurred a very long time ago, even by the standards of the

Elvenlords, and nothing, not even ghosts, could linger for that long. But she fancied she caught a whiff of ancient death, of bone-dust and terror, and she couldn't keep her imagination from painting scenes that were not at all comfortable.

Nevertheless, as she picked her way across the floor, she avoided looking too closely at anything large enough and white enough to be bone.

Were there whispers, out there in the dark? Was that a movement, not *in* the shadow, but *of* the shadow? She told herself resolutely that she wasn't afraid, that only stupid slaves believed in spirits, but—

There *were* sounds out there in the darkness, sounds that could be echoes, but could be something else as well. She couldn't even imagine what could have killed so many Elves, so quickly—and the slaves said that the spirits of those who died violently lingered, hungering after the life they'd lost and eager to avenge their deaths on anything living.

She found herself starting at every unexpected sound, and longed for the moment when she reached the far wall and the entrance deeper into the caves.

She had assumed that once she got to the entrance into the next cave she would find her path clear. In fact, she found nothing of the kind.

What had been litter on the floor of the cave was a tangled blockage here; someone, Kyrtian and his people, she assumed, had cleared a pathway through, but if the artifacts there had not already been ready to fall apart at a touch, it couldn't have been done in less than a week. Here the carts of the refugees had jammed at the entrance, and there were many, many more bones, enough so that it was no longer in her imagination that they imparted their own dry hint of ancestral corruption to the air. Big bones, these, the bones of dray-animals long since forgotten, for they had perished along with their masters, tangled in the shafts of disintegrating carts in attitudes that suggested a tide of unreasoning panic had washed over them and sent them scattering before it.

And more elven bones, this time ones without armor. Women? Old men?

A disintegrating wagon that had been laden with small, slender creatures—it took her a moment to get past the disbelief to understand that this had been a wagon full of children.

It was hard to imagine. One seldom saw elven children; they were usually kept in nurseries until they were considered old enough to mingle with the rest of society. She could hardly imagine so many in one place. What sort of spirit would a child leave behind? Something wispy and melancholy—or feral and vicious?

Whatever had sent the Elvenlords into flight had terrified their beasts as well. Triana began to feel a certain relief that the few scraps of information she'd gleaned had *not* been more specific, that legend now painted the Crossing as a matter of triumph rather than the tragedy it had so clearly been. She didn't *want* to know the details now; there were already too many details writ large in the bones of those who had not survived to become her ancestors.

She reached out her hand to steady herself, and wood went to dust at her touch, enlarging the passage that Kyrtian's people had already made. Her very skin flinched away from that dust, but it rose in clouds about her and dried her mouth and throat, as if the dead themselves rose to make claims on her. . . .

Don't be such a superstitious idiot! she scolded herself, but without effect. Her pounding heart, the blood rushing in her ears, her very skin were rebels to her reason.

But she forced herself past, and once out of the jam-up, the way suddenly cleared. No more bones; or at least, none that flashed whitely at her in the circle of her light. Just—things. Belongings, discarded, unidentifiable. She could cope with *things.* Especially things that went to atoms at a touch, collapsing in on themselves and leaving nothing behind that called up uncomfortably familiar images in the mind.

The path that Kyrtian's underlings took was plainly scribed in that litter, a trail where only bits of metal shone dully in the dust. She paused a moment to listen, and thought she caught the faintest of murmurs from somewhere far ahead; covered her light, but saw no glimmers in the distance. Wherever he was, if that was, indeed, the sound of him and his people, it was far ahead of her. She hurried on, suddenly hungry for the sight of something living, even if it was an enemy. A living enemy right now was preferable to the whispers in the dark.

"This place makes my skin crawl," Lynder muttered to Shana. "I don't see how *he* can stand it." He was pale, freckles she hadn't noticed before standing out clearly across his cheeks. She also hadn't noticed how young he was before this; all of Kyrtian's people were so competent and confident that she'd taken them all for mature adults. Now she saw Lynder for the beardless boy he actually was, newly jumped-up from a page, perhaps. Well, fear did that to people.

Shana didn't see how their leader could seem so unaffected by the place, either. Kyrtian had mage-lights floating silently over their heads, set to avoid collision with the ceiling but otherwise lighting up this series of smaller caves with pitiless clarity. The tangle of carts and beasts at the mouth of this complex had been the worst, of course; Shana had been so tempted to flee screaming away and swarm right back up the rope into the clean rain outside.

And the cart full of what had been children! No matter what the Elves had done to her, to the Wizards, and especially to their slaves—the thought of that cartload of children dying tangled up together in the dark—

It had made her throat close and her eyes sting, and she didn't care that it had happened hundreds of years ago.

They think I'm fearless, she had told herself. And that had made her clench her teeth, thrust out her chin, and pretend that her whole body wasn't flinching away from the wreckage, the bones. She squared her shoulders, and tensed to keep herself from shivering. These were men she *had* to impress; they weren't Wizards, they weren't slaves. She was a legend to them, and if they lost faith in the legend—they would lose faith in the cause. She needed them; more, probably, than they needed her. If all it took to keep their faith was to pretend to be utterly fearless, it was a small price to pay for that faith.

But Kyrtian had only directed the enlargement of a passage already there . . . a passage showing the imprint of a single pair of narrow feet in the dust.

His father made it; he must have. Kyrtian knows that. This is what he's been looking for, and all he can see is those footprints leading us deeper.

Kyrtian had spent a long moment studying those prints . . . then he had taken the lead, face immobile and expressionless, as the rest had to stretch to keep up with him.

"I've never seen him like this before," Lynder continued, wiping sweat from his face with his sleeve, leaving behind a smudge of the dust of the dead obscuring the freckles scattered across his cheeks. He shuddered.

"He's not thinking about you—or about anyone," Keman said slowly. "He's completely inside his own head."

The three of them exchanged glances; she read in Lynder's face that *he* at least would rather not be privy to what was in Kyrtian's head just now. She rather agreed with him.

It was bad enough being out here. The deeper into this string of caves they got, the more the feeling of doom—whether lingering or impending she couldn't say—increased. She'd *never* been claustrophobic before, but she felt the walls of these little caves closing in on her—or was it that they seemed to pulse and heave, slowly, as if they all traveled down the gullet of some impossibly huge, sleeping monster? If the walls clearly *hadn't* been rock, the floor clearly the same, it would have been all too easy to succumb to the illusion.

"Do you feel it?" Keman murmured, for her ears only. "That kind of drone in the back of your brain? Like there's something just barely awake out there and we're touching the edge of its dreams? Or there's something singing a nasty dirge in its sleep?"

She nodded. She did; had, in fact, since they'd been here. It wasn't getting any stronger, and if Keman hadn't said anything, she'd have put it down to nerves—but it was there, a sound so deep it could only be felt. She wondered what else Keman heard; he had the benefit of senses that could be enhanced without any immediate limit.

"There's nothing alive down here, either," Keman continued, and shivered. "Not even slime."

Nothing alive. Unheard of. Caves *always* had their own little community of creatures: insects, bats, mice, and the fungi that the littlest fed on before they in turn became the prey of the biggest. Where were they all?

And what drove them away?

She couldn't see Kyrtian's face from her place at the rear of the group, but Lynder's was bleached as white as the bones they'd left back there, and she fancied her own was, as well. Life leached out of them with every step they took deeper into the maw of the mountain.

Shana suddenly felt that they would never leave this place; that they would continue to stumble along in Kyrtian's wake until they dropped in their tracks and died. That *this* was what had happened to Kyrtian's father—no accident, but the mountain sucking the life out of him as he plodded deeper into its depths, lured by its promise and threat until he stumbled and could not rise again.

Then, without warning, Kyrtian stopped.

The mage-lights under Kyrtian's control shot past them out into some vast space ahead, and they kept from blundering into him only by swerving to his right or left. Which brought all of them to stand next to him at the edge of an abrupt drop-off, staring out into a cavern that could have swallowed *any* cave Shana had ever seen without a trace. Her pulse racketed in her throat: how nearly she had gone over the edge!

At least, that was her initial reaction. As she teetered on the edge and her eyes adjusted, it became clear that the drop-off was not nearly as far as panic had made her think. She might have broken an ankle had she gone over, all unwarned, but no worse than that—the illusion of a sheer precipice was just that, illusion. After the initial drop, a steep slope slanted away from them to the floor of this new cave. It was what bulked here in ordered rows, off in the distance, that drew the eye and confused the mind.

Objects. No. Constructs. Things of metal, gears, wheels, things that might be arms or legs or neither. Big as a house, some of them. Row upon row of them, three abreast, leading back to the biggest construct of all, a huge arch of some dull green stuff that *looked* deader than the bones they passed but *felt* alive and full of brooding menace.

Over everything lay, not merely a film, but a thick shroud of dust, obscuring the shine of metal, softening angles into curves. Thick as a blanket in some places; so thick that sections had actually broken off and fallen from the sides.

"What—are—those?" Shana asked, her voice high and strained.

Kyrtian only shook his head. "I don't know. There isn't anyone alive who could tell you. Oh, I know what they are *collectively,* they're things the Ancestors made to serve them in all the ways that slaves do now. Magic is what made them work, but once the Portal closed, they wouldn't work anymore and they were abandoned. As to why they wouldn't work, I can't say."

"Serve them?" Lynder said, puzzlement in his voice.

Kyrtian's tone was as dry as the dust lying over everything. "Of course. You don't think our Ancestors ever put hand to tool themselves, do you? They created these things—to plow and dig, build and tear down—"

"And make war?" Keman asked, harshly.

Kyrtian glanced at him, mouth set in a thin line. But his tone was mild. "Make war?" he replied, softly. "Oh yes. That, *certainly.* Above all other things. The Ancestors made war among themselves, war of a sort that makes everything we did to the Wizards seem the merest game."

Shana looked away from Kyrtian's face back to the rank upon rank of constructions, and shuddered. Under the dust, metal gleamed with cruel efficiency. Were those blades? Was that a reaper of corn—or of lives? A digger of ditches—or of graves?

She decided not to ask a question to which she did not want to know the answer.

But Kyrtian made a strangled little sound, and abruptly jumped down from the edge of the cave-mouth, landing in a crouch only to sprint off to one side of the huge cavern, where there were a few of the mechanisms that were not in such ordered rows. With a muffled oath, Lynder followed, then the rest of them, trailing along behind.

Aelmarkin cursed the men who lowered him down every time he collided with another rock, lashing them through their collars with the punishment of pain. It was not enough to satisfy him, but he dared to do no more; too much and they only became clumsier. He'd assumed—foolishly, in retrospect—that they could simply lower him down comfortably to the bottom of the place. Instead, he was having to practically walk down the tumbled slope of rocks that was the mirror of the pile outside; just as difficult as being hauled *up* that slope, but more painful, since the idiots above kept dislodging rocks that fell on his head and they kept lowering him in a series of jerks. Each one ended in a collision with more rocks since each time he was caught off-guard and off-balance.

Idiots! He would *certainly* leave some of them behind as bait for the monsters in this benighted place, and at that it was better than they deserved. He'd suspect they were doing this on purpose except that his punishments were worse than anything *he* was enduring.

When he finally bumped down with a painful *thud* onto the floor of the cave, he gave them all a final reminder of his power over them that made them yelp. The echoes of four howls of pain reverberated long enough to give him a fleeting moment of satisfaction. He picked himself up out of the dust and kicked the trash he'd fallen on out of his way angrily before sending his mage-light up to illuminate more of the area.

No point in looking up to glare at them. They were gone, of course, scuttling back to the shelter of their tents and their fire, where they would stay, probably lazing about and trying to find non-existent supplies of wine among his belongings. He knew they wouldn't leave the camp; they were more afraid of the forest than they were of him. Foresters they might be, but this wasn't *their* forest, and they were superstitiously terrified not only of the very real monsters among the trees, but the spirits they swore they'd heard in the night. They'd be waiting for him when he returned, all right . . . not knowing that if his hopes were fulfilled, he wouldn't need them. He'd have power enough to blast this place open or create a Gate home. Or fly, if he chose. That would be novel; there were old legends of how the Ancestors flew, on the backs of metal-beaked birds with razor-tipped wings and scythes for talons, how they would duel in the air until blood fell like warm rain on the faces of those below. Perhaps there were constructs like that waiting here. . . .

Well! He wasn't *finding* them standing about and kicking trash. Nor was he discovering just what Kyrtian was up to if it *wasn't* hunting relics of the Ancestors or the Wizards he was supposed to be pursuing.

He turned. It was clear enough where Kyrtian had gone, the path through the debris was plain enough for a woman to pick out. It was also clear that this cave wasn't littered with just the trash that the wind had blown in. So—Kyrtian *had* found the place where the Great Portal had made an entrance into this world!

"By the Ancestors!" Aelmarkin said aloud, and his own voice repeated his astonishment in echoes that whispered in the cave as if a crowd mimicked his surprise.

A skull—an *Elven* skull, by the high-arched forehead and the narrow jaw—lay directly in his path, glaring at him, as if daring him to pass.

Aelmarkin sneered at it. What matter a few bones? Bones were nothing. Those of the Ancestors that died here weren't Ancestors at all, were they? They hadn't gotten their bloodlines any deeper in this world than the floor of the cave. What matter that Aelmarkin's path led over those bones? That way lay his fortune, and he wasn't going to let the bones of a few dead fools stop him.

"You," he told the skull, contemptuously, "are a nothing. A dead-end. You can't even manage to block my way."

He brought his booted foot down on the skull deliberately, smashing it. It broke with no more effort than destroying an egg. His next step took him past the fragile fragments, and he didn't look back.

The demi-barricade at the tunnel's mouth didn't stop him, either; in fact; he took a great deal of grim pleasure in bullying past it, kicking at the carts and the bones of the legendary dray-*lanthans* and seeing them disintegrate. Not as much pleasure as he might have, since the wreckage pretty much fell to bits at a touch, but enough.

Some fools might find all this horrifying. All he felt was more contempt for the weaklings who had been so afraid of pursuit—for of course, it could only have been pursuit that they feared—that they allowed their panic to turn what could have been an orderly procession into a rout. And for *what?*

So their bones could rot on the floor of a cave before they even saw the light of their new world, that's what.

He wondered, as he penetrated further into the cave-complex, if all of the legends of harmony and cooperation were so much rot after all. It was obvious from this decayed chaos that there had been panic, fighting, but there was no sign of whatever was the cause. Unless, of course, the Ancestors had brought the cause with them. . . .

What if they'd begun fighting amongst each other for ascendancy as soon as they got safely to the other side?

That would certainly explain the rout—

In fact, such an explanation made more sense than the official version of the Crossing.

Suppose, just suppose, that not *all* of the Ancestors had given everything they had to the creation of the Great Portal? That was what *he* would have done, come down to it. Now, suppose that faction-within-a-faction had then turned on the rest, when they were out of magic, depleted, vulnerable?

He grinned savagely, kicking a bit of debris out of the way. Of course—that was what *must* have happened! It explained all of this, *and* explained why no one had ever come back here until the secret of just where the Portal was had been lost to memory. After all, those clever bastards who'd won wouldn't want to chance coming upon a survivor amid the wreckage, or chance on someone uncovering the real version of what had happened! And besides, things had been hard enough on those who survived, creating their strongholds, waiting to see what perils lurked in this new world and trying to defend against whatever might come.

Then, of course, the Ancestors had discovered the humans, and realized they didn't *need* constructs when they could have slaves instead, slaves that didn't need repairs, could breed their own replacements, and could be controlled with a bare minimum of magic.

Proper conservation of resources, that. It spoke well for the cleverness of the Elvenlords who had survived to become *his* Ancestors. Clever, clever fellows indeed; they would be proud of him now, who had retraced their footsteps to rediscover the secrets of *their* power and take what rightfully belonged to him.

Of course, that would only be the beginning. Once he had taken Kyrtian's estates, he'd consider his next moves. There were, after all, *many* possibilities for the future, and everything would depend on just what he learned here. Only one thing was certain; Aelmarkin, and not Kyrtian, would be the one to have the benefit of whatever lay here.

And what was more, Kyrtian wouldn't be coming out of here at all if Aelmarkin had anything to say about it.

At least, not alive.

Lynder took off at a run after Kyrtian, his feet slapping on the rock floor of the cave and kicking up puffs of dust, but Shana and Keman hesitated, exchanging first a glance, then a guarded thought.

:I have a feeling that something's about to go horribly wrong,: Shana began, not at all hesitant to look like a fool—if indeed she did—in front of her foster-brother. After all, he'd seen her do and say stupid things plenty of times in the past.

But Keman nodded, confirming her apprehensions—which, of course, only made them worse. *:So do I. It's not just that hum. There's something down here, asleep maybe, and I don't want to disturb it.:* He paused, and his eyes flicked to one side. *:Fire and Rain! Look at the mage-lights!:*

Shana bit her lip, when she followed his direction and realized that Kyrtian's mage-lights were slowly pulsing, waxing and waning in strength ever so slightly and very slowly. Had Kyrtian noticed? Would he?

:I think something's draining them a little at a time,: Keman continued. *:Then Kyrtian increases the power to them without thinking about it, and it all begins again. And I* don't *think it would be a good idea to use any stronger magic in here. It might . . . wake something up.:*

Wake something up . . . so he felt it too. The sense of presence was stronger now, although the droning in the back of her mind was not. *:We'd better follow Kyrtian, then,:* she said reluctantly.

They followed his tracks in the dust across the floor of the cave, passing among the odd and articulated shapes of metal and glass and stranger substances. They loomed, these objects.

They bulked above Shana's head, exuding unsubtle menace. Although how that was possible without possessing eyes or faces . . .

She felt her skin flinching away from them, noting a few moments later that the *constructs* were not arranged in quite the orderly fashion that they had first thought.

Nor were they undamaged.

Deep in the middle of the pack, they passed two tangled together, as if they'd blundered into each other. Then came one that had been smashed beneath a massive rock, perhaps detached from the roof of the cavern. Then another, fallen over on its side.

Then one that looked—melted? Yes, all down one side the construct sagged, and there were places along the leading edges where the thing looked like butter that had begun to run, then hardened again.

A low murmur of voices from the other side of the thing gave a clue to Kyrtian's whereabouts, but there was something harsh and desperately unhappy in that murmur that made them both slow their paces and edge, with great care, around the corner of it.

Kyrtian stood facing the rock wall of the cave, every muscle as rigid as the rock he faced, and for a moment, all that Shana could understand was that the rock looked as if it had melted like butter in the sun, just as the metal of the construct had.

Then, slowly, her mind encompassed the shape in the rock. *In* the rock, like some obscene bas-relief, like a hapless insect coated in wax and preserved for all time, like a fancy pastry enrobed in a thin glazed shell. Like, most horribly of all, like something caught in an ice-storm, preserved perfectly beneath a thin sheath of ice that replicated every detail of the no-longer-living thing.

There was a man, an Elvenlord, embedded in the satiny-smooth, melted and re-solidified rock. Not carved—not unless there had been a sculptor working here who was utterly mad. Not with the expression of utter, blinding terror that she saw on the subject's visage.

Shana could not see Lord Kyrtian's face, and for that, she was profoundly glad. The eloquent line of his backbone told her more than enough—too much, truth be told.

Desperately unhappy? That was too tame. This was a man who should, by all rights, break into a howl of despair at any moment.

This could only be Kyrtian's father. Bad enough to find bones and only wonder at how he had perished—this was infinitely worse, the moment of death caught and held on show for all time.

She didn't know Kyrtian well enough to offer comfort, but he clearly needed it at the moment, and just as clearly would not accept it from anyone standing about him now. She could hardly blame him; if she had been searching for Alara all these years only to find her like *this*—

All of them stood in awkward silence, a silence that stretched on and on until it became unendurable. Shana's nerves shrieked under the strain of waiting, and longed for someone, anyone, to break it—so long as it wasn't her. Kyrtian could not possibly bear this—no one could!

But it was Kyrtian himself who finally did so, and with utterly unexpected words.

"Light the lanterns," he said, the words emerging as a strangled croak, but clear enough for all that.

"M-m-my lord?" Lynder stammered, without comprehension.

"Light the lanterns. I'm going to kill the mage-lights. Something's feeding on them and I don't want to give it anything more—"

He didn't finish the sentence, but with *that* in front of them, he didn't have to. Lynder and the other hastened to obey his order, breaking out the candles, the oil, and the lanterns, and the moment that the first wick was kindled, Kyrtian extinguished his mage-lights completely.

This, of course, left them huddling around a lantern that in no way gave a fraction of the light that the mage-lights had, while the others hastened to light the rest of the wicks with a spill kindled on the first. Shana was just glad that Kyrtian had had the foresight to order lanterns brought in the first place—

and that even in the midst of a grief she couldn't even begin to understand, he hadn't lost himself to mourning, madness, or both.

She hurried forward to help the others; the lamps were kept dry until needed, so she filled them while the others lit them and set the transparent chimneys in place to protect them from drafts. When she looked over at him, Kyrtian still hadn't moved, except to place one hand on the breast of that terrible figure in the wall.

She still couldn't see his face. She still didn't *want* to.

But she wished with all her soul that he would weep.

Triana was surprised when the glow of mage-lights ahead of her winked out.

She dimmed her own light in automatic response, lest it be noticed. Now there was barely enough light coming from her little metal cone to let her see her way without stumbling, and she used one hand on the cave wall to steady herself as she crept along. Why had Kyrtian doused his lights?

Then, as a faint yellow glow came from the opening ahead of her, she understood that although he had doused his lights, he wasn't in darkness. The light coming from ahead was poor and weak, and she wondered if some disaster had befallen Kyrtian, or his men, to make him *lose* control of his mage-lights.

The feeling of unfocused horror that had stalked her from the moment that she entered this place washed over her in redoubled strength. It was only by stopping long enough to take a few deep breaths and swallow a sip of water from a flask at her belt to ease her fear-dried mouth that she forced herself to go on. Whatever was out there hadn't devoured Kyrtian yet, or where would the light be coming from?

As her pulse pounded in her temples and her hands grew cold, she reached the mouth of the next cave, and as she extinguished her own mage-light lest it betray her, at last she heard voices. One of them was Kyrtian's, with a harsh, grating tone to it she'd never heard before, but the low tone and the echoes made it impossible to understand what he and the others with him were saying. Still, he was *talking,* and he wouldn't be doing that if something had attacked him. She wondered wildly for a moment if he was talking *to* something that belonged here—

But no. That didn't make any sense. There had been no signs of life here at all, not even bats, so what could such a thing live on? And there were no tracks in the dust except Kyrtian's people, so nothing was going into or out of this cave-complex.

In the flickering and uncertain light she barely made out the bulky shapes of huge objects the size of garden sheds and larger ranged in utterly still and silent ranks in front of her. Great hulking shapes—frozen into immobility now, but somehow not dead; they crouched, waiting, watching. And at the edge of her vision, the arch of the Great Portal—for that was all that the soaring arc of greenish-black at the rear of the cave *could* be—brooding over them all. Moving shadows of men performed an incomprehensible pantomime against the right-hand wall, where lanterns must be. There was a whisper of acrid scent to the air here, a faint taste of metal and the flavor of lightning.

Everything instinctive in her screamed to go back, forget what she saw and go, flee, *now.* This was nothing like what she had expected—there was something horribly *wrong* here, and if she stayed she'd find out what it was. All of those things out there, staring without eyes, waiting for just the right trigger, the right action to set them free. . . .

But . . . but if she left, she would leave empty-handed. Only Kyrtian would know the secrets that lay here. And that was insupportable.

Will triumphed over instinct, and she forced herself to go on. She decided at that moment to approach the place where Kyrtian and his people were by taking the long way around the edge of the cavern, dropping down from the ledge as silently as possible, then making her way around the cavern with one hand outstretched against the rock wall to guide her. She would pass by the Great Portal, and that alone might hold some useful information. And she wouldn't have to walk among those—things.

The Great Portal—it had enabled the Ancestors to travel from another world. Perhaps it still held enough magic to take her home—after all, some of the oldest Portals could be used to go anywhere that one held a key, and she had the Prime Key to her own Portal in the form of the signet ring on her right hand. If that was true, then she *wasn't* trapped here; if anything went wrong, she could escape in a heartbeat!

That thought, when it occurred to her, brought a sudden ease of her fear that almost made her stagger, and she caught herself with one hand on the cavern wall. Relief suffused her, making her a little lightheaded. The hulking shapes of the Ancestors' chattels no longer seemed to stare at her with insensate menace. They were just—things. Old, dead things. No matter what Kyrtian had found, or *thought* he had found, these relics couldn't threaten anything or anyone—if they ever had. Her imagination had run away with her, and she was as bad as any nursery-bound child in conjuring up nightmares for herself.

Whatever had slaughtered all those people back in the main cave couldn't have come from *here,* anyway. When the Portal closed, the constructs had all died. Everyone knew that. It was in every version of the Crossing that she had ever read. That was why it had been so important that the Ancestors find or create a source of slave-labor, since they no longer had their constructs to do their work for them.

With renewed confidence, and a purely internal laugh of scorn at her own foolishness, she continued on, feeling for each step as she took it, since she could no longer see where she was going. And all the while, she strained her ears for some hint of what Kyrtian was saying, watching the enormous shadows cast on the opposite wall by the wavering light of his lamps moving in a gigantic puppet-play.

Aelmarkin doused his mage-light with a curse when he realized that the faint glow ahead of him must be caused by Kyrtian's people in the next cave. He'd finally caught up with them—only to come perilously close to blundering into them. He swore at himself for being so stupid—how could he have let something that simple catch him? He only hoped that none of them were bright enough to have noticed *his* light behind them.

The rough circle of light ahead seemed awfully dim—and *very* yellow. Odd, that. Why would Kyrtian go out of his way to create a yellow light when the natural blue-white of mage-lights was so much better and truer?

Then again, it was Kyrtian. It might be firelight; he might have found what he was looking for and decided to camp. It might be lamplight, because he *wasn't* as good a mage as Aelmarkin had thought and he was running out of energy to keep the mage-lights going. He was perfectly capable of doing without mage-light altogether, for some other peculiar reason of his own.

It was only when Aelmarkin actually reached the mouth of the next cavern and only *just* saved himself from tumbling over the edge that he understood that the lights were indeed lanterns, and that Kyrtian *had* elected to use them instead of mage-lights, and he cursed again (but only in his head) when that simple fact came near to undoing him.

It was a very near thing; one moment, he was easing himself along the cavern, and the next, his questing foot met empty air, and unfortunately, he had already trusted some weight to it, not anticipating that there would be a drop-off. Aelmarkin teetered on the brink for a heart-stopping moment before his flailing hand caught the edge of the wall and he was able to steady himself.

He burned the air with a flurry of mental curses before his heart stopped racing and he was able to really *look* at what lay below him. But then—oh then, his heart raced for an entirely different reason!

There below him, ranked and waiting like so many placid, sleeping bullocks, were the ancient *constructs* that the Ancestors had brought with them. Row upon row of them, waiting for the proper touch to bring them alive and call them to service.

His touch. Never doubt it. He could hardly wait to get down among them! What need would he have of slaves or gladiators or even armies with *these* powerful creations at his command?

His mouth gone suddenly dry with anticipation, he ascertained that the drop was nowhere near as long as he'd thought, and eased himself belly-down over the edge. The rock scraped him even through the tough leather of his hunting-tunic, but he hardly felt it in his haste to get down among those things out of another world and time.

Besides, he needed to get under cover, in case one of Kyrtian's slaves came snooping. It would be a disaster to come this far and then be tripped up by one of Kyrtian's wretched slaves.

He felt better with the bulk of several of the things between himself and Kyrtian's lamps. Safe enough to kindle a very, very dim hand-light of his own, one which could be hidden in his fist and used only, held close to the metal sides of the *constructs,* to see if he could decipher any of the ancient script. He hoped to find instructions there—surely not *everyone* who was asked to control the things in the past actually learned how to do so before attempting to operate them! Failing that, he hoped for labels, or some evocative name that would tell him what the things were used for.

But as he moved silently from one huge bulk to the next, brushing off a literal coat of dust that fell to the ground in a sheet, he was disappointed. Though he looked as high as he could reach, instructions there were none; nor names, either—at least not on the sides that he examined. He didn't dare move to the side facing Kyrtian's lamps; bad enough that he was a moving shadow among unmoving ones! The murmur of voices suggested that all of Kyrtian's people were still with him, but was by no means a trustworthy way of telling for certain.

He cursed the Ancestors now—how stupid could one be, to neglect to leave instructions for the uninitiated? Unless those instructions had been in one of the books back in the main cave, books that crumbled at a touch. . . .

For a moment, he despaired. But then came a stroke of luck so incredible he hardly dared believe it.

As he closed his fist around his hand-light in disappointment at—again—finding nothing, he caught a fugitive hint of glowing green out of the corner of his eye.

He turned, with painful slowness, to his left, and for a moment felt nothing but a wash of disappointment when there didn't seem to be anything there except another *construct,* and this one utterly without anything like writing on the side. It did have a set of blades and claws that suggested warlike intentions, not that knowing its purpose would do him any good unless he could get it moving, which he obviously *couldn't* without instructions. But then as he stared, his eyes adjusted, and he saw it.

A faint glow of green, in the midst of the blank side of the construct, exactly like the glow of an activated Elf-stone.

He sidled up to the thing, staying in the shadows, and quested over it with a finger. Only the glow and a subtle change in texture from metal to stone informed him that the thing was there at all! It had been inset flush with the surface, and in the dim illumination from the hand-light, he wouldn't have seen it except for the glow. It *was* an Elf-stone, or something very like one. And when he opened his fist to bring his hand-light up to it—the hand-light dimmed, and the green glow brightened.

He could have pummeled himself for stupidity. *Of course!* Why would you need instructions to manage one of these things? All you needed was the Elf-stone, both to power it and to control it! And, of course, that was why all of the things had collapsed into inertia when the Great Portal closed! The magic powering them that was a part of the Aether of Evelon ran out, and the Elvenlords who'd built and sustained the Portal had nothing left to supply them! Utter simplicity, but, of course, the Lesser Elvenlords who'd held back their own power either hadn't known how the *constructs* worked, or had been so busy eliminating their dangerous rivals that they hadn't bothered to try to learn to use the things!

Or perhaps they had been so afraid of pursuit that they just abandoned the brutes.

Or—well, it didn't matter. The point was, they *had* been

abandoned and they *were* there for the taking and now Aelmarkin knew how to take and use them!

It couldn't be any simpler. And it didn't matter *what* this behemoth was originally intended to do, either. It was big, it had to be brutally strong, and it was certainly brutally heavy. It could kill Kyrtian simply by stepping on him.

Aelmarkin smothered a howl of glee, and placed the hand holding his hand-light against the Elf-stone embedded in the construct's side. It sucked in the power greedily. The hand-light vanished.

And then—Aelmarkin *felt* it wake and—look for more. And felt its fierce concentration focus on *him.*

He tried to pull his hand away in a flash of alarm.

But by then, of course, it was already too late.

Kyrtian had finally allowed Lynder and Keman to lead him to a seat on a nearby outcrop of rock. He felt—hollow. And exhausted. As if he had wept for a year, although he was dry-eyed.

At least mother isn't here. That was all he could think of. *At least she can't see—this. I don't think she could bear it. I think she'd go mad.*

"No, don't try to chip—it out," he said with difficulty in answer to Lynder's question. "I don't ever want Lady Lydiell to see him. Not like that, anyway. Maybe we can find a way to cover him over—"

He shuddered, a spasm of a thing that left him sweating and shaking. *What must have happened? He must have somehow wakened one of those—things. Maybe it fed off his mage-lights, and he didn't realize what was happening. He must have been so excited—too excited to think clearly.*

He buried his head in his hands, shuddering all over, in spasms he couldn't control. He *wanted* to howl, to rail at fate, and above all things, to weep. Why couldn't he weep?

Which one of these hulks had done the deed? He wanted to know that, suddenly, with a fierce anger that took him and left him shaking. That, above all, he *had* to find out! He'd find the thing and take it to bits with his bare hands, and grind the bits to dust and scatter the dust over the barren desert, by the Ancestors, he would!

He stood up, still shaking, and turned towards them—just in time to see one of *them* slowly rising up from among its fellows, towering higher and higher, with something doll-like and screaming clenched in one fearsome claw.

34

Fear struck tines of ice deep into his gut, but Kyrtian had not spent all these years training for battle in vain. Before the thing had finished standing, he barked an order, which, if his voice cracked, was nonetheless loud enough and authoritative enough that *everyone* reacted.

"Take cover!" he shouted, even while he himself was diving for shelter beneath the sloping front of the nearest construct.

Even Lynder and Hobie, though they had not actually fought with Kyrtian's troops against the Young Lords, had trained long and hard with all of Kyrtian's men and reacted immediately to his barked order. By the time the construct had gotten to its full height, Kyrtian, Lynder and Hobie were all out of its field of vision—or so he hoped—under a slope of metal that cast a deep, black shadow.

And I only hope this thing doesn't decide to come alive, too—he thought, squeezing as far out of sight as he could, though his skin shrank from contact with the chill and slightly greasy metal.

When they had all tucked in and gone immobile, he risked a glance at the wall and the half-circle of lanterns. Shana and Keman were nowhere in sight, but at least they were nowhere *in* his line-of-sight. He had to hope that if he couldn't see them, neither could the construct. If it "saw," that is. It might use other senses. . . .

"Now what?" Lynder hissed into Kyrtian's ear. He sounded as desperate as Kyrtian felt.

"I'm thinking!" he hissed back. He wasn't worried about that *thing* hearing them; the victim it had in its claw was making enough noise to cover just about anything. The screaming was horrible, but worse was the feeling that he knew the tortured voice.

The victim—An Elvenlord; he'd seen enough in that moment of horror to know it wasn't a human. But who? Who could have followed him here, and why? Not any of Lord Kyndreth's people, since none of them knew where he was going, precisely, and surely none of his own.

The victim blubbered between the screams, incoherent in his terror. It was sickening to listen to.

No, none of them would have trailed after me, simply because none of them could *have. They're all totally unsuited to tramping about in the wilderness, thank the Ancestors.*

As frightening as the screams was the *silence* beneath it. The construct made no sound at all.

The only person *likely* to have followed him, and with the skills to do so, would have been Gel, and it certainly wasn't Gel in that monster's claw!

Yet the voice *was* familiar.

Who then? He strained to make out anything in the screams and babbling to give him a clue, as his mouth dried with fear and his insides seemed to turn to water. An enemy, then? But what enemy would have followed him on what was *supposed* to be a fairly dangerous mission to hunt out Wizards? An enemy looking for something to discredit him with—perhaps? An enemy planning to find, or plant, something to Kyrtian's harm. Or even an enemy hoping to arrange an "accident" out here where there would be no witnesses? That was something that Aelmarkin—

Ancestors! he thought, stunned, now *hearing* what was familiar in those screams and wails echoing across the cavern. *It's Aelmarkin!*

That Aelmarkin hated him enough to try to discredit or murder him was no surprise, but that he'd actually dare the wilderness to do so was something so out-of-character that he couldn't berate himself for not thinking of it before. His worst enemy—

Who has managed to blunder into this.

Fortunately, he did not have the time to battle his conscience over whether or not to attempt a rescue; there was a whine, and a flash of light sweeping across the cave floor, and the screams cut off with dreadful finality. The three sheltering beneath the still (thankfully!) lifeless construct became very quiet, hardly daring to breathe, as silence descended with leaden suddenness.

Kyrtian fought down the urge to bolt for the mouth of the cave that had brought them here. Who knew what sort of weapons this thing had?

No magic, Kyrtian decided. *Especially not levin-bolts.* If this monster was what had been feeding on his mage-lights and draining them, what sort of power would a levin-bolt give it? Or worse—what if another of the constructs absorbed the power and came awake? He was fairly certain that this one *wasn't* the one that had gotten his father—though his father must certainly have awakened one or another of the behemoths, probably by using mage-lights. This one was now a proven killer; they certainly didn't need to awaken a second!

So what *could* he use against this monster, if not magic?

Not bows and arrows. Not swords. And we've precious little else.

There was a whir, a creaking of metal, and suddenly something like an enormous upturned bowl attached to three metal struts slammed down onto the stone where he and his men had just been, sending up a cloud of dust. A second followed the first, smashing one of the lanterns.

A moment later, Aelmarkin's limp body dropped down beside the second disk. There was no mistake, now that Kyrtian could see the terror-twisted features. It was Aelmarkin, all right. And there was no doubt in his mind that his cousin was quite, quite dead. Not when his backbone bent *that* far, or at *that* angle.

Kyrtian froze; almost directly above them, he heard that peculiar whining again. He couldn't see anything but those two metal legs, but his imagination painted a picture of the construct somehow turning the top part of itself to peer down at the ground below, searching for them. He felt like a mouse hiding in a log in a field, watching the legs of a cat. Only he had no idea just what arcane senses this monster was using to look for them.

And as if to reinforce that imaginary image, twin beams of light swept over their hiding place and passed over the floor where they had all been standing.

If I knew what its weapons and its abilities were, I might have a better chance of figuring out what to do about it—

A shout broke the ominous silence, making all three of them start and clutch at each other in involuntary reaction.

"Hey!" Shana called from somewhere to the right, her own voice cracking.

The whine became a whir; something *clacked* angrily overhead—and in mere moments, the thing had taken two earth-shaking strides that got it out of Kyrtian's field of vision. He heard and felt each footstep; it was bipedal, from the sound. And it was *definitely* after Shana.

Shana! What are you doing?

It wasn't quiet in the cave any longer. The construct must not have been a very graceful thing; it sounded as if it was stumbling into or kicking aside every obstacle in its path in its effort to get to the Elvenbane. Lynder winced with each crash; Hobie just sat as frozen as a frightened sparrow.

Then it stopped. The whining noise began again, and it sounded frustrated. Kyrtian held his breath again, and so did the other two. If it heard them—

"Ho!"

It was Keman's voice this time, from another part of the cave. The construct was away again, blundering its way through the lifeless forms of its fellows. It might be bipedal, but it obviously wasn't unstable; he hadn't heard anything that sounded like a stumble or a misstep yet.

What are they doing? Not knowing what they were up to was maddening! Not being able to see the monster was worse!

"Should we try and get a look?" Lynder whispered in his ear.

"Not yet," he whispered back. Just then the crashing and

thrashing about stopped, and the whining recommenced, sounding more frustrated than before. It couldn't find Keman any more than it had been able to find Shana. *If magic feeds it—could I make it go dormant by draining magic power out of it?*

It was worth trying. The only trouble was, in order to drain something, he had to actually be in physical contact with it.

And just how am I going to do that without ending up like Aelmarkin? He shuddered, and kept his eyes averted from the remains of his cousin.

"Hey!" That was Shana again, from yet another part of the cave. It *sounded* as if she and Keman were working together to lure the construct away from where he and Lynder and Hobie hid. Was that what they were trying to do? Get the thing away from the cave-mouth so that the three of them could escape?

He couldn't deny that chance to his men. And it would be throwing the blessing back in their face to have them risk so much and not take the opportunity. "Start working your way back to the mouth of the cave," he whispered under cover of the crashes and *thuds.* "But don't move unless the construct is moving, too. Get out of the caves altogether, then bring back the rest of the men, and any equipment you think might help. I'll stay here and help Shana and Keman distract the thing."

"But—" Lynder began.

"That's an order," he hissed fiercely, and to enforce it, took a chance and scuttled from under their shelter into the space beneath another—heading in the opposite direction of the cave-mouth.

He slid under it just in time; the noise stopped again, and the whining began.

This wasn't where he'd have gone by choice; the thing was wheeled, something like a hay-wain, but the clearance between the cave floor and the thing's bottom wasn't more than half that beneath a real wagon. He had barely enough room to hide, and he couldn't help having nightmare visions of the thing waking up and deciding to squash him by lowering itself down on top of him. He was sweating and ice-cold at the same time, and fighting a panic that threatened to keep him from thinking at all. If anything, the view from under here was worse than the first shelter, and it seemed to take forever before he heard Keman's echoing *"Ho!"*

The construct crashed off in pursuit, and Kyrtian scrambled out from under the "wain" to take shelter, not under, but behind yet another behemoth. This time he wanted to *see* what the thing looked like, what it was doing.

It looked like a box on two legs, with a pair of blunt crab-like pincers on arms attached to either side of the box. It wasn't very fast, and it wasn't at all graceful, but it *was* powerful. Some of those crashes hadn't been because it was plowing into obstacles, it was because it was picking them up with a pincer and tossing them aside if they were small enough.

Ancestors! I hope those two aren't anywhere under what's being dropped!

Two lights—were they mage-lights?—at the front of the box projected the beams of light that he had seen sweeping the ground looking for them. They swiveled, looking uncannily like eyes, and the resemblance made him shiver. His tunic clung damply to his back and his hands ached where he clutched the sides of his hiding-place.

It stopped and swept the ground around it with those light-beams. So—where were the other two, and why wasn't it able to spot them?

He frowned, thinking; Keman and Shana *must* be popping up, shouting, and moving off again while it blundered its way towards them, but the thing must not have very good vision, or surely it would *see* them getting away. That was something to keep in mind.

"Hey!" came the expected cry—and that was when Kyrtian realized that Shana and Keman were being even more clever than he'd thought. They *weren't* "popping up" where the construct could see them—instead, a piece of debris went flying through the air and landed on top of another construct with a clatter—at some distance from where the shouter was. The construct's light-

beams snapped across the length of the cave and focused on *that.* And where the junk landed was where the construct headed. No wonder it wasn't able to find what it so fervently hunted!

He dashed out of cover long enough to get a piece of debris himself, laboring under the double handicap of not wanting to distract the thing from its current hunt, and being careful not to go where he might inadvertently cast a shadow or move across the lantern-light. Maybe it didn't have good vision—and maybe it did. This wasn't the time to find out.

He kept one eye on the cave-mouth. *I can't start bringing it back over here until Lynder and Hobie are safe through. . . .*

"Ho!" A much, much bigger piece of debris went flying. That was Keman, who must be very much stronger than Shana.

Well of course—he's a dragon! Kyrtian thought of the immensely-strong shape Keman had taken to bring Shana and the gear down into the caves. It wasn't much bigger than a human, but no human could have done what Keman had.

The thing fastened its light-beams on the junk while it was still in the air, and started after it.

Kyrtian glanced over at the mouth of the cave, just in time to see twin shadows slip over the ledge and into the dark hole that was the start of their road to safety.

Relief made his mouth dry. At least *they* were out of this.

That was the good news; the bad news was that the thing was moving faster, and more surely, every time it crossed the floor. Instead of running out of power, it seemed as if movement was permitting it to loosen up joints long held immobile. It was a good thing he had decided to join this little game. It looked as if it was going to need three players.

The construct reached the spot where the debris had landed—but this time it stood as if it was considering something, then slowly moved its lights along the path that the junk Keman had thrown had taken—

Oh, Ancestors. The thing can think. It's finally figured out that the debris isn't what it wants, and that someone must have thrown it.

He dropped down out of sight, looked hastily around, and picked a place to hide. Far enough away—and near enough to reach. He hoped. *"Ha!"* he shouted with all his might, and flung his own piece of junk.

He was already running flat-out for his hiding-place when the piece left his hand. He dove and rolled beneath the construct and lay there with his mouth clamped around his sleeve to muffle his panting as the footsteps crashed nearer and nearer. . . .

"Ha!" Shana heard, and knew immediately that it wasn't Keman. So Kyrtian had decided to get into the "game." She spared a moment to "feel" with her mind for Hobie and Lynder, and to her immense relief sensed them in the vicinity of the cave-mouth. And their "presences" were receding. Kyrtian was no fool, though he might be brave to the point of foolhardiness.

Still, she was glad of his aid, and gladder still he'd gotten the two weakest members of the group out of danger.

:Keman—he's sent them for help!:

:Or at least he's sent them away.: Keman replied, as the construct crashed its way across the floor. *:I don't know how much help the rest of his men could be . . . even if they get here before this thing catches one of us.:*

Well, neither did she. But right now, that was second on her list of concerns. The first was how to keep herself, and Keman, and Kyrtian out of the claws of the monster. Fear seemed to sharpen all of her senses, and made her thoughts faster. Once this was over—if she lived through it—she'd collapse. Now she was all calculation.

:What is that thing, anyway?: Maybe the way to figuring out how to get rid of it lay in what it was *supposed* to do. The Ancestors made the wretched things as slaves—to do all their work for them. Which was why when they found this world full of humans they hadn't needed the things that had gone dead on them and presumably hadn't bothered to retrieve them.

But the monster was silent again, and it was her turn to distract it. She had her piece of trash ready, a nice light piece of something metallic that should make a lot of clatter. *"Hey!"* she yelped, and tossed it backwards over her head as she sped off in the opposite direction, scooting under the platform of something that vaguely resembled a hut with a porch.

The Ancestors made them as slaves—What could they possibly have wanted with *that* thing? Two-legged, piercing through the gloom of the cave with lights, huge pincers—

She cringed back into her shelter as those twin beams of light swept a little too close. The thing was getting faster, and more nimble. That was *not* good.

And this time it hadn't gone for the place where the trash had landed, but for somewhere nearer the place where she'd been standing when she shouted. That was worse.

"Ho!" shouted Keman, and the thing whirled and lurched off.

What could that monster possibly be good for? She ducked out of her shelter and took a quick look around, just in time to see it pick up another horse-sized construct and toss it aside, for all the world like one of her farmers, tossing aside a stone or a brick that was in the way of the plow.

Her eyes widened involuntarily as she imagined the thing picking up—say—the load on a wagon, and moving it to a barn.

Of course . . . that's what it's for.

:Keman—that monster—it's meant to move things.:

:Well, it's doing a good job of it!: Keman responded acidly. *:It almost dropped that last bit it threw away right on top of me!:*

:No, no, I'm telling you what it's meant to do! That's the job it's meant for, to move things. *That's what the Ancestors made it for!:*

The thing stopped, and started hunting for Keman, sweeping its lights over the increasingly-chaotic and increasingly-tangled ranks of constructs. *:So—what does a thing like that need—to do its job?:* came Keman's reply.

"Ha!" shouted Kyrtian, and the monster was off again. Shana noticed that Kyrtian hadn't bothered to toss any junk this time. He must have seen that the monster wasn't fooled by it anymore.

:A strong back, strong legs, strong arms. It's got to learn, I suppose,: she ventured.

:Well, this one's learning! It's figuring out it shouldn't chase after the decoys we've been tossing. Don't bother throwing

things. Just yell, and run,: he replied. *:What else, do you think?:*

:Kyrtian's already figured out we aren't fooling it anymore. Um. It would need good balance. Not easy to tip over, no matter how heavy the thing is it has to pick up—: she suggested.

:So much for my idea of tripping it.: The monster was definitely getting more nimble as it moved. There was less blundering into things now, more picking them up and tossing them aside. Why was it chasing them if it was supposed to be a cargo-mover? Could the enemies of the Ancestors have something to do with that, or had the thing just gone—well—crazy in all the centuries of inactivity?

:You likely wouldn't want it to cut things up, so those pincers must be blunt.: She was trying to think of anything useful.

:Yes. It didn't have to cut that Elvenlord in half, only crush him,: came the sardonic reply. *:Whoever he was and whatever his business was.:*

:Following Kyrtian, at a guess. Maybe the Great Lords didn't trust him as much as he thought they did.: She shook herself to get rid of the distracting speculations. It was her turn. She got out of her shelter, picked up a flat piece of 'glass' and chose another hiding place. Maybe if she threw it in a different way than just tossing it anyhow, it might still distract the monster.

"Hey!" she screamed, sent the thing spinning off like the saucers that the children played with, and dashed for cover.

She reached it just in time, and was alarmed to see that this time the construct aimed for the center of the arc, not the place where the glass landed. Too close!

:Keman! Can that thing reach behind itself, do you think?:

She sensed Keman's head popping up cautiously, and got a brief glimpse of what *he* saw before he dove back down into hiding. *:I don't think it can!:* he replied with excitement. *:I don't think it can see behind it, either!:*

So. That was one weakness. No, two!

:If you took dragon-form—: she hardly dared suggest it, and Keman would need time to take the form—but in dragon-form Keman was just as big as the monster was. Could he be a match for it?

:I could leap onto its back and keep it occupied,: Keman

replied firmly. *:Then you get to Kyrtian, and both of you get into the tunnel. I'll follow once you're gone. I'll be right on your heels.:*

:But—: she protested—she hadn't intended that at all!

:You might as well, since I'm *going to do what I want to anyway.:* And he closed his mind off to her.

Damn him! she thought with a flare of anger—and shook that off, too. No time, there was no time for anything now but action.

She sensed where Kyrtian was, and waited.

"Ha!" the Elvenlord shouted hoarsely, and made his move. She did the same as soon as the monster was out of sight, planning her run to end near his.

The monster came to a halt almost directly between them, and she froze, holding her breath. Light swept over her hiding-place. Once. *Twice.*

Did it guess? Were dim senses waking up, becoming keener as its movements grew surer? Instinct shrieked at her to shrink back, further into hiding; sense told her to keep absolutely still.

"Ho!" Keman shouted, and the thing lurched off. Before Kyrtian had a chance to move, Shana did, diving under the wheeled vehicle that concealed him.

She found herself nose-to-nose with the Elvenlord, whose white face held an expression of utter shock at seeing her. "We need to get it to turn as soon as it's on top of Keman," she whispered without preamble. "He's going to take dragon-form and jump on it from behind."

"And do what?" Kyrtian asked, aghast.

"How should *I* know?" she snapped. "He's decided that's what he's going to do so we can get out the way your two men did. He says he's going to follow—"

"Well *I* think I can drain that thing if he can get it immobilized—" Kyrtian began, and the crashing footsteps stopped.

Before Kyrtian could do anything, Shana rolled out from underneath the construct and stood up. *"Hey!"* she screamed, waving her arms this time. *"Hey! Stupid! Over here!"*

Barking his elbows on the stone floor in his haste to get out, Kyrtian scrambled from under the construct just in time to see the monster turn towards them.

It was not an encouraging sight. And it got rapidly worse.

Shana just stood there, waving her arms at it, and the two bright spots—far too much like glaring, angry eyes—on its square, flat front panned over the space between them and pinned her in a circle of white light.

His mouth went dry, and fear ran down his backbone like a trickle of icy water. The thing emitted an angry whine, and lurched forward.

But before it had taken more than a single step, something moved in the darkness behind it, a shadowy form he barely made out against the glare, that wavered and surged upwards all in an instant—and then lunged.

Keman!

Monster of flesh against monster of metal. The dragon landed squarely on the construct's back, claws shrieking against its sides. The monster's legs buckled beneath the dragon's weight as Kyrtian stared in frozen fascination—

And that was all he had time to see, as Shana grabbed his wrist and wrenched him around, pulling at him. *"Run!"* she shouted, showing her heels as a good example, and he didn't need a second invitation. The monster might be encumbered, but it certainly wasn't defeated, and behind them the sounds of it thrashing about and Keman's claws scrabbling to take hold were proof enough of that.

Fear gave him a new burst of energy. They sprinted across the cave floor with Shana slightly in the lead—not because Kyrtian was playing the gentleman, either. The girl must have spent her childhood scrambling across rough ground like this; where he stumbled, she skimmed over obstacles like a frightened deer.

She must have a separate set of eyes in her feet. . . .

Behind them, crashes and earth-shuddering impacts testified that Keman was still in the fight. *Ancestors bless you, dragon. But get yourself* out *of it as soon as we're clear!*

She reached the ledge first and vaulted up onto it like an expert acrobat, turning just in time to offer her hand to help him scramble up beside her. Her hand was hard and tough, with surprising strength in it.

Keman— A quick glance over his shoulder showed him that the dragon still clung tenaciously to the back of the construct-monster, and nothing the monster could do was shaking him off.

He grabbed Shana's hand and hauled himself up beside her, turning immediately to face the fight, hoping that Keman had somehow gotten clever enough to outwit the thing.

And his heart leapt. Although the monster's "arms" flailed desperately, it couldn't reach the dragon with them, and those pincers were, next to its feet and weight, its best weapons. Keman had his hind claws lodged firmly all over the thing's back half, and his foreclaws clamped over the front edge. Kyrtian felt a smile as he saw what the dragon had done—wisely, he was *not* making any further offensive moves. Instead, he was content to let the monster wreak further damage on itself as it blundered about, trying to dislodge him. Keman had his tail curled tightly between his legs and out of harm's way, his wings folded tightly across his back, and his legs all tucked in so that the construct couldn't scrape him off without first scraping protruding sections of itself off as well.

The lights on the front swiveled independently as it tried and failed to illuminate the dragon on its back. It threw itself repeatedly against the walls, and bucked like a green horse, but couldn't get rid of him. It hadn't yet thought to roll over on its back—but maybe it couldn't. Keman was winning just by virtue of sticking on it like a burr.

In fact, it had taken some visible damage, not only from the walls of the cave, but from all of the other constructs it had blundered into. The right leg had a sort of hitch in its movement, now, and the sides were scarred where it had bashed its skin against the rock. Kyrtian winced as it flung itself into the wall of the cave, crashing into another construct in the process, and wondered how Keman managed to stay wedged onto the thing. What made the battle all the more uncanny was that aside from the crash of metal on rock and metal on metal, and an underlying, angry whir or hum, the entire battle was taking place in silence. It felt as if one or both of them ought to be giving tongue to terrible battle-roars.

He felt Shana tense up beside him. Then, suddenly, Keman made a move.

While the monster was still off-balance, he let go with his foreclaws and stabbed them down viciously at the lights. He caught them. With a grinding shriek as if the metal itself screamed, he wrenched first one, then the other, off the front. Metal and wire snapped and tore, and Keman tossed the lights aside, like a cruel boy pulling the legs off a beetle.

If the monster was ever going to display a voice, it should have then—

The lights went out as they fell, leaving only the lanterns he and his men had lit as illumination for the cave, and huge shadows sprang up behind the construct and its draconic burden, writhing and twisting as the thing thrashed and Keman took a new position on its back.

Now what—

"Run!" Shana shouted again, and as he turned to do so, he saw Keman fling himself off the monster's back at last, half running, half flying, straight for the cave-mouth where they stood.

That's what!

He didn't wait to see if the monster was going to follow, or if by taking its lights Keman had also blinded it. He ignored his aching side and put everything he had into a flat-out dash for the main cave. Within moments, they were fleeing through the darkness, with nothing more than the grey light at the end of the series of demi-caves to tell them where their goal was.

A scrabbling noise behind him made the hair on the back of

his neck stand straight up, and somewhere deep inside him he found another burst of speed—

It was inside the tunnel.

It was closing the gap between them!

It was right on top of him!

Something grabbed him, closing around his waist and spinning him over on his side as it carried him forward! Air rushed past him as his captor picked up speed. He flailed at it with fists and heels—

"Shto tha!" said a muffled and indignant voice at the back of his neck. *"Ish ee!"*

Keman?

Teeth shrank away from him even as he realized they were sticking into him, and as Keman ran, his jaws formed themselves around Kyrtian's body.

Keman made greater speed than any smaller, two-legged creature possibly could; from his inverted position in the darkness, Kyrtian couldn't see much, but when he twisted his head, the dim, round light that represented the place where the last set of small caves met the entrance cave was getting bigger. And it was doing so a lot faster than it had when he was running.

He couldn't tell where Shana was, but Keman wouldn't have left her behind, so she must be with them. Probably she'd been able to catch hold of his neck on the run and vault herself into place like a trick-rider.

Behind—

A metallic crash that deafened him for a moment and shook small rocks loose to rain down onto their heads proved that the monster wasn't blind—and was still coming for them. From behind came the scrape and groan of protesting metal, and more crashes as the monster forced itself into the opening.

Keman found more speed somewhere; hot, metallic breath panted in and out over Kyrtian's body, and Kyrtian pulled in his arms and legs and tucked his head in to keep as much of himself inside Keman's mouth as he could.

"Anks," Keman said shortly.

The noise from behind wasn't falling away. Either the thing was still trying to follow them, or it had succeeded in getting in and *was* on their heels.

A violent impact—a dust-storm—Keman burst through what was left of the barrier of tangled carts and bones and relics, and out into the main cave—

And suddenly tossed his head up in a slewing, sideways motion, letting go of Kyrtian as he did so.

"Aiiiiiiii!"

Kyrtian screamed as he flew through the air, and screamed again as something snatched him out of it as easily as a child catches a ball, then slammed him down on a bony, scaly surface that inexplicably had a *saddle* on it.

He clutched the leather, dazed, and even as his eyes took in the improbable sight of a dragon neck and head stretching away in front of him, strange and skeletal in the dim light, the dragon lurched into a run.

Ancestors! More *of them?*

Ahead of him—Keman, with Shana clinging to his neck; he must not have paused for a single stride as he tossed his burden of Elvenlord to the other. Keman scrabbled up the rock-pile at the entrance first, with no regard for niceties, dislodging anything that was loose in his haste to get *out.* As they followed, lurching and slipping while rocks went tumbling beneath and around them, Kyrtian ducked as more rocks showered down on them, and the dragon he rode cupped its wings forward to deflect some of the falling debris from him. His heart pounded, and his fingers were clamped so tightly to the saddle that they hurt, and all the while he heard the screech of protesting metal echoing behind them, coming, coming—

Then they were at the top, miraculously widened—then out—

Kyrtian gasped instead of screamed, as the dragon threw itself into empty space.

It glided heavily down the slope, wings wide-spread around him, and skidded into an abrupt landing at the bottom.

Kyrtian wasn't ready for that. He lost his grip, and tumbled awkwardly over the dragon's shoulder and down to the ground. The dragon spun around on its hind legs, nimble as a goat, and raced back up the slope to join the others, *three* of them, who were all clustered around the opening.

Kyrtian looked for Shana—and found her in the embrace of another wizard, shaking like a leaf, and whispering what sounded like a name. The wizard, who looked vaguely familiar, stroked her hair comfortingly, but spoke straight to Kyrtian.

"I hope you don't want to get back in there. Ever. The dragons are sealing the entrance."

Shana relaxed against the support of Lorryn's shoulder and cradled the wineskin in both hands; she didn't usually drink much wine but after today—

If anyone deserves a drink, I do.

She had never been so glad to see anyone in her life as Lorryn—in fact, she hadn't realized that the other dragons were there until they were all *out* of the caves.

Keman, Alara, Dora, and Kalamadea had sealed the entrance past *anything* other than another dragon getting through. They'd brought down half the mountain, it seemed, then fused the rocks together until they were exhausted and limp, their bright colors gone pale, their scales dull. The work had been urgent enough; they'd only just brought the rocks down when something began attacking the pile from inside the mountain, audible even down below. That was when they'd begun fusing the rocks together, and the moment that the monster contrivance encountered the fused section, the blockage was obvious even to an idiot—or a construct—for it began bashing something—itself? its claws?—against the rockfall. But if it intended to loosen those rocks, it was going to meet with failure.

The dragons worked the pile from the top down, creating a plug of rock that was not going to move. The only way to get out now was to blow out the top of the mountain, or tunnel out at another place.

There was no way—they hoped—that the construct was going to get at them now.

The sound of battering still came from within the pile, but it was weaker now, and slower. Maybe—hopefully—it was running out of magical energy, and would relapse into its quiescent state.

Whatever; we're not going to wait around here to find out.

She took another pull on the wineskin, and closed her eyes. *Lorryn. Oh, thank you, Lorryn. Thank you for thinking, for being here.* It was perhaps at that moment that she really, truly realized how much she cared for him.

Lorryn had just finished explaining the situation with Caellach Gwain to Lord Kyrtian—who, at this point, was stunned and battered enough to accept just about anything. He just nodded—at all the salient points, so at least he was listening—and took it all in as if the affairs of Wizards were everyday things to him.

Huh. Then again, after the politics of the Great Lords, our little quarrels probably seem small beans.

Kyrtian's men had bandaged their scrapes and bruises, applied remedies inside and out, and supplied all of them with food and drink. Including the dragons. Bless them, they'd gone out and dragged back three dead deer—a small meal by draconic standards, after all that exertion, but enough to help revive them. The fire they'd built was immensely comforting, and for once, it wasn't raining.

". . . so after we made sure he *couldn't* come straight back to the Citadel, we waited. When he didn't come back at all, I finally decided that he'd either followed you, or he'd finally let his arrogance take him into a situation he couldn't get out of," Lorryn said.

"And good riddance to bad rubbish, if you ask me," Keman grumbled under his breath. He—and the others—were too bone-weary to shift; they'd curled themselves around the entrance to the camp, making a formidable barrier between the camp and anything that might even consider going after what was inside it. Kyrtian's men were still wide-eyed and a little nervous about being surrounded by dragons, but were handling it all remarkably well. Keman was flank-to-flank with Dora; the sight of two young dragons being as affectionate as any two young lovers seemed to go a long way to reassuring Kyrtian's men.

I suppose it makes them seem more human. . . .

"Keman has been talking with me, at night," Dora said, and the bare skin around her eyes and mouth flushed a delicate pink. Shana saw two of Kyrtian's men exchange a knowing look, and hid a smile. When humans who'd never seen dragons before this could recognize a shy blush on the face of one, things would be all right. "We can speak over greater distances, mind-to-mind, than you can. And—we miss each other when we're apart." She eyed Shana with guilt. "I'm sorry Keman didn't mention it before, but—we didn't want you to feel badly because we could talk and you and Lorryn couldn't."

"Of course," Kyrtian said, with a slow smile. "I can certainly understand *that.*" He passed his wineskin to one of his men, and settled back against the bulk of Keman as comfortably as if he used a dragon as a backrest every day.

Dora flushed again. "So I knew where you were, generally. And, of course, Lorryn had already been to the place where Shana and Keman transported to in the first place and he knew how to get there himself."

I should have known the lovebirds were chatting instead of sleeping, she thought—with a little envy. It would have been a lot nicer if she'd been able to do that with Lorryn without the aid of Keman. On the whole though, it was a damned good thing they *had* been billing and cooing every night. If they hadn't been, she might not be here right now.

"So when Dora told me that you had found the cave and when Caellach Gwain didn't come back, I decided it was more important to get out here and see if we could find him before he found you," Lorryn said with a shrug when Shana tilted her head up to give him a measuring stare.

"You supposed he'd been able to follow us, then?" she asked.

"I couldn't take the chance that he hadn't," Lorryn replied. "I figured that bringing three dragons along would make certain he didn't try anything if—or when—we caught him."

"I knew they were coming of course," Keman put in. "But all they were *supposed* to do was to look for the Old Whiner. They weren't going to butt their snouts in on us, why should they? There was no reason to. When we got back, you'd have just found out they'd caught the wretch, so I didn't see any reason to bother you with it."

"You left me in charge to deal with Caellach," Lorryn told Shana, meeting her gaze frankly, and she gave his hand a little squeeze. "Without Caellach, there was no one to organize discontent. Frankly, knowing where he was and keeping him from making conspiracies out of half-truths was more important than my being directly in command for a day or so."

She nodded, and smiled. How could she *not* agree with him when he was obviously every bit as competent as she was? She left him in charge; that meant to *be* in charge and make decisions without consulting her if there was no need to. It would be pretty absurd to be angry with him for doing just that.

But she could tell him all that later, when they were alone. For now it was enough to know that *she* didn't have to be "the Elvenbane" alone anymore. . . .

"We transported in this morning and flew here, but we never, *ever* expected you to wake up a monster! And let me tell you," Lorryn concluded, "those last few moments when that *thing* attacked you and we were still in the air were the worst in my life."

"They weren't any joy for us, I can tell you," Keman grumbled.

"So that was why you went ahead and attacked the thing!" Shana exclaimed.

"You surely didn't think I'd be stupid enough to do that without being pretty sure I knew what I was doing, did you?" Keman replied indignantly. "I think I did all right without their help, thank you. We didn't even *really* need them to get out of the cave, and I know I could have at least blocked the entrance enough by myself to hold that monster, long enough for us all to transport out of here, anyway! I'll admit I was glad to see them, and it made getting that thing bottled up easier, but we three were perfectly able to deal with it on our own."

"You might have at least told me that there was help coming," Shana pointed out—reasonably, she thought, but Keman only snorted, and for a moment, she was irritated.

"I didn't exactly have time to discuss it with you!" he said, looking just as irritated as she was. "And we weren't in any trouble, anyway!"

She decided not to quarrel with him—but this new attitude on his part was something she hadn't expected. Not from Keman the gentle, Keman her little brother—

Keman the not-so-little-anymore. . . .

She'd have to take that into her calculations from now on. *Males,* she thought. *He was so much more* reasonable *when he was still a dragonling!* It had to be all of the courting and cooing with Dora, she finally decided.

He wasn't a "kid" anymore and it looked as if he was going to be like every other adolescent male and start proving it.

Now he'd behave like most of the other young male dragons she knew. Wizard males and human males, for that matter. Next thing, he'd be flying mock-combats and doing acrobatics for Dora's admiration.

Lorryn must have guessed at her thoughts—or maybe she was thinking them a little too loudly. *:No worries,:* he said, squeezing her hand. *:He'll get over it. And I assure you, I'm past it.:*

:Thank the Ancestors!: she replied, her humor coming back. *:I think I'd send you to the Iron People to get it beaten out of you if you weren't!:*

"All *I* can say is that I'm glad you came," Kyrtian said fervently, with a grateful slap to Keman's flank. "Whatever is in there can remain in there forever, so far as I'm concerned." He shuddered, and said nothing more, but Shana could only wonder if he would feel that way some time in the future. After all, his father—or what was left of his father—was still in there.

Well, it wouldn't be *her* problem. He was forewarned now, and if he decided he had to go back, he knew he'd better come with plenty of help.

And, being *without* a lady friend to impress, he just might act in a sensible manner, unlike certain young dragons.

She cocked her ear to listen for a moment to things outside the camp. The sounds from inside the mountain were definitely weaker. "Did you find any sign of Caellach?" she asked, belatedly recalling that this was why their rescuers had come in the first place.

"We found where he'd transported in—so he *did* manage to learn the spell—and then we found ambush-beast tracks on top of his," Lorryn said grimly. "We didn't bother to follow them back to the den; there was enough blood to pretty much guarantee that Caellach must have been the beast's dinner."

Her mouth formed into a soundless "O" but she couldn't think of what else to say. Lorryn waited for a moment, then continued. "My thought is to just let him vanish. If the other Old Whiners think he's gone off to the old Citadel or somewhere else to live in luxury with their belongings and with luxury goods lifted from the Elvenlords, they're not going to make a martyr out of him."

"Whereas, if they found out his own stupidity killed him—?" she countered. "Wouldn't that destroy his credit with them?"

"Then someone *might* try and make it look as if you arranged for his death," Lorryn replied, with a grimace. The fire flared up for a moment and gave them all a look of rapt concentration. "It'd only be our word for what really happened."

"A sufficiently clever fellow could even make him out to be a martyr if they *did* believe that an ambush beast killed him," Kyrtian said unexpectedly. "After all, he was the last supporter of the Old Ways, and he was trying to get information that would show the others that you and your New Ways were fomenting treachery to your own kind. It wasn't stupidity that killed him, it was a willingness to sacrifice himself to prove the truth."

Shana stared at him for a moment, astonished.

Where did he get that? It's possible—it's even likely—but I wouldn't have thought of it!

Even Lorryn looked surprised. "I'm glad you're on our side," Lorryn managed, after a moment. "If you can think of things like that—"

Kyrtian shrugged, his eyes bleak in the firelight. "I didn't always think this way," he pointed out. "I suppose I can thank my late cousin Aelmarkin for my education—and my loss of innocence." Then he smiled, and he looked more like himself again.

"Well, your cousin got exactly what he deserved," Keman said.

But Kyrtian shrugged. "Much as I'm glad I won't have to worry about him any longer, I wouldn't wish the death he got on anyone."

Shana compressed her lips; she wasn't feeling that generous. Especially when—now that she came to think about it—it was entirely possible that it had been Aelmarkin who woke that blasted construct. "I doubt he would have said the same of you," she said brusquely.

Kyrtian sighed, and looked weary and pensive. "You're probably right. No, you *are* right. But it would make me more like him to think that way, so I won't." His jaw firmed. "I refuse to descend to his level. So I'll forgive him."

"Now that he isn't here to make any more trouble for you, eh?" Keman said shrewdly.

"His men are shivering with fear in an ill-made camp, out that way," Father Dragon put in, unexpectedly. "Shall we rescue them, do you think?"

"Yes!" said Kyrtian and Lorryn.

"No!" said Shana and Keman at the same moment. All four exchanged glances, and it was Shana who broke the deadlock.

"All right," she said grudgingly. "I suppose we can round them up and take them back to the new Citadel when you've left, Kyrtian. Zed can probably find a use for them."

"We'll leave the way we came," said Kyrtian, with a sigh.

"Having found nothing but empty caves. We have a larger plan to think of."

"Indeed," Kalamadea rumbled, and it seemed to Shana that he spoke for all of them. "And now—rest. We have a great deal of work ahead of us."

Indeed we do, she thought, as Lorryn helped her to her feet, and led her to the tent that two of Kyrtian's men had vacated for them.

Kyrtian stretched, feeling every single scrape, bruise, and pulled muscle. But just as much as he longed for home and a hot bath, he dreaded facing his mother with the news he had.

Absently, to distract himself from his own gloomy thoughts, he patted Keman's side. "I don't suppose I could talk you and your lady-friend into turning up in a few days, could I?" he asked. "I'd love for mother to see you for herself."

And it would do her good to distract her from my—bad news. Oh, of course, she had been assuming all these years that his father was dead—but it was one thing to assume, and another to *know.* When you assumed, there could always be that little hope lurking in the back of your heart that you couldn't quite give up. . . .

He knew he was never going to actually tell her what he had found. It would be enough to tell her that he'd found his father's remains and not get any more elaborate than that.

And tell her that, yes, he did *find the Great Portal just as he'd always expected, but that he was killed in an accident. That it looked as if he was taken completely by surprise.* That would leave her with the comfortable impression that he'd never known what was going to happen to him.

Keman laughed. "Of course you could! In fact, I think I will ask Lorryn and Shana if Dora and I can be the Wizards' liaisons with you. They don't need us particularly to spy on the Great Lords, and the advantage of having *us* with you rather than Wizards is that *we* won't disguise our true nature with illusion. We can pose as a Lesser Lord and his Lady. Should you have any more visits from—say—Lord Kyndreth, no matter how many illusion-dispelling magics he casts, we'll pass his test."

"I hadn't thought of that!" Kyrtian said, in weary surprise, feeling a renewed stirring of pleasure. "Consider the invitation tendered, then. That would solve any number of problems."

Dora nudged him with her snout affectionately. "I think that would be lovely, my Lord," she replied. "I don't suppose you have any caves on your property, do you?"

Kyrtian repressed the automatic shudder; after what he'd just been through, he never, ever wanted to go underground again—

But he looked over at Lynder, who grinned sheepishly, and answered for him. "Quite a few, mi—ah—your—"

"Just Dora," the female dragon said, in a kindly tone of voice.

"Ah." Lynder rubbed the side of his nose with his hand, self-consciously. "Dora, then. Yes, Hobie and I have found quite a few. Limestone caves, water-carved, with lots of formations."

"Lovely!" the female dragon said with enthusiasm. "Lord Kyrtian, you wouldn't mind if we took over one, would you?"

"We," is it? he thought, holding back a chuckle at the way Keman's expression changed from startlement to pleasure. *No wonder the young cock is starting to strut! Might be a very good thing for all of them to separate this young fellow from the rest of his peers, so he's less tempted to act—well, like a young cock.* With the current state of things . . . best to get him settled. The next time there was a situation involving young Keman, the urge to try and prove himself could have some serious consequences.

"I would consider it an honor," he said, to both their satisfaction.

"Shana's so used to depending on me, you know, and I think it would be better for her if she got out of that habit and started—well—depending on Lorryn instead," Keman said in a slightly patronizing undertone, with a glance at the now-occupied tent. "I practically raised her—with Mother's help, of course, but I did most of it."

That concept made his head swim for a moment! "Ah—really?" he asked.

Keman chuckled. "I had all sorts of pets. So far as the others of our Lair were concerned, she was just one more! Until she started talking and acting like a person, of course."

It made Kyrtian's head swim a little more. "In the very near future—when you're settled on my estate and we have the time—you are going to have to tell me all about that," he said, as firmly as he could.

He was not going to disabuse the young dragon of his notion that Lashana "depended" on him. He did feel a pang of jealousy though, over that young Wizard, Lorryn. . . .

No, he corrected himself. *Not jealousy. Envy.*

It wasn't that he wanted Shana—she was a handsome young woman, but not, well, not the type he was attracted to, really. Except, perhaps, for those characteristics of mind and spirit that he admired. No, what he wanted was the kind of relationship that she and Lorryn so clearly shared. What his mother and father had once had together.

Ancestors. Won't that be a surprise for Mother. But he didn't think he'd give her free rein to go hunt him up a wife. Not at the moment. There were a lot of difficult days ahead of them; they were all going to have a great many more important things to occupy their time.

Like how to survive, for one thing.

He was under no illusion that with Aelmarkin gone, all of his troubles were about to vanish. Quite the contrary. He was now *into* the morass of the politics of the Great Lords, he had the Young Lords to worry about and—

And I'm technically a traitor. I'm conspiring with the Wizards to create a slave rebellion.

All that, in addition to trying to keep his own people safe. If he thought about it too long, it seemed impossible, and he began to doubt he'd even manage that last, and in some ways most important task, much less all the rest.

But he wasn't alone in this, now. For once, it didn't *all* depend on him and his paltry skills. *We'll be doing it together, dragons and Elvenlords, Wizards and humans working together. At last.*

And with that formidable combination—he had to believe there was no problem that they could not ultimately defeat.

EPILOGUE

Triana had never been particularly afraid before she'd entered these caves. She'd only *thought* she'd encountered terror before the construct came alive.

But the moment that the thing arose out of the rest, like some terrifying metal insect with a screaming Aelmarkin in its claws, she knew true and paralyzing horror.

By then she had been beside the Great Portal, and as the thing blundered back and forth across the cave in pursuit of Kyrtian and his people, she shrank into the shelter of one of its curved sides, praying that it wouldn't see her, wouldn't blunder into her. That was *all* she could manage; her knees scarcely held her up, and she couldn't have run if she wanted to. She was drenched in a cold, cold sweat; every time the thing came anywhere near she held her breath until she nearly passed out, lest it hear her breathing.

She was sure she was going to die. For the first time in her life, she stared mortality in the face, and realized that she couldn't bear it. . . .

She couldn't bear it. In a moment, she was going to faint, or scream and betray herself. She trembled and sweated, and clenched her fists until her long nails bit into her palms and made them bleed.

One moment, there was the metal monster. Then the metal one—was attacked by a dragon.

It was impossible. It was too much. She clutched at the Portal side, and turned her face into it and refused to look. It didn't matter which one of them won—the survivor would find her and kill her—she'd die like Aelmarkin, screaming in terror and pain; she didn't stand a chance—

She fought down the scream that threatened to escape—tears

scorched her face and her throat ached with the need to shriek and shriek, but if she did, she'd die then and there, and she wanted to *live*. . . .

Something snapped inside her. Her mouth opened, but nothing came out. She felt herself start to collapse, then blackness swooped down on her like a dragon, and took her senses.

When she woke, the cave was quiet, and she lay sprawled at the foot of the Great Portal. The cave was still illuminated by the uncertain yellow light of Kyrtian's lanterns, or what was left of them.

Suddenly, she did not want to know if Kyrtian had met the same fate as Aelmarkin. It was one thing to see mere human slaves die; it was another thing entirely to know, to *see* the hand of death cut down another Elvenlord.

No. The caves were not entirely quiet . . . in the far, far distance, out in the entrance cave, perhaps, something battered monotonously at the stone. Since the "something" sounded like metal, it must have been the metal monster that survived.

So it was between her and the only way out.

For a moment, she thought she was going to faint again, but as her hands closed convulsively and her nails bit into her palm, so did the band of the heavy signet ring she wore—

The ring. The ring! It was her Portal key—and she lay in the biggest Portal of them all!

Shaking in every limb, she got to her feet somehow, and dismissed the illusion she wore. If this was going to work, she would need every morsel of power.

She faced the Great Portal, closed her eyes, and slowly, carefully, began to weave the lines of energy that would open a long-dormant Portal like this one. It was going to take a lot—this one had been made by the concerted effort of dozens of mages, and she was only one.

But she also didn't have any choice if she wanted to live.

Bit by bit, sluggishly, the Portal began to respond. The lines of power oozed into place rather than snapping crisply into their positions. The patterns formed, but oh! so slowly!

And then, with no warning at all—the Portal snapped to full and vibrant life!

Startled, Triana opened her eyes.

The shimmering curtain of power within the glowing green arch shivered.

Parted.

And an entirely new horror stepped through.

Like some unsanctified melding of Elf and reptile, the thing stood twice as tall as she. It was long-limbed, sexless, and entirely naked, covered in its own blue-green scales. It had a tail that lashed back and forth restlessly, a hairless head, legs that bent the wrong way at the knees, a lipless mouth full of pointed teeth, and—most horrible of all—eyes she would have recognized on any Elvenlord. And it saw her the instant it walked through the Portal.

Before she could move, it had cleared the distance between them in a single leap, and seized her.

Its strong, scaled fingers closed around her waist, in a grip unbreakable as metal cables. *Now* she screamed, shrieked and fought, but she might as well have been fighting the metal monster. It had no expression whatsoever on the flat plate that was its face.

It even *smelled* like a snake, musty and green, and the smell made her even more frantic, somehow, triggering fears so atavistic that she tore off nails and bit like an animal trying to get free of it. Her entire body felt afire; nothing existed for her but the overpowering *need* to escape—

All for naught. The thing never even winced. It was impossibly strong and utterly implacable; the moment that she tired, it flung her over its shoulder.

Reduced now to mindless panic, she renewed her fight, but her shrieks made no impression on it, and she might as well have been fighting with the stone of the cave.

It carried her to the Portal, which shimmered with activity. She screamed as they approached the shivering curtain of light.

They touched it. And passed through it.

And the Portal closed behind them again.

Lord Kyndreth steepled his fingers together and stared at his son Gildor, who had just brought him news that was—well—peculiar. He wasn't certain what to make of it. He was even less certain what to do about it.

He had young Kyrtian's report on his desk, a written copy of what Kyrtian had told him via the teleson, and although he could find no fault in it, it had left him feeling vaguely unsatisfied. Granted, everyone knew what the forest bordering Cheynar's estate was dangerous, full of alicorns and the Ancestors only knew what sorts of worse things. And there was no real reason why Kyrtian should have actually *found* the purported den of halfbloods in there. After all, they'd been hiding for centuries with no one suspecting their presence, so why should one young Elvenlord find them now?

But—the report felt incomplete. As if Kyrtian was hiding something from him, although he could not even begin to guess what that "something" was.

And now—Gildor, poor dullard that he was, walked into the study with the astonishing news that Lady Triana *and* Aelmarkin were missing. That they had left their estates with camping gear and a train of slaves that included (in Triana's case, at least) slaves trained as foresters. And now, both were missing, their estates in confused disarray, their slaves left with no orders, uncertain of what they should do now. Gildor and his friends had turned up at Aelmarkin's estate for a planned event—one at which Lady Triana was also supposed to appear—to find that both were gone, vanished.

"Thank you, Gildor," Kyndreth told his son, with the gravity due to a major piece of intelligence. "Thank you *very* much. Would you care to invite all of those friends of yours who were disappointed of their amusement *here?* I will be happy to entertain them for a week, if you like."

As he'd expected, Gildor's dull face brightened at the prospect; Kyndreth summoned his steward and sent his son off with the lesser Lord to organize the entertainment. That is, Lord Belath would organize the entertainment, and Gildor would summon his friends . . . it would be a great disruption to Kyndreth's work, in fact, he might have to retire to the hunting-lodge or the old Dowager-House while the young roisterers romped through his halls. But that would be a small price to pay if Gildor continued to bring him tidbits like this one.

Was *this* what Kyrtian was hiding?

That didn't fit with his reading of the young Lord. Kyrtian was not likely to conceal the fact that his cousin had come to grief, and even less likely to have murdered Aelmarkin himself. Kyndreth could readily see why Aelmarkin would follow Kyrtian into the wilderness—Aelmarkin would be perfectly happy to engineer an "accident" out there. But if, in the course of trying to set up such an accident, it was Aelmarkin who perished, and Kyrtian found out about it, why would Kyrtian hide it?

Why would he *want* to? If Aelmarkin were hoist upon his own petard of treachery, Kyrtian should be only too pleased to trumpet the fact to all the world.

And as for Triana vanishing at the same time—well, the only thing that Lord Kyndreth could imagine was that for some reason *she* had gone chasing after Kyrtian as well. Although he could not imagine *why*.

Kyndreth ground his teeth, feeling frustration well up inside him. This was an entirely new experience for him—and he didn't like it. Always, *always,* from the time he first came to power and took his Council seat, he had known who was doing what, and why. *Especially* why. And now things were happening that he had not been told of, had not anticipated, and worst of all, he had no real notion of the motivations that lay behind these incidents.

Motivations—what in the world could have brought Aelmarkin out into the wilderness *besides* hatred for Kyrtian? Or, for that matter, Lady Triana? What could the two possibly have in common?

He closed his eyes for a moment, emptied his mind, and violently suppressed the emotions that came welling up in the wake of that frustration. Emotion was not useful. He needed logic and reason—and above all, planning.

And once he cleared his mind of emotion, something else occurred to him at long last. The one thing that Triana and Aelmarkin *did* have in common was the group that they associated with socially—the younger sons, and some few younger daughters. Until the Young Lords' Revolt, that had included—the rebellious Young Lords.

What if, rather than trailing after Kyrtian, Aelmarkin and Triana had gone—quite coincidentally—into the same area, intending to meet with the fugitives?

What if Aelmarkin and Triana had been the spies within the ranks of the Old Lords for the youngsters?

If that was the case—no *wonder* Aelmarkin had been so intent on fostering the impression his cousin Kyrtian was dotty! And no wonder he'd been so disgruntled when Kyrtian was placed in charge of the army!

It was only a theory—could by no means be proved—but it wouldn't hurt to keep the theory in reserve. It might be useful.

Meanwhile, he should be the one to spread the news to the rest of the Council, if at all possible. How many other Council members had offspring likely to be invited to that aborted party? Not many—and none were likely to have mentioned the disappearances yet.

Good. He might be swimming in a sea of uncertainties, but he *could* make something out of this yet.

He straightened his back, called for strong wine, and began to plan what he would tell the Council. And as he did so, he felt a faint smile cross his lips.

At the very least, *he* would gain something. Triana had some ancient cousin or other who would swiftly claim *her* estate, but Aelmarkin's nearest relation was Kyrtian . . . and Kyrtian was unlikely to want Aelmarkin's tiny holding *or* his business of breeding pleasure-slaves. When an estate went unclaimed, it traditionally went to the Head of the Council.

Which was, of course, Lord Kyndreth.

And if there was any question of whether or not it should be confiscated, well, Kyndreth could bring up that theory, branding Aelmarkin as a traitor, and overturning all possible objections to confiscating the property.

Kyndreth nodded to himself, feeling firm ground beneath his feet again. Good enough. He knew where he was now. He would call the Council Meeting, announce the disappearances, and see who reacted, and how. *That* would tell him a great deal—and in the meantime, he would send his stewards in to take control of Aelmarkin's possessions.

He took a long breath, and keyed the teleson. Shake the tree, and see what fruit fell—and how far.

And whatever happened, to make certain that it profited him.

"Well, Anster," he began, when Lord Anster's servant had summoned him to the teleson-screen, "it seems we have a mystery on our hands. . . ."

ABOUT THE AUTHORS

For more than fifty years, **Andre Norton**, "one of the most distinguished living SF and fantasy writers" (*Booklist*), has been penning bestselling novels that have earned her a unique place in the hearts and minds of millions of readers worldwide. She has been honored with a Life Achievement award by the World Fantasy Convention and with the Grand Master Nebula award by her peers in the Science Fiction Writers of America. Works set in her fabled Witch World, as well as others, such as the Time Traders, Solar Queen, and Beast Master series, to name but a few in her great oeuvre, have made her "one of the most popular authors of our time" (*Publishers Weekly*). She lives in Murfreesboro, Tennessee, where she presides over High Hallack, a writers' resource and retreat. More can be learned about Miss Norton's work, and about High Hallack, at www.andrenorton.org.

Mercedes Lackey has enjoyed bestselling success with her many fantasy works, including her much acclaimed adventures set in the fabled world of Valdemar. While much of her work lies in epic fantasy, she has enjoyed successful forays into dark fantasy, with her Diana Tregarde books, and contemporary fantasy, which includes her recently published *Sacred Ground*. She is one of today's most acclaimed and popular fantasy authors. She lives with her husband, artist and author Larry Dixon, in Tulsa, Oklahoma.

Available in Fall 2003
from Tor Books

The Outstretched Shadow

(0-765-30219-5)

Book One
of the Obsidian Trilogy

Mercedes Lackey and James Mallory

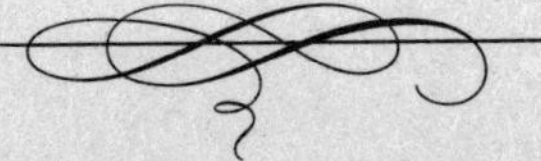

Chapter One

In The City of Golden Bells

The Garden-Market positively *thronged* with people, clustered around the wagons just in from the countryside. *What a fuss over strawberries—you'd think they were made of solid ruby.*

Perhaps—to some—they were. Certainly the number of superior kitchen-servants that filled the streets of the Garden-Market, their household livery enveloped in spotless aprons, pristine market baskets slung over their arms, suggested that the gourmets of the City treasured them as much as if they were, indeed, precious gems.

"Out of the way, young layabout!"

A rude shove in Kellen's back sent him staggering across the cobbles into the arms of a marketplace stall-holder, who caught him with a garlic-redolent oath just in time to keep him from landing face-first in the cart full of the man's neatly heaped-up vegetables. Behind Kellen, the burly armsman dressed in purple-and-maroon livery and bearing nothing more lethal than an ornamental halberd dripping purple-and-maroon ribbons shoved another man whose only crime was in being a little too tardy at clearing the path. This victim, a shabby farmer, went stumbling in the opposite direction, and looked far more cowed than Kellen had. A third, a boy picked up by the collar and tossed aside, saved himself from taking down another stall's awning by going into the stone wall behind it instead.

All this rudeness was for no greater purpose than so the armsman's master need not be jostled by the proximity of mere common working-folk who *had* been occupying the space that their superior wished to cross.

Kellen felt his lip curling in an angry sneer as he mumbled a hurried apology to the fellow who'd caught him. *Damn the idiot that has to make a display of himself here! He picked a* fine *time to come parading through, whoever he is! The Garden-Market couldn't be more crowded if you stood on a barrel and yelled "Free beer!"*

Then again—maybe that was the point. Some people couldn't see an opportunity to flaunt their importance without grabbing it and wringing every last bit of juice out of it.

Father, for instance. . . .

Kellen turned just in time to see that the Terribly Important Person in question this time was High Mage Corellius, resplendent in his velvet robes and the distinctive hat that marked him as a High Mage and thus a creature of wealth, rank *and* power. Quite a hat, it was, and Corellius held his scrawny neck very upright and stiff, supporting it—a construction with a square brim as wide as his arm was long, that curled up on the right and the left. It had three gold cords that knotted around the crown and trailed down his back, cords ending in bright golden tassels as long as Kellen's hand.

The official ranks of Mage-craft progressed from the Student, at the very beginning of the discipline, to Apprentice, to Journeyman, to Mage, to Great Mage, to High Mage, to Arch-Mage. Kellen, as a Student, was beneath Corellius's notice under the usual circumstances. But Kellen was no "ordinary" student. Not with the Arch-Mage Lycaelon—head of the High Council, and therefore Lord of all the Mages in the City—as his father.

"That'd be a High Mage, then?" asked the stall-holder, conversationally. "Don't suppose ye know which one?"

Kellen shrugged, not at all inclined to identify himself as someone who would know High Mages on sight. He'd worn his oldest clothes into the City for just this reason.

Kellen moved on, taking a path at right angles to Corellius's progress. He didn't want to encounter the High Mage again, but he also didn't want to fight his way through the wake of disturbance Corellius had left behind him. The Garden-Market, with its permanent awnings which were fastened into the stone of the warehouse-buildings behind them and unfurled every morning, was full every day, but other Markets were open only once every Sennday, once a moonturn or once a season. The Brewers and Vintners Market was open today, though, over in Barrel Street, for instance. The brewers were in with Spring Beer today, which, along with the new crop of strawberries, probably accounted for the heavy traffic here in the Market Quarter.

Probably accounts for Corellius, too. Kellen knew the High Mage's tastes, thanks to overheard conversations among Lycaelon and his friends; Corellius might *pretend* to favor wine, a much more sophisticated beverage than beer, but his pretence was as bogus as—as his apparent height! Just as he wore platform soles to his shoes, neatly hidden under the skirt of his robe, to hide his true stature, his carefully-cultivated reputation as a gourmet concealed coarser preferences. His drink-of-choice was the same beer his carpenter father had consumed, and the stronger, the better. He might have a reputation for keeping an elegant cellar among his peers and inferiors, but his superiors knew his every secret "vice."

They had to: only a convocation of Arch-Mages could invest a High Mage into their exalted ranks, and it behooved them to know everything about a potential candidate. Little did Corellius know that a frog would fly before he was invested with the rank he so coveted. The Arch-Mages would have understood and accepted a man who clung to his culinary roots openly—but a Mage who dissembled and created a false image of himself might find it easy to move on to more dangerous falsehoods. So Lycaelon said—loudly, and often.

Magic infused and informed this city, often called "Armethalieh of the Singing Towers" for all of the bell-spires piercing the sky. Magic ensured that the weather was so controlled that—for instance—rain only fell between midnight and dawn, so that the inhabitants need not be inconvenienced. Magic kept the harbor clear and unsilted, guided ships past the dangerous Sea-Hag's Teeth at the mouth of it, and cleansed the ships of vermin that entered it. There was magic to reinforce any construction, so that (in the wealthiest parts, at least) the City looked like a fantastic confection, a sugar-cake fit for a high festival. The City stretched towards the sun with stonework as delicate as lace and hard as diamonds, be-towered and be-domed, gilded and silvered, jeweled with mosaics, frosted with fretwork. Things were less fanciful in less exalted quarters, but still ornamented with gargoyle-downspouts and carved and glazed friezes of ceramic tiles. Magic reinforced these, too, and nearly every block boasted its own bell-tower, with still more magic ensuring that all of the songs of the towers harmonized, rather than clashed, with each other.

Magic set the scales in the marketplace and ensured their honesty. Magic at the mint guaranteed that the square coins of the City, the Golden Suns of Armethalieh, were the truest in the world, and the most trusted. Magic kept the City's water-supply sweet and uncontaminated, her markets filled with fresh wholesome food at every season, her buildings unthreatened by fire. There were entire Cadres of Mages on the City payroll, dedicated to magic for the public good. If they were well-paid and well-respected, they had earned both the pay and the respect. Even Kellen, no friend of Mages, had to admit to that. Life in the City was sweet and easy.

As for the private sector, where the *real* wealth was to be made, there were far more opportunities for a Mage to enrich himself. There was virtually no aspect of life that could not be enhanced by magic. Domestic magic, for instance. If you had the money, you could hire a Mage to thief-proof your house or shop, to keep vermin out of it, to keep disease from your family and to heal their injuries. If you had the money, you could even hire a Mage to create a winter-box where you could put perishables to keep them from spoiling. And there were even greater magicks to be had—magicks which melded brick-and-mortar into a whole more solid than stone and harder than adamant. Magicks which kept a ship's sails full of favoring wind no matter what the real conditions were. Money bought magic, and magic made money, and no matter how lowly-born a Mage was—and the Mage-gift could appear in any family, regardless of degree of birth (Corellius, for example)—he could count on becoming rich before he was middle-aged. He might become *very* rich. He might aspire to far more than mere wealth, if he was powerful enough: a seat on the High Council, and a voice in ruling the City itself.

Most important of all of the folk of the City were the Mages, and the most important of all the Mages were the those High Mages who formed the elite ruling body of the City, the High Council. They were considered to be the wisest of the wise; they were certainly the most powerful of the powerful. If there was a decision to be made about anything inside the walls of the City, it was the High Council that made it.

And that was what stuck in Kellen's throat and made him wild with pent-up frustration.

If there is a way to fetter a person's life a little farther, it is the High Council that puts the pen to the parchment, Kellen thought sourly, as he made his way past the Tailor's Mart and the stalls of those who sold fabric and trimmings. His goal was the little by-water of booksellers, but he would have to make his way through most of the markets to get there, since Corellius was blocking the short route.

Kellen was seventeen, and had been a Student for three years now, and although that was probably the acme of ambition for most young men in this city, he would rather have foregone the "honor" entirely. It would have been a great deal easier, all things considered, if he had never been born among the Gifted. On the whole, he would much rather have been completely and utterly ordinary. His father would have been disgusted.

And I could have gotten out of this place. I could have gone to be a sailor. . . . It would have gotten him as far as the Out Islands, at least. And from there, who knew?

Mages weren't *always* born to Mage fathers, and certainly not *only* to Mages, but in Kellen's case, if he *hadn't* been among the Gifted, Lycaelon would probably have had apoplexy—or gone looking for his wife's extra-marital interest. Or both. The blood in Kellen's veins contained—as he was reminded only too often—the distillation of a hundred Arch-Mages past, half of which had held the seat of a Lord of the High Council at some point during their lifetimes.

That was difficult enough to live up to, but he was also the son of the Arch-Mage Lycaelon Tavadon, ruler of the City and the current Arch-Mage of the High Council.

That made his life so unbearably stultifying that Kellen would gladly have traded places with an apprentice pig-keeper, if there were such a thing to be found within the walls of Armethalieh.

Wherever Kellen went in his father's world, there were critical eyes on him, weighing his lightest deed, his least word. Only here, in the "common" quarters of the artisans, the shop-keepers, and the folk for whom magic was a rare and expensive commodity, here where no one knew who he was, did Kellen feel as if he could be himself.

And yet, even here, the heavy hand of Arch-Magisterial regulation intruded.

For these were the Markets of Armethalieh, and Armethalieh was the greatest city in the world, after all. This should have been a place where wonders and novelties abounded. The harbor welcomed ships from every place, race, and culture, and caravans arrived at the Delfier Gate daily laden with goods from every conceivable place. There should be a hundred, a thousand new things in the market whenever it opened. And yet—

And yet the High Council intruded, even here.

They, and not the merchants, determined what could be sold in the marketplace. And only products that had been approved by the High Council could make an appearance here. Inspectors roamed the streets, casting their critical eyes over the stalls and stores, and *anything* that looked new or different was challenged.

In fact, there was one such Inspector in his black-and-yellow doublet and parti-colored hose just ahead of Kellen now. The Inspector was turning to look at the contents of a ribbon-seller's stall with a frown.

"What's this?" he growled, poking with his striped baton of office at something Kellen couldn't see.

The stall-holder didn't even bother to answer or argue; he just slapped his permit down atop the offending object. Evidently, this Inspector was a fellow well known to the merchant.

"Council's allowed it, Greeley, so take your baton off my property afore you spoil it," the man growled back. From his look of offended belligerence, Kellen guessed that the merchant had been targeted by this particular Inspector in the past.

The Inspector removed his baton, but also picked up the permit and examined it minutely—and managed to block all traffic down this narrow street as he did so. Kellen wasn't the only one to wait impatiently while the surly, mustachioed official took his time in assuring himself that the permit was entirely in order. Granted, some merchants had tried—and probably would continue to try—to use an old permit for a new offering, bypassing the inspection process, but that didn't mean the old goat had call to block the street!

"It's in order," Greeley grunted at last, and finally moved away from the stall so that people could get by again.

"Interfering bastard," the merchant muttered just as Kellen went past. "Even if it wasn't, what difference would a new pattern of woven ribbons make, for the Eternal Light's sake?"

Kellen glanced down curiously to see the disputed objects that had so raised the Inspector's ire. The merchant was smoothing out his wares, and Kellen could easily see why the Inspector's interest had been aroused. The ribbons in question were of the usual pastel colors that custom decreed for female garb, but the patterns woven into them were angular, geometric, and intricate, like the mosaics made from square ceramic tiles by the Shanthin farmers of the north. There wasn't a hint of the flowers and leaves usually woven into such ribbons, and although he wasn't exactly the most expert in matters of lady's dresses, Kellen didn't think he'd ever seen ribbons like this before. Well! Something new!

And the merchant was right—what difference *could* this make to anyone?

Despite the Council's eternal restrictions, the Market Quarter was still a lush, rich place to wander through, from the heady scents of the Spice-Market to the feast for the eyes of the fabrics in the Clothworker's and Trimmers Market.

But though there was a great deal of *abundance,* and it was all wonderfully extravagant (at least, in the markets that

Kellen's class frequented), creating an impression of wealth and plenty, it was all the same as it ever had been, or ever would be, except in the minutest of details. It was the same way throughout the entire City—throughout Kellen's entire *life*—tiny meaningless changes that made no difference. A pattern here, a dance-step there, a scarf added or subtracted from one's attire—someone who had lived in Armethalieh five hundred years ago could come back and be perfectly at home and comfortable now.

And if the High Council continued to govern as it had, someone who would live here five hundred years *hence* could return and find nothing of note changed.

Is that any way to live?

Somehow, that chance encounter with the Inspector had given form to Kellen's vague discontent. *That* was what was wrong with this place! That was why he felt as if he was being smothered all the time, why he was so restless and yearned to be anywhere but here!

Abruptly, Kellen changed his mind. He was *not* going to the Book Market. Instead, he would go to the Low Market. Maybe among the discards of generations past he *might* find something he hadn't seen a thousand times. He hadn't *ever* been to the Low Market, where (it was said) all the discards of the City eventually ended up. It was in a quarter inhabited by the poorest workers, the street-sweepers, the scullery-help, the collectors of rubbish, the sewer-tenders—people who had a vested interest in allowing those merchants of detritus to camp on their doorsteps twice a sennight.

Yes, he would go *there* and hope to find something different. And even if he didn't, well, at least being in the Low Market would be something akin to novelty, with the added fillip of knowing that if Lycaelon found out about where his son had gone, he would be utterly horrified.

There were no "stalls" as such in the Low Market, and no awnings sheltering goods and merchants, only a series of spaces laid out in chalk on the cobbles of Bending Square. The "square" itself was a lopsided space surrounded by apartment-buildings of four and five stories, centered by a public pump. Within each space each would-be merchant was free to display what he had for sale in whatever manner he or she chose. No Inspectors ever bothered to come *here,* and in fact, it wasn't even "officially" a Market.

Some of the sellers laid out a pitiful assortment of trash directly on the stones, some had dirty, tattered blankets spread out upon which to display their findings, some presided over a series of wooden boxes through which the customers rummaged. The most prosperous had actual tables, usually with more boxes piled beneath.

At the farther end of the Square, Kellen spotted a bookseller—one of the prosperous individuals who had tables *and* boxes of books beneath. The errand that had originally sent Kellen to the Bookseller's Market had been to find a cheap edition of one of the Student Histories—Volume Four, "Of Armethalieh and Weather," to be precise. Lycaelon's personal library had one, of course—how could it not?—but Kellen wanted one of his own that he could mark up with his own notes in the margins. This was a practice that infuriated his tutor, Anigrel, and frustrated his father, but as long as he did it in his *own* books, rather than in the pristine volumes in Lycaelon's library, there was nothing either of them could really say about it. He was, after all, studying.

I might as well see if there's one here. It'll be cheaper, and besides, if it's full of someone else's notes from lectures, I might not need to take any of my own.

Besides, it might be amusing to read what some other student had thought of the Histories.

He didn't go straight to the book-stall, however, for that would be advertising his interest. Instead he worked his way down the aisle between the chalk-lines, examining a bit of broken clockwork here, a set of mismatched napkins there. It had the same sort of ghoulish fascination as watching the funeral of a stranger, this pawing over the wreckage, the flotsam and jetsam of other peoples' lives. Who had torn the sleeves out of this sheepskin jacket, and why? How had the hand got bitten off this carved wooden doll? What on earth use was a miniature funeral carriage? If it was a play-toy, it was certainly a ghoulish one. If those rusty stains on this shirt were blood—then was *that* slash a knife-wound?

Eventually he got to his goal, and feigning complete disinterest, began digging through the books. The bookseller himself looked genuinely disinterested in the possibility of a sale; from his expression, Kellen guessed that he was suffering either from a headache or a hangover, and would really rather have been in bed.

Luck was with him. Kellen found not only the Volume Four he was looking for—in a satisfyingly battered and annotated condition—but Volumes Five, Six, and Seven, completing the set. They had stiff, pasteboard bindings of the cheapest sort, with the edges of the covers bent and going soft with use and abuse. They looked as if they'd been used for everything *but* study, which made them all the more valuable in Kellen's eyes, for the worse they looked, the less objection Anigrel could have to his marking them up further. And the more Lycaelon would wince when he saw his son with them.

I can hear him now—"We're one of the First Families of the City, not some clan of rubbish-collectors! If you must *have your own copies to scribble in, for the One's sake, why couldn't you* at least *have bought a proper set in proper leather bindings!" And I'll just look at him and say "Are the words inside any different?" And of course he'll throw up his hands and look disgusted.*

Baiting his father was one of Kellen's few pleasures, although it had to be done carefully. Pushed too far, Lycaelon could restrict him to the house and grounds, allowing him to leave only to go to his lessons. And an Arch-Mage found enforcing his will a trivial matter—and one unpleasant for his victim.

He was about to get the bookseller's attention, when a faint hint of gilding caught his eye. It was at the bottom of a pile he'd dismissed as holding nothing but old ledgers. There were three books there, in dark bindings, and yes, a bit of gilding. Rather out-of-keeping with the rest of these shabby wares.

Huh. I wonder what that is—

Whatever it was, the very slender volumes bound in some fine-grained, dark leather, with just a touch of gilt on the spine, seemed worth the effort of investigating. At the worst, they'd turn out to be some silly girl's private journals of decades past, and he might find some amusement in the gossip of a previous generation.

If he'd been in a regular bookseller's stall, Kellen might not have bothered. But. . . .

It might be something interesting. And it's bound to be cheap.

If it wasn't a set of journals, the books might even do as a present for his father if they were in halfway decent shape. An obsessive bibliophile, Lycaelon was always looking for things for his library. Literally anything would do so long as it wasn't a book he already had, and his Naming Day Anniversary would be in two moonturns.

It would be a bit better than the usual pair of gloves I've gotten him for the past three years.

It took Kellen some work to get down to the three volumes on the bottom of the pile, but when he did, he found himself turning them over in his hands with some puzzlement. There was nothing on the spine of each but a single image—a sun, a crescent moon, and a star. Nothing on the cover, not even a bit of tooling, and the covers themselves were in pristine condition—

Odd. Definitely out of keeping with the rest of the wares here.

He opened the front covers to the title-pages.

Handwritten, not printed, title-pages. . . .

The Book of Sun. That was the first, and the other two were *The Book of Moon* and *The Book of Stars.* Journals after all? He leafed through the pages, trying to puzzle out the tiny writing. The contents were handwritten as well, and so far from being journal-entries, seemingly dealt with magic.

They shouldn't be here at all! Kellen thought with a sudden surge of glee. They looked like workbooks of some sort, but books on magic were very closely kept, with Students returning their workbooks to their Tutors as they outgrew them, and no book on magic that wasn't a part of a Mage's personal library was supposed to leave the grounds of the Mage-College at all.

Perhaps some Student had made copies for his own use, and they'd gotten lost, to end up here?

But they weren't any of the recognized Student books, or anything like them, as far as Kellen could tell. The handwriting was neat but so small that the letters danced in front of his eyes, and the way that the letters were formed was unfamiliar to him, slightly slanted with curved finials. But it seemed to him that he recognized those three titles from *somewhere.*

Father be hanged. I *want these.* Without bothering to look through them any further, he put them on the top of his pile and caught the stallholder's eye. The poor fellow, sweating furiously, heaved himself up out of his chair, and got a little more lively when Kellen made only a token gesture at bargaining. Profit, evidently, was the sovereign remedy for what ailed him.

He got out a bit of old, scraped paper and even began writing up a bill-of-sale with the merest stub of a graphite-rod, noting down titles and prices in a surprisingly neat hand.

"Ah, got younger sibs at home, do you?" the man asked, when he got to the last three, special volumes.

"No—" Kellen said, startled by the *non sequitur.* "Why do you ask?"

"Well, children's stories—" the man gestured at Kellen's three prizes. "I just thought—" then he shrugged, wrote down three titles and prices, and handed the receipt to Kellen, who looked down at it in confusion.

There were his Student's Histories, Volumes Four, Five, Six and Seven—but what was this? *"Tales of the Weald," "Fables of Farm and Field," and "Hearth-side Stories"?*

There was nothing like that, nothing like that *at all,* inside the covers of those three books.

He thought quickly. Perhaps he had better go along with this. . . .

"Cousins," he said briefly, with a grimace, as if he was plagued with a horde of small relatives who needed to be amused.

"Ah," the man said, his curiosity turning to satisfaction, and stuffed the purchases in the carry-bag that Kellen handed to him without a second look.

There was something very odd about those books . . . and Kellen wanted to get home *now,* before his father returned from the Council House to plague him, and give them a very close examination. An examination that could be made without any danger of interference. Armethalieh held many magical oddities, but where had he ever heard of a book which could disguise itself? *How* was a very interesting question—but more pressing than that was—

Why?

Night had fallen over the City while Kellen puzzled his way through the books' peculiar crabbed handwriting in the safety of his room. He'd skimmed through all three of the Books once quickly, finding little that made sense to him. *The Book of Sun* was composed partly of philosophy, partly of spells, but the spells were not of a kind that he recognized, and Kellen was doubtful that they could actually work. They seemed to verge on wondertale superstition. Burn this leaf. Say those rhymes. He could imagine nothing further from the abstruse disciplines of the High Magic.

But at least *The Book of Sun* did contain things Kellen recognized as magic. *The Book of Moons* didn't even seem to contain any actual spells, just hints at spells—as far as he could tell from a quick skim, it was something halfway between an etiquette book and a philosophy text—and *The Book of Stars* made no sense to him at all. He had the odd feeling, though, that there was *something* there, if he could only figure it out.

The house was utterly silent, with all of the household in bed, from which comfort no one would stir until they had to. That Lycaelon was a stern master was no secret; he did not approve of his servants "prowling," as he put it, during the bells of proper sleep. This included Kellen, of course, and after having been caught by Lycaelon once or twice, he kept to his own part of the mansion when restlessness kept him awake.

Tonight was one of those nights.

He had his shutters open on the small balcony that overlooked the gardens, and across the gardens he could see the lights of the other homes of the Mage Elite. Soft globes of pastel colors lit their gardens—you could tell where one garden took over from the next by the color of the lamps. Only a few lights were burning in the homes themselves, and those were probably night-lights, not an indication that anyone was wakeful or working. In the distance he could see the Council House, facing the Delfier Gate which opened onto the forest road.

The Council House stood symbolic guard over the gate and access into the City. Or was it more than merely symbolic?

There were a few farming villages in that direction—the City claimed extensive lands outside itself. Certainly soldiers were sent out there, and tax collectors, the latter to feed the City's prosperity, and the former—perhaps to ensure the City's prosperity?

But Kellen had never been there, and emigration between village and City was strongly discouraged, or so he'd been told, though never *why*.

He could understand why the Council wouldn't want too many people trying to move *into* the City; conditions were crowded enough without adding more people. But why keep citizens from leaving if they wanted to?

It was a puzzle for which he had no answer. Unless it was simply that City-dwellers had few, if any, skills that would be of use in a rural or agrarian society. Perhaps the idea was merely to save them from inevitable failure. . . . Still, shouldn't people be allowed to learn this for themselves?

If would-be Cityfolk-turned-rustics came trailing back with their tails between their legs after failing some bucolic experiment to the ridicule of their former neighbors, surely that would be more effective than any reprimand from the Council.

The Council House itself was ablaze with light, for Mages worked there all night, every night, weaving spells for the good of the City. It was the only place in the City that never slept. Of course, all those lights so nearby meant that the stars were hard to see from the gardens of those living nearby.

Someday Kellen would spend his nights there too, if his father's plans for his future went according to Lycaelon's oft-expressed wishes.

A night-owl by nature, that hadn't seemed so bad in the past, for he would be well out of Lycaelon's purview most of the time once he went to night-duties—but for some reason now, the thought seemed stifling. As stifling as the High Magic itself had seemed of late, for it required a finicking obsession with detail that, applied to anything else, would be considered unhealthy. Kellen had come to realize of late that High Magic was *boring*, that—once certain tools of memory and power-manipulation were mastered—it was entirely composed of written spells which were descriptions of the change in reality that the Mage would like to produce. Very exact descriptions, very *minute* descriptions, down to the smallest detail, written in a kind of mystical shorthand and forced into the face of reality-as-it-was by magical power.

Frankly, if the simple spells were enough to induce yawns, the advanced spells that he'd managed to glimpse looked to Kellen a very great deal like abstruse mathematical problems expressed in words and symbols of the sort that drove schoolboys mad—"If *A* leaves his house on the corner of Bodhran Street and approaches Taman Square at the same time *B*—"

Learning how to read, write and thoroughly comprehend this sigil-language and apply it to the world in the form of memorized spells was what the Mage-in-training first learned. Only then was he allowed to *do* anything with his knowledge.

It was bloodless and terribly boring, when it came right down to it. There was *so* much preparation and memorization and detail required to do even the simplest thing that by the time you actually accomplished what you'd set out to do, you were probably so bored with the process that the accomplishment came as an anti-climax. And in any case, the tiny things Kellen was allowed to do now—and so far, all he'd managed to do successfully was light a candle once or twice—were so simple and so insignificant that he hardly knew why anyone had ever bothered to write down the spells for them.

He looked out at the City, looked at what little he could see beyond the City walls from his third floor balcony, and it gradually came over him that not only was he not happy, but for most of his life, save only a few, stolen moments, he had *never* been happy. Other people were happy—why wasn't he? Why wasn't any Mage, really?

He *knew* they weren't.

His father wasn't, and his father was Arch-Mage, the highest and most powerful rank any Mage could attain. But Lycaelon was perpetually dissatisfied. When was the last time he'd ever seen his father *enjoy* anything? Other than finding an excuse to browbeat his son, that is. . . .

And none of Lycaelon's colleagues seemed any more content with their lives, even though they had wealth and power and the envy of everyone in the City who wasn't them. When was the last time he'd seen *any* of the Mages take pleasure in anything, other than humiliating one another?

Being a Mage doesn't make you happy, Kellen realized with something very much like fear.

He'd never thought about it before.

He hated the lessons, was bored by the memorization, and didn't like his fellow Mage-students very much. But he'd always, well, sort of assumed that he'd get through all of it somehow, become a Mage, and things would get better.

What if they didn't?

Suddenly, staring out at the brightly-lit Council House, Kellen confronted his own life, and the prospects for the future, and he didn't like what he saw. And the more he pondered it, the less he liked it, and he began to come to some uncomfortable conclusions.

One of which was that his studies were going to drive *him* mad before too long, all this obsession with pointless detail. He brooded on the view without seeing it, wondering why *anyone* would choose to be a Mage when a Mage had so little room in his life *for* life. If he did as Lycaelon wanted, Kellen would only trade the stultifying life of a Student-Apprentice for the tedious life of an Apprentice, and then for an even more restrictive and obsessive life of a Journeyman, and then what? Spend his entire life like his father, with a fantastic home he never saw, a garden he never went into, possessions he never used, and colleagues—not friends—he couldn't stand? Was he to live a life so measured, so controlled, that all the juice was sucked out of it?

He shuddered, appalled by the prospect of becoming like one of them—with a dry little mummified excuse for a soul, spending his days contriving ways to control other peoples' lives for them, his evenings spent building baroque and convoluted spells, or equally baroque and convoluted schemes for the downfall of his political rivals. Where was the joy, the life, the *pleasure* in that?

There *had* to be some other alternative. . . .

His mind turned naturally to the Books of the Wild Magic, which seemed, from the little he'd managed to understand so far, to be all that the High Magic was not.

And if they were—if they were, in fact, the very opposite of High Magic—it would be very surprising indeed to find that Lycaelon looked upon them with favor. . . . Furthermore, there might, there just *might* be something in them that would lead him to freedom.

And that alone decided him. He got them from his hiding place, lit a single, well-shielded candle, and began to read *The Book Of Sun* in earnest.